THE GIN SISTERS' PROMISE

Also by Faith Hogan

My Husband's Wives
Secrets We Keep
The Girl I Used to Know
What Happened to Us?
The Place We Call Home
The Ladies' Midnight Swimming Club

THE GIN SISTERS' PROMISE

Faith Hogan

An Aria Book

First published in the UK in 2022 by Head of Zeus Ltd,
part of Bloomsbury Publishing Plc

9 7 5 3 4 6 8

A catalogue record for this book is available from the British Library.

ISBN (TPB): 9781800241374
ISBN (E): 9781800241367

Typeset by Divaddict Publishing Solutions

Printed and bound in Great Britain by
CPI Group (UK) Ltd, Croydon CR0 4YY

Head of Zeus Ltd
5–8 Hardwick Street
London EC1R 4RG

WWW.HEADOFZEUS.COM

This is for the Scannan Girls and the Beehive Gang – the very best tribe a girl could wish for. It is also for Anne Regan, always a Beehiver – kind, considerate and just lovely.

'There is another world, but it is in this one.'

W.B. Yeats or Paul Éluard

The G(georgie)I(Iris)N(Nola) Sisters Club

RULES:

1 No boys allowed
2 Always use the Secret Code Knock
3 Never tell the Secrets of the GIN Sisters Club
4 Secret Ice-Cream Fridays
5 Forever Friends

We the

G – Georgie
I – Iris
N – Nola

Sisters solemnly swear to abide by the rules – always.

20th August 1993

Prologue

Ballycove, Ireland, Twenty-Eight Years Ago

The saddest funeral I was ever at. That's what the mourners had whispered as they'd left the remaining Delahayes standing by Iseult's grave. And now, perched at opposite ends of the living room, Iris and Georgie were drowning in their own grief, but it was little Nola – just seven years old – who needed her father the most and there was no way round it; there was nothing left of him to give. He was suffocating when he knew he should be comforting his children.

The cry that emitted from Nola came as gasping gulps, as if she was going under, smothering in the cold waters of despair. She was far too small for her feet to touch the bottom of her grief, far too young to navigate these treacherous waters.

Iris heard her first. The choking sobs startled her from her own wretched melancholy. 'Nola,' she cried, fearing the worst. Panic gripped her; she couldn't remember seeing Nola since they set off for the funeral earlier. But that wasn't right. Of course she'd seen her. Nola must have sat in the church pew at the end of their row, stood next to her and Georgie by their mother's grave. She must have been there in the car when their father had driven them back to Soldier Hill House.

Sheer horror propelled Iris from the window seat. How could she have forgotten about little Nola? In the hall, Georgie too was racing to find their youngest sister, panic etched across her features, only just edging past the devastating grief overhanging each of them. They crashed into each other at the foot of the stairs.

'Where is she?'

'Oh, God.' Georgie was frantic, her eyes wide, a slight odour of sweat emanating from her clothes, a mixture of the painful day and the near-consuming fear reflected in Iris's eyes. Another gulp came from the alcove, just outside their father's study, and their eyes dropped to the pathetic bundle of dark clothes lying on the floor. Nola. In her best dress, the one their mother picked out for Christmas Day. Maroon velvet, too heavy for a July afternoon, too festive to mourn your mother in.

'He just left me here.' Nola wheezed between disconsolate sobs. 'First Mammy and now Daddy. All I wanted was for him to put his arms around me, like Mammy did, and tell me everything would be all right, but it won't be all right now, will it? It'll never be all right again.'

'Come here.' Iris pulled Nola into her chest roughly. Georgie too fell on top of them, bundling Nola in their weeping cocoon so she could hardly breathe. But somehow, the familiar scents of her sisters – washing powder, the faintest remains of their mother's perfume, which they'd all applied that morning, and that slightly tangy end-of-day smell that you only got in the summertime – were strangely comforting. 'We're all here together. That's the main thing, Nola. That's all that matters now. We'll be okay. Everything will be fine – you'll see.'

'But you're going to leave. You'll go off and forget about me and then I'll be here alone, with Daddy, and I can't stand it.' She was gulping down the words now, almost hysterical with grief and pain and maybe fear too.

'We're never going to leave you, Nola,' Iris said, 'I promise. How could we possibly ever leave you?'

'We couldn't,' Georgie said solidly in that way she had of saying things that let Nola know she'd never let her down. 'We'll always be the Gin Sisters, remember?' Georgie said using the abbreviation of the initial letters of their names that their father had coined.

'Oh my God, yes! We can make our own little club, just us, with a promise that means we're always going to be together. Nothing will ever come between us.' Iris was flushed, trying hard to make things better for her younger sister. There had been too much sadness already today. She found herself smiling at her own silly idea.

'Really, our own club? The G-I-N Sisters – get it, gin sisters?' Nola scraped her hair from her eyes, drying off some of the tears that stained her cheeks. 'I love that idea.' She breathed out slowly.

'We'll need a constitution.' Georgie pulled a mock-serious

face to make more fun of it. She could always be depended on to be the strong one.

'Yes, Georgie, you can write it up. Now, quick, go and get some paper and a pen, Nola.' Iris fell back on her heels; she'd do anything to make Nola feel better. The poor kid, they were all too young to lose their mother. But Iris felt she had some additional gravity because she had just become a teenager, even if Georgie always tried to rub it in that she was one year older, but Georgie would never be the maternal one among them – they both knew that. Whereas everyone said Iris was cut out to be a wonderful mother someday, and in truth it was the only ambition she had in life.

Beyond the door, she heard the muted sounds of her father shuffling about, and Iris imagined him filling up a tumbler of whiskey and slouching in the large armchair with that photograph of their mother that he'd taken long before they'd ever had children or, it seemed, worries. Still, it was better that he was here and not down in the distillery where it seemed he could lose track of time entirely. Delahaye Distillery, his life's work, was becoming an all-consuming distraction, maybe his only way to cling on at this stage.

'And no boys.' Georgie was scribbling down the club rules to Nola's subdued delight. Georgie already knew that Iris was in love with a boy called Myles who didn't even know she existed and probably never would.

'Eugh, of course no boys.' Nola scrunched up her face.

'And ice-cream every Friday.' Iris tried to make her voice sound as if she really could be happy again one day.

'Just for us,' Nola said on a breath that was still ragged,

but at least her little body had stopped shaking. 'And you'll never leave me?'

'We promise we'll never leave you,' Georgie and Iris chorused together. Anything else was unthinkable.

1

London, November, Present

Iris closed her front door behind her with a kick that felt like a final exclamation mark on a very long day. It had been that way for a while. Her sister Georgie would probably say that work should fulfil you but, Iris thought irritably, not everyone could be as lucky as Georgie when it came to finding a career that could jam up all the other cracks in her life. She pushed the notion of her sister from her mind as quickly as it had arrived. It was automatic now. She didn't waste time thinking of either of them anymore. What was the point when there was no forgiving or forgetting the hurt they'd caused her all those years ago? It was much better not to think of them at all.

Iris groaned. Her head was throbbing. She wasn't tired, just irritated with another day like every other. She was sick to the back teeth of reminding people to turn up to dental appointments they didn't want to keep. She was bored of having the same conversations about the cost of root canals and crowns and children's braces. Becoming a receptionist at a busy London dental practice probably wasn't anyone's burning ambition. It was a job, a way to make a living – nothing more, and if she could afford to throw in the towel she would have left years ago. But someone needed to earn a steady wage in the house. In fairness, her employers were generous with her wages and a hefty Christmas bonus was always thrown in to keep her there for another year. Maybe she was expecting too much from life.

She was early. She'd meant to stop off at the fish market – they were having homemade fish and chips for dinner. Myles's favourite. She hoped it would pull him out of the distanced silence he'd put between them over the last few weeks. But in the rush to catch her morning train, she had forgotten her purse and so she'd come directly home.

Though she didn't think so at the time, later, she wondered if maybe she knew that this was it. The day she'd dreaded since the very first day of her marriage to him.

His bag stood ready at the foot of the stairs. Myles was a cameraman, freelance for a news channel. It paid a pittance but gave him access to all the big news stories and held a certain glamour he'd leaned on more these last few years, now that his looks were beginning to fade.

'Iris.' He stopped, dead still in the hallway, as if he'd been confronted by a raging lion on the savannah instead of his wife home from work on a wet and miserable Wednesday afternoon. 'I...' he started. 'You're early. I wasn't expecting you yet. I'm...'

'Yes?' Iris waited, working to keep her face blank while the words *please, please, please don't do this* exploded in her mind. Iris folded her arms about herself. Perhaps it would stop her trembling when she heard the worst. Of course, she knew what it was. It was a woman – younger, prettier and probably with enough money to make up for the loss of the house and their savings that leaving her would cause him.

'I'm leaving you. I've met someone else.' His words were faltering, but she hardly noticed because it felt as if the world had already started to spin away from her. 'She's called Amanda... She's—'

'Please, Myles, please don't do this. Don't leave me for some bit of skirt that's going to be by the wayside in a matter of weeks. Come on, we can work through this...' She was pleading, but she might as well have been reciting a shopping list, because he just went on gathering up his belongings. His keys. His watch. And then in the kitchen, he hovered for a minute before picking up four of the fresh scones she'd baked that morning. She watched him, wordlessly now, because she'd run out of things to say, or was it that she didn't know where to start or where to end?

'It's not like *that*... This is different.' He dragged a hand through his hair. For a moment, his expression seemed to dip into something like anguish and Iris experienced a dart of panic. Could he really be in love with someone else?

'I'm begging you, Myles, please, don't do this. What do you want me to do? I'll do anything, anything for you to stay.' She was shrieking, unable to control either the words or the desperation. Hysteria pummelled against her ribcage where her heart should have been.

His restraint silenced her, suddenly, as if a plug had been

pulled from the very heart of her. And for a moment, the only sound in her world was the low buzz of the refrigerator.

'You need me, Myles, don't you see?' She took a step closer to him, and tried not to notice that he took a step back from her. 'This is us, Myles.' She waved her hand around their little semi. 'Twenty-three years of us! We're meant to be together. Think of everything I've given up for you, everything—'

'Oh, please, Iris, I'm sick and tired of hearing the same old saga. No-one asked you to follow me to London or to cut your family out of our lives.' He spun around with a look of pure disgust as his eyes travelled over her. She felt the power going from her legs, could hardly stand straight beneath his loathing stare. 'That was all you, all your doing. We might have been millionaires if your old man included us in his will, but that's never likely to happen now, is it?' He shook his head, as if it had been that simple, when they both knew there was so much more to it all than that. There was so much more to them. 'And as for those crazy sisters of yours – you can't blame me for falling out with them.'

'All right, all right, let's forget Georgie and Nola. This isn't about them; it's about us. Look at how far we've come. Most couples don't make it past...' She stopped, because suddenly, she knew there was something else. Something she hadn't figured into this scenario in all the times she'd played it out in her worst nightmares. If it was possible to imagine anything worse than Myles leaving her, she had a feeling that there was even worse to come.

'No. I can't do this anymore. Iris, there's something you should know...' His voice became almost a whisper and she had to lean forward to hear him properly. 'Amanda is pregnant.'

It felt as if she'd been slapped across her face. She reeled backwards and fell against the wall, felt herself drift slowly towards the ground. Could you actually die of shock? Or of a truly, truly breaking heart? 'Pregnant? How on earth could that be?' Myles wasn't ready to be a father. He'd told her that so often, it was like a mantra. It was always next year, or the year after, or after I get this job finished or when we have more money. Of course, there were times when she had pined for a child, but she told herself nothing was more important to her than Myles.

'We are having a baby.' He said it so simply, he might as well have been talking about the football results.

'But...' She felt the words that she had intended to say trickle away from her. Myles was going to be a father. It had all been for nothing. It was the annihilation of her very soul. She let her body go, floated up above it and watched as it fell about her like a puddle to the floor. Pathetic. He bent and picked up his bag, stepped over her, like someone else's rubbish on the pavement. He stood for a second that could have lasted a lifetime or might not have happened at all. And then he was gone.

The house was desolately quiet. The hours somehow drew themselves out into days and then one week fell into a second and there was still no contact from him. The stillness clawed at her imagination. Here, in the pristine tidiness of a life spent ignoring the ever-widening gap between hope and acceptance, it seemed as if the silence was taunting her. Could she really go on like this forever? She was still a young woman, just forty. Forty, had seemed to be ancient to her when her own mother died of septicaemia all those years ago, but now, women her age were starting companies, starting families, starting over. Women her age were looking forward, but all Iris could do was look back.

She played her relationship with Myles over in her mind from that very first day. She'd had a crush on him long before he ever noticed her, but then at the village fete, it seemed the sun shone extra bright and he'd ambled up to the Delahaye Distillery table. Iris still felt butterflies in her stomach when she thought about that first time he'd walked her home and kissed her at the gate. Long and lingering, much too grown up for her age. She'd been a kid, just sixteen and never been kissed. God, how had they ended up here?

He'd been gone a month and still wretchedness flooded her; it felt as if she was drowning most days. And strangely, she knew, the worst part wasn't losing Myles, rather it was the fact that he'd betrayed her so badly. A baby. She had always wanted a family but somehow, for Myles, there had never been a *right* time. Today she rolled out of bed after midday and staggered towards the hall mirror. She examined her reflection: prematurely grey hair, pallid complexion – the most fresh air she got these days was rushing for the London Underground. She tried smiling, but it didn't seem to fit her anymore, rather it was an unnatural use of her muscles, which had gotten out of the habit of joyfulness. She'd even lost weight, not that she needed to, but her wedding ring slid up and down her finger now as if it too wanted to get away from her. What did it matter if she faded away, miserable and alone, really? She should reach out; she should have people to reach out to. Wasn't that what you did in times of crisis: find a shoulder to lean on, share your misery and halve it in the process? Friends and family. Hah!

She hadn't really made any close female friends over the years, or none that had actually stuck. Her own fault. She'd become jealous and distrustful of any woman coming too close to Myles. As for family, Georgie and Nola were the last people she'd call; she wouldn't give them the satisfaction of turning their backs on her as she had so willingly done to them all those years ago. They hadn't spoken in ten years, not since that disastrous party at the family distillery when they'd had the mother of all fallings-out. Perhaps, she should have reached out to them, just as her father had reached out to her a few months earlier. They were *In Touch*. Something she'd never expected would happen again, but the letters he'd started to send her months earlier had found a chink in the armour she'd worn against her family for the last two decades. They had graduated to phone calls. God, who'd have thought these would become the highlight of her otherwise empty life?

Outside, a tapping noise broke into her miserable thoughts. She looked out the window to see a crow, digging in the eaves opposite, as if he might eventually come across nuggets of gold. Iris found herself wishing he might find something worthwhile. His beak went up and down, *tap, tap, tap, tap,* and all the while dark, voluminous clouds loomed heavier over the rooftops with each passing minute. That meant only one thing. London weather was nothing like in Ballycove, Ireland; everything – even the storms – were far more civilised here. Why was it that after so many years, she still compared the two places and always Ballycove came out the best? She sighed, flicking across the lock on the window – not that it was likely to so much as rattle. This little semi hadn't enough personality to make a sound she couldn't identify.

It would have to be sold, of course. Wasn't that what happened when people got divorced? It had been her home for the past twenty-plus years and despite its lack of character, the thought of losing it made her heart ache.

Or maybe Myles would want to buy her out of it somehow. Suddenly, she wasn't sure that she wanted to hand it over to Myles and the new family he was embarking on – not that he'd suggested it yet. As far as Iris had managed to glean from his Facebook page, he was living with this woman, Amanda Prescott.

Sometimes she saw her whole situation with terrible clarity. What if her sisters had been right all along? All those years, when she'd believed they were jealous, maybe Nola hadn't wanted to take him for herself and maybe Georgie really had seen him steal from the distillery? Perversely, that only made her hate them all the more. Well, at least it was unlikely she'd be running into Georgie or Nola anytime soon.

As Georgie Delahaye approached the shiny glass doors of Sandstone and Mellon, she felt a pleasant fizzing sensation in her stomach. Today was the day. She was a shoo-in for the job. God knows, she'd sacrificed enough for it. She had aced the interview last week. She knew even as she walked out of that room that it was a done deal. Getting this would make her the youngest director at the table and the only woman among a board of men who, in her opinion, bore their privilege far too lightly. Of course, it was easy when you'd been to public school and sailed into every opportunity in life with the doors held open for you by the guy who went before.

No such nepotism for Georgie Delahaye. It took staking her claim in the world of London marketing with a bespoke award-winning campaign for a jewellery company that was years before its time. Her campaign had sent the fashion world into a tizzy and made Sandstone and Mellon the new 'must-have' marketing firm for the world's biggest brands. And, she thought as she saw her reflection in the glass wall that separated her office from the grunt workers beyond, she hadn't lost her bite. She threw her shoulders back. She was walking on air this morning, buoyed up by the certain knowledge that in a very short time they'd be making the announcement to the whole company. And rightly so – she was still coming up with the most innovative campaigns and the snappiest lines, still had the canniest ability to sniff out a market where buyers hardly knew they needed what she wanted to sell them. And she had loved it, every single second. But somehow, she knew she wouldn't miss it.

She didn't want to pitch anymore, fighting off the snapping of younger, hungrier marketing executives biting at her heels. She had put in her time swimming with the sharks and now she was ready to take her place on the boat – or in this case, a corner office, long lunches and watching other people do the dirty work for once.

She'd just sat at her desk when her online diary pinged. Almost time, not that she needed to be reminded. Georgie checked her reflection in the little silver plate she'd won last year. She kept it buried in her desk drawer – what else was she supposed to do with it? Second place in the industry awards was hardly worth hanging on a wall. It was almost an insult. She rubbed her tongue along the surface of her teeth and flicked her hair from around her collar. She stood up, pulling her body up by that invisible string that made her feel six inches taller and then she marched into Paul Mellon's office.

'So?' They both knew what this was about, but she kept her features neutral as if it didn't much matter to her either way. Of course Paul Mellon had known for years that she wanted to run this company. This promotion was rightfully hers. Even if they'd gone through the motions of leaving the interviews open so others could apply, it was a formality. There was no-one else with her experience, her track record or indeed her proven dedication to the company.

'Sit down,' he said, his voice as cold as usual. Although she knew from overhearing some of the temp staff that he fraternised with work colleagues, between them it had always been strictly professional. 'Georgie.' He clicked closed whatever computer files he was working on before turning to give her his full attention. He cleared his throat, as if gearing up for a performance that had to carry far beyond the two of them. A light tap on the door made her turn and obvious relief flooded his features when Cole StJohn took a seat beside her. It was then that something close to a warning bell began to sound out in her gut. 'Good of you to join us, Cole.' Mellon looked across at the young man at her side as if he'd just been thrown a life jacket.

'Is something wrong?' Georgie asked, keeping her voice clear and unconcerned. 'Has something happened?' Because, suddenly, it seemed that she could only have been brought here for the most devastating news. 'Is the company folding?' But of course, she knew, it couldn't be that. They'd had their most successful year on record, due in no small part to her securing two of the biggest accounts they'd ever had on their books.

'No. Nothing has happened. I just wanted to have a chat with you before I go out and make the announcement about appointing our new director to the board.'

'Ah.' She exhaled a relieved sigh. 'I see.' Although she didn't see, not really. After all, giving someone a job – or rather, giving them the promotion they deserved above anyone else – hardly called for legal assistance, did it? 'So, you've crossed all the T's and dotted all the I's?' It was funny, but she'd thought this moment would be euphoric but now she was here it felt like a bit of an anticlimax. 'So, shall we tell them together? I hope there's going to be bubbly – it is a Friday afternoon after all...' Then suddenly something in Paul's eyes stopped her mid-flow.

'I'm afraid you weren't successful in your application to be made a director, Georgie.' His voice dipped and she supposed it was meant to sound sympathetic or maybe supportive, but it didn't. It sounded patronising. 'It's just... we had to give it to the best man for the job and the interview showed us that—'

'The best *man*?'

'Well, no,' Cole butted in quickly. 'I think what he means is the best candidate.'

'Now, we want to acknowledge the sterling work you do for the company, so we're putting together a very attractive package that's going to mean a considerable increase in your salary, additional leave allocation and of course a bigger number of accounts for you to call your own. You'll also get another assistant on your team and...'

'I'm sorry.' She put her hand up to stop him talking – whatever he was saying was just white noise to her at this point. 'I'm sorry, but let me get this right: you're not actually making me a director?'

'No. We're not.' He held eye contact with her for too long, as if he'd practised this moment all week. She imagined him now, in front of his bathroom mirror going over the words, giving them exactly the right weighting and firmness while remaining empathetic.

'Well, bra-bloody-vo.' She began to slow clap.

'I'm sorry?' He leaned forward, his brow folding in confusion.

'I mean it. You've done a marvellous job in passing on the bad news. And, Cole, obviously you pulled the short straw this morning. Damage limitations? Never an easy task.' She shook her head bitterly. 'So, it'll be all the boys around the table for the foreseeable, right?'

'We haven't told the successful candidate yet, but yes, it's—'

'What are your reasons for this?'

Cole cleared his throat. 'I'm sorry, but it was a fair decision, based not just on the interview but also on each candidate's track records.'

She took a deep breath and forced herself to remain calm. She would not shout. She would not give the lemmings outside the satisfaction; instead her voice remained dangerously low. 'How can it be fair when we both know that nobody here has worked harder to make this business more successful than I have? Nobody has pulled off the genius campaigns that have brought ten times more business to our doors than you could have dreamed of when I started out here.'

'You've been an exemplary employee. Dedicated and talented, it's just—'

'It's just what?' She stood up, her hands on her hips. She'd always seen him for what he really was: a little man who couldn't see past the fact that she wasn't wearing trousers like him, or hadn't gone to quite the right school. She managed not to say this, managed to keep her cool because she knew Cole was there to take down and use any comments she made against her. She wasn't giving him that sort of ammunition.

'You're not a team player, Georgie. You never have been. Your assistants never last any longer than six months and—'

'Yes, because they are mostly the worst imbeciles who I have to train from scratch, but when they leave me they actually know something about marketing. My assistants have all gone on to work in the best jobs in London, thanks to the training I've given them.'

Paul stood up too, and his voice took on a new, steely tone. 'Some of them have left here virtually traumatised by you.'

'Is it my fault that you keep sending me oversensitive ninnies?' she spat, remembering all the assistants she'd had over the years. But then a smidge of doubt crept in. Had she been a complete and utter bitch? No. It was exactly what Paul wanted, for her to cave in with some sort of misplaced guilt. A man wouldn't have to feel guilty for being brilliant at his job, so why should she? She dug her fingernails into the palms of her hands. It wasn't true, she told herself. Every one of them reminded her of her sisters: content to stay in their own lane, leaving the heavy duty lifting to people like Georgie.

She felt a treacherous tremor at the back of her throat, as if the hurt her sisters had inflicted on her might spill over into this present moment in the form of tears. She had convinced herself she'd gotten over this. Iris's complete and utter betrayal of their whole family when she turned her back on them for a man who would happily have robbed them blind given half a chance and Nola's letting her down when she'd gone out on a limb for her – it was all so long ago. She'd left this pain behind when she'd walked away from them at what was meant to be a centenary *celebration* for her father's distillery. She took a deep breath, steadied herself and pushed the pain they'd caused her from her mind. She couldn't let them ruin this, too.

'And then, there's the way you treat the rest of your colleagues, always shutting them down in meetings if they dare to disagree with you. You've managed to insult each and every one of them over the years, whether you realise it or not.'

'It's business,' Georgie barked. 'This is the real world, not some lovey-dovey kindergarten that we're running here. For God's sake, if they can't take a strong woman's opinion maybe they should go and get jobs as church wardens or lollipop ladies.' She walked towards the expanse of glass, beyond which stretched a view across the city she had envied for as long as she had worked here.

'Yes. I think you said something like that to one of your assistants before and we all know where that ended up,' Cole snapped, reminding her suddenly of those days they'd spent in the employment court. In spite of his easy smile, he was not a man to be trifled with.

'The insurance covered all of that and I've fulfilled the mediation requirement down to the very last letter.'

'Still doing the therapy?' Paul smirked, but she could easily rise above this. Even now, she wouldn't allow him to goad her, even if she badly wanted to take a swipe at him about accounts lost and office affairs that were hardly discreet, much less professional.

'I want a review of the interview process and a reversal of this decision.' She kept her voice low, just menacing enough to raise the tension further in the air between them so that it felt like even the slightest movement could set off a bomb that could blow the whole company apart. She waited, staring out as London packed up for the weekend in the streets and buildings far below her.

'That's not going to happen,' Paul said, his voice icy and his eyes boring through her like steel. 'The decision has been made, it's been ratified and our legal team have been with us through every single stage in the process.'

Georgie surveyed Cole's reflection in the glass. He was sitting far too confidently for her to question the legitimacy of Paul's words. 'I see. So, it's all sewn up nice and neat.' She mentally flipped through the various options open to her at this point. She couldn't bear the idea of having to go back out and face her colleagues knowing that some whippersnapper had taken her seat at the table. 'I could just leave,' she said then, a little absently.

'Yes. You could,' Paul said, and in that one devastating moment, she knew that was exactly what he was hoping she would do.

Nola looked out the café window. Raining. Again. Why did it always start just as she was finishing her shift? The last of the evening crowd were shuffling into coats, and an old man who couldn't afford it was leaving her a tip. Nola watched three office girls, gossiping in a corner – she could have been one of them instead of delivering their coffee and depending on their tips. If Georgie had come through for her all those years ago, would she be in a nice safe office job now, wearing a smart suit and sitting on a comfortable pension? Probably. Would she have been happy? *Well, what is happy anyway?* she thought. At least she'd have had security, a future. She wiped the counter fiercely. No point thinking of what might have been... but damn Georgie, anyway.

Shalib, the owner, was deep in concentration, counting up the day's takings. A mini cab pulled up outside, disgorging a shrieking hen party arriving for the nightly performance of *Guys on Tour*. Distracted, Shalib looked up at them, scowled, and started counting the sheaf of notes again.

Nola turned to gaze back out of the window. She'd applied for the job in this shabby café precisely because it was next to the little theatre that looked like it might one day be one of those hidden London gems. Nola didn't want to think about how long ago that was exactly. It was meant to be a filler, between acting jobs, but she was still waiting tables, serving coffee to smart office workers while her own dreams died a little more with every passing hour. These days the nearest she got to show business was a customer commenting on how much she resembled someone who used to be on the telly. Nola had lost the heart to tell them that it *was* her, Nola Delahaye, who had once been famous enough to be recognised from her part in one of the country's most popular soaps. Meanwhile, next door, the Stockton Playhouse had changed hands twice and hadn't staged anything more arty that a drama summer camp for disadvantaged kids about a year ago. She sighed. The nine-hour shift she'd just completed was enough to suck the soul out of Laurence Olivier, never mind Nola, who'd happily sacrifice her eye teeth for a bit part at this stage.

And she was getting older. Maggie, her agent, put it bluntly, when she phoned for her regular badgering session; '*Frankly, Nola, you're too old. They all want Saoirse Ronan and you're never going to be that package*.'

'I'm sure she didn't mean it like that,' Shalib said when she told him about the conversation, her face etched with misery. Dear Shalib, he listened patiently every time she wanted to let off steam about the career that had so easily slipped through her fingers. But even Shalib must be sick and tired of listening to her talking about what her life had been like once. The parts she'd turned down, the people she'd met and the parties she'd attended. She only talked about it because otherwise it felt as if it had never really happened at all. He handed her a cup of extra-strong coffee. It was like heavily scented aromatic sludge but she drank it, welcoming the tingling shock of caffeine hitting her system.

'I'm not giving up.'

'I never said you should, but you should listen to your agent. This idea of trying another way to be involved in the industry you want to be a part of? It might be sensible.'

'But I've spent a fortune on acting classes – I'm meant to be in show business; it's what I'm trained in.'

'And you still can be.' He smiled and his kind eyes wrinkled into a thousand familiar lines. 'Don't all actors just want to be directors anyway? What is the difference which part of the elephant you begin to wash, so long as he's clean at the end?'

Nola gave a reluctant smile. 'Oh, Shalib, you are funny.' But the truth was, if Nola could have got a job in any part of a theatre, she'd have taken it in a flash – after all, when it came to cleaning tables, who wouldn't prefer to be wiping down in the Barbican?

'It's only funny because it's true,' he said, touching the side of his nose. 'London is changing; the world is changing. When my father came here, things were simple. He worked and saved and managed to scrape enough together to start this café. Now my children are—'

'I know you're really proud of them,' and Nola thought it was lovely that they were both doing so well in their chosen careers, 'but I still don't want to give up on my dream...'

'That's not what I meant. When you started here, the theatres in this area, they put on plays, proper plays. And I know some of them were *only* community productions.' He gave an awkward little cough because at that stage, Nola wouldn't consider doing an acting job that wasn't paying some small amount. God, times had changed. How many others had taken those opportunities and were working in the West End now, she wondered? 'Now, it's all strip clubs and peep shows. The culture is gone and it's not coming back here anytime soon.'

'You're right. Of course, you're right.'

He shrugged sadly. 'I don't want to be. But I have to say it, because otherwise you could spend years waiting for something that isn't going to come knocking on any door around here.'

'I know that,' she said, and what had been biting away at her thoughts for ages became as real as the tables and chairs in the café. Suddenly the dainty cup seemed to weigh a tonne, and she no more had the strength to hold it in her hand than she had the courage to face the alternative future that seemed determined to pan out before her. How could it be that one moment you had everything you'd ever dreamed of and the next it could slip through your fingers like water? She wiped away a stinging tear from her eye. This was what defeat felt like: heavy, empty, crushing her from the inside out. Really, deep down, she knew it was over. It was either keep going as she was and slowly wither into a tragic has-been, or do something to break out of this prison she'd managed to build for herself.

Shalib cleared his throat loudly to break into her thoughts and bring her back to the present moment. He handed her an umbrella from beneath the counter. It was time to call it a day. And with that thought, she stepped out into the rain.

She woke the next morning to more rain and four bills she could not afford to pay. She would be thirty-five years old in a few days' time. Thirty-five years old, and what had she to show for it? A waitressing job that covered her rent and would never allow her to see any more of the world than the Tube could take her. Her acting career had peaked in her twenties with a starring role on Britain's second-most-watched soap opera. Things could have been so different, if she'd set her cap at something else all those years ago. She was too old to change track now.

Wallowing in her bitterness was a luxury she couldn't afford. Her TV career was over; that was just that. Her character had died under the crushing weight of a falling toilet. And yes, she'd heard every joke going – truly, the sh*t really had hit the fan. She didn't even pretend to laugh anymore. Since that less than glittering finale her greatest achievement was three words in an overplayed series of television adverts for teabags. Ugh, even thinking about that and the court case that followed just made her fists curl. She had thought she'd be a poster girl for pay equality, pave the way for more serious roles, give her some much-needed gravity. How naïve she'd been. Far from elevating her character, it had only emptied her bank account and made her the most unemployable actress in London. She wanted to thump the crumbling plaster of her bedsit wall. She stopped herself for fear of whacking right through to the rap-music-loving weed-smokers next door.

She sat there, letting her thoughts roll over endlessly in her mind until she wanted to scream with the sheer waste that was her life. As her tea grew colder, instead of dreaming as she once had of the glittering promise that seemed to lie before her, she descended into the now familiar regrets that had taken up residence in her mind. It seemed as if those thoughts had not only moved in, but redecorated every room, so there was no longer space for anything but bitterness at what had slipped away.

What if she had married Oliver Hughes? She'd be a *Fabulous London Housewife* now, with a show streaming to millions of viewers around the world like bloody Carly Miller with her fake boobs and her terracotta tan. Except he had dumped Nola along with everyone else when her career had hit rock bottom. Mind you, she knew now, looking back, that she hadn't loved Oliver Hughes, and she couldn't imagine having to put up with him for the rest of her days. No. That thought actually cheered her. Even here, with the constantly dripping bathroom tap and draughts that felt as if they were sneaking in directly from Siberia, Nola knew she was better off. She might spend the rest of her days having '*tea for me*' called after her in the street, thanks to that rotten advertising job, but it was better than tying herself up to the dry vacancy of a man she didn't love just for a shot at C-list television 'stardom'.

It took almost a week to push back the advancing bleakness that seemed to constantly shadow her these days. It was as if it was waiting for a moment of careless vulnerability to strike, engulfing her in a depression she wasn't sure she had the ammunition to defeat. Oddly, at times like this over the last couple of years, work felt almost like a respite.

Then, one morning shone sunny and dry through the gauzy curtains of Nola's bedroom window. At around ten o'clock that Tuesday, something seemed to click and she felt a little better, as if she was ready to take life on again in some small way, rather than just lie there and take its punches. Maybe it was just fleeting optimism, but, in that moment, she settled on a course of action. She would go and have things out with Maggie. Obviously, they just needed to reset her portfolio, pitch her towards older parts. She'd march into Maggie's office and tell her it was time to get serious. Or perhaps it was time to get a new agent.

Nola plucked her green velvet cape from the hook on her bathroom door, which doubled up as most of her wardrobe space. She dithered over wearing the bright green beret to match, knowing it brought up her eyes, but the last thing she wanted was to look as if she'd made too much of an effort. She decided that her best approach was to be as nice as she could, while still driving home her point. As she sipped her morning tea, she wished she had a little of her sister Georgie's fire in her belly.

Funny, but for a moment, it almost felt as if Georgie were standing next to her, cheering her on as she would have when they were kids. That thought alone brought an overwhelming sadness over Nola and she felt as if she might cry, but she fought hard to keep it at bay – the last thing she needed today was an attack of the waterworks. It would get her precisely nowhere with Maggie. Instead, she bit her bottom lip and squeezed her eyes shut, determined that her estrangement from her family, the intense dislike that had festered between them over the years, would actually propel her to tackle Maggie with even greater strength, not hold her back.

Her sisters only lived a few miles apart from each other as the crow flies. Of course, in reality they lived in completely different worlds. She, here in her dingy little bedsit with her low-paid job might as well have been living on a different planet to Georgie,who had a sky-high apartment in one of the city's fanciest blocks, or Iris, who was settled into domestic bliss with Myles in a cosy suburb, whose address she'd tried hard to forget over the years.

She wasn't jealous as such, but it was hard not compare the lives they'd all made for themselves. There was no getting away from the fact that of the three of them, she was the big failure – Iris and Georgie had managed to get everything they'd set their hearts on. But it wasn't her petty envy that had meant they hadn't spoken in years. No, that was their fault entirely.

Damn it. She'd upset herself now. There was nothing for it but to wipe her eyes, and tug the beret on. Drawing her hair about her face, she pushed up the corners of her mouth into a smile and hoped by the time she got to Waterloo, her expression might actually look as if she hadn't a care in the world.

Shining Light Theatrical Agency was a one-woman show. Maggie had set up her office in the back recess of a former hotel where the rent was cheap and the natural daylight scarce. The office always looked as if it was in a state of turmoil. Maggie's desk, a too-small Victorian writing table, was bordered on both sides by long orange Formica-topped catering tables. Every space, except – Nola presumed – Maggie's chair, was covered with old newspapers and manila file folders that looked as out of date as the flocked wallpaper that covered two and a half walls.

The lady herself sat primly behind her desk and today, assessing her in a strangely remote way, Nola thought she could have played a good queen, if only circumstances were different. She had the poise for it, even if her cheap peroxide hair and everywoman features fell short. That was the thing about Maggie Strip: what defined her was all of this. She loved being a theatre agent because, essentially, it was the only thing that made her stand out from a million other women who lacked any sort of talent or charm to mark them out as special.

'I don't have you in the diary.' She glanced at a suspiciously empty page before her when Nola sat on the seat opposite, having removed a stack of papers first.

'No, I was just passing.' Nola smiled what she hoped was sweetly. 'It seemed a shame to just walk by when I haven't seen you for so long.'

'Humph.' Maggie took the coffee that Nola had purchased for her from the vendor on the street and stirred it deliberately before sipping it.

'Anyway, now that I'm here, I wondered if we might have a rethink about how we're going to pitch me for the coming season.'

'Look, Nola, there's no easy way to say this, but—'

'Don't say a word; just let me do the talking for once.' Nola smiled with a degree of calm she certainly didn't feel. 'I've been thinking about roles that have come up over the last year and I think I know the problem. It's my Irish accent, isn't it? I can't do the British twang, not well enough to fool the English, but I could do the French accent – *mais oui?* We could change my name, get new head shots done, I could reinvent myself: Sophie Du Paris or Isabella D'Ville or…'

'It's…' For the first time ever Maggie actually looked startled.

'It's bloody genius, I know, isn't it?'

'That's not what I was going to say.'

'Oh?' Nola felt that delicate ball of hope inside her begin to crumble, softly, achingly.

'What is it they say? It's not you, it's me.' Maggie laughed, that gravelly sound that gave away her habit of smoking forty a day for more years than she'd care to admit.

'Oh, God.' All Nola could think was, *She's dropping me. I'm finished. Please don't do this.*

'I'm going to retire. Maybe not this very minute, but certainly this year. It's time. I've met a nice man and we have plans.' She smiled now and it did something odd to her face. It transformed her. 'He has a bar. In Spain.' She threw her hands up in the air as if it was all still a revelation to her. 'And I'm going to move there in a few weeks, so…'

'But you can't. You're my agent, my only hope…' The words were out before she had a chance to stop them and then she began to cry, huge big ugly sobs that no Frenchwoman would ever turn out.

'I'm afraid I can, and I am.' Maggie sat back and waited for the crying to stop, which eventually it did.

'I…' Nola was working hard to pull herself together. 'I'm happy for you. Congratulations.' And maybe in a way she was, because the old girl deserved her shot at contentment too. 'How exciting for you,' she managed finally, because of course, she could see now, the change in Maggie was more than just a new pair of earrings or some piece of gossip she was dying to share. This was what happiness looked like in someone who'd given up on it.

'Thank you.' She smiled and leaned forward. 'I'm actually trying to make my way through my client list to tell everyone and some of them have been not so nice.'

'Do you have a plan for the… er business?' Nola asked, because if Maggie's clients worked as infrequently as Nola did, there wouldn't be much of a business to leave behind.

'Not really. I don't own anything – this place belonged to an aunt of mine, but it's just one room and her son is going to let it out, I think. He'll be delighted if he can make some money on the place for a change.'

'And your clients – has anyone asked if they can take over the books?'

'Hah.' It was a high-pitched sound that cut through Nola like glass. The pain must have showed on Nola's face, because Maggie hastily rearranged her features and had the grace to look sheepish. 'Sorry. No. I'm afraid not. I did contact a few people I know, but most of them are in the same boat, looking for a way out, not looking to make their own ships even more likely to sink.'

'So, that's that,' whispered Nola. She was officially

without an agent. The only connection she had to the world she so desperately wanted to be a part of had been severed and there wasn't a thing she could do about it.

'Oh, darling, maybe it's time to give up on it, don't you think? I mean, I told you from the start, it's a dog fight just getting that first job and then from there, for as long as you're trying to get work, every single round of auditions, it's like you're starting over every time. Perhaps you could see this as your chance to try something new or different?'

'But I don't know what else to do,' Nola wailed. 'Don't you see? This is the only thing I have that's worth anything to me.'

'Oh dear, I knew this would happen eventually.'

Nola stared at her. 'What does that mean?'

'It means that you haven't been listening to me, over the years, when I've tried to manage your career.'

Nola snorted. 'What career? Since I was dropped from the soap, you got me one job in an advert that still bloody haunts me and paid enough money to get my hair styled and take a couple of days' holidays in Barcelona. That's it!'

'Well, I tried to manage your expectations, planning for the eventuality that has turned out to be the case. I have suggested a million times over that you go back and get some sort of formal training: hairdressing, make-up, costume design or even mending—'

'I thought you meant go back and take more acting classes!' Nola sobbed again.

Now it was Maggie's turn to stare at Nola. 'Why on earth would I suggest that?'

'Because you're a bloody actors' agent! If I'd wanted to be

a hairdresser to begin with I wouldn't have come knocking on your door, would I?'

'Look, you're upset, but this isn't the end of the world. You have to see it as a new beginning.' Maggie got up from behind her desk and placed Nola's beret on top of her head and shepherded her towards the door.

'I was coming over to suggest that we try and pitch me differently, and now it's all over. My life is over,' Nola said between heaving sobs.

'For goodness' sake, don't be so melodramatic,' Maggie snapped. 'It's just a job, and not even that most of the time. You need to get on with life. This thing, this career that you've set your heart on, it's clearly not for you.' Nola stood in the doorway, tears rolling down her cheeks, her dreams disintegrating before her eyes. Maggie looked at her now, held her eyes before she spoke. 'Listen to me: you're not an actress anymore. You had your shot, and now it's over. It's brutal, but better to hear it now than in a decade's time. Go home, Nola, make a new plan and start living a life that has a chance of leading you somewhere better.'

2

'He's a child!' Georgie wailed. She could do that here; God knows she was paying Sylvia Lombard enough to listen to her.

'But from what you say, he's got a first-class degree from Oxford?' Sylvia slipped in. She had the irritating habit of being direct and soft-spoken all at once. That was what you got when your employers chose a therapist originally from Galway. Sylvia walked about in a cloud of essential oils and jangling silver bangles, seeing the world from her esoteric vantage point, which was all too often at odds with Georgie's practical world view.

'For the last time, Crispin Biggley-Downes stealing my job has nothing to do with his degree and everything to do with his father being one of our biggest clients.'

'I'm sure that—'

'He was the office joke! We all called him CBD – or Mr

Cannabis, to give him his full title – and not even just behind his back.'

'And he took the joke in good spirits?'

'He didn't have much of a choice.' But then, Georgie thought, maybe that was it. Even Paul had been in on it. Was that how Crispin had managed to ingratiate himself with him? 'Oh, God.' She buried her head in her hands. How had she been so stupid? Georgie remembered them now, guffawing at whatever joke Crispin had delivered. He was unnervingly ubiquitous, slipping in and out of groups in the office. Now that she thought about it, there wasn't one person who worked at the firm who hadn't liked him.

'So he didn't take himself too seriously?' Sylvia said slowly.

'In many ways – all right, in every way – he's the complete opposite of everything I think it's important to be as a director. It's not meant to be a popularity contest.' It was true, but just because they had different approaches, didn't mean hers was automatically wrong. 'To be honest, if someone treated me the way Crispin treats his assistants, I'd be livid. It's nothing short of patronising. It's please this and thank you that. Honestly, all that gushing, you'd swear he was at a tea party with the Queen half the time.'

'And what's the problem with that?'

'He always tries to be everyone's friend – it's inappropriate. Whereas I have boundaries...'

'But perhaps your boundaries are as much about your past as they are an appropriate approach to a leadership role?' Sylvia's voice was too gentle. Georgie never fully trusted her when she spoke like this; it felt as if she was being led into some sort of trap.

'This isn't about me and my sisters – why do you always bring it back to that?' Too late she realised she'd taken the bait.

'I didn't mention your sisters, you did.' Sylvia looked up now from her notepad as if surprised by the entrance of Iris and Nola into their conversation.

'Well, you needn't think I'm talking about them now. I want to figure out what happened to my promotion.' It was bloody infuriating sometimes, all the money this woman was earning for sitting there and leading her in endless circles, never ending up anywhere properly.

'Fine. So you were saying… boundaries?'

'Yes, boundaries. You need to lead from the front with these people; otherwise they're in danger of going off on all sorts of tangents.'

'So, your relationships with your colleagues are only professional.'

'Always.' Wait a minute, Georgie wasn't sure if they were going back over old ground and the bullying charge that had been levelled against her or if this was leading them somewhere altogether more difficult.

'And so, you never let anyone in…'

'Of course I let people in,' Georgie snapped.

'But, your colleagues never get to see a vulnerable side to you, do they?'

'That would be very unprofessional.'

'No, Georgie, that's what we call being human.' Sylvia kept looking at her. If it was going to be a staring competition, Georgie wouldn't be the first to break the connection. 'It's okay to let people know if you're struggling and it's good to ask for help. Sometimes, it can create bonds, relationships; it can even build respect.'

'So, if I'd been one of those women who regularly cried her eyes out in the communal bathrooms I'd have been a shoo-in for the promotion. Is that what you're saying?'

'Of course not, but you haven't managed to get the job anyway, so what have you lost out on on the way?' She stopped, glanced at the clock, although Georgie had a feeling she knew the time down to the millisecond once a session started.

'You think I should be more like Crispin, jollying everyone along, organising karaoke nights and meditative art sessions during lunch hour...' Georgie stopped for a moment, realising that she'd wrinkled her nose, and so she concentrated on moving her features back to some sort of neutral passivity. Was this woman actually suggesting that they were right to pass her over for the job? It was true that Paul had called her into his office a few times over the years because she'd upset some so-called assistant, but as she'd explained to him a hundred times over, you can't make an omelette without cracking some eggs.

'I think you need to be yourself, but a joyful atmosphere is always more productive. What I'm saying is that it would be a good thing to examine exactly why you have had to create these boundaries in the first place, because I think we both know that it has more to do with shutting yourself away from pain. Isn't it that you don't want to end up being hurt again?'

'Oh, please!' Georgie couldn't answer, but she wasn't going to admit there was a huge lump at the back of her throat that threatened to spill over and break into a reserve she'd spent so many years building up.

'You can pretend you don't know what I'm talking about as much as you like, but we both know it's true. You've been badly hurt, Georgie, and you haven't taken the time to heal, you haven't even tried to rebuild those bridges again.'

'You really want to know the truth?' It was gone; that steely cold reserve had cracked and there was no stopping the anger shooting through. 'The truth is, I told my sister Iris that her husband was stealing from our father's distillery and she chose to believe him over me. I probably pushed them together more than they had been before and after that she wanted nothing to do with me. She followed him out of Ballycove and that was that.'

'And Nola?'

'Nola.' Georgie thought of her youngest, sweetest sister sadly and then she remembered how things had turned out between them. 'Nola asked for my help and then she threw it back in my face. She found fame and fortune and friends in London and that was the last I've heard from her.'

'I'm sorry,' Sylvia said. 'I know this is painful, but, Georgie, can't you see that the people you're working with may want a more inclusive work environment? They may want a workplace that's...' she paused for a moment as if considering her next word carefully '...harmonious. And that's about having good relationships, everyone being part of the team.'

'You don't make the grade with harmony. You get results with hard work, with stretching people beyond what they thought they were capable of, not by mollycoddling them.'

Georgie scoffed. But even as she said it, a memory came back to her. It was a few years ago. She'd been off work for a few weeks with double pneumonia. It was one of those stupid things; she'd been sicker than she thought and hadn't stopped. She was far too busy to make time in her schedule to see the doctor and ended up in ICU.

When she'd eventually made her way back into the office, she'd decided to get an early start. She'd turned up at four-thirty in the morning to find the office transformed, the desks pushed back and the space between them empty as if freed up for dancing. It took her almost an hour to get those desks all pushed back into place again. By the time the first of her colleagues turned up for work, she had the place looking spick and span again and though everyone welcomed her back, even at the time she could tell that behind their words she detected something else. Was it disappointment? Resentment? She found out later they'd been having daily yoga sessions organised by one of the young interns.

'Har-bloody-monious.' She felt the word fall in a whisper from her lips.

'Yes, Georgie, harmonious,' Sylvia repeated, and there was a note of guarded triumph in her voice.

'So, say you're right and what Paul wanted all along was not someone who pushed people to reach their full potential – how can I still manage to get my job back from CBD boy before it's all set in stone?'

'I'm not sure you can,' Sylvia said. 'And I'm not sure you should even try. It may be that there's something far better you could be doing with your time.'

Georgie raised her eyebrows. 'Like worming dogs in Battersea, I suppose?'

'If it gives you joy, then maybe.' Sylvia picked a stray thread from her skirt and laid it carefully on the arm of her chair.

'Well, it doesn't. The only thing that gives me joy is the idea that I've got what I deserve fair and square.'

'What you deserve is a very ambiguous thing. For example, a child might deserve pudding for doing some particular good deed, but if the child is overweight, pudding might be the last thing he needs.' She smiled, as if Georgie might somehow find this analogy helpful. It was infuriating.

'I'm not a child and I have zero desire for pudding.' Georgie looked out the window and she knew, even as her eyes skipped across the various wind chimes and bird feeders that covered the sickeningly sweet lilac block work opposite, she sounded just like a child. And worse, she sounded like the sort of child she'd always detested: petulant, spoiled and whingey. Had the years turned her from single-minded to downright obstinate? No, she was determined, that's all. They wouldn't be saying all this about a man, would they? A surge of fury coursed through her.

'All I'm saying is that your company have given you a fantastic opportunity. Of course, you can stay and continue to do exactly what you've always done, but it's not making you happy.'

'It *is* making me happy,' Georgie retorted, feeling the exact opposite of happy.

'But, Georgie, don't you remember our first sessions? Why you came here?

'That's not relevant to this at all.' Georgie stopped her. 'You have no right to bring that up now. It was a completely separate incident and that airy-fairy mediator only sent me here because the company wanted to wriggle out of having to make a payout to a disgruntled ex-employee.'

'You really believe that's why you came here? A paper exercise to reduce your employer's liability?' Sylvia sighed, as if they were trudging up a hill and there was no chance of ever reaching the summit. So much for being an expert at neutrality. 'Georgie?'

Silence stretched out between them. Georgie glanced at her watch as if she didn't know exactly how long was left in this session. At this point, she was expected to say something agreeable, conciliatory even, but she was damned if she was eating any more humble pie today. 'You're just twisting things about to suit yourself. You think you can convince me I actually need to be here? None of this is exactly rocket science. It's easy to see – it's a boys' club and I'm on the outside, and—'

'Maybe you're right, but I have a feeling that being on the outside is something you've created all by yourself and it has as much to do with the past as it has with the present.'

Georgie had a feeling all this woman wanted was a reaction. She wanted to see her shout, or cry or maybe – and this was the most unlikely outcome – to agree with her. 'What's that supposed to mean?'

'Oh, come on, Georgie, you've always skirted past any mention of anything beyond work.'

'That's right.' There was no way Sylvia was getting her claws on the fact that Georgie hadn't had a proper relationship since she'd left Ballycove all those years ago. There had been flings, casual affairs, but nothing that stuck. The only man in her life was her father and for now, that suited her just fine. 'Moving on.' She glared at the woman opposite. 'What would you suggest I do now?'

'Anything you want.' Sylvia smiled. 'Open a goat farm in the outer Hebrides, start up a B&B back in Ireland, buy yourself a sizeable chunk of London property and live off the rent – it's entirely up to you! But do something that gives you real joy.' She stopped for a moment, gauging Georgie's blank expression and perhaps realising that this was too radical a proposal for her. 'Why not start by taking a holiday? Just a little break away from London, somewhere to clear your mind and set your refresh button. It would do you the world of good, I promise.'

'Well, if you feel that strongly about it, I'll do it; it's the first time you've ever told me to do anything that wasn't an open question.' Georgie harrumphed. She would go on holiday. She would pack up her life for two weeks and escape to somewhere with sun and sea and lots of alcohol – so much alcohol that she would wipe Sandstone and Mellon clear out of her mind for fourteen solid days.

It was only as she left the consulting rooms that she saw the missed call on her phone. Ireland. She rang back immediately and was answered by an unfamiliar woman's voice.

'Ah, Georgie, thank you so much for calling back. I'm Lucy Nolan and I've recently taken over the Ballycove doctor's surgery from Dr O'Shea.' There was a pause at the other end of the line, and Georgie had the sudden urge to hang up, to stop this woman saying whatever it was she had called to say. 'I'm so sorry to tell you that your father passed away during the night. It was peaceful…' She went on speaking; her voice soft, measured, kind, but Georgie didn't hear the words. All she knew was that her father had died alone while she was tossing and turning, worrying about things that suddenly didn't matter.

She swayed, unable to engage with the increasingly urgent voice coming down the phone asking if she was okay, if there was anyone she could call.

No, there wasn't, Georgie thought absently. She was now, truly, alone.

Shalib placed a cup of his strongest coffee before Nola. It was laced with a mixture of spices she knew were meant to calm her down, but she had a feeling that there was no blotting out this pain.

Her father had passed away peacefully at home. The news washed over Nola like a freezing tide, numbing her, so it felt as if she was looking in at everything from somewhere just beyond her own reach. She'd hardly talked to him for years, until he'd reached out a few months earlier. His letters had become something she looked forward to, one a week, a small highlight in the grey vista of her existence here. She hadn't been home in a decade, not since that awful party when she'd run out and sworn she'd never set foot in the same room as her sisters ever again.

But her father was dead and she couldn't believe it. Now, so many years later, she could close her eyes and remember exactly what it felt like when he carried her on his shoulders down the beach on sunny afternoons in Ballycove. The memory filled her with intense, bleak loneliness. Nola knew she would have to travel back to Ireland for the funeral. Was it so bad to want to wriggle out of it?

'What now?' She had just begun her shift at the café when the call came through. It was the only address her father had to reach her. Somehow, a few months earlier, he'd tracked her down to here. She could imagine how it was – some cousin of a neighbour had probably spotted Ballycove's once-famous actress clearing tables in a slightly shabby Moroccan coffee house. Yes. She could imagine it; the village news-bags would have had a field day with that nugget of gossip.

'Of course you will have to go home,' Shalib said, his voice firm but gentle. 'Some things are more important than saving face, Nola.' He smiled, shaking his head sadly.

'Oh, Shalib, it's not just that…' She stopped for a moment. She couldn't even cry. What on earth did that say about her? 'I'm not sure I belong there. So much happened and, well, I haven't been much of a daughter these past few years.'

'He would want you there.' Shalib's voice was low and certain.

'You don't know that,' Nola said, her voice hollow.

'I know he was proud of you.'

'After my mother died he hardly noticed any of us for ages and then my sisters left home and I just sort of got on with life as best I could.' She thought back to that dark time, and shuddered. Everything had gone to pieces and Nola was too young then to know how to put it back together and ever since, even if she'd wanted to, she still wasn't sure how to go about making things right.

'Nola. He had lost the love of his life; he was a man drowning in grief. That doesn't mean he loved you any less.'

'That's not the point. He was my father, my only remaining parent, and he was supposed to look after me. Anyway, how do you know he still loved me? You sound so sure...' Nola looked into his eyes, wanting to believe him more than anything.

'I know what it is to be a parent. We don't always get things right, but that doesn't mean your bond was any less important to him.'

'Oh, Shalib, we made a terrible mess of things, but I did love him.' Now, she'd never be able to tell him. That made her gasp – the finality of it taking her breath away for a moment, as if some traitorous part of her was falling into unknown depths of sadness without her permission.

'Nola, everyone just does their best. We may want to have done better, but we do our best.'

'I haven't gone home to see him in ten years.' She was ashamed to admit it.

'I'm sure he knew why that was.' Shalib's face creased into a thousand lines of kindness. 'He would want you there now, supporting your sisters and showing the village that he still has a family to be proud of.'

'It upset him so much that my sisters and I don't speak to one another. He probably gave up hope long ago that we'd ever support each other the way proper sisters should.' And then she was crying, great big tears leaking down her cheeks and falling onto the table, overwhelming her too much to even try and figure out whether she was crying for her father or the sisters she missed far more than she'd ever admit. She rubbed her eyes with a force that had less to do with drying her tears and more with heaving herself by sheer force out of this crushing sadness.

Shalib wouldn't hear of her finishing her shift. As he gently ushered her out, he said, 'There is no rush to come back to work. You will always have a place here.' He pressed two weeks' wages into her hand and she heard the latch pull across when he closed the door behind her.

That night after she booked the cheapest flight to Ireland she could find, sleep evaded her as her mind shuttled between memories of the past and thoughts of what lay waiting for her in Ballycove. Of course, her sisters knew that she wasn't going to be up for an Oscar anytime soon, but that didn't mean she couldn't let them believe she wasn't a jobbing actress in the West End. She began to cook up a plausible biography of her life in London. After all, thousands of people were employed in theatres all the year through. And she could be doing anything from understudy roles to bit parts to front-of-house – not that she hadn't tried all these options in reality, but it seemed her meagre fame had worked against her. She was too well-known for some roles, not enough for others. She could even say she was acting as an agent for other actors. Georgie would probably be most impressed with that, even if she wouldn't admit it.

Nola smiled, in spite of herself. She really could lose herself in this pretend life she was dreaming up for the benefit of her sisters. Although, was it really for their benefit? More likely it was for her own – after all, *they* had managed to get their hearts' desires. Iris had got her comfortable suburban home and husband who she put up on a pedestal so long ago that she'd never see through him even if she wanted to. Nola shivered when she thought of Myles, even all these years later. The thought of him still made her skin crawl. How was it that she'd done nothing wrong, but she was the one left feeling guilty and somehow soiled by him? And Georgie? Georgie had achieved all that she'd ever wanted; Nola was quite sure of that. By now, she was probably the CEO or managing director or whatever the top job was at her company. She had oodles of cash and her bathroom was probably three times the size of Nola's whole flat.

No. She deserved this. A little white lie or two couldn't hurt for just a few days, could it? And already, just thinking of this dreamy make-believe life was lifting her spirits enormously.

Georgie rang. *Georgie rang.* Iris stood by the phone until it almost went into messages because Georgie hadn't telephoned her in years. And even if the rational part of Iris knew her older sister wasn't ringing with good news, still she felt her insides fight with each other in an eruption of joy and dread that even if she wanted to contain it, she couldn't help which came out on top.

'Hello.' Iris heard her own voice, as formal as if she was answering the phone at work.

'Iris?' Georgie asked, as if she hardly recognised the person she'd just rung.

'Yes.'

'It's me, Georgie.'

'I know who it is,' Iris said softly and she realised that if it was a few weeks earlier she might have snapped – no, she corrected herself now, a few weeks earlier she probably wouldn't have picked up the phone at all.

'It's Dad. I've just had a call from his GP. I'm afraid he…' Georgie stopped a moment, as if there was someone pulling at her sleeve and then she sniffled. 'Bloody sinus,' she said more gruffly.

'What's happened to Dad? Has he had a fall?' It's what happened to old people, living on their own, and their father had been rambling about in a house too large for him for far too many years for the odds to be stacked any other way but against him.

'I'm afraid he's died,' Georgie whispered so quietly that Iris wasn't sure if she'd heard her properly.

'He's… but he can't be…' And then Iris dropped to sit in the nearest chair and let her sister's words wash over her while her body went numb with what she supposed was grief.

Two hours Iris sat there, until the light began to fade outside. Her tea turned cold; the biscuits she'd placed on the coffee table still lay there, looking even less appetising now. She'd been lost in memories of her childhood in Ballycove. And then, occasionally, a creaking gate or a parking car would rouse her and remind her she was still sitting in the near-darkness of her too-tidy London sitting room. She could hear her father's voice, fragments of conversations that had been buried so deeply in her memory; she wondered if they'd ever been real to begin with.

He felt very close to her, as if he'd just stepped into the room. And she thought back to that day long ago when she was hardly six years old and he'd brought her to the shops, promising her an ice-cream at the end. She'd wandered off, dazzled by the sweet counter and then before she knew it, she was lost. Suddenly, she could feel that rising childhood panic battering her ribs, hollowing out her insides. The feeling had been so overwhelming; she could recall the ghost of it even now. Fear had pushed tears and snot down her face. She had brushed them away but she couldn't stop wailing as if the world had ended. And then he'd scooped her up and wiped away her tears, and all at once everything was right again. He'd told her then that he'd always find her if she was lost.

And suddenly, she wanted to be back in Ballycove, back with her father, in that grand old house where she could convince herself that everything was okay and that he would wipe away her tears, making sure she was never lost again.

It took her over like a yearning so strong it might be rooted in the relentless tide at the bottom of the village, a sort of primal call that she needed to go back there. She needed to make things right, not just with herself, but with her father too. And then she remembered. He was gone. Georgie's phone call – the first time she had called in years – had put an end to any possibility of making things right ever again.

She was numb. Of course, apart from grief, it was guilt. She'd spent so many years trying to desperately hold onto a husband who couldn't be held and in doing so, she'd missed out on her father's last years.

At least it had been peaceful. In the end. Perhaps that

would eventually make some difference to how she felt, but not yet. For now, she felt just as lost as that day in the shop. And this time, he wouldn't be coming to find her.

The day she was due to fly, Nola's alarm didn't go off. Bloody typical! She leaped out of bed and made a lunge-fall-dash towards the bathroom. She scrubbed her teeth vigorously but quickly, grabbed her bags. She was starving, but there was no time; she'd have to get breakfast on the way. She was a ball of sweat by the time she was ready to leave. Only she, Nola Delahaye, could oversleep by an hour and put the flight home to her father's funeral in jeopardy.

As she flew around her bedroom stuffing clothes into a bag, the realisation that he was gone hit her anew. Suddenly, on the morning when time was against her and she needed to hold it all together, her grief hit her like a tsunami and all she wanted to do was sit in the middle of her cluttered flat and bawl her eyes out like a baby. But she couldn't, because she had to get to the airport.

As she was locking up, she felt a hand on her shoulder and a deep, gravelly voice said, 'Miss Nola Delahaye?'

She whipped around, her heart pounding, to find a tall man far too close to her. 'Dear God!' she gasped. 'Are you trying to give me a heart attack?'

'Sorry, I just…' He took a step backwards. 'I wanted to catch you before you left for work. Here.' He shoved an envelope into her hands. 'I'm supposed to deliver this to you,' he said, before turning on his heel and heading towards the flat upstairs.

'Right,' she said, just relieved that he wasn't going to mug her. She stuffed the envelope in her pocket. She hadn't time to think of it now. She had a plane to make.

An hour later, she was sandwiched between an elderly half-deaf woman who was intent on saying the rosary and figuring out who the patron saint of flying was all at full volume, and a kid who looked like he was on a gap year and smelled as if he'd spent most of it deprived of any sort of shower facility. Nola buried her nose in her phone and hoped that they would make it to Ireland in record time.

The plane was already stiflingly hot, so she peeled her coat off and handed it to an already put-upon stewardess who was securing the overhead baggage holds.

'I think this is yours,' the stewardess said, handing her the letter. Nola hadn't thought about it since she'd stuffed it into her pocket.

'Thanks,' she said easily. She pulled open the envelope to find it was a single page from a solicitor she'd never heard of. It took her two reads to figure out what they were trying to say between the lines of legal jargon. They were evicting her, wanted her out of her flat in a month's time. There was a demolition order on the building and they'd helpfully (pah!) attached a cheque for two thousand pounds as compensation for any inconvenience caused. And oh, yes, they hoped that she would consider buying a high-end apartment on the site when they came up for sale late next year.

She felt herself begin to shake. She couldn't cry (perhaps, she thought, she'd cried herself completely out), just felt cold and empty and scared for the future that looked as if it was being ripped up from every corner possible. Oh God, how could this be happening to her? She was going to be homeless. Homeless and alone in London. She took a deep breath, praying maybe it was some silly mistake. She pulled out the letter again, skipping from line to line, as if in doing so she could change what it said. But no matter how many times she went back over it, the sick feeling in her stomach made a mockery of her. *This is what real fear feels like,* she thought – like standing on a precipice. She was about to be pushed over the edge and, yet again, there was no-one to save her.

Nola held the letter in her hand for the whole flight, trying to make sense of where her life was going to end up. She couldn't afford another flat in that area; she'd barely been able to afford the run-down one she already had. Two thousand pounds would be about as useful to her in compensation for upturning her life now as snow boots would be in the Sahara.

As the flight touched down on the Dublin runway, Nola crumpled up the letter and stuffed it into the pouch on the back of the seat before her, along with the various airline magazines. She folded the cheque carefully, tucking it into her jeans pocket with deliberateness at odds with the shaking, quaking foundations of her life.

It was greener. Iris was sure it was greener than she remembered, but then, perhaps that was because she hadn't been back for so long. She had taken the first flight she could arrange into Knock airport, and now she was standing outside the small terminal, looking out at the glorious landscape of her childhood. Her employer had been very understanding and given her time off, telling her to spend as long as she needed in Ireland. They were very kind, but really she had no intention of spending any longer than she had to in the company of Georgie and Nola.

Since hearing the news, it felt as if she hadn't stopped crying. She hadn't expected her father's death to hit her so badly. For a long time, she thought she'd never forgive him for saying that Myles was only after the distillery. He had taken Georgie's word that Myles had been selling on bottles of whiskey to his friends after her father had promoted him to being his right-hand man. That had been the beginning of the end for Iris and Georgie and her father. The more they ran him down, the more determined she'd become to hang on to Myles.

Then, three months ago, her father had reached out to her, completely out of the blue. His letter had arrived one damp depressing morning and she must have read it a hundred times before she'd even had her elevenses. There was honesty and rawness to her father's words. His pen had shook as it moved across each letter. It was, she knew, heartfelt and it touched her deeply in a way she'd never have expected. Very soon, it felt as if they were feeling their way back towards one another. It was as if he was guiding her heart back to Ballycove, if not quite forgiveness. On their last call, she'd almost promised to visit him. And now, she was back here and it was too late.

Since Georgie's call two days ago Iris found herself gasping at the overwhelming sense of loss his death provoked. It caught her out when she was least expecting it. Making her heart pound, her stomach churn and filling her with an overwhelming sense of loneliness that felt as if it might suffocate her completely. She would have sworn that Myles's betrayal and the news of his baby had been the final straw – but it turned out she was wrong.

A light misting rain breathed its filmy breath on her face as she left Knock airport. The sensible thing to do now was run and catch the next bus for Ballycove. She wasn't feeling very sensible though and part of her just wanted to walk in the soft, dewy breeze and feel it cleanse from her the stain and stench of London.

'Iris?' she heard a broad familiar voice call out. 'Iris Delahaye, is it yourself that's in it?' She swung around to see Moira Barry making her way towards her, accompanied by her husband Eugene. She was unchanged – a little older, a lot wider, but the same open face, full of welcome and warmth. 'I can't believe it! It's too long since we've seen you. And your poor father – we're so sad to hear it. He'll be badly missed about the place.'

'I know, sad times indeed,' Iris said, her voice hollow in her own ears. Moira Barry was a hugger; there was no point fighting off the embrace. At least Eugene settled for a manly handshake and friendly nod.

Moira looked at her with a critical eye. 'You look tired and you need feeding up, but you're still the same girl; I can see it in your eyes. A few days here and you'll be right as rain. There's nothing the sea air can't fix.' She was not being unkind – or not intentionally, anyway – just solicitous in her motherly way, and Iris knew she'd say no different to her own girls when they arrived back at her farmhouse just a few miles along the road from Soldier Hill House. 'You're not thinking of taking the bus, are you?'

'Well—'

'Absolutely not, we wouldn't hear of it. It'll take you half the day and a third of the county to get home. Our car is just over there. Come on, now, Eugene will have you home before you know it.' And then they were making their way towards the car park and loading her bag into the back seat before she could even thank them. She was glad, as they drove through towns she hardly recognised now. It was nice, travelling along in their little car, listening to all the latest news from Ballycove, even though it was mostly about people she'd hardly given a thought to for more years than she cared to remember.

'Ballycove hasn't changed much,' Eugene said stoutly.

'No. There's no danger of you getting lost, anyway.' Moira laughed. 'New doctor, and of course the old Corrigan Mills have changed hands, but the hotel is still going strong and the sea is slowly trying to eat away at the pier when we're not looking.'

'And your family are…?'

'Scattered to the four winds, apart from Aiden – he's making a great fist of the farm,' Moira said proudly as she gazed out across green fields that had been subdivided almost to the point of postage stamps. Aiden was the middle child in the family, but older than Iris, and she had almost forgotten about him; Georgie would probably remember him much better.

'That must be nice,' Iris said, thinking wistfully for the first time in as long as she could remember that it must be something special to have family about you as you got older. Actually, it must be lovely just to have a family in general. Iris looked out the window, concentrating on the scenery passing slowly by. The sky overhead had papered in a pewter colour that pressed down on the darkening hills rolling into the distance.

They were right about Ballycove. It hadn't changed a bit, and the road along the bay seemed like it was extending a welcome home to her that she knew she didn't really deserve. She'd loved it here, but that was something she'd managed to disregard when she fell in love with Myles. Back then, like everyone else her age, all she'd wanted was adventure and excitement. God, if only she'd known then where the road she was on would take her. Now, she rolled down the window and inhaled the sea air as if it was precious oxygen to a drowning woman.

'You can't beat it,' Eugene said, proudly surveying the Atlantic Ocean below them. Perhaps, that was the secret to happiness, Iris thought: relishing what is on your doorstep, never having to leave your own backyard to find the kind of contentment that in her experience had only grown more distant as she'd tried to chase it down.

'Aye, it'll soon put a colour back in your cheeks,' Moira said confidently.

'It's good to be back.' Iris surprised herself by realising she actually meant it. Even today, with the sky a gloomy grey and the sea a molten cold steel and black, there was no mistaking the sweetness of the air and the enveloping welcome of coming home to somewhere she knew she had once belonged. They passed by the tiny cottages facing across the sea wall and then on up towards the top of the village, passing by the old Georgian houses that had stood proud but shabby when she was here last. Now, they looked as if someone had come along and spruced them up to their former glory. 'The surgery is gone,' she said softly.

'No, it's still here; the new doctor has opened up a brand-new practice at the back. It's out on the market square – much better. There's parking and no hanging about, not like in the old days,' Eugene said as if he was giving tour guide information to a day-tripper.

From there the little car weaved through the two miles of bendy roads to take Iris back to the house where she had grown up. The avenue alone was enough to let her know that here, at least, the hand of reinvention had not yet waved its magic wand. A high growth of grass sprouted in the middle of the narrow avenue and on either side beech trees stretched lacy fingers towards the darkening sky.

Soldier Hill House stood tall and majestic, if a little worse for wear – her father had never been a man to notice much if it needed paint or pruning. Now, sleeping wisteria hung from the front façade waiting for the summer to bloom again in purple glory. Still, even in the overcast afternoon, she could see that the windows gleamed and the ancient brass adorning the old front door shone even in this grey light. Then she spotted the plumes of smoke rising from two of the chimneys, and unexpected warmth suffused her whole being.

She was home. The question was, what on earth was waiting for her now she was here?

3

Ireland, December

Iris was first to arrive, which was a relief; it gave her time to get her bearings. It seemed someone, probably Mary Lynch, her father's housekeeper, had thought of everything. The larder was full, the fridge was stocked and the whole place had a lingering aroma of either lemon or pine. Even the beds were aired. If the house was dated and a little faded, it still was fresh and clean.

Iris walked from room to room, allowing the nostalgia of memories from happy times so long ago to wash over her, then she stepped out to the garden. She sat on the swing that still hung from the huge oak and thought about both her parents, gone now, and she let the tears that were never far away these days flow freely.

Sitting there on that swing, Iris realised she had to make a plan. She couldn't waste any more of her life in the way she'd squandered the last twenty-odd years. This place seemed to be whispering something on the sea. She couldn't make out the words, but a tiny ray of sunshine cut through the clouds above her, lighting up a thin path along the grass. A soft warmth flowed along her skin, pricking up the fine hairs at the back of her neck. It was little more than a glimmer, but somehow, for the first time in weeks, she had a sense that there was room to hope for a better life. She took a deep breath. She could choose to do things differently – if she wanted.

There would be an inheritance. She wasn't a greedy person, but there was no getting away from the fact that her father had worked hard and built up a considerable number of assets over the years. He would have left everything between the three of them, equally – wouldn't he? When everything was sold, they would all be wealthier than they'd been before.

A light wind brushed past her, sending a tingling sensation through her and clinking through the tiny bottles that they'd hung years ago from the branches overhead – a homemade wind chime that had miraculously survived all the storms over the years. She felt a little light-headed. It had been so long since she'd felt she had a choice in life.

If she returned to London, put some time and effort into how she looked and waved her small fortune beneath Myles's nose, she knew she might have some chance of stealing her husband back. Was it stealing if he was meant to be hers to begin with? She didn't feel as excited as she'd have expected at the prospect.

On the other hand, if she could face down the tsunami of questions and curiosity about the end of her marriage, she could come home. That thought made her laugh out loud – the possibility of coming back to live in Ballycove had never been one she contemplated. No, it would be far more sensible to fight for the life she'd carved out for herself in London. Much better to keep to the road she'd set out on with Myles all those years ago, for better or for worse. Wasn't that what they'd promised?

An insistent growling from her stomach interrupted her thoughts. When she checked her watch, she realised it was almost dinner time and she hadn't eaten since the cereal bar she had for breakfast on the plane. She trotted up the garden path. Every crack along it was so familiar, it felt as if she'd stepped back in time. How often had she and her sisters raced along here, eager to get to the beach or the village on long summer days that seemed destined never to end?

As Iris entered the hall, she caught a glimpse of herself in a mirror hanging on the wall, and stopped. She grimaced at her reflection, tucked her hair behind her ears. It looked as brittle as she felt. She patted it down. She should have made time to go to the hairdresser's. Iris sighed. This evening, when she was due to collect Georgie from the airport, was not the time for thinking about things like her hair. A trendy new cut might have made her feel more confident, but it was too late now. She had decided that the best way to deal with the awkwardness of seeing her sisters again was to just be friendly. It was only for the funeral, and then she'd never have to stand in the same room as either of them ever again.

The most important thing was to keep the truth from Georgie. If her sister knew the truth of her life, Iris knew what she would say: *I told you so*. And she had, to be fair; she'd said it before Iris had even packed her bags to follow

Myles to London all those years ago. Wise before her time, that was Georgie; no wonder she'd made such a huge success of things. Always such a know-it-all.

As she drove to the airport, parked up and waited for Georgie to emerge, she felt that familiar mixture of anger and hurt that both her sisters brought up in her. She would have to pretend it wasn't there this one last time, just for her father's sake. If she pretended her life was ticking along as planned, maybe she could rise above the niggling little remarks that always set her off.

Iris spotted Georgie stalking through arrivals – classic Georgie, the first passenger off the plane, cool as steel. You couldn't miss her. She was six foot tall and still gangly, with a shock of red hair that refused to be tamed or tidied – much like Georgie herself. It had dulled a little; perhaps her colourist had chosen to tone things down as the years had passed.

Georgie's eyes met hers and it felt as if a knot that had tightened in her stomach years before pulled even tighter. She strode over with the sort of confidence that marks people out, but then stood there for a second eyeing Iris warily. What was the protocol, Iris wondered, for how to greet estranged sisters after all this time? Georgie settled for a curt nod.

'You made it.' Iris impressed herself by managing a stiff smile.

'Of course I made it. What's that supposed to mean?' Georgie was on the defensive immediately. Iris suppressed a sigh.

'Nothing, nothing at all. It's just that you're so busy and

I know it must have been tough to have to drop everything at a moment's notice, so—' She was blabbering, too nervous to even string together a proper sentence, much less one that didn't sound as if she wanted to take up the arguments they'd left off the last time they spoke.

'I've never been too busy for Dad.' She pinned Iris with a look that said far more than any words. For a moment, Iris couldn't look away. There it was, the inescapable truth: Iris should have visited, she should have made things up properly, when there was still time. She felt her cheeks flush.

'Right.' Iris grabbed one of her sister's bags and soon they were making their way out to the old Mercedes her father had hardly used for the last couple of years. It smelled of nothing more than the stubborn hint of the pipe their father smoked every time he drove it.

'I can't believe you decided to drive this old thing.'

'It's officially vintage, apparently.' True enough, it was ancient, but her father had kept it in excellent condition. The housekeeper told Iris that he hadn't properly driven it in years, but he'd still had it serviced every six months. 'It drinks petrol as if it's an alcoholic in an open brewery and I don't suppose we want to think of the damage it's doing in terms of emissions every time I rev the engine.'

Next to her, Georgie sighed as they made their way out onto the open road, green fields stretching off into the distance, interrupted by stubborn rock and packed down by dreary skies. 'God. This place,' she said, her voice quieter than Iris ever remembered. 'It hasn't changed much, has it?'

'No,' Iris said softly. 'It's hard to decide if that's good or bad, isn't it?'

Georgie said nothing for a while, and they continued in an uncomfortable silence until she cut into Iris's thoughts with: 'So, I suppose Myles is back at the house already?'

Iris felt her palms grow clammy against the steering wheel. 'Ahm, no. He – er – couldn't make it this time… A big story, he's abroad for a few weeks, and, well, you know how it—'

'He's not coming to Dad's funeral?' Georgie shot a sideways glance at her and Iris felt her cheeks redden under the scrutiny. 'Oh, well. I suppose Dad's not going to mind either way.' She shrugged. If she was thinking that he would be as well pleased if Myles had never been part of the family to begin with, she didn't say it, and Iris was grateful. Perhaps she'd also decided to call a truce for the next few days.

'Anyway, never mind all that,' Iris said as brightly as she could. 'What about you? Still taking the world of marketing by storm? I bet you're top dog at this stage…' She tried hard to bite down any trace of resentment or cynicism at Georgie's success. After all, everything Georgie had made of her life had been completely down to herself; she had earned it fair and square.

'Actually, things are going really well…' Georgie's voice sounded far away and she tailed off, as if she was thinking about other things, and Iris remembered her father telling her a few weeks earlier about the last time her sister visited. Apparently, she'd spent all her time working on some account and hardly saw beyond her computer screen for the whole weekend. Not so perfect after all. Iris knew only too well that you could be in the same room together, but in completely different worlds if the other person was so wrapped up in a computer screen that they didn't see you anymore. In her experience, that was almost worse than not having the person there at all. At least whenever he had rung Iris in the last few weeks, *she* was there – present – listening to him, talking to him. But this wasn't the time for point scoring.

'So, only Nola left to arrive now,' Iris said, changing the subject. Nola. Their youngest sister, so different to the other two. She'd always been beautiful, the popular one, a little out of hand. Iris felt herself gag. Why couldn't she put aside that memory of catching her younger sister and Myles together, if only for the next few days? She could try. After all that had happened with Myles over the last few weeks, surely there was room to doubt everything that he'd convinced her of so thoroughly now?

'Yes. Nola,' Georgie said shortly, as if even the mention of Nola irritated her. 'I thought I might bump into her on the plane. She is coming, isn't she?'

'Of course,' Iris said with more conviction than she actually felt. 'Apparently, she has an audition in Dublin for some new sitcom. It all sounds very promising, so she's stopping over there before she takes the train down. I'm collecting her tomorrow morning if you want to come along to meet her too?' Even as she offered it, Iris sincerely hoped she wouldn't. At least driving into town for a few minutes on her own would provide some respite from pretending everything was fine.

'We'll see. I'm quite tired; it's been a long week…'

'Of course,' Iris said, trying not to sound too relieved.

***

Arriving at the airport, the familiar journey home, even the lasting aroma of her father's pipe in the car... It was the cloying familiarity of it all that stopped Georgie in her tracks. Nothing had changed, and yet, with the loss of her father, the very fabric of the place would never be the same again. She tried to be composed about it, but even seeing Iris, standing there at the arrivals gate, had been a shock. Georgie had stomped about looking for a woman who didn't exist anymore. When she'd pulled up in front of Iris, it had taken a moment to register that it was her sister beneath that gaunt frame, pasty pallor and those slightly dead eyes. Iris was prematurely grey. She had somehow allowed herself to become an old woman – not in a wrinkly, twinset sort of way, but in something deeper, as if the life had been faded from her. Perhaps that's what comes of getting your heart's desire...

Or had she? Thinking back to the awkward exchange they'd just had, Georgie had a feeling that Iris was no more content with the life she'd left behind in London than Georgie was herself. At the same time, there was a measured composure about her, as if she had made up her mind that there would be no silly arguments this time. It was only at the mention of Myles that she sensed a tension driving between them that she could tell Iris was trying very hard to avoid. She had not been her usual biting self, who couldn't take so much as a comment without having a meltdown and accusing them all of wanting Myles for themselves.

So, Georgie decided, in that sticky moment as they drove, that would be the last mention she'd make of Myles until their father's funeral was well behind them. It was a relief that he had not travelled over; they should leave it at that. It was time to think about her father, not about the petty squabbles that had worn away at the relationships between his daughters until there was barely anything left. Georgie sent up a silent prayer, promising her father that she would try to be good and not provoke any more arguments.

It occurred to Georgie that their father's death was almost like a final loosening of whatever ribbons still joined the sisters together. She experienced the thought as a weight being removed from her shoulders, and then felt immediately guilty. How had things got so bad? Georgie's eyes shot across to Iris when she spoke of Nola and she could feel it, writ large between them. Nola hated both of them and even if Georgie and Iris managed to rub along together until this ordeal was over, Nola was quite a different matter.

Georgie shifted uncomfortably in her seat. When Georgie thought of Nola she had to admit that her feelings for her youngest sister were complex. There was always a hint of jealousy. Everything seemed to come so easily to Nola. She gathered up friends as effectively as Georgie pushed the chance of any away. She sighed deeply, elbowed her way further down in the passenger seat and pretended to sleep for the rest of the journey home.

The sun was dipping low, just peppering spots between the grey clouds behind Soldier Hill House as they drove up the avenue. Georgie felt a sting of tears well up in her eyes. She scrunched them closed and pretended to wipe the sleep from them, yawning loudly at the same time. Everything looked so perfect, as if beyond the familiar front door life as it had been when they were children might just carry on as usual.

'God, this place hasn't changed at all,' Georgie said as she got out of the car. 'I had expected...'

'That without him the whole place would feel different?' Iris smiled sadly. 'I know what you mean. It feels as if he should be coming back across the fields from the distillery at any moment.'

'It does look a little tired, maybe?' On her occasional weekend visits here, Georgie never took much notice of anything beyond her father. They would both work all day, him pottering about the distillery and her glued to her laptop. In the evening, they'd sit down for dinner together and drink aged whiskey in the sitting room and talk until the fire died in the hearth.

Today, in truth, Soldier Hill House looked as though it was being held together by wisteria branches and trellis. Mind you, it was very old, almost three hundred years in places. The first Delahaye had settled on this patch of ground after landing in Killala Bay with the French. The intention had been to spread the breaking down of barricades to the furthest reaches of Europe, but of course, the uprising had been quickly trampled down. Legend had it – or at least, her father's story was – that the first Delahaye had stood here, put down his bayonet and decided he would not go another step. Instead, he bought the land and put down roots. The house then grew with each generation that came after him, until it resembled a rambling hall any of the English gentry would have been proud to call a bolthole.

'We probably should order something from the village for dinner and—' Georgie started.

'Oh, no, it's all organised, a roast with all the trimmings—' Iris said as she pushed open the front door and Georgie pulled her bag into the hall.

'Really, you shouldn't have gone to so much bother,' Georgie said. The last thing she wanted to do was sit around the kitchen table and pretend to play happy families with Iris.

'I didn't. Father has kept the housekeeper on until everything is settled, apparently.' Her tone was chilly, but then she turned, looked towards the photograph of both their parents on the wall and took a deep breath. 'But I do think it would be good for us all to catch up... After all, we have just lost our father and whether we like it or not, that grief is something that bonds us together – for a while longer, at least.'

She turned away and headed for the staircase, and Georgie stood for a moment and remembered back to when they were children, one on either side of the wide sweep, racing each other as they slid down the banister. In that moment, she almost thought she could hear their whoops of laughter echo out in the belly of the old house. It sent a small, reluctant shiver through her and she heard herself say, 'Fine, that will be lovely. I'm on wash-up.' Then she climbed the stairs behind Iris, preparing herself for the little room that had been hers at a time when everything in life had seemed to be far simpler.

An hour later, dinner was proving to be just as uncomfortable as she had expected. At least the housekeeper had had the good sense to set them up in the kitchen rather than the more formal dining room that reached too far back into happy memories of Christmas lunches and family parties than Georgie suspected either of them could stand.

'So?' Iris looked at her. It seemed to Georgie every possible topic of conversation she could think of was off limits.

'So,' Georgie replied because she wasn't sure where the invisible boundary between politeness, cordiality and the danger of breaking into another civil war lay.

'The pudding is good,' Iris settled on in the end.

'Yes.' Georgie nodded and wondered how long they could squeeze out of a conversation around rhubarb and raspberry pie. 'I might take a walk tomorrow morning. I have a key, so you don't need to worry about letting me in again, if you have plans to go out.' It was a stab at marking out an hour's freedom for them both, maybe longer if they dawdled.

'Aren't you coming to collect Nola with me at the train station?' Iris asked, but it felt like she was throwing down a gauntlet.

'Of course. I forgot about collecting Nola. Absolutely, I'll go along too,' Georgie managed through gritted teeth and a tight smile.

The train station, like everything else in Ballycove, had hardly changed since last time she was here. If anything it was even more like itself than before, although Georgie wasn't sure that made sense. It was only when she spotted the little plaque put up by the tidy village committee that she realised she was actually right. The rough local stone had been washed and repointed. A proliferation of heathers sprouted from large planters on the platform. It was as much as you could depend on for the winter months to brighten up the place. The brasses gleamed in the absence of any great sunshine overhead and the arrival of anything less than a full steam engine felt as if it might be completely out of step with the whole atmosphere of the place.

One thing that had changed was the arrival time. Or rather, the fact that it arrived on time; as far as Georgie could remember that had never been the case in the past. They waited as the train disgorged its few passengers. Ballycove was literally the end of the line.

Nola hadn't changed either, it seemed. Georgie spotted her as she got out of the carriage, a flurry of long copper hair, breezy clothes – and she could have sworn she could smell her strong perfume from where she stood. Somehow, at almost thirty-five, Nola still looked carefree. She pulled off the Boho-babe look as if she was born to the role. Georgie could feel the resentment – okay, maybe it was a touch of jealousy – digging a deeper furrow in the thin line that cut into the space between her eyebrows.

Along the platform, Nola stopped for a moment, dropped her bag and ran back to the carriage, then alighted again with a separate set of cases, followed by an elderly man who looked as if he might be a hundred and four years old. Typical Nola. Everyone's friend, so easy-going. From where Georgie was standing, it seemed everything just fell into her younger sister's lap.

***

Oh God. Nola just wanted to race back onto the train. Sweat oozed out of her every pore and panic erupted in her stomach so it felt as if she might throw up right there when she saw Georgie and Iris standing on the platform. In blind panic, she turned back in the hope that they hadn't spotted her, praying in one mad moment that she might be able to hide in the toilets until the train pulled out of the station again and headed back to Dublin for its afternoon journey.

But then, she'd seen the old man standing there. Honestly, he looked like Professor Dumbledore in a golfing jumper that had managed to outgrow him before he got a chance to change it. He must have been a hundred years old, hardly able to manage the step down to the platform, never mind actually get his bags off. He looked nothing like her father and yet, as she helped him with his cases, she felt a rising bubble of loneliness lodge itself at the back of her throat, tossing up even more devastation than she'd bargained for. Bless him, but he was so thankful. In the end, there was nothing for it but to stride down the platform with as much confidence as she could muster.

She had spotted Iris first. Standing there, looking as if butter wouldn't melt in her mouth, pink sweater and too-baggy jeans. Perhaps she'd recently lost weight. She'd certainly lost something of the woman she'd once been – Nola could tell that just from one glance.

She tossed her hair and with that felt an unfamiliar wave of self-possession. She could fool herself into thinking she was the same girl who left here all those years ago. It was no harm if it gave her a little extra confidence for dealing with her sisters. Oh God. Her hands were sweating already at the thought of what lay ahead.

And then right on cue, Georgie. As cool and collected as ever. Nola felt a thrill of anger at the sight of her, but fought hard to suppress it.

'Hello,' her two sisters managed in a tight chorus that certainly didn't give way to anything like welcome.

'Hey.' It was all she could manage. Her stomach was flipping somersaults. How on earth would she get through the next few days with them both?

'We haven't had breakfast yet,' Iris nattered as they made their way to their father's ancient Mercedes.

'Iris thought you'd be famished, long journey and all that.' Georgie grabbed one of her bags and tossed it in the boot.

'Well, yes, I suppose I haven't eaten since…' Actually, she hadn't been able to face food since she'd read that letter, and everything here was so bloody expensive. Honestly, Dublin prices – she'd nearly need to take out a loan to buy dinner and a decent glass of wine.

'Good. Pancakes back at home so…' Iris said and it felt as if a tuning fork had been touched on the words – it was so long since any of them had been *home*, or certainly in Nola's case had considered it to be home.

Awkward stabs at conversation followed by long silences punctuated the journey back to Soldier Hill House. Nola hid behind her giant sunglasses, even though the day was overcast. This meant that everything was cloaked in even greater shadow, which suited her mood perfectly, even if she had no intention of letting either of her sisters guess she was anything but fine.

It was depressing; looking out the window. How on earth could so many years have passed and Ballycove seemed to have stood still? The long line of houses, leading from the quay end of the town to the well-appointed houses on the hill, they were still standing, crumbling but holding on like obstinate old men, glaring out at the bay. She rolled her eyes at the humdrum rhythm of it all. God, she couldn't wait to get back to London and sort out her life once and for all.

They gave her half an hour to unpack before Georgie called upstairs that breakfast was ready.

'So, how have things been with you?' Iris took a careful step into what might have been a normal conversation between most sisters.

'Great. Things have been really good.' Nola flushed slightly, but the kitchen was dark and she figured her sisters were coming to an age where flushing would soon be normal.

'Oh?' Georgie raised her eyebrows and then quickly lowered them.

'Yes. I've been working, mainly in the West End, but busy you know.'

'Acting?' Iris's voice was high-pitched, surprised.

'Well, of course, acting. What on earth else would I be doing?' Nola shot back.

'Any more TV work in the pipeline?' Why wasn't anything ever good enough for Georgie? Nola felt a surge of resentment.

'Actually, yes,' she lied. 'I'm pretty confident that I aced my audition, so I could be back on the small screen again in the autumn.' The lies really did just trip off the tongue. Well, Nola supposed, she was probably playing the finest role of her career. It had started out with an off-the-cuff remark about the possibility of a role on a new Irish television series. Unfortunately, she'd hinted at names that were too big not to warrant further interrogation. She should have known better. Iris probably spent most of her married life glued to the telly. That was what came of being married to a man who liked to socialise while she stayed at home keeping his dinner warm. To be fair to both her sisters, they were managing to keep up a civil front, even if she did sense the thread of disbelief from Georgie.

'Well, that would be good. Is it with RTE or Virgin Media?' Iris asked.

'Virgin,' Nola said absently.

'I have some contacts there – we book a lot of advertising over here.' Georgie hesitated.

'No. Please don't contact anyone,' Nola almost shrieked with panic. She'd be mortified if Georgie ever found out that she'd been lying through her teeth. 'I wouldn't want it on anything but my own merit.'

'Well, fingers crossed for you,' Georgie said evenly. 'Are there many other actresses going for it?'

'I don't need fingers crossed,' Nola said icily. 'I'm not completely without talent, you know.'

'I think what she meant was break a leg, you know, or whatever you showbiz people say,' Iris said quickly – she tried to do jazz hands, but they just didn't work – before looking nervously at Georgie, who'd never liked to have words put in her mouth. 'Anyway, of course you'll get it,' she went on, more assuredly than they all knew was merited, but Nola was grateful for it.

'We'll see.' *If only*, but the truth was, there were no auditions and there wouldn't be any, not without an agent.

The more Nola took in her surroundings, the more she realised that someone had cared for this house in her absence. Her father had kept it as a place to welcome them. It certainly made a pleasant change from the creeping odours of mould and mildew that had been eating away at her flat in London for as long as she'd lived there. Still, there was no getting away from the fact that they were here for their father's funeral and every time Nola thought about that, she felt new waves of grief well up inside her.

They managed to stay out of each other's way for the rest of the day, which suited everyone. Nola spent the day walking on the beach. Her sisters had taken off in opposite directions and later each had pleaded exhaustion in an effort to escape having to spend time together. But there was no avoiding seeing each other again at dinner. They muddled through until dessert, and Nola could practically see the finish line.

'So,' she said as they were finishing their dessert. 'When is Myles getting he—?'

'He's not.' Georgie cut her off, and Nola glanced at her, baffled.

'Ahm, he's actually really busy at work.' Iris fidgeted with her napkin. 'I'm bushed. I think I'll turn in for the night, if nobody minds.'

'Absolutely.' Georgie's voice was uncharacteristically soft. 'Leave the washing-up to me, both of you.'

'Thanks.' Nola slipped away from the table before Georgie could change her mind.

That night, it was actually a relief to sink into the narrow single bed that had been hers so many years before. This room, like all the others in the house, felt as if it had been preserved, wrapped up in a prism of nostalgia and soaked in pale memories so everything felt as if it had been washed to a shade more welcoming than she remembered.

She yawned widely. It had been a hell of a long day – hellish, even, when she thought about it from the very start. But lying here, on the cusp of sleep, she sighed because in all the anxiety about meeting her sisters and hiding from them the reality of her car-crash of a life, only now as she lay drained and empty she thought again of her father. And all of a sudden, she was sobbing, shaking with great convulsive gulps, drenching her pillow and emptying her out so she felt as if she'd never be whole again.

As she eventually drifted off to sleep she imagined her mother kissing her goodnight and whispering in her ear just as she had when she was a little girl...

The following morning, lemony light slid through the narrow slit in her curtains and woke her. She stretched her legs and arms the full length of the bed and yawned with the delicious feeling of having slept soundly. Downstairs, she heard the radio on. One of her sisters – or perhaps both of them – had evidently already risen and were up for breakfast.

She slumped back onto her pillows and closed her eyes, thinking of the day. It had gone off quite well, considering. Of course, it was obvious that they were all measuring every word each of the others said, each of them doing their best not to step on one of the many tripwires that could detonate the explosive row that had marked their last time in this house together. But at least they were making an effort.

Georgie especially would be finding all this hard. She'd always been so close to their father – not that he had favourites, per se, but it was as if she'd connected with him in a way that neither Nola nor Iris had ever quite managed.

She heard Iris's voice downstairs, and her thoughts turned to her second sister. It was strange having Iris here without Myles; she'd hardly even mentioned him. It used to be she couldn't manage a sentence without slipping his name into it. It was Myles this and Myles that. Maybe nowadays, he wasn't the catch he had been all those years ago.

Nola closed her eyes. Who was she to judge Iris? After all, wasn't she the one lying through her teeth from the moment she'd set foot on Irish soil? She sat up in the bed, picked up the hairbrush from where she'd dropped it on the locker the night before and began to mindlessly pull it through her hair.

All she had to focus on for today was her father's funeral and keeping a lid on the fractious emotions that would surely surface as the day wore on. She drifted from her bed to her unpacked travel case and pulled out the neat black jersey dress she'd picked up in Camden Market a few years earlier. She'd bought it for an audition when she'd been going for a stage production of *Breakfast At Tiffany's*. It hadn't been lucky then, but it still looked good and her wardrobe didn't extend to a huge choice for formal occasions. She held it up to her now; it would just have to do.

'Knock, knock.' Iris's voice at the door surprised her.

'Come in,' Nola called, turning from the mirror.

'I just brought you coffee. Thought you might,' then she

looked at Nola and Nola could almost see the thoughts churning about her brain. Iris had long believed that all her younger sister thought about was preening herself in front of a mirror. 'For goodness' sake, Nola, it's a funeral, not a fashion show.' Iris turned on her heels and closed the door with a bang.

Funerals in Ballycove could go on for days. Granted, Nola was only seven when her mother died, but the wake alone stretched out over five days and then there was the burial and a get-together for the mourners afterwards. At least her father had been considerate enough to contain the affair to two parts. This afternoon, he would be laid out in the little sitting room that had once been a small library at the front of the house. Tomorrow, after a short ceremony at the local church, he would be buried next to her mother in Shanganagh Cemetery.

The undertaker arrived with just an hour to spare. He worked quietly while they sat about the hall, each lost in their own thoughts. Nola tried hard not to think about what was actually going on behind that closed door. Instead, she focused on the flamboyant pattern of the wallpaper that ran along the stairs. The bright pink peonies on their glistening green stalks and rich navy background that felt like silk in her childhood had gently faded so now it had a velvety, comforting feel to it.

'Ladies, if you'd like to follow me.' Nola caught Iris's eye, and saw that there were tears brimming on her lashes, but she rubbed them fiercely and her mouth drew up into a thin, tight line. Georgie stood back, respectfully letting them through the door before her, but Nola had a feeling she too was only putting off this moment for as long as she could. The undertaker opened the door; the room was darker than in Nola's memory. Two wax candles flickered at each end of an array of photographs on the narrow fireplace behind the casket. 'It's important to take a little time with him, before the village turn out. It'll be a big crowd, so…' He trailed off softly and gave them a sad little smile.

It seemed their places were already written in the sand. Nola stood at her father's feet, Iris in the middle and, of course, Georgie at his head. Suddenly Nola felt like a complete outsider in this strangely familiar place. She kept her eyes pinned on the pristine white polyester that was arranged across her father's legs and feet. She knew she would have to look at his face but she wasn't ready for that yet. Instead, she worked her way along the line of photographs. Her father was in every image, across many years, from a toddler wearing what looked like a dress coat, sitting on a stool at the front of Soldier Hill House, to his instantly recognisable smile among the baritones in the local choir. Then there was one of him as a young man, standing in the distillery. God, he was so vital then. Iris touched her arm, her earlier outburst forgotten about. Now she pointed to a photograph second from the end. Their parents' wedding day. They looked so happy, their father dapper in the black-and-white print, their mother almost lost beneath billowing lace. He was gazing at her, as if she was the sun, the moon and every star in the galaxy and he couldn't believe he was lucky enough to call her his wife.

Nola felt a tremor run through her. Beside her Iris was heaving great big sobs, each one felt as if it was harpooning her own resistance. She had promised herself she would not cry. She stole a glance at Georgie. Nola felt as if she'd been punched, deep and unexpectedly from behind, taking her breath away. Georgie's composure had finally crumbled, the façade collapsing, so she looked almost inconsequential beneath crushing anguish. Deep furrows lined her forehead, and her lips trembled as though she was holding in her grief so it didn't dare make a noise. And then, Nola spotted her hand, Georgie's fingers, lovingly caressing their father's cheek, as if she was wakening him gently from some deep, distressing dream.

Their father.

'Oh, God.' The words escaped Nola before she could pull them back. She felt her legs buckle at her knees; her limbs had decided to give up on her. She was literally giving at the seams, and so the only thing she could do was stumble backwards, her head spinning with the enormity of it all. Her father was dead. Both her parents were gone now. She felt Iris's arm at her waist, gripping her, propping her up so she wouldn't drop down into the coffin before them. Then Georgie moved to the other side, a strong arm about her shoulders, so she was yanked back on balance.

They stood there for what was probably only a second or two, but it felt like an eternity. Nola found herself drifting back to years earlier, when they'd put their arms around her and somehow made her feel better on a day when it was impossible to have really felt anything at all. She closed her eyes now, gave herself over to the tears that racked their way through her body. She managed to shuffle so she knew she was steady on her feet. Her sisters were still holding onto her, both of them, supporting her for just long enough so she didn't end up splayed across the sun-lightened rug, which was too thin now to pad out any bruising from the hard parquet beneath.

And then, when she took a deep steadying breath, Iris slipped her arm away again, as if its straying there had been some sort of accident. Georgie too stepped back, cleared her throat and said, 'Well, I suppose we should probably pull ourselves together for what comes next.'

Georgie thought it felt as if they stood there for a long time, close enough to touch, but with a million miles and broken promises making them so far away from each other in every other sense. Today, it seemed that her father, like everything else about Soldier Hill House, had become smaller, more faded – still like himself, but at the same time, not.

'I didn't know he'd grown a beard,' Iris said lightly, tracing her finger along the grey silky hairs that had been tamed and tapered about his face and chin.

'No?' Georgie asked shakily.

'He looks different. I mean, apart from being…' Nola stopped.

'He'd lost a lot of weight, by the end,' Georgie whispered. 'Mary said there was no tempting him no matter what she cooked for dinner. Sometimes, she'd come back to find the dinner she'd prepared sent straight to the bin and he'd have maybe had a cream cracker or two by the end of the day.'

She reached out and touched his hand gently, lingering just a little, but his skin felt waxy and Georgie missed the warmth of him so much she thought it might double her in two.

From four o'clock, villagers began to arrive and it seemed like everyone who pushed open the front door was an old friend. To Georgie, they were mostly foggy characters. Her weekend visits had just been to the house; she hadn't involved herself in the village for years.

'Dear God, deliver us,' Georgie said under her breath when they spotted Boo and Everina Swift arriving in the front hall. The twins had been in school with her and even when they were very young, Georgie had been able to mimic them expertly. 'Looks like they're still leading out the hunt every year.' They were still bandy-legged in breeches.

'I always thought he fancied you.' Nola leaned in closer and tried to stifle a giggle as Georgie nearly choked on the dainty cup of tea she was drinking.

'Don't get me started,' Georgie scoffed because she could so easily fall back into that habit of making fun of them just to make her sisters laugh.

It felt as if they shook hands with every villager for miles around that afternoon. People came and spoke about their father in a way that made him seem even further away than he already was.

'Aye, he was a changed man these last few years.'

'Never seen the likes of it, couldn't do enough for the village.'

'Best man in a pickle.'

'Never leave you stuck – that's for sure.'

And on it went, as if they had nothing better to do, but stand over him, giving him the last of their best wishes.

By the time the last of them left, she could see the same worn-out quality in Iris and Nola as she felt in herself. It was as if they'd been washed over by an ocean of other people's grief for a man who meant more to her than anything or anyone else in the world.

'Well, that's part one over, I suppose,' Iris said softly as she closed the front door of the house after the last of the mourners left. Then came the removal of their father's remains. And instead of the hushed sympathy of strangers murmuring what were meant to be words of encouragement and solace, the house echoed with the creaking of screws being turned slowly and deliberately as the coffin lid was fastened closed across their father. Georgie sat with her sisters in the hard chairs that lined the opposite side of the room, feeling each turn of the screw spin her insides back to front. She wanted to be sick and still she sat there, knowing that to leave would be like abandonment. It seemed to take forever, one painful creak at a time, as if they were winding up some invisible pressure – the question was, which of them would crack first?

And then, the undertaker touched each corner of the coffin with a narrow tap from a miniature hammer and Georgie wasn't sure if it was some old wives' tale tradition, or if the tiny metal hammer would in some way secure their father for the next part of his journey to the local church.

Outside, four strong men waited to carry their father to the hearse, and the sisters stood together silently on the doorstep as he made his final journey down the avenue. Georgie's breath caught in her chest as the starlings filled up the sky in a coordinated soaring and diving cortege.

She stood there for a while after the hearse had rounded the final bend and moved out of sight. It felt as if his spirit lingered, reluctant to leave them just yet. Maybe that was why her sisters stayed there too, until the final starling had disappeared from the sky and the moon was an oblique shadowy light picking through the tall trees beyond. Silence tripped across the hall between the three sisters, none of them quite sure what they should do next.

'Have any of you thought about what will happen to this place?' Iris murmured, her eyes travelling up the staircase, taking in everything as if she was seeing it for the very last time.

'We'll sell it, of course, and then split everything evenly between us,' Nola said, shivering against the evening cold in her flimsy dress.

'You say that as if it's already been agreed.' Georgie couldn't imagine pulling apart her father's life – at this moment, even talking about it felt like a betrayal and then, just to spite them both she said, 'For all we know, he may have made a will and left it to just one of us, or maybe none of us at all.'

'He wouldn't do that.' Iris didn't sound very certain. 'It'll be divided equally between the three of us, I'm sure.'

'And when it is, the only sensible thing to do is sell it on and divide the proceeds three ways,' Nola said.

'You can't wait to take everything he worked for and

hightail it back to London, can you?' Georgie said, and there was no mistaking the fact that the day had torn into the reserve of composure she'd been wearing like a flimsy mantilla.

Nola bristled. 'I wasn't the one who brought it up.'

'No, but I didn't mean it like that. I meant...' Iris put her hands up as if to stop the argument before it began.

'What did you mean exactly?' Georgie stood a little straighter.

'Come on, Georgie. You can't say that you haven't thought about it?' Iris said. 'It's three hundred years of Delahayes, the end of an era.'

'Obviously not as much as you have, or...' Georgie smiled, realising that it wasn't Iris who wanted what she believed was her share. 'Or perhaps it's Myles who has plans for it? A nice little windfall he's been just waiting for all these years? I'm surprised he's not here with his measuring tape and calculator. Or has he sent you to do his dirty work?'

'That's not fair.' As usual, Iris was straight to his defence. *Some things never change,* Georgie thought.

'It's pointless arguing about it,' Georgie said loudly. 'Knowing Dad, he'll have made his own mind up. And what does it matter, anyway, whether we sell it or keep it? None of us ever wanted anything to do with it when he was alive – even when I came here, I wasn't interested in the house or the distillery. He may have decided to pass it on to someone who loved the place as much as he did and—'

'He wouldn't!' Nola gasped.

'I can't talk about this now,' Georgie muttered. She spun on her heel and stalked off to the kitchen. She had to get away from that pair before she said something she'd really regret; although, with all that had been said over the years, she wasn't sure there was anything much left to say ever again.

4

For the first time in her life, Iris looked around the little church and thought there was something consoling about it. It seemed like everything else in Ballycove: nothing here had changed. Perhaps there had been a lick of paint, the walls were certainly a shade whiter than she remembered from her youth, and overhead the beams seemed blacker, stouter, lower. The pews shone too, as if an army of local women had spent all night polishing them. But apart from the surface trappings, everything was the same. A lingering scent of beeswax was a welcome relief to Nola's sickly sweet perfume, which had wafted before and behind her this morning. Iris wanted to ask if she'd fallen into the bottle, but she knew that even the tiniest remark could have them all at each other's throats.

'So sorry for your loss.' Anonymous locals shook her hand as she knelt and pretended to pray to a God she'd all but forgotten about. A couple who might have once been familiar told her what a decent man they'd known her father to be and far from being a consolation, it actually made her sad that she hadn't appreciated him more when she had the chance.

Iris took a deep breath and sat back in her pew. She tried to pray, but it was no good. All she could do was sit here, letting the organ music wash over her. 'Nearer, My God, to Thee'. It was meant to be consoling, but she suspected her father would have preferred 'When the Saints Go Marching In'.

And then, the ceremony began, with the organ groaning out the final note and the ringing of a bell somewhere out of sight. The priest's words washed over her. At the end, she could only remember fragments – but she may have just imagined those. *A good man. A community man. A happy, if tragically short marriage. A family to be proud of.* Seriously?

Iris's footsteps, in line with her sisters, tapped out a thin staccato as they followed the rubber-soled men who had shouldered their father's coffin. She couldn't help but remember the day her father had walked her up this aisle – everything seemed to be full of possibility then.

Later, after what felt like one of the longest days of her life, Iris waited for the kettle to boil. She wanted a proper drink, but she was making do with tea for now. She had thought that if she could just get through the next few days, she could probably survive anything.

It was turning out to be even harder than she'd expected. It was obvious they were all on their best behaviour, but still the tension simmered too close to the surface to ever really relax. She felt it now, crawling along her spine, wrenching up her muscles, so when she spoke her voice was tighter, her words measured and sparse. She could see the others were feeling it too. Georgie, once generous and garrulous, had become measured and clipped, and Iris almost felt as if being in the same room as her was like waiting for a volcano to erupt. On the other hand, Nola, far from being the directionless dreamer who had once got on Iris's nerves, had become withdrawn and sensitive to any remark about her life in London. At least it looked as if she was having some success. Iris supposed that brought its own pressures, but she could do without Nola taking it out on her.

Taking a mug from the cupboard, Iris automatically ran her finger round the inside rim, checking for spiders or cobwebs – just in case. She had a feeling that her father only used one or two mugs regularly. God, this place. She found her gaze travelling about the kitchen now she had it to herself for once. Nothing had changed here, and if she closed her eyes, she could imagine her mother standing in this very spot, making tea for her father or just gazing out the window at what had then been a flourishing kitchen garden beyond. She ran her finger along the cold glass of the window and it sent a shiver of anguish through her – regret? Possibly. And now, when Iris looked out that same window, she realised everything had changed. She sighed, weary of it all and knowing that there was more to endure yet.

Iris thought back on the funeral with a serene kind of sadness. It had gone off without a hitch. Their father had planned it down to the final psalm, with readers and pall-bearers picked out in advance. It was all taken care of so his daughters could turn up and leave if that was all they wished to do. They had stood for longer than he would have expected at his grave, trying to process the strange reality of being there together.

And there was more to come. A funeral lunch and then, in a day or two, the reading of his will. She hoped that Georgie wouldn't be awkward about things. Her father would not have wanted them falling out any more than they already had – probably the worst way they'd all managed to let him down.

Iris would miss him. Although she felt she had no right to think that; after all, she hadn't been back here in a decade. But she now knew, with a certainty that had never been there before, that she could have come back here to get away from the mess she'd made of things in London. Gerald Delahaye had been a decent man and he would have welcomed her back like the prodigal son – well, daughter –and given her time to heal.

What a pity she hadn't realised it just a little sooner. She took her tea and moved towards the drawing room. At least there, she thought, she might be reminded of happier times. Unfortunately, her sisters seemed to have had the same thought. Georgie was sitting on one chair, eyes closed, and Nola was curled up on the other.

'And then there were three,' Georgie murmured, so there was no turning on her heels and pretending she'd been about to go upstairs.

Iris sighed, kicking off high heels that had grown too tight over the course of the day. Why on earth did they all wear dressy shoes to stand at gravesides when a solid pair of walkers would have been far more practical? She sunk gratefully into the deep sofa and stretched out her aching legs.

'It seems unreal.' Georgie looked around the room. She looked sapped, as if the grief of the last few days had wrung her out.

'It's being here, isn't it? Maybe when we all get back to London, it'll feel more... I don't know...'

'Oh, God. London,' Nola moaned longingly, and Iris realised that she was the only one among them who was in no rush to go anywhere because, at this stage, there was nowhere else that really felt like home.

'Well, don't book your flight just yet,' Georgie said drily. 'Dad would want us all here for the reading of his will. I spoke to Stephen and he'll be up to visit in a day or so and we can make some plans about it from there.' Stephen Leather was her father's solicitor and the executor of his will. It didn't matter that he should have retired a decade earlier – they had always been friends and Stephen had been there to the very end.

'It seems he's thought of everything,' Nola murmured.

'In the end, he cared that everything was taken care of for us. I think he wanted to make sure that everything went off without a hitch, you know, in case...' Georgie didn't need to finish the thought. *In case they let him down again with the ongoing feud that had almost broken his heart and wrecked the centenary celebrations a decade ago.* The same old resentments had bubbled over and they were still hanging between them, like old ghosts waiting to come out again. They probably always would, Iris realised sadly. 'He very much wanted us to have good lives and for this to be...

as easy as possible on each of us...' Georgie stopped for a moment, distracted by the unmistakable creak of the porch door.

Who on earth could be calling at this hour? The sisters glanced at each other, puzzled and slightly unnerved.

'Hello?' A deep voice came from the hall. 'Is anyone home?'

'In here,' Iris called out and jumped up to open the door for Robert English. He looked different to when she'd seen him earlier at her father's funeral. He had changed from the formal suit he'd worn as one of her father's pall-bearers and was dressed to go walking instead. He had the air of a man who walked fast and stood at intervals to enjoy the scenery around him.

'Sorry.' He glanced at each of them and nodded his greetings. 'Sorry, I don't want to intrude, but I have this for you.' He handed a box and card to Georgie, who was nearest to him.

'A gift?' she said confused and looking at it for a moment.

'Yes. But not from me, I'm afraid. Your father left instructions that I was to bring this to you on the evening he was buried. It's for all three of you. You're to open it together and raise a glass to the future. I think it's probably all in the note.' He smiled at each of them and then turned back towards the door.

'Won't you join us?' Nola asked. She'd tucked her feet beneath her on the armchair and was peering over the deep cushions, and Iris tutted. It seemed even in grief, she couldn't help batting her eyelashes at any man who came her way.

'Not tonight. I'm under strict orders from your father. It's a very special gift, just for you three,' he said. And then he was gone, pulling closed the porch door with a loud bang, and it felt as if the house echoed back a whole new sort of emptiness now it was just the three of them again.

There was something unnerving about the gift arriving just after the funeral and Georgie had a feeling that the others were as thrown by it as she was. She moved to sit next to Iris, and Nola too slid from her chair and perched next to them on the sofa. Georgie watched as Iris gingerly went about unwrapping the box, setting the card aside for a moment.

'Oh, come on – just peel the bloody wrapping off,' Nola said impatiently, and she reached out and tore away a strip of paper.

'Oh my God,' Iris breathed, almost dropping the box. Luckily, Georgie swiped her hand beneath it before it crashed to the floor. 'I can't believe he actually did this,' Iris murmured. She had turned completely pale.

'It's a blast from the past, all right,' Georgie said, examining the box. It was a bottle of Iseult Gin. Named in memory of their mother, her father had spent a long time experimenting with it after she died. 'I never thought he actually bottled any of it, or...' She studied the home-made amateurish label. It was old-fashioned, staid, not how she would brand a product for the current gin-drinking market, which had shifted dramatically over the last decade. No doubt her father believed Delahaye Gin should be marketed towards little old ladies who liked a tipple, or afternoon drinkers who solidly stuck to pep or lime. He would have no idea of the huge resurgence in popularity gin had been having for the last few years. Her father liked things as they were. *Old dog, new tricks* and all that. She looked over at his empty chair. She could see him now, a twinkle in his eye as they raised their glasses to the end of a long day's work. Georgie took a deep breath. She would not cry again. Not now.

'He made it for our mother?' Nola's voice dragged Georgie back to the present.

'He made it in her memory. I hadn't thought about that in years,' Georgie explained.

'Well, he obviously wants us to taste it,' Iris said, standing up and taking down three tumblers from the sideboard. She rooted about beneath it for a bottle of tonic water and, when she found one, she set out the glasses and then opened the box carefully. It felt as if she was uncovering something holy, a relic of sorts.

'It's purple!' Nola squealed.

'It says on the box that it's been infused with lavender,' Iris said, frowning. 'Can you actually drink lavender? I thought it was just handy for smelling up sock drawers and attracting bees to your garden. Anyway, you can pour,' she said to Georgie and she handed the bottle to her now to take charge.

'I think we should all sip together,' Georgie said when she'd poured out three small measures.

'In case it poisons us?'Nola was only half joking.

'Oh, don't be so ridiculous,' Iris said scornfully. 'He wouldn't have left us poisoned gin. And besides, it's obvious this isn't about the gin. Father wanted us to sit here for a short while and take time to think about our mother, and about him. He would have wanted us to spend time just reminiscing about our happiest memories of them both. It's what families do.' After another tense moment, Nola relented and picked up her glass. The others followed suit and they sipped together, savouring the taste for a moment before any of them said a word. Then Nola exhaled, as if the alcohol had somehow neutralised some of her nervousness.

'It's actually very good,' Georgie said, holding up the glass towards the light. She was trying to figure out if she liked the colour or not, but there was no denying, the gin itself was probably the best she'd ever tasted.

'It's better than good.' Iris sipped again, savouring the mixture of alcohol and lavender. 'It's like taking a holiday in each sip, isn't it? It feels as if it's almost washing away the stress of the day.'

'I think we should read the card.' Georgie leaned forward and handed it to Nola.

'Why me?'

'Why not? You're the actress,' Iris said, sinking back into the depths of the old sofa.

Nola reached forward and took up the card, opened it a lot more gingerly than when she'd swiped at the box. 'It was written almost a year ago.'

'Well, do go on, read it aloud,' Iris said. Her eyes were closed, as if she wanted to concentrate on every single word. Georgie leaned back next to her. Nola took a deep breath and began.

'*Dearest Girls, I am so glad you're all together to read this card and share a bottle of my Iseult Gin. Of course, it's named after your darling mother, but the truth is, it's been inspired by each of you – my dear GIN girls. It's taken an age to get the recipe exactly as I wanted it. I hope you all enjoy a glass or two and it gives you a chance to sit for a while and perhaps look back, but more importantly look forward.'*

'What does he mean by that?' It seemed Iris couldn't help interrupting.

Nola ignored her question and continued reading aloud. '*I could make this a letter of apology and waste pages saying sorry for all the things I regret when it comes to each of you, but know this: if I feel I have fallen badly short in being the father you deserved, that doesn't mean I didn't love each of you with all my heart. It's too late for all that now and I don't want anyone wallowing on my account. But I do have one request. My greatest regret is the fact that you three have not managed to remain close. I want nothing more than to know that when I'm gone, at least you will be there for each other. We all made promises. I promised your mother that I would do my best for each of you and I did try, but I can't help feeling that the divisions between you spell out my biggest failure in life. Darling girls, don't forget that we all made promises – now I'm going to ask you to keep one of yours…*

'*So, in the next few days, Stephen will arrive to read my will. I want you to bear in mind that it's set out to try and bring you together – not to divide you. There's a future here for all of you, if you want it, but there's no obligation on any of you to give up the lives you already have. I'm only asking that you each make a little room for the other as you move ahead with whatever lives you decide to have going forward.*

'*All my love,*

'*Your father.*'

As Nola fell silent, Georgie felt that all too familiar cavern of loss open up in her again. She sipped some gin to cover how close she was to crying; she couldn't let her sisters see the floodgates open. There was far too much that could rush out alongside her grief, things she'd promised herself she wouldn't tell them.

'So, we're no wiser now than before we opened it?' Nola looked at Georgie and Iris.

'You know as much as I do.' It was all Georgie could manage if she wanted not to drown in the well of longing for her father that threatened to engulf her.

'Well, I say we should have another glass of gin,' Nola said, and topped each of them up. The fire, dying in the grate, needed stirring and feeding up. As if she had noticed it at the same time, Nola put her glass down, picked up the poker and prodded at what was left of it, scattering the ash and adding fresh firewood, stoking and blowing it back to life.

'Are you cold?' Iris reached behind the sofa and pulled out one of the heavy woollen rugs from the Corrigan Mills.

'Cold? No.' Nola took the rug and spread it across them. 'It's just… that letter. It felt as if…' She shivered.

'As if he was still here?' Iris smiled.

'I don't know, exactly,' Nola said, and a small tear ran down her cheek. 'It just all seems like such a waste, doesn't it?' She looked into Georgie's eyes and then towards Iris.

'It was too long ago for it to make any difference now.' Georgie heard her own voice much surer than she actually felt.

'I'm sure he wanted it to make all the difference in the world to us,' Iris said quietly, and her voice cracked. 'Right up to the end, he just wanted us to be there for each other.'

'It's too much.' Nola stared ahead at the fire.

'I've often thought about you both – you know that...' Iris said softly. Georgie assumed she was tipsy.

Georgie kept her eyes on the glass of gin in her hand. She was suddenly uncomfortable sitting here on the sofa next to her sisters. She wanted to jump up and fold herself into the armchair, but somehow doing so felt almost disloyal to her father's wishes, so instead she sat rigidly on the sofa with a woollen rug over her knees, and felt completely at odds with herself.

'He's not asking for very much, just that we look out for each other... that maybe we could become...' Iris's words faded away.

'Friends?' Nola asked, and there was no missing the cynicism in her tone.

'Maybe, eventually...' Iris's voice trailed off again, and Georgie knew they were all thinking the same thing: no matter how much they wanted to do the right thing by their father's wishes, being friends was more than any of them could ever realistically imagine.

'Or maybe just sisters.' Nola sounded wistful, perhaps the gin was stronger than they realised. Wordlessly, she raised her glass, and after a moment's hesitation, Iris met it with hers, Georgie held her glass to theirs and a tight silence stretched between them for a moment. Still, it felt as if it would be churlish not to toast, even if it was the one promise they couldn't keep.

***

They sat for another hour, sipping their drinks in what Nola supposed might have been companionable silence if it wasn't for the fact that she, for one, was counting down the time until she could escape up to the sanctuary of her room. She wasn't used to gin and was tipsy before she knew it, but then an unexpected sense of loneliness began to creep in around the edges of her thoughts. She wondered if the others felt the same.

The fire was roaring up the grate and the only sounds in the house were the once-familiar cranks and rattles of old pipes and worn floorboards. She listened as outside, somewhere in the distance, the seagulls cried their last for the night. Maybe she was imagining it, but she thought she heard the tide turning and the rocks on the shore crackle against each other as the current dragged around them. She sank back into the deep sofa. It was strangely anchoring, sitting here, and she snuggled further beneath the rug that stretched across all three of them. She almost felt as if Ballycove and this house could pull her back. Perhaps it was the gin, but instead of racing upstairs and packing her bags as fast as she could, she found herself wondering if perhaps there was something more she needed to do before she cut her ties forever.

'It seems wrong to say it, now Dad is buried, but it feels a little bit like it used to, years ago, being home,' Iris said softly.

'That's the gin talking, for sure.' Nola laughed at the other two. They were each on their fourth glass and there was no mistaking the stuff was potent. Nola knew that too much of it could make her let her guard down and whatever else was going to come out of this, that was the last thing she wanted to happen. She put her glass down.

'Do you remember when we were young and Mammy would throw her big Christmas parties?' Iris said wistfully.

'We'd spend days trying to figure out where we could hide so we didn't have to miss out on any of the fun.' Georgie shook her head.

'I remember that,' Nola said. 'I remember both of you stuffing me into one of those cupboards in the hall – I thought I'd never get out.' It was the vaguest memory.

'Mammy nearly lost her mind trying to find you,' Iris said and then she started to laugh, looking across at Georgie. 'And we forgot we'd put you in there.'

'You'd fallen fast asleep,' Georgie said shaking her head. She was laughing so much, there were tears rolling from her eyes. 'When you finally crawled out, even you had probably forgotten we'd put you in there.'

'You were a great kid.' Iris looked across with near affection in her eyes for a brief moment. 'You never told a soul it was us and we all got to stay up as late I can ever remember for one of those soirees just because Mammy felt so bad about having lost you.' She threw her hands up in the air. 'God, we were terrible. How on earth did they put up with us?'

'We all snuggled up in your bed afterwards, Iris,' Nola said. It was all coming back to her now. Even then, Iris had always been the mammy of the three girls and Nola wondered now why on earth she'd never had a family of her own.

'God, I'd almost completely forgotten about that,' whispered Georgie, looking down at the blanket thrown across them.

It actually felt as if they could be back there again. And suddenly, Nola was brought back to that feeling of warmth and camaraderie they'd shared together – the sisterhood. She'd thought it would never end. She had been such a silly kid. Because of course it had ended, and when she really needed them most, they'd turned their backs on her.

'Do you remember Aiden Barry?' Iris asked Georgie.

'There's a blast from the past.' Georgie shook her head. Aiden had been Georgie's graduation date. They'd been great friends, but nothing more. 'He was at the graveside today. I wonder whatever happened to lead him back here.'

'Quite a bit, as it turns out. He's been all round the world and he came back to Ballycove a couple of years ago to take over the family farm.'

'But that was a tiny place. He'll never make a living at that, surely?'

'Apparently he's bought up every square inch of land that's come up for sale over the last few years and he owns half of Ballycove now,' Iris said. 'I got a lift from the airport with his parents – they haven't changed a bit, by the way.'

'Oh, I adored Moira. She was so kind after…' Nola said, remembering the woman who had been like a mother to her when her sisters had left her behind.

'Of course, Nola, you were friends with Helen Barry, weren't you?' Iris said. 'I almost forgot that.'

'Yes, but you know, looking back, we didn't have that

much in common. I think the thing I liked most about her was going to their house for tea. It was like…' Nola didn't finish the sentence; there was probably no need. They all knew that after their mother had died, this house had lost something so vital it didn't really feel like a home. You could feel it in the very fabric of the place, as if Iseult Delahaye had breathed one final sigh and inhaled with it every drop of joy, not just from her husband and daughters, but from Ballycove itself. 'I used to go over there whenever I could. I think I loved Moira Barry. I used to wish that she'd adopt me.' Nola threw her eyes up to heaven, but even saying the words drew a tight knot in her stomach. 'Crazy kids' thoughts, of course.'

'No, Nola, not crazy at all,' Iris murmured. Nola felt that familiar tug of childhood – the need for her mother and later, the need to replace that figure with people like her sisters and Moira, who just hadn't been able to fill that void.

'There was no replacing Mammy after she died,' Nola said softly. It was only now, after all this time that it was dawning on her that her father had felt that so acutely. It was probably a miracle he hadn't died of a broken heart years ago. She'd been selfish – the worst daughter her father could have asked for. How on earth could she have left him here for so long without so much as a visit? He was so utterly alone at the end. A small tear scudded down her cheek and she wiped it away.

'Oh, come on. What's the point in crying now?' Georgie topped up each of their glasses again.

'She didn't want that,' Nola whispered, thinking of her mother making them promise her before she died. *No sadness, no thinking of what might have been, no regrets.* That was how Iseult Delahaye had made her way through life and it was how she had slipped away from them in death. She expected the same from her daughters.

'You should go visit her,' Georgie said suddenly.

'Who?' Nola had been lost in her own world.

'Moira Barry, of course.' Georgie rolled her eyes as if she was talking to a toddler.

'Oh, yes, you really should – she'd love that,' Iris said. 'She mentioned you in the car, asked for you in particular. She was really fond of you, you know. I think she always hoped you'd come back—'

'Stop it, the pair of you. I'm sure no-one in Ballycove has given me the slightest thought since I walked out of here all those years ago.' Nola laughed, because really, she was certain of that. 'But I might drop in to see her, just before I go back to London. It'd be nice to catch up with her and see how Helen is getting on...'

'You really should,' Georgie murmured, she seemed miles away, but then Nola spotted a small smile creeping up around her eyes. 'The Gin Sisters?' She shook her head in apparent wonderment.

'That's right. Little did we know, eh?' Nola said softly. They'd set it up one wet afternoon and it became the default game for miserable days when there was nothing else to do, until her sisters grew tired of it and moved onto more grown-up things to become bored of.

Georgie walked to the fireplace, stoking up what was left of the blaze. Then she turned to them, smiling, and for a moment Nola looked at her, thinking how much it completely transformed her sister to see her so relaxed. 'What is it?' she asked sleepily.

'I'm thinking of whatever Dad has in store for us tomorrow with the reading of his will. I have a feeling it's not going to be straightforward.'

'Oh, it won't be too bad,' Iris said. 'He'll want us to promise to look out for each other. I expect that's about it.'

'Of course, it'll be how he wants things divided between us and maybe, if we're lucky, another bottle of this lovely gin.' Nola shivered, even though it wasn't cold, but she couldn't shake the feeling that Ballycove was not quite finished with them yet.

5

Stephen Leather was nothing if not punctual. By eleven o'clock they were all sitting down, Nola and Iris on one side of the dining room table, Georgie on the other and Stephen at the head, in what Iris couldn't help thinking of as her mother's seat. After she'd died, they'd stopped using this room, apart from a couple of Christmases when they pretended to celebrate with forced seasonal cheer. This thought prompted something in Iris that for so long she'd worked hard to ignore. What had Christmas been like for her father all these years since? Suddenly flooded with guilt, she knew that, sitting here now, waiting for his will to be read, she had let him down in a way that she couldn't ever put right.

'Well, then, I suppose we'd better get started.' Stephen checked his watch against the chime of the grandfather clock across the hall. He opened up the sealed envelopes with an air of ceremony that was almost reverent, then he looked at all three of them, as if checking that they were ready for what lay ahead.

The will began with various small gifts and instructions their father had made to acknowledge people like Mary, his housekeeper, and her predecessor, as well as the secretary who'd worked at the distillery for almost forty years and retired a year earlier and, of course, a small bequest to the local tidy towns association, who volunteered for everything from cleaning old people's gardens to maintaining the church grounds.

'And so, we move onto the bulk of the estate,' Stephen was saying, and Iris tuned back in. 'The remaining estate, such as it is, is made up of the main residence, Soldier Hill House, and all of its contents: the farm – almost two hundred acres, running from the house and including all outbuildings and machinery currently held, and the Delahaye Distillery.'

Stephen stopped for a moment and looked from one to the other of them again. It was clear to Iris that there was no fair way of dividing things up equally without selling everything off and splitting the money received from them. Suddenly, that seemed an unbearable thought. This house was their last connection with their mother, and now with their father too. It was irrational, she knew, but even though she'd hardly set foot in the place for years when her father was alive, somehow she couldn't bear the idea of being parted from it.

Stephen was still speaking, measuring out her father's wishes in gentle tones. *Three daughters, each loved equally. To be shared in equal parts, but one request... the estate to remain in testate until this request is fulfilled... six months...*

this house... Georgie, Iris and Nola... It all faded together like an old record playing on long after the partygoers had stopped listening. Iris's thoughts drifted far away, beyond the rattling windowpanes, out across the expanse of land that rolled off green and empty in the distance. It was only when Nola gasped next to her that she was jolted back to the present moment. On the other side of the table, Georgie's cheeks had that flushed appearance she'd always got when she thought the world needed to be put right again.

'I'm sorry,' Nola said shortly. 'I don't understand. How are we going to receive the value of our inheritance if we can't actually sell it? I mean, he can't have thought this through. Does he mean to leave one part to one of us and another to the other? There's a huge disparity between the value of the farm and the value of the distillery, surely?'

'Your father's will is quite unusual.' Stephen pushed his glasses back up over the bridge of his nose. 'In the plainest of English, Gerald's wish is that you girls all come together and stay in the house for six months, and that, at the end of it, you are all agreed on how the estate is to be divided between you.'

'Oh my God.' A sharp pain seared across Iris's forehead. 'And if we don't?'

'Haven't you been listening at all?' Georgie said shortly, an irritated edge to her voice. 'Basically, we have six weeks to straighten out our lives in London and then he wants us to come back here and live together, in this house, for six months. If after that time we still—' she rolled her eyes theatrically '—want to sell the place and all the other assets, we can do that and divide it three ways. If we can't agree what to do with it, it all goes into a trust, managed by the executor.' She nodded towards Stephen.

'Well, not me exactly, it's my firm – well, my son's firm at this point.' Stephen pushed his chair back a little from the table, raised his hands as if to ward off their anger. 'I did try to explain to your father that it's most irregular, but his request was within his rights.'

'Well, I can't just throw away my career in London to come back here and play at being a farmer or a distiller or whatever other crazy idea he had in mind for me,' Georgie said crossly.

'But what if we can't come back?' Nola asked in a small voice. And of course, Iris assumed, she was thinking of that screen test. Nola couldn't turn her back on a part in a sitcom – it could be *the* part. She wouldn't do it, not for every blade of grass in Ireland. And nor should she be expected to.

'Oh, yes, that's right, Nola, so you're the only one here with a career and a life you want to get back to,' Georgie said sarcastically.

'Actually, maybe yes.' Nola met her sisters' eyes and Iris could feel the tension in the room expand between them. 'Certainly more than sitting it out in this God-forgotten place with—' She stopped herself, just in time before saying something she might regret. 'I'm not sure a share in anything is worth that.' She looked as if she was fit to cry.

'Ladies, ladies.' Stephen calmly broke the stand-off. 'I understand it's not what you expected. I did try to explain to your father, but he was adamant. He wanted what he always wanted: for you to put your quarrels behind you and be a proper family, and even though he was quite sure that in the end you'd all return to London, he wanted to give you a final chance to reconcile and move forward with a clean slate.'

'Hah,' Nola snorted, but for all her angry words and her skilful make-up the colour had drained from her cheeks. Of course, Iris realised, she may have been depending in some way on some sort of immediate windfall from the estate.

'Look, it would be the easiest thing in the world for me to appoint an estate agent and put the whole place on the market, for all of you to pack your bags and take a photograph or a clock to remember him by, but really, I think there may have been far more wisdom to his thinking than I realised at first—'

'Surely, if we all agree, we can overturn this stupid will?' Georgie cut him off.

'The estate will be held in trust indefinitely, tied up until your grandchildren's grandchildren can come together and reunite the family.' It was an exaggeration, but Iris knew that no-one – least of all their father – would want it to go that route. 'In my experience, you may well win the case, but ultimately, you'll effectively lose up to half the value of the estate, maybe more, if you can't agree between yourselves.' He smiled at Iris kindly, but it was clear that he was indeed her father's friend, and wanted them to comply with his last wishes.

'And if one of us decides not to join in this silly charade?' Nola looked up from examining the empty table before her.

'Then you are automatically throwing up any claim you have on the estate,' Stephen said simply. They all sat for a moment, digesting this stark alternative. It would be, when all was said and done, a sizeable fortune to run away from.

'So, what about you, Iris?' Nola turned to her expectantly and of course, what she meant was, '*What about Myles?*' Her mind – and heart – started to race. Her sisters knew all too well that she would hate leaving Myles for five minutes, much less contemplate six months without him, if they were still together. But they weren't together anymore and now no-one would miss her in London if she never went back. The truth of how alone she was turned over in her stomach like a knife, wielding its worst. And of course, it would be almost impossible to avoid telling her sisters about Myles leaving her, if she agreed to stay.

'I...' Iris sighed. There was no choice. Myles did not want her as she was, but with the Delahaye legacy in her bank account, child or no child, she knew him well enough to know that he would think again. The very fact of it made her feel nauseous. She wasn't sure if she was sickened more by the fact that she still wanted him back so badly, or at the idea of having to pay such a heavy price to win him over. She shifted uncomfortably under the excruciating gaze of their sets of questioning eyes. 'These are our father's wishes. I think we need to respect them.' She cleared her throat. She needed to stay calm. Whatever else, there was no way she was letting either Nola or Georgie know that she had so much riding on this whole shambolic exercise. 'Can we have a copy of the will? I think a lot of it has gone over my head.' She managed to smile at Stephen. 'Late night, father's gin.' She shook her head and wondered if she was the only one sitting at this table who felt as if the world had been whipped from beneath her yet again.

⋆⋆⋆

'He can't have really meant we were to come back here and live for six months, can he?' Nola asked once Stephen finally closed up his briefcase and headed out the door. She was so pale, she looked in danger of fainting. 'I mean, I kept expecting him to jump up and shout *Surprise*! This can't be right, can it?'

'I'm afraid it's no joke; it's all laid out exactly as Father wanted it,' Iris said softly, and Georgie wondered if her sister wasn't in shock, considering she was taking the news so calmly. Perhaps she and Myles really needed the money, Georgie thought. Iris was still working in that little dental practice and Myles was never going to make much of a living – that had been obvious from the get-go.

'But… what about my job, my auditions, my flat…' Nola's hand flew up to cover her mouth, as if she'd said too much, and Georgie thought she looked like she might burst into tears. 'How could he do something like this to us?' She looked from one sister to the other.

'He wasn't trying to punish us,' Iris said with utter certainty as she pushed her chair back and walked towards the bay window that overlooked the front avenue of the house. 'He's given us a gift of sorts, or at least that's what he believed he was doing. Come on, this is our father – all he wanted was for us to be happy.'

'For goodness' sake, why couldn't he just have made things easy for everyone?' Nola was almost in tears.

'Maybe it *is* a gift of sorts, but it's not a very practical one,' Georgie said cynically. She should be back in London tomorrow, getting going with... The truth was, she wasn't sure what she should be doing anymore. It wasn't as if she actually had a job to go back to. But she had an apartment and that was home to her now, wasn't it? God knows she'd spent enough money buying it and then having it designed so it reflected the lifestyle she'd aspired to, even if she never quite felt at ease there. 'What on earth would we do here for six whole months?' she asked. That meant long, dark evenings, rainy days and not a lot to do unless you fancied being blown away while you walked along the beach. 'I'm not sure I can do it...' she whispered, her voice almost cracking. She hated this, the vulnerability she was showing. She cleared her throat; there was no way anyone was going to see her become weak.

'Of course you can't bloody do it; you have a career. You live in London, for heaven's sake. You can't just throw up your whole life for six months. None of us can. It's not like we're all students on a gap year,' Nola raged.

'I think I possibly could...' Iris said and it sounded to Georgie as if she was talking from a place very far removed from the reality of this shocking moment. 'I mean, on a practical level, I think I could.'

Georgie and Nola turned to stare at her. 'But what about Myles? And your job? And...' Nola threw her hands up in the air '...your mortgage?'

'Oh, don't worry about any of that. I don't see why I couldn't sort all that out easily enough.' She put her finger to her lips and turned back towards the table again, holding each of them with her gaze for a moment, as if she was thinking of something that was not exactly unpleasant.

'Myles will be working away for a few months and, to be honest, I've needed a change from being a receptionist for quite a while now. It's hardly been a vocation for me.' She almost smiled at this. 'I don't see why I couldn't rent the house out, which would cover the mortgage and give me a bit of spending money. Father has laid on everything here for us – it's in the will. There's an account at the local grocer's and all the bills are going to be paid anyway. It might be an opportunity to stop and reset the clock for a short while.'

It seemed to Georgie that Iris was doing her best to convince herself, but as the words drifted towards her, Georgie realised that really, the same logic applied to her own life. What was in London waiting for her? Who? Nothing and nobody – that was the cold reality of her life. Normally it never bothered her, but things were different now. The fact that her career had taken a nosedive had suddenly brought all those other things into stark relief so in this moment, all she could think was: why on earth wouldn't she take the offer of a six-month break with no more stresses than sorting out her sisters' jealous squabbles? At the end of it, she could go back to London and easily set up her own firm. She'd have the start-up cash to go it alone, without partners or investors, just the way she liked things best.

As if she was reading her mind, Iris turned directly towards her and examined her with narrowed eyes. 'What about you, Georgie? Could you walk away for six months and be comfortable that everything you've invested in over the years is solid enough to be waiting when you return?' She was throwing down the gauntlet, an irresistible challenge, but of course, what Iris didn't realise was that Georgie's house of feathers had already blown away on the wind.

She squared her shoulders and returned Iris's gaze coolly. 'Of course I can. I can spend a few weeks clearing the desk, handing over my biggest accounts to one of the senior partners and then take some of the time off that's been building up for me over the last few years.' She smiled easily. Neither Iris nor Nola need ever know her life had become a bonfire of half-truths and outright lies.

'Good, well then, that's two of us settled,' Iris said, looking pointedly at Nola.

'That's not fair,' Nola shot back at them.

'What's not fair?' Georgie knew she was taunting her.

'You're both so much more... your lives are more... Look,' she said, bunching her hair on top of her head, and pulling it tight as if it might clear the brain fog that Georgie felt was the only legacy that any of them had been granted after the meeting with Stephen. 'It's different for me. My career is so much more precarious.'

Georgie snorted. 'You could always go back to the coffee shop?'

'I only help Shalib out occasionally, but we've become friends and he depends on me. I told you, I've been working for the last couple of years between various productions on...' Nola snapped.

'Yes, yes. Of course you have...' Iris said sarcastically.

'Oh my God. You two are unbelievable. How bloody smug you both are, with your solid marriage and your big career.' Nola's voice grew thick and her eyes brimmed with tears. 'I can't just throw everything I've been working for up in the air on a whim—'

'This could change your life, Nola. We're not talking about a couple of hundred pounds. It could mean you have the money for a flat in a very nice part of London – that's security for life,' Iris said.

'And it's our father's last request of us. We will probably never be friends, but the least we can do is walk away knowing that in the end we did as he asked. We can at least try.' Even as she said it, though, Georgie knew it was hopeless. She had long believed that their bonds had been so badly severed, they'd never be able to reconnect; she'd just never had the courage to tell her father.

'So we shack up here for six months and then flog the lot before returning to real life again?' Nola's voice was shrill. 'But that's fine and dandy because we've done what he's asked? He means for us to do more than live together, Georgie. You know that he means us to reach some sort of reconciliation, make some sort of relationship.'

'Well, I'm up for trying it, if you're both in,' Iris said, managing to sound as if she meant it while fiddling with the thin string of pearls at her throat that had been left to her in their mother's will.

'I can't take any more of this nonsense,' Nola shouted at no-one in particular and everyone in general. 'I'm going for a walk.' She pushed her chair back with such force that it went flying from beneath her and crashed against the ornate sideboard running along the wall behind her. 'On my bloody own,' she said as an afterthought, as if either of her sisters would want to join her. Then she stalked through the door and banged it so hard behind her, Georgie almost expected the plaster around it to crack and fall to the floor. She looked at Iris and suddenly, they both burst out laughing, as if the tension of the whole morning had been pulled from the room with their younger, wilful, still slightly out-of-hand sister.

Nola yanked the front door closed behind her with an almighty crash. The noise reverberated in her ears, but she knew that had as much to do with the fact that her nerves were shattered. She had to get out of here, out of this house and away from Iris and Georgie. She wanted to race down to the station, jump on the first train and never come back, but that was impossible. Her sisters were impossible. Nola didn't need to spend six months with them to know that much.

She took a long, deep breath, her back still leaning against the front door of the house. She shivered under the clawing fingers of a passing chill breeze. She needed to breathe; she needed to get past this panic that was rising up in her at the thought of having to turn her life over to Ballycove for six months. Another deep breath, filling up her lungs with air sweetly scented with witch hazel that reminded her of her mother and happy times that were so faded she sometimes wondered if they were ever real or just a hazy dream.

Another deep breath and Nola stepped away from the door, tossed her hair back from her face and set off down the avenue. Moving one foot before the other, she could forget that her legs felt like jelly, her heart was racing and her head was spinning. All she needed was fresh air and there was never any shortage of that in Ballycove. She had over-reacted, and the beginnings of embarrassment started to awaken in her.

It was just nerves, she knew. After all, it wasn't as if there was anything to go back to in London. She *could* do this. She *had to* do this. The words kept turning about in her brain like a ticker tape. Six months. It was all right for Georgie – she could probably afford to walk away from her huge monthly salary for a year or two if she felt like it. She probably had millions in the bank for all they knew and there was no doubt in Nola's mind, but her company would be turning somersaults to take her back whenever she felt like returning to her high-powered career.

In some ways, it was the same for Iris. Nola might not think very much of Myles Cutler, but at the end of the day, they'd stuck it out. And it looked like their relationship had only gone from strength to strength. After all, there was a time when Iris wouldn't have left London for five minutes without him, probably because she knew she couldn't trust him not to chase the first woman he saw as soon as her back was turned. Now, here she was, seemingly content and secure in the knowledge that if she threw away her job in the morning, he had her back.

It was a heck of a lot more than Nola had managed to garner after the years spent in London chasing a dream that seemed determined to give her the slip. The truth of that stabbed at her heart with a ferociousness that almost took her breath away. She was so bloody miserable and the last thing she needed was to spend six months comparing herself to Iris or Georgie.

She tried to tell herself, she should be bloody thankful to have somewhere to live for the next six months. Maybe that was the problem, though, because she knew that coming back here meant she was cutting ties with London and there was nothing there to call her back. She was anchorless, unlike her sisters who had homes and jobs and loved ones in the city. That was besides the fact that it was *Ballycove*, the place she couldn't wait to leave all those years ago and worse, she'd be stuck here with the last two people in the world she'd want to be living with.

Before she knew it, she was thundering down the small lane that provided a shortcut into the village. Her emotions drove her, a mixture of grief, devastation and, yes, she could admit it to herself, jealousy of her sisters and the lives they'd made, which seemed to be so secure compared to her own. Her life was already a mess and this just felt as if she was kicking the can of sorting it out down the road for another six months. She was walking blind and it was little wonder that she wasn't killed when a huge tractor careered around one of the narrow bends.

Nola felt herself fall backwards in a slow-motion dive that seemed to last for much longer than it possibly could have. One moment she was lost in thought and the next, she had landed in an ungainly heap in the ditch and was a little more than dazed when the farmer who was driving the tractor jumped down to pull her out of the long, wet grass and thorny brambles.

'Are you all right? What in the name of all that's holy were you thinking, walking along the middle of the road like that?' he barked as he straightened her up, grabbing her deftly by her upper arms when she lost her balance and began to slide backwards again. She was, she knew, in complete shock. A matter of inches and she'd have been flattened beneath the huge machine. 'I'm so sorry, people normally have the good sense to stay on the side of the road. You could get yourself killed with that sort of carry-on,' he said then.

'Excuse me? You were the one taking up the whole road and driving like a bloody lunatic.' She pulled away from him, still slightly swaying.

His face contorted in disbelief. 'Look, when you walk in the middle of a narrow lane—' He stopped suddenly and stepped back, as if he too needed to take a long breath. 'Nola? Nola Delahaye?' He waited a beat. 'It's me, Ai—'

'Aiden Barry,' she said, her mind all of a sudden slotting his vaguely familiar face into place. 'So, I should feel better that I might have been killed by a neighbour instead of some random stranger?' Nola did her best to straighten out her clothes. She smoothed her hair and then looked at him. He was almost bloody smiling, as if there was something amusing in nearly mowing her down on the road. 'I'm fairly sure this lane is still on our land, so it could be that apart from dangerous driving, you're actually trespassing,' she said haughtily.

He took a step back. 'Well, now, is that right?' He rubbed his chin and she had the distinct impression that far from being sorry for almost flattening her in the ditch, he was laughing at her. She felt a flash of anger.

'Yes, that's right. And another thing, if you're going to drive that thing like a maniac, well, you should really…' She ran out of words because as the shock was wearing off she realised that only an idiot wouldn't have heard the roar of the tractor coming round the bend and only a fool would be standing here arguing with someone they hadn't seen in years. She felt herself starting to blush.

'Well, it seems there's not a lot wrong with you that a teaspoon of common sense wouldn't cure,' he said, looking her up and down once more. 'It's a pity, but it seems London didn't do a lot to put manners on you after all this time.' He shook his head once more as he turned back towards the tractor. 'It didn't do a lot to give you much in the way of road sense either. God knows how you survived in a city with buses and trains when you're not safe on a country boreen.' He heaved himself up into the cab and pulled away, leaving her standing open-mouthed by the side of the road.

Nola watched as the tractor made its way back up the avenue towards the entrance to the farmyard at the back of the house. She felt that surge of loneliness for London, for the life she'd lost, for her father, well up in her and she started to cry, hot salty tears for so many things she couldn't even begin to process. Here, in Ballycove, where she should feel at home, she was utterly lost. So much for being the city sophisticate back in the sticks.

When she got to the sea, she immediately felt her spirits lift a little. She walked the length of the beach until it felt as if everything had settled within her. It was really very simple. Even if she wanted to return to London, she couldn't possibly afford to live anywhere near the café or the centre of London on the wages she was currently earning. There was no agent, no auditions, and no acting career to go back for.

It seemed the further she was from London, the more Nola could see what a flimsy foundation her whole acting career had been built upon. She hadn't even found an agent on the basis of her talent, rather Maggie Strip had found her one dreary morning in Hammersmith as she queued outside an open audition for extras. Right place, right time. Maggie had needed a redhead for what was supposed to be two episodes in a soap. The two episodes had continued first to a month and then to a year, then longer. For a while, Nola had been a star. Until she wasn't anymore.

Shalib would understand her having to go home. He was always saying that family is everything.

And she did have to come home. She knew that for certain as the wind whipped cold about her ears and the sand dug into her already stinging eyes. It was the very least she could do for her father. Apart from which, if she could just do this one thing – stay here for six months – and then they sold off the whole estate, Georgie was right: she would be able to afford to buy an apartment somewhere in London. It would mean at least some small piece of security in her life going forward. Otherwise, what was her option? Go back and rent somewhere even further out, probably for more money each week that she clearly couldn't afford as things were. She sat for a while on some rocks, looking out to sea. Far out, a fishing boat bobbed on the water, weaving its way in before the weather made a meal of whipping up the waves about them and making unloading their catch ten times harder than it needed to be.

Yes. For once in her life, she would do the sensible thing. She would return to London and pack up her flat.

Later, when she returned and pushed open the door of the house, there was no mistaking the aroma of baked trout coming from the kitchen, and her stomach responded with a groan. She pulled the jacket from her shoulders. It was soaked. She was soaked.

'I'm back,' she called out as she walked into the kitchen. The blast of warm air that greeted her took her by surprise. They'd lit the stove and someone had taken down two candles and placed them on the table. A bottle of wine sat open on the worktop and Iris was squeezing lemons for the sauce at the dresser.

'Ah, so you are. Nice walk?' she asked, not lifting her head from what she was doing.

'I've opened some wine.' Georgie appeared at the door that led to the dining room with three of their mother's heavy crystal wine glasses in her hand.

The whole place – the heat, the aroma, her two sisters here together waiting for her, as if they were looking forward to sitting down to dinner together – brought a lump to Nola's throat. An almost overwhelming flow of gratitude flooded through her, to be here, warm, safe, home. In that moment, she couldn't think why on earth she'd reacted so poorly earlier. What a spoiled brat she had been. Six months with these women in this gorgeous house couldn't be that bad, could it?

'I'll do it,' she heard herself say. 'I'll come back and stay here for six months, if that's what it takes.' And somehow, she managed to ignore Iris's triumphant smile as she took her glass of wine from Georgie.

6

Ireland, January

Georgie was delighted to find Soldier Hill House empty when she got there. The radiator in the hall welcomed her with a rumble and a blast of soft heat that promised to negate the cool mist that had settled on her clothes as she'd made her way from the taxi into the house. After lugging her cases upstairs and putting her clothes away, she sat on the bed for a moment. She had arrived early, with two weeks to spare. Well, when she'd looked about her in London there hadn't seemed much point in hanging about. There wasn't anything to keep her there now. She hadn't let anyone know she was coming, so there was no hot dinner prepared today, but as she walked past the sitting room, she'd spotted kindling and wood for the fire. Later she could sort herself out for dinner. But she wasn't hungry yet. Perhaps it was the excitement – was that even the right word? – of coming here, but it set her on edge a bit, so she felt she couldn't settle just yet.

Instead, she decided to put on her walking boots and go for a long tramp in the rain. She couldn't remember the last time she had just gone for a walk in the countryside when it was raining.

Rather than heading towards the beach, Georgie opened the gate and veered through the field that bordered the property. It was a shortcut down to the distillery, and on the spur of the moment, she decided that she might just pop her head in and see what the old place looked like these days. She couldn't remember the last time she'd gone down there. It had probably been to call her father up so he could have dinner with them all when they'd been young and sitting around the kitchen table was the one ritual that kept them on track after their mother died. Back then, the distillery was little more than a huge, ramshackle outbuilding, painted in various shades of red as bits had been added to it or patched up after storms that had bitten down hard on anything that jutted far enough from the landscape to sink windy teeth into.

She checked her watch: just before five. Surely there would be someone about to let her in if she knocked on the door.

Wow! Georgie could hardly believe her eyes as she stood outside the distillery. *There was a main front door now?* To her best recollection, there had only ever been huge garage doors that had taken two men to open and close at either end of the working day. It seemed the place had quietly undergone a complete facelift. It looked – well, *beautiful* was the word that sprang to mind. Notwithstanding the fine gin her father had produced and gifted them that night of his funeral, she had still expected the place to be almost dilapidated. How naïve of her. Quite aside from dabbling in making gin, the Delahaye Distillery produced a world-class whiskey that was carried in some of the finest American hotels and bars. It was a boutique product, but there was a loyal customer base and in any food or drink production setting, Georgie knew there would be rigorous health and safety standards to be adhered to. It seemed that even if the gin packaging hadn't, the Delahaye Distillery had moved along with the times and her father, or whoever was overseeing operations these days, had done it with vision and style.

The whole building had been spruced up, painted a crisp white over pebble-dash walls with accent panels of ash between long gleaming windows giving a tantalising view of the huge vats within. She walked about the perimeter and at the other side, she could see inside long picture windows, the huge silver and copper drums where the whiskey sat waiting to be barrelled. A brand-new roof sloped down on one side to just about eight foot off the ground and it gave the building a slightly dapper air, as if it had just had one gin too many. The place looked great – well, apart from the sign. Everything about the logo and what she'd seen of the packaging made her wince.

'Hey.' A voice behind her startled her and she turned around to see Robert English. 'Remember me?'

She found herself smiling and extended her hand. 'How could I forget you, after you personally hand-delivered the most delicious bottle of gin to us.' He had a strong handshake; it was easy to warm to him.

'Want to come in for a guided tour?' he asked, holding the door open for her. 'Not that you need to be shown around, but I'd imagine it's a while since any of you were here – not since the renovations, I think your father said.'

'No,' Georgie said softly. 'When was that?' It was too long ago – she was certain of that much. She wasn't really sure she wanted to know exactly how long.

'Let me think, it must be five years or so,' he said easily, and from the way he looked around the place, she could see he had as much pride in it as if it was his own. 'We had to talk your father into it. He was thinking of letting it go altogether, but then the government started to hand out grants to small businesses, everything from building repairs to upgrading the marketing spend. Once we got going, he really enjoyed sprucing the place up.'

'It looks amazing; my memory of this place is that it was little more than a glorified spirits-still in a shed.' She laughed softly at the silly notion of it being able to continue into the twenty-first century in that state.

'No, we wouldn't have been able to operate if it was just left like that,' he said, and then he turned to her. 'So, what did the three of you think of Iseult's Gin?'

'Seriously, you have to ask? It's gorgeous. I'm surprised you haven't changed the sign over the door from whiskey to gin.' She laughed.

'No, I'm afraid we're not quite there yet.' He started to lead her up the cast-iron steps to the little office she remembered so clearly her father sitting in. That too had changed completely. The last time she was here, her father's desk had dominated the room and from every spare inch of wall, receipts and notes had been pinned, as if it was being held together by BluTack and sticky tape.

Now, there were two desks, with gleaming white computers on each. Had her father learned how to use a computer? She couldn't imagine it and didn't want to let herself down by having to ask. There was no mistaking his desk though. It had a photograph of her mother, one she remembered clearly from the house, taken one afternoon as she'd walked along the shore, the sun amber on her skin, her eyes dancing in that way they did when she expected to laugh at something that hadn't yet been said.

'And anyway, we'd be mad to give up on the whiskey; it's kept us all in jobs and allowed us to expand when other businesses were falling by the wayside.'

'And the gin?'

'It's a new product.' He smiled now and Georgie found herself smiling back at him. He was easy to like. 'Well, when I say new, it's never been launched. It's been a labour of love for years with your father, but he knew he had completed his work on it before he…'

Georgie pushed past the sticky moment. 'He was happy with it?' That meant a lot; Georgie knew her father was a perfectionist.

'He was.' Robert smiled sadly. 'Anyway, it's going to be up to you and your sisters what comes next.'

She couldn't help it – there was that niggling feeling that always crept along her spine at the prospect of a new project. Except it wasn't hers. She couldn't do a single thing here without Iris and Nola agreeing to it, and that thought brought her back to earth with a thud.

He looked out at the distillery floor beyond the office. 'We'll keep the place running until you decide exactly what you want to do with it,' he said, and she had to admire him for not pushing for any firm answers.

'That'll be a decision for a few months' time.' It seemed wrong to have people working here not knowing what would happen to their jobs, but it couldn't be helped. 'I'm sorry I can't be clearer.'

'Oh, don't worry. I'm sure we'll still have jobs. Your father was beating away the offers to sell this place over the years and now, with the new product line, I'd say you'll have no shortage of buyers. Delahayes will keep distilling; the question is whether you or your sisters are going to continue to be involved or if you'll decide to sell it on to one of the bigger brands.'

'That's a question indeed.' Georgie felt a twinge of sadness at the thought of handing over her father's life's work to some corporate suits that would see nothing more than a bottom line. In some ways, it was a pity they were planning to sell.

A light mist descended across the fields on the walk back up to the house, but Georgie hardly noticed because she was so lost in her thoughts. For the first time since she could remember, she wasn't agonising over her job with Sandstone and Mellon; rather, she could feel a rising anger in her towards her sisters, neither of whom she suspected would care very much one way or another about the legacy of their father's work. She assumed Iris and Myles would spend their portion of the estate on foreign cruises and perhaps a swanky new car for Myles to drive about in. As for Nola, it would undoubtedly be frittered away on parties and the social whirl of thespian London.

As Georgie reached the house, she realised that, far from bringing them closer together, her father's will could drive them further apart than ever.

7

Six Months To Go and Counting...

Iris felt decidedly thrown when she reached Soldier Hill House to find Georgie there before her. She'd been so looking forward to having the place to herself. She'd have stayed in London for a while longer if she'd realised that coming here meant being holed up with her older sister for longer than she needed to be.

'Oh, it was easy for me – all I had to do was tell them I wanted a sabbatical and shutting up the apartment just meant switching off the lights. The management company will take care of the rest,' Georgie said smugly as she took the flowers Iris had stopped off to pick up on the way.

'Lucky you.' Iris tried and failed not to sound begrudging. It was hard not to feel a bit hard done by when she thought of her whole life being boxed up in the attic, sorting through her belongings and the memories they stirred up before she left London. In a fit of crazy abandon, she'd decided to rent out the house. She'd handed in her notice at work and left a message on Myles's answer machine that she was taking a bedsit nearby to get herself together. She'd had to de-personalise their modest little semi before renting it out, and so all her mementos and knick-knacks were now tucked away. The most difficult part turned out to be finding a tenant who didn't look as if they might be doing crystal meth on her kitchen table while she was away.

The truth was, apart from her previous employers – who had quickly found her replacement – no-one else in London had a notion she was here in Ballycove. Very different no doubt to Georgie's situation – Iris imagined her sister having a big send-off from her colleagues at work. Her bosses probably begged her not to go and they most likely couldn't wait for her to get back again. What a difference to her own lacklustre exit – some cake in the break room and a card only signed by a handful of people! Sometimes, Georgie made it even easier to resent her – not that Iris didn't feel that she hadn't already got good cause.

'I'm sure it'll all be there when you get back, and there's nothing to stop Myles sorting out anything you forgot,' Georgie said without realising the irony in her words.

'Did you hear from Nola?' Iris asked, both to change the subject and because surely if they all arrived early they could talk to Stephen and see if the six months of hell could kick in immediately.

'Oh, yes, that's right, she's really likely to ring me for a long heart-to-heart,' Georgie said sarcastically.

'Well, if you'd been a half-decent sister to her all those years ago...' The words flew out before Iris could stop herself, and she braced herself for the oncoming storm.

Georgie snorted. 'I did try to help. It's hardly my fault if Nola didn't want to take me up on my offer. And that's rich coming from you, anyway. You were the one with the cosy semi – remember?' Georgie's colour rose.

'Yes, well, she didn't do to you what she tried to do to me!' Iris shot back, reddening as well.

'It's a bit late now to change what happened. Anyway, everything worked out well enough for her in the end,' Georgie said, almost under her breath.

It was dispiriting, taking all of those familiar items from London out and placing them in her childhood bedroom. When Iris had her inheritance after this purgatory, she would buy a whole new wardrobe before winning Myles back, she decided as she folded her warmest jumpers and squeezed them into the bottom drawer.

It was early evening by the time she emerged from her unpacking and there was no sign of Georgie about the house. There was fresh soup on the stove and someone had picked up a Vienna roll, so she settled down for an early dinner at the kitchen table alone, enjoying the familiar sounds of the old house around her. Georgie must have gone out for a walk along the beach, which suited Iris perfectly. She would sit here for a while, collecting herself after the last few weeks' upheaval and then amble down to the village supermarket to pick up the little essentials she hadn't bothered to pack, like toothpaste and shampoo.

It was a pleasant walk to Ballycove along the little lane where small clumps of snowdrops still pushed through the sleeping hedgerows. Overhead, the sky was sheathed in a silky grey layer and it was hard to call if there was sun or snow on the way. Iris figured she'd settle for either at this point. She walked slowly, savouring the sound of small birds rustling in the bare hawthorns broken up only by the fitful call of a seagull far out over the sea beyond.

In spite of herself, Iris had found when she was home for her father's funeral, that she still loved the village. It was a charming place to live, with the town stretching from the Atlantic's edge, hemmed back by a thick barricading wall and rising up to the gothic-looking church at the top. The village was made up of a zigzag of narrow streets etched out of the land and sheltering a small square in the middle. In the winter months there were no holidaymakers to witness the ravages of storms that hit the coast; the villagers had its ferocious beauty all to themselves. Iris wasn't sure it was any of this that she was beginning to fall in love with at this late stage, as much as it was its familiarity. At every turn there was a recognisable face with an easy greeting and a welcome that she knew with certainty was genuine.

In the shop, she was served by a girl who probably hadn't been born before Iris left Ballycove all those years ago, but still her easy manner let Iris know she was one of their own. How had she not appreciated this sort of thing back then? All she'd wanted then was to leave here and the arguments she'd had with her sisters to prove them all wrong and live what had seemed to be an exciting new life in London with Myles. She could see it now: she'd been running away, not just with Myles, but maybe from the truth of who he really was. She hadn't wanted to face it then, but maybe now she could admit to at least some of the faults Georgie had been so eager to point out. In hindsight, she'd been right all along, he was a womaniser and he had spent his whole life looking for the free ticket to an easy life. Iris had been so immature. How times had changed – these days the nearest she got to Myles was checking into the pregnancy app she'd impulsively downloaded when he first told her about Amanda and the pregnancy.

As far as the app was concerned, Amanda was in her first trimester. Somehow, Iris knew, she'd have to figure out how to uninstall it – the last thing she needed was that ticking away like a time bomb, reminding her of what Myles had to look forward to and all she had to regret.

When she left the supermarket, she decided to turn back into the village, rather than just walk directly to the house. After all, what was there to go home for, apart from stilted conversation with Georgie and the feeling that she had to walk on eggshells to avoid a flare-up? They had six months to fall out, no point starting just yet if she could help it. Instead, she sat in the square, but after a minute or two, she could feel the chill air of the sea biting against her spine. Then a first large drop of rain fell, catching her cheek, and she looked up to see that the sky had darkened ominously. On the other side of the square the hotel was open. She could wait out the shower before making the journey home again.

Like the village, the hotel had managed to retain its old-world charm, but beneath the pretty printed fabrics on the sumptuous sofas, the deep pile of the rugs, the heavy scent of very expensive coffee and behind the warbled glass of the glittering windowpanes, the place had been completely refurbished. Apparently, people travelled from far around for its top-class restaurant. Certainly, everything shone as if an army of cleaners went through the place every five minutes. She could have put her make-up on in the reflection from the brasses on the front door. A smart youngster took her order and explained that it might take a minute. They were expecting a wedding and as usual guests had arrived hoping for a room, but the hotel was impossibly small, so there was a little mayhem trying to get them sorted.

Iris didn't mind in the slightest. She was quite happy to sit in her window seat and watch the wedding guests in their finery settle down to a day of celebration around her.

Her tea with complimentary biscuits arrived fifteen minutes later. The manager of the hotel himself brought it, apologising profusely for the delay.

'I know you, don't I?' she said, not quite able to place him, but he was oddly familiar.

'Ted Rowland,' he said easily. 'We were at school together.'

'God, Ted,' she said, holding out her hand. 'It's lovely to see you again.'

'And you. I was so sorry to hear about your dad.' He shook his head. 'I'd have come to the funeral, obviously, but we were away on holidays.'

'Anywhere nice?' she asked, because he certainly had a good colour compared to what she remembered of the pasty boy who sat behind her at school.

'Corfu.' One word, but his dazzling smile told her what a great time he'd had. 'Never easy, getting time off here, but you have to make the effort while the kids are young, don't you?' He shrugged. 'And of course, the wife works in the parish office, so there's that to juggle too...'

'Life is short – you're right to make time for it.' It was lovely to talk to someone who seemed to have a normal life with everyday worries; and happy with his lot. 'You have your hands full here, I'd say.'

'You can sing that one.' He sat down in the seat opposite. 'It was all grand while the B&B up the road was running. They took our overflow, but Mrs Peters is too old now to be putting up breakfasts for twenty people at all hours of the morning, so she threw the whole thing up at the start of the season. It's left us in a bit of a pickle when it comes to weddings at this time of year, I can tell you.'

'So, where do you send them now?'

'They simply have to go to the next town over, but the hotel there is an awful dump, so I'll have to organise something more upmarket before too long.'

'Well, good luck with that,' she said, because looking around, this was a gorgeous hotel and they were lucky to have it in Ballycove, but the chances of anything even half as good opening up were slim or nil.

'Hey, you don't fancy turning that big house into a fancy bed and breakfast, I suppose?' He laughed.

'Things haven't quite come to that yet,' she joked. But when he left to sort out some other emergency, Iris found herself picturing it: she and Myles running a little country hotel together, her cooking the breakfasts, him charming the guests on the reception desk. Well, a woman could always dream. She sipped her coffee, enjoying the brief respite from real life, for just a little longer.

***

That night, outside her bedroom window, Georgie could hear the ocean roar far off in the distance. The rain, which had looked like just a spitting shower earlier in the afternoon, seemed in no hurry to leave. She heard it rush through the downpipes that ran from the creaking eaves at each corner of the house. Tomorrow, everything would have that lovely, lush look and smell to it. She was already looking forward to a satisfyingly squelchy walk before breakfast, if the rain lightened up. But it wasn't the rain, or the ocean, that kept her awake until this hour. It was something else: a nervy anticipation that sat at the bottom of her chest, an itch she needed to scratch with growing desperation.

Iseult Gin. Ever since speaking with Robert English, the idea of doing something with her parents' gin had nagged at her. For the first time in her professional career, she didn't want to do something to look good for someone else, nor to advance her career. No, this time, it was for her mother, and her father. She knew she wanted to create a legacy with it, something that would live up to the fabulous product her father had worked so hard to create and have her mother's name spoken all around the world. Apart from anything else, it would be good to have a little project to divert her in the long months ahead.

She wasn't being cocky; she knew with certainty that she could do it. With the right branding, a few phone calls to some of her old contacts and good old-fashioned hard work, she could launch Iseult Gin and catapult it to the front of the international market fairly quickly. As she lay in her childhood bed, tossing and turning with the unmistakable adrenaline of a new venture coursing through her, she pictured walking into her local London supermarket in a year's time and seeing bottles of Iseult gin on the shelves, and she smiled to herself in the darkness.

Then her smile faded as she realised she'd have to ask her sisters' *permission*. Well, get their agreement, at least. She'd run her own projects for so long that having to answer to her sisters stuck in her throat. Would they cut her down just because they could? Probably not, but with that pair, who knew?

'So, what do you think?' Georgie asked Iris over a plate of chicken casserole and vegetables the following night.

'What do I think?' Iris asked, sounding taken aback at being asked. 'Well, of course, I think you absolutely should take it on, if you feel you want to—'

'Well, it's not that I want to as such,' Georgie said a little crossly. There was no way that she was having Iris think they were doing her some sort of favour by letting her take this on. Even if she was very excited about it, she meant for them to appreciate it would be hard work and using her not inconsiderable talents. 'I mean, the product has to be branded and launched, we can employ some two-bit company over here or I can take it on and give it the best start it could possibly hope to get.'

'Of course you should do it. I didn't mean to sound as if…' Iris's words petered out, and Georgie felt a stab of regret.

'No, don't worry. I'm sorry for snapping. Thank you,'

Georgie said stiffly; apologies didn't come naturally to her. 'In that case, I'll get started first thing tomorrow morning.' She picked up Iris's plate and took both it and hers to the sink.

The evening seemed to stretch out ahead of them like the Arctic.

'I suppose we could watch the news,' Iris said, intruding into her thoughts. And so Georgie found herself sitting stupidly in front of the television and letting one programme after another wash over her until she began to nod off into a surprisingly restful nap.

'Hey.' Iris's prodding finger woke her and made her jump. It took a second to orientate herself, but then the grandfather clock in the hall chimed out and in her half-awake state she thought she counted eleven strikes clanging along the hallway and up the stairs. Suddenly, she realised she had missed that. Every sound was muffled in her plush London apartment – she'd actually paid extra for it. Here, the echoing rattles and chimes were charming and homely. Even the dry political discussion on the television was somehow soothing, and Iris had slipped a blanket across her, which blocked out any stray draughts. No wonder she'd slept so soundly.

'You should really go to bed.'

'But it's only early.' Even to her own ears, Georgie sounded like a stroppy teenager.

Iris raised her eyebrows. 'Makes no difference to me, but if you want to make the most of your night's sleep…' She smiled then, folding away the yarn and needles that she'd been contentedly knitting for most of the evening.

'I'm usually out like a light anyway,' Georgie said, not mentioning the small white pill that she'd been prescribed years earlier to help her cope with hypertension and stress. It normally knocked her out sufficiently for four to five hours every night. Since she'd come back to Ballycove almost a week ago, she hadn't taken one, she realised, as she headed up to her room. Maybe it was all that sea air.

A band of crows picking crossly at the eaves outside her window woke Georgie late the following morning. She checked her clock, checked it again. It couldn't be ten o'clock in the morning, could it? She hadn't slept that long in over a decade. What on earth was wrong with her? She tumbled out of bed, stood and stretched on the faded circular mat that she remembered so well from childhood. She dressed quickly and was met by the smell of bacon as she walked into the kitchen.

'Ah, you're up, are you?' Iris said and placed bacon and fresh bread on a plate before her. Coffee had just been brewed. There was another aroma in the kitchen and it took a moment for Georgie to place it. Boxty – Iris must have been up early to have prepared the potatoes and flour for this homely breakfast. Georgie couldn't remember when she last ate boxty although she'd loved it as a youngster. 'I was going to call you if it went too late, but I was hoping the aroma of the frying pan might do the trick.' Iris looked as if she was just back from a long tramp across the fields.

'Thank you,' Georgie said tightly. She felt uncomfortable knowing that she'd slept so late, as if it was a chink in her normally perfect armour.

'I think you're right, by the way.' Iris sat down opposite

her and began to butter a slice of bread. 'We should probably make the most of these six months to recharge our batteries – you know, take long walks, soak in the bath, enjoy spending time doing things that we don't normally get the chance to.' Then she laughed. 'Well, apart from taking on the branding of a whole new product, that is.'

'Maybe you're right,' Georgie said. 'I was certainly exhausted last night.' She couldn't remember the last time she'd slept so soundly. 'And, by the way,' she said softly, 'taking on a marketing role in the distillery...' She stopped, trying to find the words.

'I know. That is, I think I understand. You want to do it, but that doesn't mean it's going to be a doddle,' Iris said easily and then she reached down into the oven and took out a slice of boxty and popped it on Georgie's plate. 'Look, sis.' It was years since Georgie had been called that and it pulled her up short, but surprisingly it wasn't altogether unpleasant. 'I wasn't making light of you going in there and taking it on. You know, neither Nola nor I would be any good in the distillery.'

'Well, I don't know, you could both have big futures as gin testers!' Georgie joked.

'Yeah, well, I've had a lot of practice.' Iris raised her coffee as if to make a toast. 'Seriously though, I know you'll do a great job and like you said, the running of the place is down to us now. I think, quite aside from any notions father might have had of us all living happily ever after and meeting up in London every weekend, he'd have wanted us to spend our time here making the most of his life's work before we make a decision on what will become of it all.'

The generosity of Iris's words affected Georgie in a way she hadn't expected. Between the cooked breakfast and the easy atmosphere of the kitchen, it gave her a lovely warm, if unfamiliar glow.

It was only later, as she was heading out for a walk that she began to think about it differently. Of course they would want her making the gin the best it could be – it would seriously impact on the value of the place. Neither Iris nor Nola had ever given a fig about the distillery, their father, or Georgie, once they'd managed to secure their own perfect futures. Cross with herself as much as anyone else, Georgie pulled on the spare wellingtons at the back door with a vicious tug. A bloody slice of homemade boxty shouldn't make her forget it either.

It wasn't an entirely conscious decision, but Nola stayed in London until the last minute when she had no other choice but to leave her flat. She'd sent out what felt like a million query letters to agents, with head shots and her meagre list of credits attached. Yes, she was hoping against all hope that some divine power might pull her from the jaws of having to return home to Ballycove, but in the end, she knew there was nothing for it. She was running out of money and, she had to acknowledge, maybe she'd run out of time long before Maggie Strip had pulled the plug.

So, she packed up her bags, crammed what would fit into a couple of huge suitcases and donated as much as she could to the nearby charity shops. Some of the stuff she'd accumulated over the years wasn't even good enough for that, so she'd left it behind. In the end, she had to drag herself out and lock the door. It felt as if she was finally giving up on her dream. Worse, she was returning home with her tail between her legs and the unmistakable taste of failure on her lips. To cap it all, the notion of having to spend six months with her sisters was just about the only thing worse than knowing she was basically destitute and unemployable in the only profession she'd ever set her heart on.

Outside, the taxi driver had blown his horn three times now and she knew he wouldn't wait any longer. This was London; he might already be making his way towards his next fare with her bags tucked up in his boot.

The plane ride over wasn't much better. Nola felt as if she'd cried an ocean by the time she landed. Iris had offered to collect her in their father's old car, which she had to admit was kind, otherwise she'd have had the mother of all times trying to lug her cases from one bus to another just to make it home. On her way through arrivals, she nipped into the bathroom to repair as much as she could of what remained of the make-up she'd applied that morning in the flat before she'd left. The last thing she wanted was either of her sisters figuring out that she'd been crying on the way over.

'You made it.' Iris was already racing towards the exit after she met her at arrivals. They made their way quickly to the car, managing the bags between them. 'I've parked on double yellows.' Which explained the rush. In her haste to avoid a parking fine Iris pulled the car out of the tight parking space too quickly, almost slicing the nose off another passing car. She jammed on the brakes, throwing everything in the car about. Nola reached down to pick up Iris's phone, which had slid from the dash. She hadn't meant to look. She certainly wasn't one to go prying, especially in Iris's phone, who she'd have assumed would have nothing more interesting to look at than knitting patterns or maybe a sleep app. But there it was: Bumps and Grows – the baby app – had been left open. *Oh my God.* Iris was pregnant! Nola pushed the phone into the glove compartment as if it were on fire, her heart pounding. They spent the remainder of the journey in stony silence, each lost in thought, Nola trying hard to digest the news that it looked as if she was going to become an aunty.

The following morning, Nola woke relieved to see that at least the torrential rain that had been promised for the night before had passed over Ballycove. 'Make hay while the sun shines,' her father used to say. Well, she thought, she would take that advice today.

Breakfast was *almost* a pleasant affair, cooked by Iris today. Mary was due in each day to cook dinner and tidy up, but there was no reason they couldn't be civilised about breakfast too. Georgie had organised a rota; they would each have a day to cook breakfast and clean up afterwards. Swaps were allowed. Honestly, Georgie could make a luxury stay in the Ritz feel like a military operation. Still, at least Iris could cook; she wasn't sure if Georgie still remembered how. Breakfast was a full Irish, and the taste was enough to make up for the stilted conversation.

'I think I'll drop in on the Barrys this morning,' Nola

announced as soon as the breakfast dishes were cleared away.

She was delighted to see that Moira Barry's house had not changed very much at all. When she sat at Moira's kitchen table, it was as if she'd never left Ballycove to begin with and the reassuring feeling that she had landed somewhere safe was one she knew was worth returning for.

'You have to tell me everything,' Moira said as she plopped down opposite her. Nola had already heard all the details of her daughters' lives: Helen, her old chum, had recently divorced and the other Barry girl was living in a town she hated with two kids who seemed to be running rings around her.

Nola knew she could tell Moira anything; when she'd been young, it was Moira she'd come to when her own mother had not been there. 'Are you sure you want the truth of it?'

'Go on, what does the fridge magnet say?' She pointed towards the far end of the kitchen. 'The truth sets you free.'

'All right, here goes…' And so it all tumbled out of her. From the great highs of the success of being one of the most recognisable faces on British television, to sitting in a kitchen in the village she'd vowed never to return to again. 'I suppose, it sounds naïve now, but I hadn't realised how much of my life depended on that one role.'

'It was as plain as day you were the best one in that programme. I never missed an episode and I'm sure I'm not the only one who tuned out as soon as they decided to kill off your character.' Moira topped up her tea. 'Surely you could just get another part?'

'It sounds simple, doesn't it?' Maybe it should have been, but Nola remembered clearly the downward spiral her life had fallen into after her last day on set. It was strange really, because right up to the filming of her very last scenes, it hadn't really bothered her at all. 'After it was all over, I slid into depression. I mean, I didn't realise it at the time. I'd never experienced anything like it before. But one day I woke up and knew I just couldn't go on. I could hardly get out of bed, never mind brush my hair or go for auditions. My *friends* vanished one by one. They just stopped taking my calls.' Nola fought back tears, because even now, she didn't quite understand how those people who had always been there with a party invitation could have cut her from their lives so callously when she needed real friends the most. 'And of course, you'll know from the tabloids that my relationship imploded when Oliver fell for the next actress to arrive on set after I left. I was completely alone.'

'I thought you were great in that tea advertisement too,' Moira said loyally. 'It was such a pity about the court case afterwards.'

'I have no-one to blame but myself for that.' God, she still felt that stab in her stomach like a physical pain at her own stupidity every time she thought about it. She thought it would be the making of her, spearheading a case that highlighted the differences in pay between male and female actors in the industry. She had been incensed when she realised her co-star in the advertisements for Britain's Best Loved Tea was being paid ten thousand pounds more than her. 'I never bargained on losing the case, nor the fact that even taking it to begin with marked me out as a troublemaker that no-one would want to employ afterwards.'

'Surely there were other things you could have done? Writing or directing or—'

'I knocked on every production company door I could think of. In the end, I'd have done anything – worked front of house, made the tea, swept the floors – but like I say, at that point, I was marked out as trouble. London had firmly shut its doors on me. Things got so bad, I ended up in a squat for a while. I even asked Georgie for a job, but by that point, we were hardly close…' She found she couldn't go on. That was probably one of the lowest points in her life, the moment she knew that she really had hit rock bottom.

'I think we'll need another pot of tea, my dear,' Moira said gravely. She was holding Nola's hand and, mercifully, the kitchen that she remembered from her youth as being so busy had remained quiet while she spilled out every last detail of her miserable life for Moira. 'You poor, poor girl,' she said, then began to smile. 'You know, you might have arrived here at the best possible time.'

'How do you mean?'

'Well, hear me out now. Don't say no, until I've said my piece.'

'I never would – you know that.' With Moira, Nola knew that anything she would ever say would only be for her own good. There were no *I told you so's* here. Not like with her sisters. Moira was as devastated as her mother might have been for the way everything had come crashing in on her over the last few years.

'Well, I have it on very good authority that they're looking for someone to help out in the school, just a couple of times a week with their drama class. Their last teacher let them down without a lot of notice and ran off to Italy, if you can imagine. Apparently, she met some fella on the interweb thingy and that was that, packed up her bags and did a moonlight flit before anyone had a chance to talk some sense into her.' She shook her head. 'I'm not sure what it would entail, but it would be work and you'd get paid and it might be a lot better than hanging about in that big house thinking of all this...'

'Maybe,' Nola said dubiously. 'But I'm not a drama teacher; I've never even gone to college.' She sighed. If anything, she couldn't wait to get out of school when she was a kid. The last thing she'd have signed up for was the idea of actually spending the rest of her days working in one. Now, somehow, sitting here with Moira, the idea of teaching kids what she loved actually seemed like a nice way to earn a living. It was better than waitressing and certainly better than spending her time with nothing to do but mope around the house with Georgie and Iris. She'd get paid too, which was something she definitely couldn't turn her nose up at what with the inheritance being by no means certain at this point.

'Haven't you done more acting lessons than anyone else for miles around?'

'I have.' Nola had spent a small fortune on acting classes over the years.

'And that's what they want. You've even been on the telly, for heaven's sake. That's more than the last one ever had. The Easter pageant will be coming up and then the musical and they're always looking for people to cover once the flu season arrives.'

'It does sound pretty ideal.' Nola smiled in spite of herself.

'What have you got to lose, eh?' Moira squeezed her hand again. 'All you have to do is put together a little CV for yourself and drop it into the school – I'm sure they'll be snapping your hand off to get you in there as fast as they can before school starts back.'

'I don't know about that, Moira. They'll probably have loads of people applying and—'

'Well, I do, so promise me you'll get down there and start talking them into it.'

'You're impossible – you know that.' Nola laughed, but she had already decided, she was going to give it her very best shot.

'You'll thank me yet,' Moira said, then put her finger to her lips when she heard the back door open and the unmistakable sound of someone coming in and shuffling out of wellingtons and a coat. 'Are you back for dinner today, then?' Moira called out as the door opened wide. Aiden Barry stood there, windblown and looking surprised to see Nola ensconced at his mother's kitchen table. He brought with him a blast of cold from outside, as if he'd stood on the ocean's edge for half the day before arriving. 'You remember Nola, don't you, Aiden?' his mother asked, smiling fondly at her only son.

'I do,' he said, hardly looking at her once he'd actually come into the kitchen. 'And you're lucky she's here at all, if she keeps walking on country roads without so much as a passing regard for tractor drivers going about their business.'

'I hardly think that you have any reason to be complaining,' Nola said, her colour rising. 'After all, you weren't the one almost killed on the side of the road.'

'What's all this?' Moira asked, but she was smiling, as if she knew something more than either of them.

'Anyway, Mum, I just came back to drop this in. I met the postman on the way. It's only bills and circulars, but I thought I'd save him the journey.' He eyed Nola as he said this, as if he deeply regretted his generosity now that it meant he'd been forced into further contact with her.

'Ah, you're very considerate,' Moira said, looking at him fondly. 'Isn't he very thoughtful, Nola?' She looked across at Nola, who would have liked to say she thought he was indeed a lot of things, but considerate wouldn't be top of her list anytime soon.

Nola could have sat in that kitchen all afternoon, if it wasn't for the arrival of Aiden. She hoped he'd leave quickly but when his mother insisted he have something to eat before going back to work, Nola knew it was time to get moving. Anyway, suddenly she felt invigorated – she was eager to get her application in to the school before that job was snapped up by someone else.

The old convent school she remembered hating for most of her teenage years had long since been turned into a community building as a brand-new, state-of-the-art school had been built on a green-field site at the furthest end of the village. It was all natural light, neutral colours and muted sounds. The yard was laid out for basketball, netball, tennis – games that Nola never had much interest in when she was a kid, but she could see now that maybe, if they'd had facilities like this, she might have felt differently. Today, everything had a bright, optimistic feel to it.

The principal – Gary Cotter, a rotund man in his late forties – seemed nice enough. She couldn't help but think when she spoke to him that in a few years he'd make a great Santa Claus.

'A celebrity!' he cried, shaking her hand vigorously.

She gave an embarrassed smile and said, 'Hardly.' But, she supposed, perhaps she was by Ballycove's standards. 'I certainly have enough experience in front of a camera, though, and I'd love to put on something really special with the kids this year.' And as she said it, she remembered how much any chance at getting up on a stage had meant to her when she was young, and found that she meant it.

'Yes, it's a pretty special role. You get to work with kids and really see what a difference you're making. You will have the chance to build them up, shape them and have a hand in the adults they'll become.'

'I know. I lived for drama class.' She smiled, remembering how much she'd looked forward to that one class a week. 'It helped me to fit in when I didn't feel I could fit in anywhere else.'

When she walked down the driveway, there was an undeniable spring in her step and for the first time since she arrived in Ballycove, she noticed the birds singing and the sun shining. Gary had said he'd be in touch later in the week, and for once, she was fairly certain it would be good news.

It was by no means what she'd have imagined herself doing at this point in her life. Still, it was a job and to her own surprise, she found herself feeling excited at the prospect. Maybe there was a little sense of having achieved something, too – it was in the direction of that long-held dream and that was more than she could say for too many years in London. It was funny, but even just knowing that she'd gone in there and asked for it, somehow taken her destiny into her own hands, buoyed her up no end. She had a feeling that for the rest of the evening, even Iris and Georgie wouldn't be able to get on her nerves.

The call came the following morning.

'Thanks so much, Mr Cotter. Oh, right, yes, of course.' Nola was flapping her hands. She'd turned down the radio and shushed Iris just as she'd been offering her a refill on her morning cup of tea. 'Gary.' She smiled. 'I'm so thrilled. Thank you, I'll see you later today, then...'

'What's that all about?' Georgie looked up from reading the morning paper on her phone.

'That was the principal at the new secondary school.' Nola picked up her slice of toast and inspected it with a satisfied smile before taking a small bite. 'He just rang to offer me a job.'

'What sort of job?' Iris asked.

'Teaching, of course – drama.' Nola licked some stray butter from her fingertips and looked at her sisters defiantly.

'But you're not a teacher,' Iris said, although the very fact should have been self-evident, even to Nola.

'So, you think I should be cleaning the loos? Applying for a post as a dinner lady, is that it?'

'She never said that.' Georgie didn't look up from her phone.

'No, well, she didn't say congratulations either,' Nola snapped.

'Congratulations,' Iris said, sounding flustered. 'Of course I'm delighted for you.'

'Ditto.' Georgie looked up, her lips momentarily lifting into what was supposed to be a smile. 'Is it full time?'

Nola bristled. Trust Georgie to look for the holes in her achievement. 'No. But I'll be going in every day to teach a few different classes and maybe, if there are teachers absent, I might pick up some supervising hours between classes.'

'That's nice. It'll be good for you to have something to do. And a little pin money, for running about with,' Iris said, sounding like she was talking to a five-year-old.

Nola stood up so quickly that her chair flew backwards and hit the wall. 'That's just so bloody typical of you, Iris.'

'What? What did I say?'

'If you don't know, why should I tell you?' Nola picked up her cup and stormed out of the kitchen. In spite of herself, she felt disappointment coursing through her. She was angry with them, but even angrier with herself. How could she be so stupid as to expect them to have changed? Nothing she did would ever be good enough for Georgie, and Iris was only ever going to patronise and belittle her. And now, they'd ruined her moment.

8

Iris wished to God that she didn't have to watch every single word she uttered. If it wasn't bad enough to have Georgie being prickly about taking on the marketing for the distillery, now she had Nola taking offence at her sincere attempts to be nice about her new job. Looking back, she realised how what she said about pin money could have sounded condescending – but really, Nola should have known Iris didn't mean it like that. Where on earth was the lovely girl that Iris remembered from childhood? But who was she to talk? She herself had changed beyond all recognition, too.

She decided on a walk along the beach to clear her head. Maybe she'd stop off at the hotel for coffee on the way back. That thought cheered her, so she threw on her father's old jacket and set off with a spring in her step. When she met the postman at the end of the road, she took the letter he'd been about to deliver and stuck it in her pocket without taking much notice.

It was only later, as she sat on some rocks just beneath the cliffs that overhung the halfway point in her walk, that she remembered and pulled out the letter. It was addressed to her, from London. The handwriting was unfamiliar, but then again, she couldn't think of anyone who would be writing her a chatty letter to catch up on the news since she'd been away. It had obviously been forwarded from the new tenants in the house in London; she spotted the leasing company stamp on its back.

She tore it open, an ominous feeling making her heart pound.

Her eyes raced down through the jumble of words faster than she could read them. It was from Myles's solicitor. Myles had a solicitor? Before she could process the mere fact of this shocking development, two words jumped out at her: Divorce Proceedings.

Myles wanted a divorce. She tried to read the letter again, but her eyes were full of tears, her hands shaking too much to hold the paper steady. She couldn't see the words and she knew somewhere in the back of her dazed mind that even if she could, they wouldn't make any sense to her right now.

No. No. No. No. She felt the words come from the bottom of her throat, more a groan than anything else, over and over, no, no, no, no.

This couldn't be happening. Not now. Maybe if she pretended that she'd never seen it, he might change his mind. That was it: he wasn't thinking straight. Iris scrubbed back the tears from her eyes. Her hands were sandy, which only made things worse. Far out, on the choppy waves, she could just about make out the shadowy shape of a fishing boat, overhead the circling gulls yelped a lonely sound that travelled on the tide towards her. Oh God, this couldn't be happening. She tried to focus hard on the birds, diving and soaring, catching any fleshy dinner before the fishermen threw it back into the sea again.

She would not let this happen. She folded the letter up, twice, four times, eight times and over again until it was a tiny square – how could such a small piece of paper tear her world down now? She shoved it deep into the pocket of her father's old jacket and then got up and began the journey back with a heavier heart that made a lie of the life she had been trying so hard to convince herself was real.

As she walked back along the beach, she knew the sensible thing would be to go and engage a solicitor of her own. Tell someone what was happening, do something.

No, she had made up her mind – she was going to win him back. She would win him back with her share of the Delahaye legacy and when she finally confronted him, she would pretend she'd never seen this letter. They could pretend none of this had ever happened.

By the time Iris made it back to the village, it was easier to believe that winning Myles back was as sure and certain as she had convinced herself before. The most important thing, Iris knew, was to keep a low profile. As long as he believed she was renting some tired little bedsit in London, there was a good chance he'd just assume she was getting her affairs in order – which of course she was, thanks to the fact that in six months, she was likely to be a wealthy woman with a lot more to offer Myles than ever before.

By the time Iris arrived back on the footpath and had

shaken the sand from inside her shoes, she'd managed to block out even the slightest notion of that letter. She forced her mind back to the present, which involved coffee in the hotel.

Her marriage, imploding before her eyes, had taught her to count her blessings in a whole new way. For a start, she was living in a charming old house, which she'd never truly appreciated before. It still felt as if her mother and father lingered somewhere behind the fabric of the place and that gave her more comfort than she could have ever imagined. There was the beach to walk along and the endless green fields to lose her worries in as she tramped across them early most mornings. She had even found herself revelling in the rain. What was that about? In London, she had hated the rain. It meant umbrellas and taking the bus and more often than not snagging her tights. It meant coming home shivering after a day behind that draughty receptionist's desk where no matter how long she stayed, she knew she'd never know anyone more than identifying them by their chart numbers, the state of their molars or next appointment dates. Here, in Ballycove, it felt as if she had a community around her.

Ted Rowland dropped into the chair opposite her with a steaming mug of coffee in his hand, interrupting her reverie. He was back to his favourite topic, or at least that's what she called it: the crazy notion of his that she could open up a B&B in Soldier Hill House.

'Seriously, there's a good living to be made here,' he said earnestly, probably wishing that anyone would take on the local bed and breakfast just to help with the overflow from yet another city wedding party hoping to score some tranquillity in Ballycove.

She groaned internally. This was the last thing she needed, today of all days. But she knew Ted of old, and knew that the only way of getting rid of him was to let him get whatever bee was in his bonnet out of his system. 'Yes, Ted, but you're forgetting, I can't just open up a bed and breakfast on a whim. People expect en-suite bathrooms and televisions in their rooms and homemade brown bread and all sorts...' She stopped.

'Okay, okay, you know best. I'll stop harping on at you. I get the message, no B&Bs.' He was laughing at her, but she was just relieved when he got up to sort out some emergency in the kitchen. Of course, it was all just pie in the sky. She couldn't possibly take on something so ambitious. She was just a housewife, a receptionist. She stopped for a moment, corrected that thought in her head: *a soon-to-be-divorced housewife and an out-of-work receptionist*. She shivered.

There was a delicious lamb stew for dinner. It was a pity that the company wasn't up to the same standard. Not that Iris was even sure she'd be capable of keeping up the pretence that everything was fine and dandy. There was a limit to her reserves and as she sat there, although the food was good, she found herself approaching that limit. In the end, feeling as if she might gag if she continued, she gave up, laid her cutlery on the table and switched on the kettle. The day and, more specifically, that letter, was taking its toll regardless of her best intentions to ignore it.

It seemed that Nola still hadn't forgotten their spat since earlier, and her conversation ran to one-syllable answers that reminded Iris of when she was a teenager. Georgie seemed to be completely consumed with the distillery, so she just wolfed down her food and disappeared out the back door and across the fields as if her life depended on getting back there again. As soon as the dinner things were cleared away, an operation loaded with heavy silences broken only by the sound of stacking dishes and cutlery hitting the drawer with speed, Nola locked herself behind the dining room door, mumbling something about lesson plans for her new job.

At eight o'clock, far from feeling relieved that her sisters were out of her hair, Iris felt as if she'd been cast adrift. The silence of the house, normally soothing, felt oppressive. The last thing she needed now was time on her own to mull over things she was trying to forget. What could be better than a nice walk, just as the crows were settling into their nests and the bats were leaving their roosts from the attics in the old outbuildings that separated the kitchen garden from the farmyard?

She was right. Getting out in the cold night air was exactly what she needed. At least with the breeze at her back and the rustle of nocturnal animals readying themselves for the night ahead, she could think. Or maybe, not think and that was like a balm across her fraying nerves. She realised it must be years since she'd actually walked down the avenue. It was half a mile from the front door to the main gates, but she walked slowly, savouring the cool night air. When she arrived at the gatehouse, she stood for a moment and felt a smile stretch out her lips as her eyes fell upon the old gate lodge cottage that stood in the shadowy trees dappled with moonlight.

In the half-light, it looked like something conjured from a John Hinde photograph. But of course, darkness covered over any little age lines that might mar its beauty in the less forgiving daylight hours. Iris remembered adoring it when she was a child. She'd wanted to live here like the tenants who'd kept it beautifully with roses at the door and the smell of fresh baked bread drifting through the open windows.

And suddenly, it came to her. A madcap idea, something maybe she *could* do. Then that familiar voice rose up inside her – weirdly, it sounded a little like Myles – laughing at her, telling her that of course she couldn't take on something like this, it was much too ambitious for her. She'd never be fit for it. The words ricocheted in her mind for a moment. They were so familiar, she had never interrogated them before. But this time, instead of blindly accepting them, she took a step backwards. Myles was right, wasn't he? What had she ever done in life to qualify her to take on a project like this?

The sound of an owl, hooting high up in the furry-topped pines beyond her shoulder, tipped her back to the present moment with a sharp intake of surprised breath. She laughed, suddenly nervous in the cooling darkness, but the voice in her head had been switched off for a moment and she took a deep breath. What was the harm in taking a closer look?

Of course, it was crazy to think anyone would want to stay in an old stone cottage in the middle of nowhere. And anyway, what did she know about the hospitality industry and self-catering cottages or running a bed and breakfast?

A second owl hooting in the trees behind the cottage made her jump once more, as if correcting her, and she pushed the gate open. In for a penny, she thought, her hand lingering on the peeling paint for a moment. Someone – her father, probably – had left the front door keys beneath the welcome mat. Iris shook her head at the naivety of it. Of course, here it was unlikely anyone would want to break in, so maybe he wasn't so naïve after all.

The house was a pleasant surprise and if it was too much to say that it lifted her spirits, Iris certainly felt her worries easing off as she explored the little house that she only vaguely remembered from years ago. Neither the electricity nor the water had been disconnected and the place felt if not exactly warm, at least as if it was holding out the cold of the falling evening temperatures. It could be cosy, if the fire was lit and the lights were low. Whoever had stayed here last was obviously house-proud and they'd left the place as clean as a new pin. There was no doubt that the furniture was shabby and the sofa was in need of replacing and it could definitely do with new mattresses and a supply of crisp white linens for the beds, but overall it was miles better than she'd have imagined.

For a long while, she sat in the room they'd always called the parlour, imagining the possibilities of running this as a little business and she felt a wave of something warm bubble up in her. It was a feeling so unfamiliar she found it hard to pin a name on it to begin with. But she sat there, enjoying it, welling up with it. It was the merest inkling of happiness and it was the nicest feeling she could remember having in a very, very long time.

It was after midnight when she pulled the cottage door closed behind her. She'd spent almost three hours at the house, just wandering about, sitting, thinking, planning and, for the first time in years, dreaming of something that she would love to do just for herself.

As she saw it, most of the work in setting the cottage to rights as a quaint, self-catering getaway, would mean little more than elbow grease. It was a lot of washing, scrubbing, a fresh coat of paint, new curtains and repurposing some of the furniture from the main house to replace what was too shabby to be upcycled here. Her life so far had prepared her perfectly for it.

The worst part would be telling her sisters – or rather asking them, because after all, this cottage was as much theirs as it was hers. And she wondered, for a fleeting moment, if perhaps Georgie had felt the same way when she'd decided to take on the marketing brief at the distillery. Of course not, Iris thought with a sigh and shrug. Georgie never let anything slow her down; nothing got in her way if she set her mind on something. But that was Georgie. The same set of rules did not apply to Iris. But this was something she longed to do.

She mulled over the idea for the next couple of days, fizzing with excitement all the while. In fact, by the end of the third day, it had become such a dominant thought in her mind, it had actually pushed all thoughts of London and some of Myles and *that letter* to one side for most of the time.

Iris steeled herself for the conversation she dreaded having with her sisters. She went down to the village beforehand and bought a huge bouquet of white roses and lilies and arranged them on the kitchen table. They'd finished dinner and for some reason, this evening, Georgie had opened a bottle of wine, as if there was something to celebrate before Iris even got around to sharing her plans.

'I wanted to tell you both something,' Iris began softly. 'Well, maybe *ask* is a better way of putting it. It's about the gate lodge...'

'Oh?' Nola's head shot up from examining her phone.

'Yes. I think I could make it into a really nice holiday let.'

'But isn't it almost derelict?' Georgie said without a moment's thought.

'Well, that's what I thought too, but I've had a look around and it's in much better shape than I expected. You see, I was talking to Ted down at the hotel, and he said that with the overflow from weddings alone, we could probably have it filled with guests every weekend. It could be a nice little earner,' she said.

'Let me say, right here, I'd have absolutely no interest in being a chambermaid to some yobs arriving down here for stag nights,' Georgie said, but when Iris's eyes met hers, something in her features softened. Perhaps she realised that just as she had the distillery and Nola had the school to keep her occupied, Iris too needed something more than hanging about the house all day long. 'But of course, if you want to take it on, it would be a great string to our bow, if... I mean, when we sell the place...'

'Yes. That's exactly what I thought...' Iris said, and then she looked across at her younger sister. 'Nola?'

'Fine by me, just don't expect me to cook breakfast for your guests anytime soon,' she said, going back to browsing the internet on her phone. Then her head darted up, as if she'd remembered something. 'Are you sure it won't be too much for you, I mean…' she stopped '…well, we're meant to be taking it easy, enjoying…'

Iris felt herself stiffen. Trust Nola to pour cold water on things. 'Of course not. I think I'm more than capable of putting a house together and making sure the place is nice for someone coming to stay,' Iris bit back. It wasn't going to affect either of her sisters. After all, it was just something to keep her busy for the next six months. They'd all be rushing back to London as soon as they could afterwards.

And so, it was settled. Iris had the strange sensation that she was about to take a tentative step towards her future. And, she had to admit, that future looked just a shade brighter than it had in a while.

A week later, Georgie was sitting at her father's desk when her phone pinged, but she ignored it. Unlike in London, she didn't feel she had to be 'on' all the time. She could ignore emails and messages because for the most part, they didn't have any great power over her anymore.

And this morning, she had important things to consider.

Periwinkle, Savoy Blue, Blurple or Midnight Blue? She had narrowed it down to just four – no mean feat when she had started off with ninety-two various shades of blue for the packaging of Iseult Gin.

'You're asking the wrong man,' Robert English said as he placed two digestive biscuits beside her stout cup of tea.

'I could get used to this.' Georgie smiled. Yesterday, they'd brought her cake. Somehow, they'd found out it was her birthday and one of the women – June – had made the cake the night before. It was uneven and filled with far too much cream to be anything but messy, but they'd sang her happy birthday and Georgie had felt a warm glow like she hadn't felt in a very long time. It felt as if she was among not just colleagues, but maybe even friends if she stuck around long enough. She couldn't help but compare it to the leaving party that never happened at Sandstone and Mellon – there she knew the only celebration would be because she'd left, not because they'd miss her. 'So, what do you think?'

'Blue is blue to me. You might as well be putting different types of fairy dust before me. I wouldn't have a notion.' He smiled, and while Georgie laughed, it brought her no closer to a decision.

'Well, I need to choose soon. They've been on my desk for three days now.' Never, in all her professional career, had she been a woman to dither. The Georgie of old would have known, just as if told by some divine voice, which to go with.

'You're overthinking it.'

'Hmm.' He was probably right, but this wasn't just any product. This was the Delahaye brand and it *had* to be right. Somehow, over the last few weeks, the late nights, the early mornings and the time she'd spent with just the whirring sounds of the distilling lines for company, she had become invested in the future of this place in a way she'd never been before. 'Once we make the choice, it's there for a very long time,' she said. She held a line of silver samples against the Midnight Blue. It was classic. But then she knew, if she held it against the Periwinkle, it could be iconic. 'Bloody hell, when did this get so hard?' She flopped into her chair, took up a biscuit and chewed it slowly. Perhaps the sugar would loosen something in her brain.

'Why not put it to a vote?' Robert asked.

'A vote?' She laughed at the suggestion. 'And who would we ask to vote? The cat's mother, I suppose?'

'If you want, but I was thinking, more like your sisters? Or the lads on the floor? They all have vested interests in the place, after all.'

'Really? But...' Georgie felt that old familiar feeling rise up in her again, a sort of tightening of the muscles around her neck. She knew what it was, of course: it was a reaction to the idea of losing control. She'd never been very good at handing over her work to anyone else. Wasn't it half the reason she'd driven away every assistant who'd ever made a suggestion in the past?

'After all, you're not going to be here, Georgie.' Robert's words unexpectedly hurt like a gut-punch. Maybe he was right. If she was going to be handing over the Delahaye Distillery to the new owners, she should just make a decision and have done with it.

'I really think I'm leaning towards the Midnight Blue,' she said, though with less enthusiasm now.

'And maybe Iris and Nola will also.' He was smiling at her now, the merest twitch of his lips.

She looked at him suspiciously. 'What?'

'Nothing.' He held his hands up. 'It's just, you're so much like your father. He couldn't bear to let anyone else have a say either.'

'I am not,' she said, sounding much more outraged than

she felt, because she didn't want to admit what had been patently obvious to her for years and what may have marked her out as a great success but also the office pariah when it came to making friends or having relationships. 'Anyway, he was a great distiller,' she said, avoiding his eyes.

'He was, but he was stubborn as hell too and he'd never have been able to run this place with partners, silent, temporary or otherwise. And I have a feeling that the same applies to you too, even if you don't want to admit it.'

'Humph.' Georgie gave the trademark Delahaye response of a shrug, then peered at him over the rim of her mug. 'So you think I could make the distillery into a great success?' she said casually, flicking through the colour patches on the desk before her.

'I think if you hung around you could probably be the best distiller of the whole Delahaye family, but that's not on the cards, is it?' He drained his cup, picked up the checklist and set off to do his eleven-thirty rounds.

The 'rounds', as Robert referred to them, were probably Georgie's favourite task in the distillery. It was very simple really, just a matter of checking temperatures and pressure valves, and identifying and correcting any deviations he noticed.

This was a job normally carried out by the master distiller, but she'd taken on the role the previous day when Robert had been busy and there was no-one else to step into the breach. Georgie was becoming slowly but surely obsessed with the whole process. In the evenings and at the weekends, when she wasn't in the distillery, she devoured books on the subject. Everything from how to set up your own distillery to the industry bibles, she was learning about making anything from bourbon to poitín and everything in between. It wasn't that she was planning on sticking around or anything, but it was good to keep the mind occupied, she told herself.

'Georgie,' Robert called out from the behind one of the aged vats near the end of the factory floor. 'Georgie, come here!' There was an urgency to his voice that brought Georgie racing down the stairs.

'What? What is it?' In her mind's eye, it was something terrible. She'd twisted a gauge and destroyed the contents of the entire vat or the copper had finally worn thin. Could it do that, she wondered? 'What's wrong?' She was panicking now, her heart racing and sweat seeping through the palms of her hands.

'Nothing's wrong.' Robert smiled at her. 'I'm just wondering who switched this gauge to one-seventy-five?'

'Well, I did. I checked it late last night and it seemed to be…' What? She just had a feeling that it needed to be moved down a degree or two. God, she'd made a total mess – she bet it would cost thousands to recoup.

'Why did you turn it down?' He was gazing at her steadily now, keeping eye contact and it was slightly unnerving. She hadn't felt this nervous under anyone's gaze in years.

'I just…' She stopped. 'I did as you said: I checked everything, made a decision…' She stopped again, not sure now it was such a bad thing after all, as Robert began to smile. 'I used my nose as well as my brain?' she said, remembering something her father said about the true 'art' of distilling.

'Good work, you might have saved the day.' He

mock-saluted her. 'That gauge has been acting up since before I can remember. It goes to show one thing though.' He was smiling at her again.

'Oh?'

'It looks like you've got the touch as well as that stubborn streak from your father. And thank goodness, because I think you might have saved us from losing the entire vat. We'll make a distiller of you yet.' He slapped her back, as if she really was one of the team. And Georgie, rather than feeling that disgruntled sense of incumbent grouchiness at *having* to save the day (because she was surrounded by imbeciles and halfwits – which on reflection, may not always have been strictly true in the past) this time felt instead a lightness of spirit that she had made some small difference. And here, that difference meant far more to her than she'd ever imagined possible.

She still hadn't settled between the Midnight Blue and the Periwinkle, and Robert had jokingly (she hoped) made up a suggestion box and placed it on her desk. He'd put in a bit of work on it, with the colour combinations on the outside and a single line – all suggestions welcome – in great big red letters along the side, as if to goad her. But there was no goading her these days: she was much too busy and maybe, even almost too content to let anything bother her.

'You don't have to take their suggestions; you can still make up your own mind,' he said as they were finishing up one evening.

'Then what's the point in a suggestion box?'

'It makes people feel valued, involved, invested.' He said. 'Ultimately, the decision has to be yours. After all, you're the marketing guru.' He smiled at her again and she wondered if he wasn't somehow making fun of her, but his eyes crinkled up and there was no missing the kindness that lingered there.

'Perhaps, even gurus need a little help now and again, it seems.' She was learning it slowly, but maybe late was better than never.

'Don't we all?' he said gently before letting himself out the door and leaving her with the suggestion box – and the decision about whether to use it – in her hands.

She set it up in the mini canteen. She sighed grudgingly; if she was doing this, she'd have to ask Nola and Iris too. After all, whether she was the expert or not, they were still equal owners in the distillery and as such, they deserved to have their say, even if Georgie had begun to secretly enjoy running the show on her own.

A loud bang at the other end of the distillery woke her from her thoughts. It was dark outside and normally the only sounds here were the ongoing whirr of power and the vats occasionally rumbling. Georgie jumped from what had quickly become her chair. For a second, she was unsure whether to run and see what or who had made the noise or just ring the guards in case it was an intruder.

'Who's there?' she shouted in the most commanding voice she could muster. Again, the sound of shuffling and unseen noise reached her ears. 'Who's there?' she called again.

'Hey!' a friendly voice came up from down below. 'It's only me.' Nola stepped into the puddle of light from the office overhead.

'You nearly gave me a bloody heart attack.' But Georgie

laughed, feeling a wave of relief, and walked down the steel steps to her sister. 'What are you doing here, anyway?'

'Nothing. I just thought I'd come have a look. The door was open and I wasn't sure if it was supposed to be or if someone had left it open by mistake.' She sounded a little defensive.

'Well, thank you for checking it out,' Georgie said, suddenly feeling as if she didn't want Nola intruding here, but she had to remind herself that Nola had as much right to be here as she had. She should just be grateful that she wasn't part of a masked gang breaking in to do untold damage to the place.

'You're welcome,' she said stiffly, looking about her and taking it all in. 'This place has changed.'

'It has.' Georgie smiled with an absurd pride she knew she had absolutely no right to feel, as the changes Nola was talking about had been made by their father. 'Is it your first time in here since we came back?'

'Yes.' Nola looked a little embarrassed. 'I just never felt as if... Well, this place... It always felt off limits, didn't it?'

'Did it?' Maybe Nola was right. Certainly, it felt very often as if their father spent as much time as he could here to escape the emptiness left at home when their mother died. Of course, Georgie had pushed her way through that when they were kids, but then, she didn't have Myles or Moira to fill the gap.

She looked at Nola now in the half-light, standing there wet and windblown, and she could see that fragile little girl she remembered from years earlier. It made her catch her breath for a moment, as if she'd been thrown back to some earlier time, before they'd all fallen out so badly. 'You know, he'd have wanted you here as much as he wanted me. I think a lot of the times, I only got in the way, but unlike you, there was no point sending me to dancing or singing classes.' They both laughed at that because it was true. Georgie had two left feet and a voice to put the crows out of business. 'Fancy the grand tour?'

'Yes, all right,' Nola said. Georgie brought her through the distilling process from beginning to end, explaining as much as she could from what Robert and her own research had taught her.

'Goodness, you seem to know so much about it all,' Nola said.

Georgie peered at her sister suspiciously. 'Is that your way of telling me to shut up?'

'Not at all!' Nola held her hands up in the air. 'Why do you always have to assume the worst?'

Georgie sighed. 'You're right. I'm sorry. I suppose I do go on a bit, but I find it all fascinating.' That was the truth. She spent more time down here learning about the process than she had on the marketing plan. If she put her mind to it, she could put together a top-notch plan for the whole factory in two weeks flat.

Nola seemed to accept her apology with grace, and they came to a silent truce. 'What about the marketing work you're doing here? Do you have any drawings, or is it secret until it's all done?'

'No. It's not secret at all; in fact I was going to bring up three different ideas I've been working on one of the evenings this week, for you both to take a look,' Georgie said, feeling unexpectedly nervous.

'Oh, well, that's exciting,' Nola said softly. 'I'll look forward to it.' As her eyes met Georgie's, Georgie could see that she really meant it. But then she looked away, the hint of a smile drawing up across her pretty features, revealing just one dimple in her left cheek. Georgie remembered that look from when they were kids. Back then, it usually meant that Nola had a secret she was bursting to tell them.

'What is it?' Georgie asked.

'Nothing, it's nothing.' Nola bit her lip. But it clearly wasn't, because she got up now, rubbed her hands together and laughed. 'I never was any good at keeping secrets from either of you, was I?'

'Come on, whatever it is—'

'I wasn't going to say anything, but I just can't stop thinking about it.' She turned to face Georgie now and took a deep breath. 'Iris is pregnant.'

Georgie felt as though she'd been slapped, hard, across her face. 'What? She can't be pregnant. Can she?' But all she was thinking was, she'd left it late; she was forty now. 'Of course, what am I saying? Sure, she was always going to be a mammy, the only mystery is what took them so long to get around to it, isn't it?'

'I know, I thought that too, but—'

'I wonder why she didn't say anything to me?'

'Maybe it's early days—'

'When did she tell you?' Georgie couldn't help but feel a bit put out that Iris had confided in Nola and not mentioned a word to her. Nola had just as prickly a relationship with Iris as she had, didn't she?

'No, of course she didn't tell me.' Nola nudged Georgie with her shoulder and rolled her eyes. 'As if she'd tell me anything… No, she has an app on her phone. It seems she's in the first trimester. I looked it up and the only thing she might be feeling now is morning sickness, but—'

Georgie gasped. 'She's been working like a bloody horse down at that cottage.'

'Well, you were all for it and then she almost bit my head off when I tried to talk her out of it.'

'I was all for it because I didn't know she was pregnant.' She stopped for a minute, tried to get her bearings. 'You knew then? How long have you known?'

'Since the day she collected me at the airport.'

'But she's been drinking wine and—'

'Maybe she needed to.' Nola rolled her eyes. To be fair, they were having a glass every evening to take the stress out of living together.

'So, what do we do now?'

Nola ran her hands through her hair. 'Nothing, I suppose. I mean, she's definitely old enough to know what she's about. I think all we can do is try and make sure she doesn't go lifting anything too heavy or drinking too much. But she'll do what she wants, either way.'

'You're right.' Georgie nodded slowly. 'Crikey, we could have done without this on top of everything else.' She shook her head, but at the same time, she could feel a tiny smile trace up along her mouth. A baby.

'We'll be aunties.' Nola smiled too, breaking into her thoughts.

'Huh. Only if Myles will let us anywhere near them,' Georgie said, suddenly remembering that theirs was hardly a conventionally happy family. Myles had hated Georgie forever, or at least since all those years earlier when Georgie had told Iris she'd seen him kissing Denise Hawley when he was meant to be dating Iris. The final straw had been when she caught him selling stock from the back door of the distillery. That had ended up in not only the mother of all rows, but also in halting any ambitions he might have had for the distillery one day. Mind you, he probably hated Nola even more for the stink she'd caused! They stood there for a few moments, silence stretching their thoughts out between them until the pipes began to rattle loudly overhead as they tended to do for no good reason that Georgie could figure, pulling them back to the real world.

'Would you like to see the marketing plans?' Georgie asked, surprising herself.

Nola looked surprised, too. 'All right, go on so; I'd love to take a look.'

Georgie led her sister up the stairs to the rook's nest that was the office she shared with Robert these days.

Georgie pulled out her drawings. There were almost a dozen, but she had whittled them down to five. Robert had been kind in his feedback, but the truth was, he didn't represent the lion's share of the market they were going for. Gin was a woman's drink, always had been, and if they were going to make a real impact on the market, it was the twenty-five to fifty-five-year-olds they had to target. Women with enough money to buy a quality product that was pitched directly at everything they aspired to. She laid five different images on the desk before Nola. These were the ones that had survived her own critical eye, but there was still a lot to choose from. She dug around for the colour combinations she'd been deliberating over earlier and placed them on the desk also.

'Wow.' It was all Nola could manage. She took up each one and inspected it closely. 'That's all I can say, Georgie, just wow.' She shook her head and a small tear ran down her cheek.

Georgie felt a flicker of annoyance. God, how had she managed to upset Nola now? Seriously, sometimes it was like walking on eggshells. 'What's wrong?'

'Nothing,' Nola said, wiping her tears. 'It's nothing, just…' She smiled then, although her voice sounded as if she might be holding back more tears. 'It's just, I feel so useless. There's Iris. Whether we like Myles or not, she's managed to stay married to him and even if it's late in the day, they're going to have a baby. She's going to produce an heir to the Delahaye legacy. And you're so talented, really making a difference, whereas, as usual, I'm just…'

'Don't be silly.' Georgie shook her head, but she could see that Nola really was upset. She shuffled up the samples on the desk before her, uncomfortable with Nola's raw vulnerability.

'You don't have to say that. I know I've just…' Nola looked away. 'All I've ever been is a pretty face and one day that's going to fade, and then where will I be?'

'Oh, come on, Nola.' Georgie had never heard her sister speak like this before; it was completely out of character. 'All this over a couple of drawings?' Suddenly, she wanted to put her arms around her younger sister, but she couldn't seem to manage to move the couple of feet close enough to touch her.

'It's not just a couple of drawings, though, is it?' Nola shook her head. She looked down at the distillery below them, which had picked this moment to fall into complete silence, and then Nola turned around to look at Georgie. 'You know, I always thought what you did in London didn't matter. I thought it was self-important bullshit, to be honest. But I was wrong, Georgie, these are just brilliant.'

Georgie didn't know what to say. Her breath had caught in her chest and she really couldn't put the words on what she wanted to tell her sister, so she resorted to the one thing she knew would break this uncomfortable tension.

'I bet the baby has Myles's nose. Think about it: if he has Myles's nose and the Delahaye feet he'll be—'

'Oh, God, don't. It's not right to be making fun of the poor child when it isn't even born yet.' But it did the trick, because now they were both laughing, ticking off all the things they'd always disliked about Myles and now there was even more to add to the list. In fact, top of the list was the fact that he'd let Iris come over here on her own into a situation that everyone knew was going to be really stressful. It only confirmed what a total creep he was.

'I don't know what's wrong with me these days. I seem to do nothing but cry like a little girl,' Nola said eventually.

'You're lucky,' Georgie said regretfully. 'I'd probably be a lot better off if I cried more often.'

'Oh, Georgie, if you cried, we'd all be sunk – you've always been the strong one.' She reached out and placed a hand on Georgie's arm, which took them both by surprise, but she left it there for a moment and Georgie smiled at her. 'Seriously, we'd have been lost without you all those years ago and even now, it'll probably be you who'll get us through the next six months.' She turned away. The loaded silence of the distillery felt completely overwhelming to Georgie, as if it had suspended them in this surreal moment of something akin to normality, or what normality might have looked like if they hadn't all fallen out so spectacularly all those years ago. Georgie wondered whether to bring up what had happened between them. The old Georgie wouldn't have hesitated, but the new one she'd become in the last few weeks didn't want to ruin the moment.

Georgie cleared her throat, cutting into the stillness. 'I bet you make a fantastic go of teaching those kids for the next few months. They'll be talking about you for years after you've gone back to London – the famous actress who turned their drama class around!'

'Come on,' Nola said, but she smiled, as if Georgie's few kind words had somehow made a difference. She reached behind the chair that had been their father's and pulled Georgie's coat from the back of it. 'It's definitely time for dinner.'

Secondary schools had changed a lot since Nola had left. On her first day, Gary gave her a map of the grounds and sent her off in the direction of the classrooms. For now, she had senior classes only, until her Garda clearance forms were returned. It was halfway through the school year, but drama wasn't an examinable subject, so she had free rein, so long as the kids learned something and they managed to get two stage shows out of what remained of the next two terms.

'Good luck,' he said, and as she walked along the seemingly endless corridors Nola had a feeling she was going to need it. Eventually, she found the classroom and pushed the door open before she had a chance to change her mind. Walking to the desk, she felt the eyes of twenty wary teenagers upon her, the silence that had fallen across their exuberant shouting was somehow gratifying – as if they were waiting for her to perform.

'Good morning, everyone. I'm... Miss Delahaye. I'll be taking you for drama' – she looked down at her timetable – 'twice a week.' She looked up and smiled. She was greeted by a mixture of expressions from mild interest to a smattering of enthusiasm and just a little truculence from one or two at the back. In many ways it was like walking on stage and the show was all hers, and she felt a surge of confidence. 'Now, we have a lot of work to do so let's take out our notepads and start with a piece of drama I want to share with you all...' She smiled and suddenly, somehow, she knew, this was going to be fine. Maybe even better than fine.

After her first day, Nola was making her way back through the village, having stopped to pick up some shopping, and she was filled with a fizzing feeling of satisfaction. It was a mixture of having thoroughly enjoyed her day's work and maybe also the fact that since that night in the distillery with Georgie, it felt as if some sort of balm was slowly spreading itself across their relationship. It gave Nola an extraordinary feeling of warmth, which of course she knew was just ridiculous; after all, it was nothing more than a moment when she'd managed to let slip her own vulnerability. But Georgie had been kind – kinder than Nola could remember her being in years.

Suddenly, a little terrier raced out of an open gate, barking like a wolf. He nipped at Nola's ankle and snagged her skin with his sharp little teeth. Nola screamed, jumped backwards and dropped the two bags of shopping. There was no sign of the dog's owner and so there was nothing for it, Nola reckoned, but to leave the bags and jump out of the dog's way before he did any more damage. The nearest thing to her was a huge off-road Defender, muddy and dusty, but needs must and she clambered quickly, if not very elegantly, onto its bonnet before the blasted dog decided to take another bite.

The dog stood on the pavement, growling and daring her to touch ground again so he could bite her once more. She was examining her leg. Two small puncture wounds marked where he'd sunk his teeth, when Aiden Barry turned out of the piano shop and stopped to look at her. Why did he have to show up at the worst possible moment? If she hadn't been in pain and scared stiff to get down off the jeep's hood, perhaps she might have seen the funny side of it. When she saw his lips twitch into something that looked like it might be a smile, she felt burning incandescent rage soar through her. She wanted to flounce off without a backward glance, but the dog was still eyeing her dangerously.

'Don't you dare laugh at me,' she said crossly.

'I wouldn't,' he said, lifting the dog up and depositing him inside a nearby gate and then closing it firmly behind him. *Bloody typical*, Nola thought, *he's even training the dogs of Ballycove to hate me*. 'Now, did he get you?' he asked, lifting her easily off the bonnet despite her protests.

'Actually, yes, he did.' She scowled at the dog, which now had the nerve to look as if butter wouldn't melt in his mouth.

'Ara – sure that's nothing.' Aiden bent to pick up her bags that had spilled across the path. 'It looks like you have more damage done to your shopping,' he said, looking at the trail of milk draining along the path.

'I'll need a tetanus shot, at the very least. What kind of person has a dog that—'

'Oh, don't be such a drama queen.' He sighed, opening the door of the jeep she'd been sitting on and throwing the one bag that seemed to have survived the crash intact on the back seat.

'Come on, we'll go back into the supermarket, get you a dry bag and a fresh carton of milk,' he said, walking ahead of her so that she found herself limping as quickly as she could behind him to keep up.

'I think I turned my bloody ankle too,' she groaned, although she had a feeling he wasn't listening. She stood at the counter while Aiden unpacked her shopping bag. She was glad there was nothing too embarrassing in there and then he flew about the aisles replacing what had been broken.

'There you go, as good as new,' he said, wiping the spilled milk off a jar of olives and setting it on top of the rest of her shopping. Then he was stalking out ahead of her and back towards his car while she paid for the milk and stuffed the receipt she didn't want into her purse. He was sitting in his jeep waiting for her when she limped back up the footpath.

'Well, do you want a lift or not?' he asked when she stopped beside the jeep.

'Sure.' She climbed into the front. It was everything she'd have expected, if she'd given any time to thinking of what Aiden Barry might drive. It was rough and functional, littered with dog's hair and an overhanging smell of cut grass and some sort of astringent aroma that she couldn't quite put a name to.

'So, how are you finding being back in Ballycove?' he asked her as they sped out of the village.

'It's fine, you know…' What did he expect? 'It hasn't really changed that much.'

'And of course, you were in such a rush to get away.' He smiled wryly.

She turned sharply. 'What's so funny?' she demanded.

'Nothing,' he said, keeping his eyes on the road. 'Have you left the house at all, apart from trying to get killed every other time I run into you?'

'Of course I have.' She looked out the window. 'I'm teaching drama in the school and—'

'Yes, but have you actually gone down to the local pub and met people your own age?'

'Well, no, I'm not sure that the pub is exactly my scene anymore,' she said because she hadn't actually stood in a pub in years. In fact, when she thought about it now, she hadn't been out to relax and socialise in as long as she could remember – her life had become little more than a trudge from her flat to the café and constantly waiting for a call that never came from her agent.

'Oh, I *see*. Too good for Ballycove – is that it?' His eyes darted sidewise at her, but his voice was deadpan.

'No. Of course that's not it.' She took a deep, calming breath to stop herself from rising to whatever bait he was dangling before her. 'That's not it at all. I just…' She let her words falter. 'I've just been too busy and anyway…' Why was she so against the idea? She supposed because she didn't actually know anyone in Ballycove – there was no-one to meet up with and have a drink and a laugh with.

'I'm sure there are still lots of people around that you'd remember from when you lived here,' he said as if reading her thoughts.

'I don't know, I'd say most of the people I knew back then are long gone,' she said softly. 'And if they're not, they're probably bogged down with husbands and kids and terrifying bloody dogs that snap when you pass their door.' They both laughed at that.

'Well, we'll have to see about that, won't we?' he said as they rounded the main gates into Soldier Hill House.

'See about what exactly?' Nola asked, but she wasn't really interested in what he was saying; instead she was looking at Iris putting the final strokes of paint to the door of the little gatekeeper's cottage as they passed by before heading up the avenue to the main house. A little dash of guilt rose up in Nola. A woman in Iris's condition should be resting and not putting a house together. Mind you, she looked surprisingly fit all things considered.

'That's coming on well,' Aiden said beside her and he

looked in his rear-view mirror to get a better view. 'Iris was always a goer, wasn't she?' He was right of course: her sister had never been afraid of hard work and signs were on the gate lodge now. The progress took Nola by surprise. She hadn't passed the gate lodge in weeks, choosing instead to take the more direct walking route along the lane to the village. It looked as if it had been taken in hand by an army of conservationists and been brought back to its charming, quirky best almost overnight.

'Yes, she's worked really hard on it. She's planning to let it out as a self-catering cottage,' Nola said and the pride in her voice surprised her, because she couldn't ever remember feeling anything but resentment for either of her sisters for so long. Then, they were pulling up at the back of the house before she could say much more.

'So that's settled,' he said as he dropped the shopping carefully on the doorstep for her.

'Huh?' she asked. She was barely out of the jeep by the time he'd swung back in and thrown the gear stick into reverse.

'Friday night, I'll pick you up after nine.'

'What?' she said, but it was too late; he was already turning the jeep around and driving out of the yard before she had a chance to figure out what he was talking about.

9

Four Months To Go...

Iris couldn't remember ever experiencing back pain as she did tonight. It had lingered at the base of her spine for the last week and she had ignored it. Instead of being sensible and resting, she'd kept on pushing herself. Washing, scrubbing, scraping, digging, planting and finally painting – it was, she knew, the painting that finished her in the end. She dropped in to the local surgery as much to say hello to dear old Elizabeth O'Shea – the former doctor's widow – as to see the new doctor. After all, she knew what she needed, really: rest. But the clock was against her and at this point, her only option was strong painkillers.

Iris felt silly for having wiped herself out so easily. How on earth would she ever have coped with childbirth? Funny how she still found reasons to try and convince herself that her childlessness was for the best. Old habits die hard. A tear raced down her cheek. It was so long since she'd cried about that child she'd longed to have. Apparently, the loss of what had never been could even at this stage feel like a cuff to her gut. She wiped her cheek with the heel of her hand. She simply must not think of Myles and what he had to look forward to now.

It was only when she spotted the colour cards peeping out of Georgie's folder that she felt her mood lightening. Liberty Blue. She reached out and pulled the card towards her. It was a gorgeous colour, velvety and rich, but soft enough to bounce light around the darkened kitchen of the cottage. It would be perfect on the kitchen cabinets. She pulled out her phone, tracked down a number for the small hardware shop in the village and placed an order for two medium-sized cans of paint to be collected by the weekend.

There was sewing, too, and even if she had to rest her back, she could still hem a curtain and fashion a cushion out of the leftover material.

'You're in your element,' Mary said as she searched for the perfect-coloured thread at the bottom of their mother's old sewing box.

'I suppose I am.' Iris smiled at her.

'Well, it's good to see something happening with the place. You know, if you don't manage to rent it out to tourists, there's plenty of locals looking for somewhere to rent in the village. That could be a lovely home for someone.' Mary smiled back and Iris had a feeling she was talking to herself, rather than making conversation. And something about the exchange settled something for her. In the end, her father hadn't really been alone. He'd always had Mary, who cooked and cleaned and chatted away and would turn up with provisions even if every shop in the country was closed. And she was wise too.

Mary was right about Iris. The fact was, she couldn't remember a time when she'd felt so fulfilled. It was a strange thing, but the better the cottage looked, the better she began to feel about herself. It was almost as if with every layer of cleaning, she scrubbed away a little of the hurt she'd carried about for so long and with each layer of paint she was rebuilding a stronger, newer version of herself.

The following Thursday, just six weeks after she had embarked on her overhaul of the cottage, it was complete.

When she told her sisters it was ready, she felt ridiculously nervous. 'You should come to see it. After all, it belongs as much to you as it does to me,' she'd told them last night, and they were on their way to see it now. This last week, she had to constantly remind herself of this fact; otherwise, she could completely lose the run of herself. Sometimes, she daydreamed about Myles coming here with her. She imagined him falling in love with the cottage, as much for the fact that it meant so much to her as anything else, and then he would carry her over the threshold and ask her if they could renew their vows and start over. Here. Just the two of them living out the rest of their days in the little cottage. A fresh start. Honestly, as she tightened bulbs and gave the lampshades a final dusting, she could almost feel herself swooning at the perfection of that happy-ever-after ending in her imagination.

'We're here.' Nola's voice broke into her daydream and she almost lost her balance on the stepladder. For a moment it swayed precariously, until Georgie dived for it and grabbed the base, holding it steady for her to climb down to the ground next to them.

Iris had been feeling that strange mix of elation and weariness that comes from completing something that you've worked so hard at and feeling inordinately proud of your efforts. She realised, now, that pride was a real thing. She'd begun to stand taller and walk with a little shimmy to her step. The place looked great – she knew that – even if she knew her critical eye was more than a little biased, but still, she was nervous. God, she never thought she'd say it but, 'I'm glad you're both going to have a look around before our first guests arrive.' They'd be here in little over an hour; two couples who had been referred from the hotel were due to stay for the next few days.

'It's cute and homely and all but it's hardly the Ritz, is it?' Nola offered. And even if she wasn't trying to be mean, it felt as if in that one sentence, Nola had cut every drop of sweat Iris had lost over this place to worthless.

'Yes, well, if anyone has seen the inside of a lot of hotel bedrooms, it's probably you,' Iris bit back at her.

'What?' Nola's jaw dropped and she stood there open-mouthed, long enough to let Georgie stand between them.

'Easy there, Iris, she wasn't trying to get at you, she's just saying that it's no harm to keep in mind that it's a small cottage in the west of Ireland; it's not going to turn us into the next Hilton family,' Georgie said, standing between them.

'Oh, that's right – it's all very well for you to say, with your fancy qualifications and years spent working with the crème de la crème of London's big corporate sector,' she hissed at Georgie.

Georgie rolled her eyes. 'Iris, stop being such a child. You could have bloody well gone to university too, if you hadn't decided to throw your lot in with that waster of a husband. Honestly, we all know that once Myles came along, you couldn't see any further than the end of your own nose.'

'How dare you?' Iris shouted. 'I might have known neither of you could wish me well. That's always been the way with both of you, as far back as I can remember. Even with Myles, you couldn't just put aside your petty jealousies and be happy for me.'

'Oh, dear God – are you really so stupid?' Nola said scornfully. 'If I ever had any feelings for Myles bloody Cutler, it was that he made my skin crawl. I actually find it offensive that you thought I was after him. The only thing either of us ever thought of Myles was that he wasn't nearly good enough for you.'

And suddenly, it felt as if all the anger Iris had bottled up over all the years was exploding within her; a huge volcano and there was no stopping the eruption. Iris staggered backwards. 'I don't have to listen to this, this – this – this *poison*. Neither of you is exactly an advertisement for domestic contentment, are you?'

Even as she shouted, a small voice whispered in her ear: *What do you know?* For all she knew, maybe they were both in happy relationships. She knew nothing about their lives. But all that mattered in this moment was keeping up the pretence that all was well and that the life she'd pinned everything on wasn't shown to be what it really was: a complete and utter failure and sham.

'And whatever you want to say about him or my decision

to marry him, the fact is that we've been together for a hell of a long time. We've stuck it out. I have something that neither of you have ever come close to. No matter whether you're a great success' – she looked at Georgie – 'or a great beauty' – she looked at Nola – 'none of those things mean anything at the end. It's about who'll want to grow old with you and... and...' And that was when she noticed Georgie was wearing their father's old jacket, which Iris had left hanging on a chair. As she reached into the pocket, in a blinding flash Iris remembered dropping the solicitor's letter from Myles in it that day on the beach. She stood there, feeling the blood rush from her head to her feet, watching in horror as Georgie took the folded up letter and began to examine it, unfolding it slowly.

Iris couldn't breathe. She whipped the letter from Georgie's hand. She was pulling the dregs of her dignity from both of them, just before all was lost.

'Hey!' Georgie said, but her surprise hardly registered with Iris, because before she even had time to decide, Iris was storming off back up the avenue, leaving her sisters standing aghast at what had just happened. Oh, God, she thought she'd die of shame now, if they knew the actual truth about what that letter contained.

It was three days since they'd had the spat at the cottage and Iris sat stony-faced at the kitchen table. Tonight, they all ate silently like a group of nuns in a contemplative order, except their thoughts were on nothing so high-minded as forgiveness and love. Rather, Georgie had a feeling that each of them was chewing on what they didn't say, what they might have said and maybe, what they shouldn't have said.

Either way, it was time to bury the hatchet. Iris was never going to leave Myles. Not when she had stuck it out this long. Not now. Not with a baby on the way. Georgie had been thinking a lot about the baby. She couldn't help but feel excited at the prospect, even if she knew she had no right to, and it wasn't as if Iris would let either her or Nola anywhere near the little one when it was born. All this fighting, it couldn't be good for a baby – it wasn't good for any of them.

Georgie, for her part, knew exactly what she should have said even before she'd reached the narrow gate that bordered off what was once an abundant flower garden in front of the little cottage. She should have gone into raptures about the cottage from the moment they came to the end of the drive, because to be fair to Iris, she'd done every bit of the work herself. She'd cleaned and scrubbed, painted, mopped, dusted and laundered every single inch of that little cottage and she'd done it happily in an effort to make some contribution to the Delahaye property. It was not Iris's after all, Georgie had to remind herself. Iris would have no interest in putting down roots here. All that this place would mean to Myles, and by extension to Iris, was probably a couple of cruises or maybe a slightly bigger car every other year. *He* was so predictable.

She should have offered from the get-go to take on some of the work around promoting the cottage. Although she was no website design expert, she knew her way around a couple of programs well enough to set up something that would outshine anything else on the market for miles around Ballycove. She should have congratulated her sister, Georgie knew. She should have *been* a sister to Iris for the last few weeks – no, for much, much longer than that.

Instead of doing any of those things, she found herself doing the worst possible thing she could have done. And why exactly? Why was she still carrying this hurt of so many years earlier? What sort of woman can't forgive her sister for choosing her husband over her sisters? Perhaps it was time to face the fact that as much as there was bitterness in Georgie's heart, that had faded long ago, only to be replaced with something else. It was a feeling that settled on her when she was alone in her expensive London apartment – envy. Iris had Myles. Nola had an army of friends. *They* both had people they could count on, people who cared that they were well and happy.

Georgie glanced around the table. It seemed she wasn't the only one to have lost her appetite. Nola had hardly touched her food either and Iris had only picked at the meat and corralled the vegetables to the side of her plate.

'I'm going to bed. My head is throbbing and I can't take another minute of this,' Iris said, getting up from the table, and Georgie couldn't help but notice the dark circles dug out beneath her eyes.

'But it's your turn to…' Nola said feebly.

'The dirty dishes can wait until the morning,' Iris said in a tone that brooked no arguments.

'Go on. Sleep well,' Georgie heard herself saying, but Iris was already making her way upstairs. She began to clear the table and handed the rubber gloves to Nola, who made a face but slipped them on with a shrug. Nola. Suddenly, the familiar resentment bristled under Georgie's skin. The argument at the cottage had been down to Nola as much as any of them. 'This is all your fault – you know that, don't you?' The words were out before she could stop them. And even as she was saying them she could hear her therapist's soft Galway voice in her mind saying *really? Seriously?*

'Excuse me?' Nola swung round from the sink.

She couldn't back down now. 'Well, you started it.'

'I'm not having this conversation with you, Georgie; I'm not ten years old anymore. It's time for you to move on. I've already given up enough to come back and play this bloody charade so we can finish this thing and walk away from each other for good,' she said, pulling off the gloves and then, before Georgie could say another word, Nola banged the door behind her and stomped up the stairs with as much anger as she'd ever pounded into those steps in her worst teenage strops.

And then, Georgie thought, there was one. So she set about putting the kitchen to rights. By the time she was finished, it was almost dark outside. Still, she knew that after the tumultuous evening there was no point in thinking she'd sleep without a good long walk. She grabbed one of the old coats that hung behind the back door and stuffed her phone in her pocket. She had no particular route in mind, but soon she was in front of the little gate house standing in the pools of faded light thrown out from the old carriage lamps hanging either side of the porch. The curtains at the windows were drawn back in even bows and from the chimney she could smell the homely scent of woodsmoke drifting out onto the evening stillness. It really was quite the most idyllic little getaway you could want.

And then, before she realised it, Georgie found she was crying, great big tears running silently down her face. And finally, she knew, there was no running from it here. Maybe this is where she was meant to be when she faced up to the emptiness she'd been trying so hard to cover up for so long. She stood there wallowing in the melancholy, which strangely felt more real than anything she had felt for a very long time, and as the tears subsided, it felt as if she'd cast off a heavy burden she hadn't even realised she'd been carrying. That argument she'd had with Nola, the miserable way in which she'd treated both her sisters – what sort of person talked to people like that?

And then in what felt like a dawning epiphany she realised, it was exactly how she'd treated everyone she'd ever worked with. This is what Sylvia had been trying to show her all along. What had happened to her? Was it jealousy? Or was it something else – the need to always be the best, the strongest, to make sure that everything turned out as it was meant to – was that what being the top dog had always meant to her? She gasped, drank in the night air like a drowning child. It was time to let it all go, the fears that had driven her since her mother had died, the obsessive need to save her sisters from themselves, which had only driven them from her, and the way she'd learned to push people away in case she'd have to suffer the pain of losing anyone again. Suddenly, she could see it clearly for what it was and it had to stop if she was ever going to be truly happy. She had to learn to be kind to everyone, including herself.

She turned back towards the main house and strode up the drive. Full of energy, she knew that she would do her best to make things right. And then a heavy feeling floated about her: *if she* could *just make things right.*

Nola managed to avoid her sisters the following morning. Friday. It was her long day at the local school. She had classes in the morning and in the afternoon. She was meant to take a couple of different groups to start rehearsing for the Easter play. She had decided on a pared-down version of *Easter Parade* and the teachers were delighted. It made a change from the usual Easter pageant, which all of the teachers – and they suspected most of the parents – were sick to death of.

Nola had spent quite a bit of time trying to track down a script that would be suitable for the youngsters; something they could deliver that would incorporate a couple of big song and dance numbers so everyone got a chance to shine.

'Well, what do you think?' she asked Gary when they were having coffee together.

'I think it's brilliant. Ambitious, but if you can pull it off, it'll be the best production we've ever put on.' He handed her back the copy she'd given him a few days earlier.

'I'm looking forward to it. Okay if I hold auditions over the next few days in the gym?'

'Better make it Mrs O'Dea's room. She's going to be off

for the next while and we're doubling up classes so you can make yourself at home there for the foreseeable.'

'Perfect,' Nola said.

'Just pop up a note on the noticeboards with audition times and you'll find you'll soon be run off your feet.' He laughed as he headed out the door.

When she heard the bell for the start of her class, Nola felt that familiar waspish nervousness in her stomach. It was the closest thing to going on stage that she could remember. She gathered up her books and strode off down the corridor as if she was walking towards the spotlight.

It was a busy day and at the end of it, Nola felt as if she'd done a hundred straight shifts in the café with no break for coffee. It was exhausting in a completely different way. But, she thought as she dragged herself wearily back through Ballycove and headed towards Soldier Hill House, it was tiring in a way that was unexpectedly fulfilling. Far more fulfilling, it turned out, than that day all those years ago she'd spent hanging about a film set saying three words that continued to haunt her. Thank God, they seemed to have taken that blasted add off the TV over here and none of the students had seen it.

A few days ago, Nola knew exactly where she was going to tell Aiden Barry to go with his pity date; although she was pretty certain that it wasn't a date. Except of course, when she'd been planning to knock him back, she hadn't been living in a house with an atmosphere colder than Siberia. Neither of her sisters was talking to her and she really couldn't face another night of frosty silence and early to bed, so the opportunity to go and have a few drinks, maybe meet some normal people and have an ordinary conversation, suddenly looked far more attractive.

So Nola tidied herself up – well, clean jeans, a fresh blouse and her best jacket. She smeared a slick of red lipstick across her lips and tucked a couple of euro into her purse. With a spritz of perfume she was ready to walk out the door at precisely the correct time. She felt a hint of happy nervousness. It had been so long since she'd been to a pub and she couldn't help but wonder if there would be people she remembered from school still hanging about the village.

'All dolled up and nowhere to go?' Iris said as she passed by her open door.

'I actually do have somewhere to go.' She pulled the brush through her hair again.

'I thought you'd have learnt your lesson by now...' Iris muttered before disappearing into her own room and slamming the door behind her. Honestly, sometimes Nola wondered what went on in her sister's head.

An hour later, she was still waiting for Aiden to arrive. There was no sign of him, not even a phone call and she wondered if she'd been stood up. She paced the sitting room, stopping every now and then to stand at the window and peer expectantly down the drive. She had the huge desire to bite her fingernails, but it had taken too long to break that habit to allow something so small to send her back there again. Well, she had two options: she could either sit up here in her ivory tower waiting for a man to come and rescue her, or she could make her way down to the village without him.

She had hardly turned out of the yard when she saw his oversized Land Rover bumping along the narrow lane.

'Sorry,' he said, reaching across and opening the door for her. 'Cow calving – nothing I could do about it,' he added and then once she was in the passenger seat he did a nifty three-point turn and had them headed towards the village.

'Never mind,' she said easily, because really it didn't matter either way. All right, so, she'd wasted an hour of her time waiting for him, but if she let him see it annoyed her, he might think that this arrangement meant more to her than just a casual lift to the pub.

'I suppose, like all women, you were only ready to go now anyway,' he said.

'Actually, no.' She kept her voice even. 'I was ready to go exactly on time, but I decided to do a little work and head out when it suited me. From what I can remember, the pubs of Ballycove only really begin to fill up an hour before closing time anyway.' It was true she had a tonne of work to get through this weekend, plays don't just happen and she wanted this to be perfect.

They spent the rest of the short journey in an uncomfortable silence, or at least that's what Nola thought, but perhaps it just washed over Aiden, who seemed to be lost in thought and hardly aware she was there at all.

The local pub had changed very little from outside, though once inside, she was surprised to see it had been opened up into a much larger space which obviously did a brisk pub grub trade as well as a brilliant traditional music session tonight. The bar counters filled one end, with a couple of groups interspersed along it, cliques that probably went back to when people were at school. It sent a shiver of isolation through Nola, because apart from loving her new teaching job and being happy to live in Soldier Hill House most of the time when her sisters weren't at war with her and each other, she could almost convince herself that there might be more for her here than in London.

But even Nola knew that a future here meant more than working and living. She would need friends, a social circle to call her own, and a group of people she could meet for coffee or go shopping with or maybe just shoot the breeze with on a Friday night in the local pub. All of those things had slipped through her fingers in London; it was something she needed to change, wherever she ended up.

'Come on.' Aiden headed for a high table on the far end of the bar where a couple of musicians were tuning instruments between sets in the music session. He fired out a round of introductions and even if she couldn't quite keep up, she got the feeling that this group were his close circle. There was an attractive blonde, holding a fiddle, a couple of redheads who might be sisters, both with tin whistles and an older grizzly-looking guy who had a long shaggy beard and a wide smile that stretched right up to his eyes.

'My round.' Aiden looked at Nola, who ordered a white wine and then he nodded to her. 'Well, come on, the drinks aren't going to carry themselves down.'

Against all the odds, actually, it was a great night. She managed to get names on the three girls; yes, they were two sisters and a first cousin. In between belting out traditional Irish tunes they had time to talk and it seemed to Nola, they loved to talk and laugh and generally have the craic.

Between them, there was a nurse – Eve, a teacher from the secondary school in the next town over – Madeline, and a postwoman – the attractive blonde who everyone for some reason called Red. Old Benny on the accordion had been playing for years; Nola hardly remembered him ever having been any different or any younger to what he looked tonight. After a glass of wine, Nola began to really enjoy herself and as she chatted to the people at the table even Aiden seemed to be a little nicer than she had first imagined. At some point, he disappeared leaving her there with the other four, but it didn't matter, because at that stage the ice was broken and a number of others had joined them too. Nola knew that if she wanted to she could turn up here any Friday night and she'd be more than welcome.

'We have it all here,' Red said when they broke up a set to catch their breath. She was talking about the village; she'd never considered living anywhere else. 'Well, almost everything – the only thing we're missing is available men.' She shook her head and laughed.

'What about?' Nola waved her hand around the bar, there seemed to be a fairly even distribution.

'Eww.' Red wrinkled her nose. 'Sure that'd be like dating your brother. We've known almost everyone here for years. No, that's the only problem with Ballycove, apart from the summer season, it's the same old same old. We've all known each other too long to find anyone here even vaguely attractive at this stage.'

'What about Aiden?' Nola asked. He seemed to spend most of the night standing at the bar chatting to the barmaid, a statuesque blonde, who looked like she belonged in a

Victoria's Secret catalogue rather than behind a counter. At a guess, Nola reckoned, she hardly looked twenty years old.

'Oh, Aiden has had his share of girls, but he's not the settling-down type. Much too busy rescuing damsels in distress and building up his empire.'

'But he's a farmer?' Nola laughed and then stopped, because she knew that most of the people here had come from farming backgrounds, including her, and very few of them probably had left to try their luck at the bright lights.

'Yes, he's a farmer, but he's a serious businessman too. He's bought up a lot of land, probably the wealthiest man here tonight, but that doesn't seem to matter to him.'

'So, what?'

'He's had his heart broken, as bad as it can be. There's no getting over some things, you know,' Red said, and she sipped her drink before running her bow across the bridge of her fiddle and starting into a lively reel.

'So you enjoyed it?' Aiden asked when he dropped her home later, turning to her when he'd parked in the backyard.

'Yes. Thank you for making me come along.'

'Sure there was no making on it. Weren't you already walking along the road when I picked you up?' He shook his head.

'You know what I mean.' She opened the door, still feeling that there was something else to be said.

'Yeah,' he said softly and when she looked at him now, she could see what the statuesque blonde had fallen for – he was ruggedly attractive. Nola felt something like an electrical volt shoot through her. For a crazy moment she thought he might lean across and kiss her. She might even kiss him back.

But then, abruptly, he turned over the engine. 'So, you'll be all right from here,' he said, checking the rear-view mirror to gauge his space before turning in the dark. And once more, she felt that familiar irritation that she'd felt from the first moment she'd met him.

'I think I can definitely manage from here,' she said, slamming the door behind her before she ran up the steps to the back door and disappeared inside for the night. He really was the limit. Aiden Barry got under her skin – and not in a good way, either.

10

It wasn't so much that Iris was in a strop with Georgie and Nola anymore. It had as much to do with being angry with herself, because their argument had been about nothing really. Like all their arguments in the past, it grew from one comment and it felt as if all the old wounds were opened wide again.

It took almost a week for Iris to calm down enough to make some kind of overture towards mending things with either of them. She couldn't go on living in a war zone. She got up early on the Monday morning and made coffee and scrambled eggs for the three of them. In fairness to both of them, they sat with grace and didn't, on this occasion, rub her nose in the fact that she was the first to give in. If anything, as she sat down with them, once the initial gesture was made she had a feeling that they were both relieved to grasp it and there was a sudden overflow of strangely uncomfortable helpfulness around the breakfast table. It almost felt as if they were trying each other out, treading carefully on a first date because this might be the 'one'.

Once the last dish was dried and put away, Georgie took down her laptop.

'If you have time,' she said a little haltingly, 'there's something I'd like to show you.'

'A website,' Iris almost gasped. 'You've set up a website for the cottage?'

'Well, only the bones of it. We need to get some good photographs, but everything is here. I've filled in the text and it's attached to the distillery, so we won't have to pay additional hosting fees or any of that. But I've included a booking facility and set up an email account so you can be in charge of it from your own phone.' She was flicking through the three tabs across the top of the site. A small link brought you back into the main distillery site at the bottom of each page.

'I can't believe it, Georgie, it's great, but how on earth?' Iris looked up at Georgie to see a small smile was spreading across her lips.

'It was actually quite easy. I've been fiddling about with the distillery one anyway, because obviously with the launch of Dad's gin, I'm looking at making a few changes to that. And so, when I was poking about behind the site I added a few extra pages for the gate lodge,' Georgie said modestly.

'It looks really professional,' Nola said, then stopped, as if fearing that she might have said the wrong thing.

'It *is* really professional.' Iris smiled at Georgie. 'Thank you, this means so much.' She reached out and put her arms around her sister, hugging her close to let her know that their silly argument was truly at an end and she really did appreciate all the work she'd done. 'I know you're saying it was easy, but you must have put a lot of work into it.' She was scanning through the text and she could see there was a great deal of thought put into selling the place to people looking for a real country getaway, quite aside from the customers they might pick up from the hotel.

'Ah, it was nothing, the very least I could do, after...' Georgie looked at her now. 'I should have made more of the fabulous job you did on the cottage, Iris. I knew it that evening even as we were having that ridiculous row over nothing. I couldn't do what you did to make something so lovely if I had a hundred years to do it and you just whipped about the place so quickly and suddenly it looked fantastic.'

'I second that,' Nola said at her side. 'I'm sorry too. It turned out really beautifully – no-one else could have pulled it together like that. I could have walked by that place a million times and I'd never have spotted the potential in it.'

'Well, that's very kind of you both to say—'

'There's nothing kind about it, it's the truth. It took vision and a lot of hard work to get it up and running,' Nola said and she leaned in too for a hug.

'Honestly, you two, I don't know when I've last felt so...' Iris smiled. She was going to say loved, but even now, here in the warm glow of her sisters' embrace, she couldn't bring herself to admit that her marriage was over, that it really was the first time in a very long time indeed when she didn't feel completely alone. And she found herself thinking against all she knew to be reasonable that it was nice, being here with her sisters.

With a feeling of deep gratitude, she spent the rest of the morning pottering about the house. Later, she planned to head down to the hotel for a cup of coffee, but there was no rush, better to wait until the lunchtime crowd left. Instead, she decided to go up to the attic and look through some of the stuff that had been stored away up there for far too long.

As she poked her head through the trapdoor her phone rang. Damn. It was Myles. She stopped for a moment, paralysed in that netherworld of feeling thoroughly sick to her stomach with nerves, fearing the worst and the slightest hope that maybe he had changed his mind and he wanted to come home to her. She stood there for agonising seconds, teetering on the edge of almost forgetting how much he'd hurt her, a feeling of butterflies in her stomach fluttering up a storm, and she was unable to answer the phone. She'd stopped breathing, conscious of just her heart, beating so hard it felt like it might break right through her ribcage, and then somehow the ringing penetrated some part of her, so she answered.

'Hello, Myles.' She managed to keep her voice even. It was strange, thinking of him in this present moment. What was he doing now? Since he'd left her that evening, she'd only thought of him in the past. She didn't dwell on the reality of Amanda Prescott and their new baby. Being back in Ballycove had played perfectly into convincing herself that maybe her marriage hadn't quite been pulled from under her just yet. Here, it was easier to imagine that this was a temporary hitch, a bump in the road that they would iron out when she inherited her share of the Delahaye legacy and returned to London. But suddenly, knowing that he was somewhere in London at this very moment, ringing her from his new world that had nothing to do with her, brought her back to devastating reality with a resounding bump.

'Hey,' he said doing his best casual voice. 'Just thought I'd see how you're doing.'

'Really? You want to see how I'm doing?' Well, that was nice. Perhaps he did still care for her as much as she did for him.

'Well, that and I've been thinking about where we go from here,' he was saying and she felt her stomach turn over with anticipation.

'Oh?'

'Yeah. I'm sure we can come to some amicable agreement about the house and between us we can organise a quick divorce? I mean, we've known each other so long, I was thinking just this morning, maybe there's no need to get solicitors involved, is there?'

'But haven't you already been to a solicitor?' she said, because even if she tried to block it out, that letter she'd whipped from Georgie's hands was real. Suddenly, it felt as if she was walking three hundred steps behind.

'The thing is, they cost an arm and a leg, and for what?' He cleared his throat, adjusted the volume of the radio that was blaring in the background.

'I'm sorry?'

'Solicitors. They're going to make a fortune from us and I've been thinking the best thing we can do is agree between us what we want and then we can make our own application and...' He was still talking but Iris couldn't hear him anymore. She didn't want to listen.

There was an expectant silence. She had no idea what he'd asked her, but it was obvious some sort of answer was required. 'Hmm.'

'Well, I'll tell you what they're charging, a small bloody packet, that's what. The way I see it, you don't need the house anymore. Let's face it, a nice little bedsit nearby and…'

A cold shiver raced along her spine. *Shock – I'm in shock,* she thought as she listened to Myles outlining how their years of marriage could be divided (not very equally!) between them. Like the soldiers casting lots at the crucifixion.

'And of course, I'll need to hold onto the car, for work—'

'Hang on, Myles.' For some reason, mention of the car that she had bought and paid for, denying herself a cappuccino most days to make the repayments, jolted her back to some sort of sanity. 'You can't just assume that you're holding onto the car?'

'But you don't need it,' he said plaintively. 'Have you even got a licence anymore? You never drive it.'

'I never drive it because you took it over from the first day it was parked in the driveway.' Now, somehow the hurt was being pushed aside to be replaced by something else: rage. Did he really believe she was a complete doormat? Did he actually assume that she would just sit back while he took their shared possessions as well as the family and the future she'd always dreamed of?

'You're just being unreasonable now,' Myles said, chiding her as if she was an infant.

Iris took a deep breath. 'Divorces are not easy, Myles. You can't have imagined this would be a simple case of you telling me what you wanted and me rolling over. These things take time and if we need expert outside help, like a solicitor, then so be it. They'll probably suggest we sell the house and the car and then divide the proceeds equally between us.'

'Whoa, hold on a minute. Sell the car?' There was a tremor of something close to panic in his voice. 'You can't think you're taking the car from me. I need that to get to work every day.'

'Of course the car, Myles. I did buy it after all, and the only benefit I've had out of it is the occasional lift to pick up the shopping.'

'But my name is on the logbook,' he snapped back.

'It is. And mine is on the loan I took out to buy it, but I'll leave the argument about that for another day,' Iris said mulishly. The car meant nothing to her really, although she definitely didn't want Myles ferrying Amanda Prescott about in it.

'And what's this with selling the house?' he wailed. 'Surely you can see that we can't go on living in Amanda's tiny flat once the baby comes along?'

'No. I don't suppose you can.'

'So I thought, maybe we could move into the house. Obviously, I'm happy to pay you half of what the buying price was and—'

'Seriously, Myles?' she spluttered. 'You're living in a dream world. Even if that was a fair deal – I've paid back more in interest rates already than we ever took out on that mortgage. If you're determined to do this, the house is going on the market and if you want to buy it, you can put up the cash to buy me out.' She sounded to herself as she imagined Georgie might sound if she was hammering out a deal – strong and confident; truly a force to be reckoned with. Except, she was pretty sure, Georgie wouldn't feel as if she was dying inside with every word she spoke.

'You've changed,' Myles said ominously. 'It's as if I don't know you at all anymore.'

'That goes both ways,' she snapped. She was tempted to hang up now, because there was nothing to be gained from this, but at the same time, it was the only contact she'd had with him in weeks and as awful as he was being, she still loved him. Georgie would be so proud of how she sounded, but she'd be appalled at the feelings whizzing around inside Iris's heart at this moment. 'You were the one who had the affair and got Amanda pregnant. You hardly expect me to lay out the welcome mat for you and let you walk all over me once again.'

'All right, I deserve that,' he said, obviously changing tack. 'But the truth is, Iris, I miss you.'

'Really?' She so badly wanted to believe him. But then she remembered why he'd called. As she listened to the background sounds of London behind him, she managed to knock some sense into herself. Was he sitting in the car with the radio still on in the background? *Her* car radio – which he wanted to take along with the house and the very last shred of her dignity?

'Maybe we could meet up and—'

'I don't think that's a good idea, Myles,' she said.

'No? But what harm could it do? Just the two of us, somewhere quiet, just for a chat? What if I call round after work? Pick you up in the car, and we could—'

'No, that doesn't suit at all.' She debated whether she

should tell him right now that she wasn't even in England, but didn't because there would be too much explaining. Anyway, if her plan of winning him back was going to work, she wanted to swan back into his life dolled up to the nines with a fat cheque in her back pocket. 'No, Myles. The truth is I can't face you at the moment,' she said and that *was* the truth too. 'I've a new job and I'm trying to build a new life for myself.'

'You've left your job?'

'Yes, it was time.'

'So where—'

'What does that matter?' It was an effort to keep the whine from her voice. She hated herself for being so pathetic, but talk of solicitors and divorces had knocked her for six. 'If you're determined to do this, I'll talk to my solicitor over the next few days and we'll see what happens next.'

'But...' He was lost for words. She knew it was as if she'd thrown a bucket of ice water over him and he couldn't quite get his bearings. 'Iris?' he said finally in a voice that sounded so thin, he could be a hundred years old.

'Goodbye, Myles.' And with that, she hung up the phone. She was shaking, felt as if she might throw up and fall down all at the same time. God, she was actually glad not to be in London, but to be here in Ballycove instead, where everything seemed so simple by comparison. She sat for a long time, her body shaking with what she supposed was a form of delayed shock. She wasn't even sure if it was because it all sounded so final with Myles. It had more to do with the fact that her life was starting again and somehow, sitting here in the dusty old attic, the reality of that absolutely terrified her.

***

The last person Georgie expected to hear from was Paul Mellon. The call came first thing on Monday morning just as she was sitting at the desk opposite Robert English in the tiny office they shared overlooking the distillery.

'Well, aren't you a blast from the past,' she said breezily, knowing full well that if Paul was ringing her it was because he wanted something.

'Hey, yourself. You sound different, relaxed – have you been enjoying your break?'

'Break?' She laughed. 'You must be joking, I'm up to my eyes.' She leaned back on the old leather office chair that had been her father's. It creaked comfortingly with every movement, so different to the designer chrome and Italian leather simplicity that had cost a small fortune to co-ordinate in her last office.

'So, you're working?'

'Of course I'm working, what did you expect? It's months since I left. I've never been busier.'

'Oh, I just hadn't heard, you know…'

'Maybe marketing circles aren't as small as you thought.' She smiled. Paul prided himself on knowing everyone on the London scene and knowing exactly what everyone was up to. She knew it would bother him that he hadn't heard where she'd landed after she walked out his door. It might even make him feel as if he was losing his edge, which would bother him more than anything.

'Well, you're being rather coy. What exactly are you up to?'

'At the moment? I've got a brand-new product, and it's going to be HUGE!' she said, drawing out the word. 'It's a speciality gin, high-end, luxury market – my favourite place to launch.'

'So, you're freelancing?' It sounded like he was chewing his fingernail; he was under pressure.

'Yes, much more fun and lucrative than I ever imagined, really, so many lovely clients to approach.' She gave a tinkling laugh. She was goading him – sweetly, but she knew how to raise his hackles.

'Well' – he lowered his voice – 'if you were to consider coming back to us now, I'd make it worth your while.'

'Oh?'

'Yeah. This place isn't the same without you.' They both knew what that meant – clients were looking for her. While she might have been considered *difficult* to work with, she knew how to butter up a client better than anyone else and she got results.

'Missing me already?' she said sweetly.

'Come on, I'm serious, we need you back here. I know you were upset about the promotion, but we had a great thing going here, good money, the best accounts in London. You were the best in the business – the queen bee of the London marketing scene.'

'Oh, but Paul, I still am.' She was enjoying this. As far as he was concerned she was a shark circling the waters and he wouldn't know how close she was until he started to lose accounts. Let him worry; it was payback time.

'Have you been trying to take our clients? You know that there are ethics involved in that…' He sounded tense.

'Paul, I haven't approached anyone; if you're losing clients, then that's down to you. You had a chance to reward me for my work and you didn't. I walked out and now I'm doing something that's giving me more satisfaction than I ever got at Sandstone and Mellon.'

'So, you're saying you won't consider coming back?'

'As a partner?' she said softly, then a little more sternly, 'Or as a director?'

'Fine. As a director with direct responsibility for some of our biggest clients. If that's what you want,' he said grudgingly.

'As a shareholding director?'

'Bloody hell, Georgie, what do you think I am?'

'I think you're desperate,' Georgie said, cutting to the chase. 'I'd say that your biggest accounts are going to walk away because between the lot of you, you can't keep it all together.'

'All right, all right,' he said and then she knew; the clients must be jumping ship like rats in a hurricane. It was nothing she couldn't sort out with a few phone calls though.

'Fine. Put something in an email and I'll get back to you by the end of the week.' She hung up the phone before he had a chance to say another word and Georgie just smiled. It was, after all, everything she had wanted to begin with, wasn't it? So why didn't she feel happier...?

It felt as if the seasons here ran into each other far more quickly than they ever had in London, although, sometimes, Nola wondered if she even noticed the changing of one season for another when she lived there. This week, as the new buds on the trees and the sea of daffodils that lined the grassy verges into Ballycove, March was marked out as much by how busy it was at school as it was by any migrating birds that Iris pointed out at the feeder in the old kitchen garden.

And it was busy. When Nola had time to think, she was in her element. She was producing and directing her first ever production and besides the sometimes stressful moments, she was loving every minute of it.

'It's the first time we haven't put on *The Passion*,' one of the religion teachers confided. 'To be honest, we're all looking forward to a break from the same scenes, the same lines, the same everything.'

'Well, our version of *Easter Parade* will certainly be different,' Nola enthused. Far from the old Judy Garland and Fred Astaire production, this would have everything from hip-hop to light opera – she was pulling in every talent the school had, even the teachers were going to do a number to help her out, since time was so tight.

'We'll have to put on extra shows at this rate.' The vice principal, a small neat woman with an eye on the bean counter, was thrilled with the ticket sales. All proceeds were going towards the arts programme within the school.

The week of the actual shows passed by in a whirr of excitement, stress and celebration. Nola had never experienced anything like it before; it was the best week of her life, even if she wouldn't admit it to her sisters in a million years. She'd spent most of the week in the school, only turning up at Soldier Hill House in time to wolf down a dinner and then flop into bed.

The following Tuesday she decided to go and visit Moira Barry. It had been a while since she'd dropped in on her, not only because she'd been madly busy, but also because she didn't want to bump into Aiden again. He just made her feel awkward and somehow as if she had missed a step, so everything seemed to be a little uneven every time he was around.

'Ah, it's yourself.' Moira was standing at the kitchen sink, busy peeling carrots for the dinner when Nola arrived in the kitchen.

'I just popped in to say hello,' Nola said, taking up a knife and finishing off the few that remained on the chopping board before emptying them into a pot on the stove.

'Do you know something, Nola?' Moira said, drying her hands on a thin towel that hung over the cooking range. 'I cook far less these days than I ever did before, but it feels as if everything takes me a lot more time. When the kids were young, I'd have these done in a flash.' She shook her head and placed a lid securely on the pot and Nola thought she was the most perfect typical Irish mammy.

'Do you need me to do anything for you?' she asked as she filled the kettle to make a pot of tea for both of them, but she could see the dinner was prepped so it was all down to the old stove now to do the rest of the work.

'Just tell me all that's been happening with you since I saw you last.' Moira plopped down into a chair and waited while Nola set the table for tea for them both.

'Oh, you know any news I have. You were at the musical, so that's been keeping me busy for the last few weeks.'

'Well, you certainly showed them how to put on a show

this year.' Moira smiled. There was no missing how proud she was of Nola. 'The kids are raving about you and the parents are delighted with you.'

'Oh, I don't know about that.' But Nola found herself blushing and it was nice to hear that she was doing a good job.

'Just you wait until the parents' meetings in a few weeks' time, that's when you'll have something to blush about, my girl.'

'I'm really enjoying it,' Nola said. 'I mean, the kids are great and even some of the parents that I've met so far…' It was true, they couldn't be nicer.

'Sure you'll know most of them anyway, from around the village. We've only had a couple of blow-ins; apart from that, if you don't know them, you'll remember their families.'

'You're right there.' It had surprised her, people calling her by her name and when she looked at them, really looked at them, she'd been able to pick out who they were or who their older or younger sister was, because Ballycove was a small place and everyone knew everyone – even it seemed if you had gone away for years, you were still one of them. 'It's actually a nice change, from London, you know.'

'Aye, I'd imagine it is, all right.' Moira smiled. As far as Nola knew she'd never left Ireland apart from the occasional holiday staying with her sister outside London. 'Our Aiden said that too, when he came back from his travels.'

'Where was Aiden anyway?' Nola asked more out of politeness than any real interest.

'Where wasn't he, you mean?' Moira laughed. 'He travelled all over after he finished his studies.'

'His studies?'

'Oh, you wouldn't remember, he went on to become a priest, first, but then turned back at the last minute. I suppose he had a lot of thinking to do, so he took a job on a cruise ship and we hardly saw him for a long time, but he's a good boy, always called to let his mother know where in the world he was.'

'So, he really did see the world?'

'He did. He saw all four corners and his fill and more of the oceans in between.' Moira shook her head fondly, thinking of her only son.

'And then he came home to Ballycove,' Nola said as if that brought the story to an end.

'Well, no, not exactly. He came back to Dublin. The cruise company he was working for offered him a big job in their headquarters here, plenty of money and terrible long hours. I suppose when you're accustomed to a life of being able to move about the place, being tied to an office chair isn't really going to make you very happy.'

'So, then he decided to become a farmer?' Nola couldn't imagine making a life choice to be a farmer.

'Well, he came home here, decided to hang about for six months, after his father had a bit of a turn.' She shook her head. 'Double bypass – the old fool was smoking the pipe and thinking it'd never catch up with him.' She smiled then, because everyone knew that Eugene Barry really was the love of her life. 'He nearly gave me a heart attack with it all, never mind himself.' She stopped then, lost in memories from that time. 'Anyway, it was probably all for luck. Aiden threw in the job without a backward glance.' She shook her head. 'That's just like him, never thinking for a minute about himself. He took over the farm and had the place shipshape in a matter of weeks. After that, Eugene knew it was time to hand it over and as luck would have it, Aiden was happy to take it on.'

'Well, that worked out well for everyone, so I suppose,' Nola said.

'Yes. It's funny, but the older I get, the more convinced I am that things always do, in the end.' Moira smiled. 'Now, all we have to do is find him a nice girl to settle down with and...'

'He seemed to be getting on very well with the barmaid the last time I was down in the local pub.'

'Little Stella Barrington?' Moira threw her head back and laughed. 'Ah, no, I don't think so, Nola,' she said still wiping the laughter from her eyes.

'Oh, well, I suppose you know more than I do,' Nola said softly. The last thing she wanted was to make things awkward for anyone, but in her experience, if a man spends the whole night chatting up a good-looking woman, no matter what her age, it was a fair bet that they weren't talking about the price of cattle.

11

April, Two Months To Go...

Georgie loved her journey to work, through the fields and across the narrow little lane where most mornings a robin perched on the fence to greet her – a bit different to her previous commute in London. The mornings were the worst, always the sausage in a sandwich between smart young suits and too-strong aftershave.

Now that the seasons had turned and the robin had become a regular feature, Georgie started to bring along a crust of bread for the journey. She watched as he hopped from post to post on the fence along the narrow lane next to her, waiting for what had become a daily treat.

Why on earth was she comparing this to London, anyway? A good question, and one that she'd been asking herself since Paul Mellon's email had pinged into her inbox a few days earlier. It was a generous offer, one that she wouldn't have dared to dream of a few years earlier.

She would have to go over there, meet with Paul and

the other members of the board. She'd agreed to a time the following week. Absurdly, Iris too had business to complete in London. Georgie hadn't asked what sort of business could send Iris trotting over to the big smoke; she really didn't want to hear about a lovey-dovey reunion with Myles.

These thoughts were clouding her mind as she made her way through the narrow gate at the rear of the distillery. She was early. No-one was due in here before eight-thirty, but Georgie loved to have a cup of coffee, mooch about the office and check any urgent emails before the day began.

It was as she was keying in the alarm code that she noticed the insistent beeping noise, like a buzzing bee, whirring with supreme urgency. It took a moment to register exactly what it was, but then she knew, even though she'd only heard it once before. It was the fire alarm. A warning signal that should be sounding in the nearby fire station to alert them that something was going wrong, something could be about to blow. And now she was racing along the factory floor. Moving from vat to vat, from still to still, checking each valve and then, stopping, checking again. With the rational part of her brain, Georgie knew she should leave, but the sensible part of her had shut down and now she was working off her gut. She was not going to see her father's work go up in smoke without doing her damnedest to stop it.

She rounded the last of the gin stills – all clear here. Then—

'Georgie?' Robert's voice came from the far end of the distillery.

'I'm here. I'm just trying to figure out where that beeping is coming from.' Somehow Georgie managed to sound a lot calmer than she felt. She shivered. A fire would be a disaster on a scale never seen before in Ballycove. *Don't think about that now,* she told herself.

'Georgie, come out now, the fire brigade are on their way, it's not safe here.' Robert's voice was moving towards her. She could hear his footsteps squeaking along at a faster pace than she'd ever seen him move. Then more voices as the men arrived to go on shift.

'Who's in there?'

'I think it's Georgie.'

'No. No.' She heard the men making their way down the factory floor behind her.

'Go back, go back,' she called to them. The last thing she needed was those people who had come to mean something to her over the last few months being led into danger because of her. 'I'm coming out now.' She took a final glance around. There was only one more still to check. Of course, this one had been giving trouble. Robert had talked about shutting it down as soon as they could to have some repair work carried out. She looked at it now; the needle was riding at twenty degrees above the others. It was simple enough to just reduce the temperature, surely? She reached in, fiddled with the dial, pulling it back down to twenty below the others, hoping that would do it. Perhaps it would just slowly cool down.

Wrong. She was rewarded with a loud thumping and thrashing sound from inside the still, as if a hurricane was brewing, building up and pressing violently against the walls around it. She could almost feel the ferocity of heat pumping out from within. Terror seized her.

Oh, dear God.

'Georgie, where are you?' She could hear the men searching for her at the far end of the distillery.

'Go back, go back, it's going to bloody blow,' she screamed at them.

And then she spotted it. Just beneath the ancient barometer on the wall opposite. A small green pulley at the base of the wall, locked behind glass, but there for emergencies. She flung herself on it, broke the glass with her elbow. She pulled the switch, immediately severing the power to that end of the distillery.

The sudden silence was ominous. Then a huge belch from the overheating still almost made Georgie jump out of her skin. The whiskey would be ruined, but she was almost certain they were now safe.

'Thank God, you're all right.' Robert was first on the scene. He threw his arms around her and held her close for a moment, before stepping back self-consciously. 'You are all right, aren't you?' She noticed then that there was an obscene amount of blood flowing from her elbow – it must have happened when she had broken the glass. But all she felt was an overwhelming surge of relief. As if, with the saving of the distillery, she had taken a deep breath and somehow, even her bones felt lighter – she felt elated to have been here in time to avert what could have been a catastrophe.

'The whole still is probably lost.' She sniffed as Robert put his arm around her shoulder and half-carried her back down the factory floor.

'Maybe, but the distillery is saved and without your fast thinking, it was only a matter of minutes until that bloody whiskey still blew the whole place to kingdom come.'

'Oh, God.' She shivered. Had it really been that close a shave?

'Really, you were very brave—' He didn't get to finish the sentence because as they arrived back to where the other workers were waiting for them, they were greeted with clapping and cheering. It was the closest she was ever likely to feel to being a hero and as each of the men shook her hand she tried not to blubber with this newfound feeling of belonging.

Later, as she sat outside, her legs stretched out on the grass waiting for the fire officer's opinion on the incident, she felt as if she was somehow changed by the experience and her eyes began to fill up with tears. It was an odd feeling, cathartic and almost a revelation, since she'd always been so keen to avoid any great show of vulnerability. She'd thought she was much too strong for any of that silliness. Perhaps she'd been wrong all along. Maybe it was only those who were courageous enough to allow themselves to feel something who could let themselves cry.

And she did feel something. She'd risked her life to save the distillery. Her work here – not just putting together a marketing plan, but on the distillery itself, the employees, the history and the future of it – meant more to her than she'd realised until it looked like it was about to go up in smoke. Georgie smiled as she thought about this and the fact that here at least, her colleagues actually cared about her, enough to risk their own lives and try to rescue her.

It didn't change the fact that she would be travelling to London to hammer out the details of her return to Sandstone and Mellon in two months' time when her father's will had been settled, but it certainly took the shine off it. If she was honest with herself, at this moment, as she lay back on the grass, with the warm sun resting gently on her skin, the very idea of going back to London felt like the last thing she wanted. *But you can't just turn your back on your life's work. Can you?*

Iris wasn't exactly sure that she wanted to make the journey to London but Georgie making the trip somehow felt like a sign and it only made sense that they travel together. She'd need a London solicitor – there was no point going to Stephen Leather or his son to sort this out. And anyway, she'd prefer a woman, not just because she wanted them to tell her that everything would work out – she actually wanted someone more like Georgie than herself. She needed someone who could be depended upon to do the job well.

She had spent three weeks trying to talk herself out of the reality of what lay ahead and hadn't been brave enough to actually do anything about it. And then yesterday, she remembered the new offices that had opened up just next door to the little coffee shop that once upon a time had been her haven each Friday for a delicious cup of coffee after she ate her packed lunch at her desk. By some divine inspiration, the practice name came to her and she made an appointment.

And now she was here in London, standing outside Muriel Huggit Solicitor's front door, everything around her seemed different to what it was before, as if the very substance of the place had changed when she wasn't looking. Iris had a feeling the biggest change had been in herself. Myles had hurt her, but Ballycove was somehow healing. Through the window she saw a woman about the same age as herself, deep in concentration on a file before her. She put it down and spotted Iris at the window and smiled as if they knew each other. She was nothing like the hard-faced, skinny-arsed ball-breaker she assumed all divorce solicitors should be. She looked normal, just like any woman Iris might have been friends with if her life had been different to what she'd allowed it to become. Something resonated with Iris and she pushed in the front door and introduced herself.

'Would you like a coffee?' Muriel indicated a room beyond the receptionist's desk and waiting area. She nodded to the girl there who smiled at Iris and then reappeared once they were sitting with two fresh coffees from the café next door.

'Lovely,' Iris said. She savoured it, enjoying the strong caffeine kick. It was invigorating. Perhaps, she mused, it wasn't the coffee so much as the fact that for the first time in years, she felt as if she was taking control. Not with going to Ballycove, but just by sitting here – she was making a plan and putting Myles on the back foot, rather than waiting for him to call the shots.

Perhaps now she was finally ready to face the truth of her marriage. She still wanted Myles back, didn't she? Of course she did, but maybe spending time with Georgie had made something rub off on her. She wasn't going to be a doormat anymore. When they got back together – okay, *if* they got back together – Iris knew with certainty that she wanted a better marriage than the one she'd settled for before. And she wanted a child of her own. That was going to be non-negotiable. With the Delahaye legacy to wave beneath

Myles's nose and pulling half the value of everything they owned from under him, perhaps it would be enough for him to see sense. And if it wasn't? Well, she'd cross that bridge when she came to it.

'So?' Muriel leaned forward on her desk, notepad at the ready.

And then the whole sorry tale of her marriage to Myles came slowly, haltingly at first and then eventually flooding out. It was the first time she'd told anyone about his affair or the fact that he wanted a divorce. As she spoke, she could hear her own words as if they were some strange woman spilling a story that she would have found pathetic, if she'd been eavesdropping on the conversation.

Muriel had to interrupt her to check that she had facts straight. 'It's a lot of history,' Iris said. She'd spent years covering up the cracks and saving face. It was why she'd never really made any friends in London. How could she be a true friend and not share what her life was really like? To tell anyone would have seemed like giving in, maybe even tempting the universe into finally pulling the rug from beneath them. She'd wasted so much energy trying to appease him, putting him first, that she'd ended up completely neglecting the things that might give her some shred of happiness. But today, as she told the story of her marriage, she found even those suspicions that had dogged her for years about affairs she'd been convinced he'd had came flooding out. She'd spent half her life trying to ignore the fact that her instinct was telling her one thing, while Myles convinced her of another. Deep down, perhaps she'd always known the truth and with every affair she felt as if she wasn't good enough, just dying a little bit more inside every time. 'And so, Amanda Prescott, it turns out she's pregnant...'

'You and Myles never had a family?' Muriel was just ticking off facts with no idea of how deeply this simple reality had cost Iris so much more than she could explain in one simple check mark.

'The time was never quite right and we put it off and put it off until, well...' Iris heard her own bitter laugh, but it hardly covered over the emptiness that filled her heart. It was this betrayal that hurt far more than Myles just leaving her. Having a child without her was unforgivable; she could see that so clearly now after finally saying it out loud. How could she have been so stupid?

'I'm so sorry,' Muriel said after a moment, her voice gentle with years of practice consoling scorned women. 'That's such a terrible thing to sacrifice for someone who obviously never deserved you to begin with.'

Her words touched Iris in a way she'd never have expected. Honestly, all she really expected was for people to say, *I could have told you so*, or maybe berate her for being so dense in the first place. *Blinded by love*. Her eyes were well and truly opened now.

'Now, I think you need to heal, but my job isn't to help you with that. It's going to be my job to make sure you come out of this with everything that is rightfully yours and as much of his as I can lay my hands on too.' She and Iris shared a laugh. It was not greed, but rather the genuineness of the woman's eyes that confirmed for Iris she had come to the right place.

'Actually, I'm not even out to get revenge... I mean, I still feel that if there was any hope to save my marriage I would,' Iris said, although even she could hear how pathetic that notion was now.

'I see.' Muriel laid her pen slowly next to the pad she'd been taking notes on.

'And the thing is, it could happen. You see, I'm going to come into a sizeable inheritance and I feel it could really make a big difference to us...' Her words petered off and perhaps it was the expression on the other woman's face, but suddenly, she felt as if she couldn't move, couldn't speak – in fact, she could hardly breathe. The reality of her situation hit her like a tonne of bricks. What on earth had she been thinking? She was drowning in her own naivety and there was no life jacket to save her. A pain in her chest almost knocked her from the chair – was she having a heart attack? Panic sent rivulets of sweat from what felt like every pore in the body. *Myles did not love her*. The truth of it came as a flash, sending a dizzying jitter through her body and making her struggle for breath, vaguely aware of a brown paper bag being placed before her mouth.

'Breathe, slowly, it's all right. You're going to be fine. It's just a panic attack.'

'It's over, isn't it?' she gasped. 'My marriage? It's over.'

'I can't tell you that either way.' Muriel was sitting in the chair next to her now, still holding the bag before her. 'I think you're going to be fine now.' She took the bag and balled it up before dropping it in the wastepaper basket.

'So now, you really do know everything.' Iris attempted a wobbly smile.

'Not quite – tell me about this inheritance.'

'My father died just after Myles left me. It's the Delahaye legacy, but there are conditions.'

'I'm so sorry about your father, but I'm interested in the Delahaye legacy.' Muriel leaned closer and listened while Iris poured out the whole story.

'It sounds as if this could be a sizeable bequest when it is eventually transferred to each of you.'

'Yes, but it's going to take quite a few months before that happens. And, of course, we sisters have to agree on what to do with it – if we don't there'll be nothing at all.'

'And does Myles know about this?'

'No. He has no idea that my father even died,' Iris said. 'But even before, we'd always expected the whole estate to go to my older sister Georgie because Nola and I had stopped visiting Dad. Also I think she was his favourite and certainly the best placed to keep the family business going, even if she only did so from a distance.' Iris stopped for a moment. 'I used to wonder, you know, when things weren't good, if the distillery was the reason Myles married me to begin with. I talked my father into giving him a job, in the beginning, but Georgie accused him of pilfering and…' In a strange twist, the further she had pushed everyone away over the years, the more she knew, deep down, that there had to be some measure of truth in the accusation. 'Dad made up his mind about Myles then and even if I had tried to talk him into another job, he'd never have left the distillery to Myles in the end.' *Oh, God.* Perhaps she'd been right; maybe the distillery was all he'd wanted all along.

'Well then, I think my advice to you is that you need to

get this divorce in motion and moving very quickly, because otherwise, he will be able to take half of any assets you own,' Muriel said softly. 'That would be the wise thing to do. If we can make this an uncontested divorce, we might be able to rush it through in six months, which would probably suit your ex anyway.'

'I don't know, I had thought...' What had she thought? She had no idea.

'Pushing it through quickly wouldn't stop you getting back together. You wouldn't be the first couple to reunite and marry again, but it would be on your terms.' Muriel shook her head. 'I can't believe I've just said that, but it's an unusual case. The terms of your father's will really throw normal practice out the window just a little. Usually, I'd be advising you to take your time, regardless of my personal feelings, but in this case...' She shook her head again and pushed her glasses high up on her nose. 'At the end of the day, regardless of what I think, it has to be your decision.'

'No, no, I think you're right. As much as I didn't want to face up to it, my marriage is over. Even if we did get back together, what's to stop him leaving me again once my father's will is finalised? I don't think I could bear the idea of him living the high life with Amanda and their child on the back of generations of Delahaye hard work.'

'I'm so sorry.'

'It's Myles who should be apologising.' Iris took a deep breath. 'He's the one who's created this terrible mess. He's the one who's going to be a father in a few months' time.' Oh God, was she going to cry again? She swallowed hard to try and stop the tears from falling again.

'That's in our favour. Divorce cases are hard to predict in terms of how long it takes to actually get to the finishing line, but in this case, with a baby on the way and if it's easy enough to work out the financials, we might wrap this up before the will goes into probate. I'm not sure how long that takes in Ireland, but I'm sure we can drag things out at that end.'

'Oh, yes,' Iris said, thinking that all she would have to do was dig her heels in and declare to her sisters that she had no interest in selling her share – that would slow things down nicely. 'And in the meantime, as I said, Myles doesn't actually know that my father has died. Well, that is, I haven't told him, so…'

'Is he likely to find out?'

'I can't imagine so. He's so loved up with his floozy at the moment, I doubt he's given me a second thought, apart from maybe getting his hands on our shared assets as they stand.'

'And you still live in the primary residence?'

'I've rented it out while I'm living in Ireland for the next couple of months. It's paying the mortgage and giving me a little pin money as well.'

'Better if all the rent just goes into the mortgage account for now; we don't want to muddy the waters with money going anywhere but where it should. It would be another issue to drag things out longer.' Muriel was making ticking marks against the neat notes she'd just taken. It seemed to take an age as she read through each note aloud to check she had everything right. 'I'll need a current address for Myles, and I'll let you know how we're going as I move things along.'

They shook hands and rather than feeling that she was losing something that had been a part of her life for so long, Iris almost felt relieved as she stepped out onto the busy street. It was as if in facing up to the truth of what her marriage was, she had opened the door to some unfamiliar freedom and far from being daunting, it almost felt liberating in the London afternoon sunshine.

Iris had rung Georgie after her mysterious appointment had ended. She said she was at a loose end for lunch and would Georgie like to meet up? Georgie had been surprised, but then she was out of sorts about this meeting with Paul. Anything to stop her fretting would be good – even teaming up with Iris.

They went for a sandwich at the deli on the corner near Sandstone and Mellon. Georgie had been tempted to suggest a drink, but she didn't want to raise Iris's suspicions that her meeting with her former employers was anything she was nervous about. So instead, she made do with a double espresso and hoped it would firm up her negotiating skills. She did want this, after all, didn't she?

It was a strange sensation being back here, looking up towards the seventh floor that she'd spent such a big part of her life working in. She almost felt as if she was somehow outside herself, looking in at a snapshot of time that wasn't quite real. She was out of kilter with everything around her, so she almost felt as if she might lose her balance just standing still. People raced past in their expensive trainers and even more expensive suits, talking on phones to people who could make or break them or tuned into earbuds to help them forget about their stress for five more minutes. She wasn't part of them today. She was a voyeur, looking on from that elevated position of having so recently been racing on that treadmill and now having a free pass. She'd come to check her ticket and it turned her stomach to think of getting back in that race.

That was it. The whole place, being here, made her feel ill, as if some part of her DNA was pulling back from it. Perhaps it would be different when she was back here? She almost had to push herself through the doors of the building, aware of Iris next to her like an excited child being brought to her parents' family-at-work day.

Georgie nodded at the security man, who checked his list.

'Go on up, Miss Delahaye.' He'd looked pointedly at Iris, who was obviously not on his list, but Georgie pulled her along with her towards the lift before he had a chance to offer her an uncomfortable seat in the foyer. For the first time in years, Georgie wanted Iris by her side. The fact that she was actually here, with her, well, she wasn't sure she had the capacity to examine what that meant exactly. Probably, the therapist would have a field day with this one! Sylvia would probably call it a sign. Okay, in this moment, she *needed* Iris by her side. Still, there was no escaping the feeling that it galvanised her as she walked across the echoing foyer.

They stood waiting for the lift for what felt to Georgie like the longest, most uncomfortable minute. Suddenly, she felt invisible in a place where she'd so recently been cream of the crop. Of course, Iris was completely unaware of this. Her sister stood there, gawping at the architecture and marvelling at the brash capitalist opulence of the place. 'Oh my God, I can't believe you work here; really, it's so much more than I'd pictured!' Iris tugged at her sleeve and giggled. When the lift finally arrived, the doors opened to reveal a harried woman in her late twenties, head buried in her phone, fingers tapping furiously. It was like looking in a mirror. Georgie had so recently been that woman, so busy and important she could barely be out of contact to rush to the loo if she was bursting to go! Georgie too had been every bit as beset and self-absorbed. The younger woman brushed past them, but in the process somehow lost her balance, having not noticed either of the Delahaye girls waiting for the lift.

'For heaven's sake,' she snapped at them as the phone slipped from her hands. Iris automatically bent to reach it, but the woman got there first.

'Sorry,' Iris said, although clearly the flying phone had nothing to do with either of them.

'Just watch where you're going next time,' the woman barked before stalking off as if personally affronted by their very existence. *Oh, God*, Georgie thought, *I really was that woman.* The butterflies in her stomach suddenly grew heavier, as if they'd mutated back to giant caterpillars, wriggling inside her and setting free an undeniable truth: Sandstone and Mellon had not been a good place for her. It had made her self-absorbed, rude and ultimately miserable.

Iris dragged her into the lift just as the doors were about to close and she wondered if she could be a different person here this time round and still do her job as efficiently as she had in the past.

'Well, she was nice.' Iris made a face, but Georgie knew her sister wanted to laugh out loud at the rudeness.

As the elevator brought them whirring upwards, Georgie felt sick to the very pit of her. The incident with the woman at the elevator felt like an epiphany. She hadn't time to process it now; she was due to meet with Paul in a few minutes. She had to stay calm and focused, but she was failing at both miserably. Sweat was seeping through the cotton blouse she'd put on, hoping to strike a balance between relaxed and professional. They arrived too soon to dampen down her panic; the lift opening to reveal the smart reception desk manned by yet another striking blonde creature. The Barbie girls never lasted very long. Georgie had stopped bothering to remember their names.

'Hello, Miss Delahaye.' The girl flashed a perfect set of what had to be expensively whitened teeth at them when they approached the desk.

'Hi,' Georgie managed. It was probably the longest greeting she'd ever delivered to a receptionist in years and it wasn't lost on her that it only marked out what a total bitch she'd been. It added to her discomfort now and she read the girls name tag. 'Rachel,' she managed. 'We're probably a bit early. I might just pop into the...' She nodded towards the bathrooms along the corridor and yanked Iris along behind her.

She locked herself into the cubicle. She couldn't be sick here; she just couldn't. She sat on the toilet with her head between her knees, trying to breathe down the panic that threatened to overtake her. This was ridiculous; of course she wanted to come back here. She needed to hammer out a deal that would make Paul Mellon's eyes water and she wanted to swan in here every day and feel that she'd made it – on her own terms, down to her own talent. She deserved it. Damn it. This was just self-sabotage, imposter syndrome. What she'd worked so hard for was just within her grasp; surely she could muster the courage to go out there and claim it.

'Are you all right, Georgie?' Iris was outside the cubicle door now. 'You looked quite pale out there...'

'I...' She clenched her eyes shut tight. 'I think that sandwich must have disagreed with me, I feel... ill.'

'Oh, no,' Iris said. The concern in her voice was obvious but rather than giving Georgie the resolve she needed, it actually made her feel as if she might completely crumple. 'Can I do anything? I could get you a glass of water, perhaps or—'

'No. No. I'll be fine, just give me a minute.' Georgie was digging in her handbag, hoping to find a wet wipe to rub around the back of her neck, down her chest, on her face. Damn the make-up she'd applied earlier – better to look clean and fresh than arrive like a wrung-out panda. 'I'll be out in a minute, just hang on.' She heard the door open to the offices outside, two girls arriving and going to a toilet on either side of her, continuing the conversation animatedly that they'd begun on the way.

'Go on, tell me, I'll never guess in a million years,' one of them squealed. 'Actually, hang on, is it Harry Styles?' She shrieked with excitement before flushing the toilet and heading out towards the sinks to where Iris was waiting.

'No. Not even close,' the other one said. 'No, I have

to tell you; otherwise it's going to be such a complete disappointment. It's only Georgie Delahaye, back from the dead; Rachel just rang to say she was here.' And Georgie couldn't help but think that Rachel might be a total bitch after all.

'The wicked witch from the west? I thought they'd sacked her – I mean, wasn't that what the party was for, Paul Mellon telling us all that she was finally gone for good?'

And then, they were gone, just like that. Georgie felt like she'd been slapped. Now the hurt that she'd buried for so long beneath anger and bitterness overtook her with choking force. Suddenly, in the worst possible place and at the worst possible time, she was a sobbing bloody wreck. Her body heaved with the grief of it all. They hated her. They hated her so much, they actually had a party to celebrate her leaving! Paul Mellon had told them he'd fired her, as if he'd ever grow balls big enough to even dream about it. Hah! A million thoughts swirled within her in what felt like a maelstrom. When she finally managed to stop crying, she opened the door slowly to reveal Iris on the other side.

'Oh, God, Georgie, I'm so, so sorry,' Iris whispered, shaking her head and bending to put her arms around her sister.

'What should I do now?' Georgie asked, child-like. But of course, this was crunch time. This was her whole life's work. It wasn't fair to put a decision like that on Iris's shoulders. 'Paul wants me to come back, has made me an amazing offer. How can I say yes knowing they all hate me so much?'

'What do you *want* to do?' Iris asked simply. Georgie had a feeling she knew what Iris wanted her to say, but was far too wise to offer an opinion that might yet turn out to reopen that wedge that had been between them for so long.

'I don't know.'

'God, but they're a pair of proper articles. I've a good mind to go out there and make them apologise,' Iris said crossly, turning to the sink and wetting a wad of paper towels. She bent down and patted Georgie's face as if she was putting out a fire.

'Maybe, but they're not telling any lies. When I was here, I was a different person.' Great big walloping tears rolled down Georgie's cheeks and she began to sob again. 'Honestly, I was the queen bee of the lot of them here and that's saying something, Iris. I was a complete and utter dragon – the meanest-spirited of the lot.' She hung her head, ashamed of the person she had allowed herself to become in the blind pursuit of success.

'I'm sure you weren't all that bad,' Iris said in a generous attempt at sisterly loyalty that Georgie knew she didn't deserve.

'We both know you're just being kind. You weren't here. I completely lost sight of who I was and let my ego drive me. But it didn't make me happy; I can see that now.'

'You've changed,' Iris whispered. 'Maybe we both have. Perhaps Dad's idea of bringing us back to Ballycove may have been wiser than we gave him credit for that first day.' She smiled, squeezed Georgie's shoulder conspiratorially. 'Come on, let's get you sorted and then you can decide whether you go in there and give him hell or we make a run for it.'

'God, the idea of having to pass by that bloody Rachel...' It made Georgie shiver with a sort of humiliation and self-loathing she'd never felt before. 'I should apologise.'

'Don't you bloody dare! Anyway, I bet they say a lot worse about your boss when they have a few drinks on them.'

'Probably not, he's the darling of everyone he meets,' Georgie said, but it didn't matter now. She stood up and walked to the mirror. She looked a sight, like a zombie emerging after spending too long in the special effects department.

'Well, whatever he is, he wants you back to work as soon as you're up for it,' Iris said deliberately.

'I'm not sure he *wants* me back, but he needs me, probably. As I said, he's looking to give me a better deal than before, but it's all about clients, getting them and keeping them. It's not really a work relationship that's founded on much more than that...'

'Well then, the ball really is in your court. You know that you've worked hard and that you're talented enough to sit at the top of your game in this city. The question you have to ask yourself is, do you really want this life anymore?'

Nola loved this, sitting in the staffroom, surrounded by the chatter of her (pinch herself) colleagues. Not that the conversation was ever that riveting, but it was the camaraderie of the mundane. Hearing about a particularly troublesome first-year who managed to pull one of the oldest tricks in the book: chalk on the teacher's chair.

'Have you had that yet?' Stephanie, a geography teacher who had transferred west from Dublin a few years earlier, nudged her while passing the biscuits along the line. Somehow, there was always one or two left to reach the end.

'What's that?' Nola asked.

'Kids' tricks,' Nigel a maths teacher on her other side said helpfully. 'Not like when I was at school. Kids these days are nothing if not remarkably gauche in how they can bring you down.'

'You talk like it's guerrilla warfare.' Nola laughed, but the idea of it made her a little nervous.

'Oh, you don't have to worry.' A teacher opposite whose name Nola couldn't remember chimed in. 'They love you. Actually, I'd say they are pretty much in awe of you.' She smiled at Nola. 'I often wish I'd gone for drama rather than staid old history – the history teacher is never cool.' They all erupted with laughter at that. 'Still, I'm always very popular on pub quiz nights.'

In spite of herself, she was actually enjoying being here. Not just here in the school either, where she was quickly making friends, but in Ballycove too. She had rediscovered her love of the sea and even went for the occasional dip when the weather was warm. Some of the women had invited her to join them in the Ladies' Midnight Swimming Club. Iris had gone a few times and she was making friends too, people she went for coffee with. Nola wasn't sure she was brave enough for the cold night-time waters yet, but maybe before the year was out.

That evening, she walked back to Soldier Hill House at a pace so leisurely she'd probably have been slapped with a parking ticket in London. She was struck once more by the sheer beauty of the place. Of course, it helped that the sun was shining. Maybe it helped too that both her sisters were in London for the day; each of them settling their own affairs, both of them cagey about exactly what those affairs were.

Unlike her sisters, Nola had nothing to settle in London. She had, in many ways, nothing tangible to go back for. Right now, she corrected herself as her mind began to drift along dangerous lines that she knew could darken her mood. Things would be different next time. She would have a lovely flat, in a nice part of the city. It would be hers, with no other name on the deeds so she could never be turfed out of her own home again. She would be a fresh face – literally, the fresh air and soft rain of the west of Ireland had washed the weariness from her. She turned back towards the village; perhaps she should pick up some supplies. Dinner would be made, but maybe afterwards she might treat herself to a tub of Moo'd ice-cream for dessert. Without Iris making snide remarks about her every time she passed a mirror and Georgie sitting there, engrossed in whatever distilling book she was currently absorbing, it would be heaven to lounge in the deep sofa and watch mindless TV and savour her ice-cream.

It was as she was passing by the community centre that

she spotted the notice on the window. At first she wasn't sure what she was looking at really, but seeing the familiar images of Thalia and Melpomene – the two masks of drama at the bottom of the notice made her stop to read it.

Due to unfortunate circumstances
the Saturday Morning Drama Club
is permanently cancelled.
Signed
Miss Lorna Tuft

'Ah yes, poor Miss Tuft.' Elizabeth O'Shea, the doctor's widow, came along the path and stood next to her.

'Why is it being cancelled?'

'Ah well. I suppose there's only so long any of us can go on for and Miss Tuft must be eighty-seven if she's a day. She broke her leg a few months back and since then she's just gone downhill. The poor old dear has been in the nursing home ever since.'

'That's a shame,' Nola said. Miss Tuft's drama class had been one of the highlights of her own week as a child.

'Well, really, I'm not sure she even had many kids in the club. It was set up more as a place for kids to drop into. They learned a few poems and sang some songs, which the old girl would rattle out on the piano, and then call it a day for lunchtime.'

Still, Nola thought as she ambled off towards the supermarket, it was the end of an era. Since she had started teaching, the idea of making a mark on the next generation had really gripped her. Without giving it too much thought, she turned left instead of right for home when she had picked up her few supplies in the supermarket and found herself standing outside the community hall once more. It was an ugly building, probably the ugliest in Ballycove, although the tidy towns committee had painted it a brave shade of maroon and fastened a jungle load of hanging baskets that would trail petunias down before the windows and either side of the main door within a couple of weeks.

Inside was as dark and dated as she remembered from her youth, but again, there were tell-tale signs that fresh paint and other little touches had been added in an attempt to keep the place as bright as it was possible to keep a building that for the most part was windowless. Nola let herself into the main hall, a space she remembered from her youth that had only shrunk a little since. It still multitasked for everything from basketball games to any local concerts or the Christmas pantomimes, which had run for a couple of years when she was still a kid.

The stage was framed by dark red velvet curtains, but above it, she noticed new lights and when she went through the stage door entrance, there was evidence that at some point the sound system had been updated also. At the back, there was a tiny green room, two dressing rooms and all the trappings of set and stage that had set her heart racing before she'd ever imagined leaving Ballycove. She walked onto the stage in the dim light that came from the emergency beacons at both sides and a shiver reached along her spine. Standing here, centre stage – this had been her dream. To work in the theatre, to hear her feet move across the boards, to feel the warm lights on her shoulders and lose herself in whatever character she was lucky enough to play. How on earth had she lost sight of it all on the way?

Of course, she hadn't come back to Ballycove to act. Nor had she come here to teach, but there was no denying that she was enjoying her new job at the school far more than she had any other job she'd had since the disastrous end of her career on the soap opera. She laughed bitterly at the memory of it all and her voice echoed strangely in the hall beyond. It wasn't cold here, but she pulled her cardigan closer around her shoulders as she shivered – someone had stepped on her grave and she had a feeling that they were trying very hard to tell her something.

It was later, as she folded herself up in one of the old Corrigan rugs, her legs drawn up on the sofa beneath her, that she began to think about the hall again. It was a nagging feeling; as if there was something she hadn't quite noticed or remembered when she was there. She switched off the TV, listened to the familiar sounds of the house creak and rattle around her. Somehow, the familiarity of home, the bruising wisteria aching with new growth against the window, the whiff of woodsmoke from the open fire and the depth of the sofa that hugged her closer with even the slightest movement made her feel safe.

She sighed, a feeling of contentment settling on her as she realised that maybe this was where she was meant to be at that very moment. London would still be there when she returned. But what if…

Nola sprang up from the sofa. What if she was to open her own drama club? What if she was to start a drama school right here in Ballycove? Temporary of course, just for the next couple of months. It could run straight through the summer holidays, while school was closed; surely plenty of parents would go for that? She could use the hall, couldn't she? It would be a lovely little earner on the side, but more than that, it would sort of be – well, living the dream. Or at least the dream she had started out with. It could culminate in a little show just before she headed back to London. She was in no doubt that just because the six months would be up in June, it would take months, probably, to free up any cash from the estate – until then, there was nothing for her in London, so why not make the most of things in the meantime? Nola sank back on the sofa, a thousand ideas whirring about her brain at a million miles an hour. She would love to work with the younger children in the village, kids who were a million miles away from the teenagers she met at school.

Could she really do this? Well, that was the question she'd have to mull over for a little while until she'd figured things out past this initial rush of excitement.

12

Rather than feeling utterly depressed at the idea of divorcing Myles, Iris actually felt a wave of relief envelop her over the next few days after they returned from London. She felt better; she looked better. Gone were the gaunt shadows on her face. She'd even put on a little weight. It must be the combination of the fresh air and home cooking.

It certainly wasn't that she was glad her marriage was over – far from it. But there was no getting away from the fact that it actually *was* over and even if it hadn't been her choosing, there was something empowering in having taken the bold step of engaging Muriel Huggit on her behalf.

The other thing that Iris noticed since she'd returned was that the decision seemed to have lifted whatever barriers there were before to her actually enjoying her time in Ballycove. This morning, she made breakfast for the three of them and they sat down in their usual chairs. She watched Nola sip her black coffee slowly as if she was carefully turning a key into wakefulness and Georgie reading a trade magazine for the Vintners Association of America and felt an unusual fondness for them both. She should tell them, but as she stood there folding a tea towel and hanging it on the Aga, she couldn't quite find the words. She just wasn't ready yet. Would she ever be ready to admit to them that her marriage was over?

'I'm thinking of helping out at the fete this year. Are either of you interested in joining me?' she asked as she topped up their coffee cups.

'Huh?' Nola asked, winding her hair in a long semi-circle across her shoulder so she had one enormous ringlet falling along her arm. Iris couldn't help but notice how striking her sister was, devastatingly beautiful really; it had been the ruination of their relationship all those years ago. 'Is that even still going?'

'Of course it's still going.' Iris stopped for a moment, lowered the radio at her back. 'It'll be the last time the Delahaye family will be here. It might just be closure, you know?'

Nola yawned.

'The distillery will always be here,' Georgie said from behind her magazine again.

'Maybe, but that doesn't mean that it'll still be the Delahaye Distillery.'

'I'm sure it will,' Georgie said lightly, then she dropped her magazine, folded it over and sighed. 'Anyway, I've already said we'll do a stall. We're donating any proceeds to the local tidy towns committee. Let's just hope it's not bucketing down with rain or we'll all be cultivating a nasty strain of pneumonia together.'

Georgie looked across at Nola expectantly.

'I'm probably going to help out on the school stall. We're looking for props for the end-of-year play and the kids are making up little crafty things to sell on the day.'

Iris for her part was hoping to get a second-hand book stall or something straightforward like that. 'Well, watch out, Ballycove fete – it looks as if the Gin Sisters are coming your way this year.'

A little later, Iris set off down the avenue with a few basic provisions and the intention of readying the cottage for the couple and a small child who were due to arrive later in the afternoon. Running the little cottage as a business had been a complete revelation. In the few weeks since Georgie had set up the website, there had been only one night when it wasn't occupied. Mainly couples, but occasionally a small family group.

Today, a lovely fresh breeze whipped through the trees, making them sway and creak as if they were chattering among themselves. The rooks high up in their branches joined in to give voice to their disapproval of the wind whipping about their nests. In the field that had been fenced out of what had once been a rather stately drive, a herd of curious cattle escorted Iris towards the cottage. Their great big button eyes watched dolefully as she turned in at the cottage gate. She was glad of the company.

It didn't take long to zip through the work, changing sheets, scrubbing the bathroom and washing down the kitchen surfaces. She left the smaller bedroom to last. It was funny, but this was the first room in the house she'd tackled and even though she'd squeezed in a double bed, she had chosen the sort of colours she'd always have imagined in a nursery room if she'd had children herself.

The room was a confection of soft buttery yellows – suitable for either a boy or a girl. It was pretty, but it still worked with the hints of pale green that accented the accessories and were stitched along the heavy Corrigan blanket that lay across the foot of the cast-iron bed. She stretched the cover out, smoothing any creases so the bed looked perfect.

Later, she would pull down the old rocking horse she'd hauled out of the attic a few weeks earlier and stored for families arriving. Last time she'd sat for almost half an hour cleaning the blasted thing only to realise that the child was sixteen and more interested in a Wi-Fi connection than an antique wooden toy. She'd been disproportionately disappointed; she'd liked the idea of the little wooden horse creaking over and back softly and the sound of a child's laughter echoing about the little cottage.

She checked her watch. Time just seemed to glide away from her here, but then she was busy, content to be doing something that was useful. The final task was placing the rocking horse in the second bedroom. She took it gently from the tiny trapdoor that led into one of three separate attics running across beneath the crouching pitched roof of the cottage. She dragged it along the floor and placed it just between the window and the side of the bed. She'd been wise enough to cover it in lose plastic last time, so now it just had that shaggy worn look that comes with age and love, but it was clean and perfectly huggable if you were a small child. She stood next to it, drawing her breath for a moment when it struck her.

This should have been hers. This rocking horse, this excitement at the idea of a small child clamouring over it and hours spent in the beginning holding him or her on safely and then later, sitting in a nearby chair while her child swung contentedly. The very idea of it brought tears to Iris's eyes and she could feel what it seemed had become a familiar swell of sadness rise up within her. Was it normal to grieve for a child that had never been hers? And now, as she reached out and stroked the familiar face of the toy from her childhood, she felt angry as well. She was angry with Myles, who had taken away her chance at having a child.

Suddenly, as the curtains billowed in the breeze wafting through the open windows, she knew that Myles had never wanted a child with her. Why hadn't she just faced up to this years ago instead of brushing it under the carpet of her fairy-tale dreams? Sadness engulfed her and she knelt down next to the rocking horse, throwing her arms around its shaggy old neck and burying her face in its soft fur. She rocked gently with it, back and forth, a rhythmic movement to the heaving sobs that were escaping out of her.

After she wasn't sure how long, the sound of a car on the gravel outside broke into her misery. She raised her head to look through the window. The guests had arrived early. She swore under her breath then rubbed the rocking horse's fur back in place, stood up quickly and straightened herself out in the mirror. She didn't look too bad. Actually, considering that a minute earlier her heart felt as if it might break, she looked bloody great. Then she caught something, a glint in her eye, perhaps a measure of Georgie rubbing off on her. She moved closer to the mirror; yes, there it was.

She smiled, because of course it was obvious now. If she wanted a child, she would never have had one with Myles. It would always have been on her own. Myles had only wanted her to take care of him, and a child would have meant dividing her attention. Being a mother would have meant she had something more to think about other than devoting her every waking worry on Myles. The question was, did she still want one badly enough to go it alone? Or did she want Myles back so much that she was willing to give up on the idea altogether?

It was a crazy idea, but it woke Georgie early the next morning and it wouldn't leave her for days. What if she bought out her sisters' shares of the distillery when this was all over? Madness – she knew, but on the other hand it was becoming harder with each passing day to come up with any good reason to return to the life she'd been living before. It seemed now she was here that there was nothing to go back to London for.

Oh, on a practical level, she knew she'd get another job. She was certain too that working in that high-pressure corporate environment, she would revert to being the same person she'd been in London and it hadn't made her happy. The longer she spent at the distillery, the more it felt as if this was where she was meant to be. She was creating a marketing and branding strategy for Iseult Gin and more than that, she was learning as much as she could about the distillery from Robert. She didn't want to go back to being the same person she was before, nor did she want to go back to that life.

It was clear to her now that she didn't enjoy the backstabbing nature of relationships she'd had with her colleagues in London. In the distillery, she was building relationships with the other people who worked there. They had celebrated her birthday together. She was as excited as any of them when Shane McCall's girlfriend went into labour and produced the most adorable baby girl. Robert would bring her coffee most evenings and they would sit for hours just going through whatever he was doing that day, and she was genuinely fascinated by it all, looked forward to their chats.

But it was the silence of the place that she loved the most. When everyone else went home and she just sat there, breathing it all in; this history, this legacy – it was in her blood. She had started to close her eyes and imagine what it would be like if this became her life's work. Could she do it? Could she throw up everything London had given her to come back here and become a distiller? God, even thinking about it brought up such a mixture of fear and excitement.

She could afford it. She was pretty sure about that. Even if she had to go up against one of the big brewers, what with her severance package, her apartment in London and her share of the house and farm here in Ballycove, she would have enough to buy her two sisters' shares out. It could be the perfect solution for all of them. It was obvious, they'd both just want their slice of the pie as quickly and easily as possible so they could go back and resume their lives in London.

Nola wondered if it wasn't a strain of lunacy. The dream of opening a drama school when she had less than two months before the instructions in her father's will had been adhered to. And what did she know about running her own business? And yet, here she was again, sitting in the middle of the dusty stage in the community hall, a slight chill in the air and musty aroma enveloping her in the darkness.

She had ducked in with a fold of raffle tickets one of her colleagues had left in the staff room that were meant to be dropped off for tonight's bingo session. But it was only an excuse.

'*Juliet* or *Lady Macbeth*?' Aiden's voice came from the back of the hall.

'I'm too old to play Juliet,' she said, and the truth was, she was too lightweight to ever be considered for Lady Macbeth.

'Shame, you would have made a fabulous tragic heroine.' He was pulling out stacks of chairs. 'Well, are you going to supervise or lend a hand?' He laughed at her.

'But I...' There was no point telling him that she'd only popped in for a moment – she'd been there almost an hour already when she checked her watch. 'Sure.'

'We're trying to get a rota going, you know, to keep this place in shape. Old Jack Coveney died last year and since then...'

'God, I remember him from when I was a kid coming here

for Irish dancing classes. He must have been ancient by the time he passed away.'

'He probably was, but he turned up here every single day to ready the hall for whatever was going on.' Aiden rolled out stacks of chairs in a neat line and Nola started to lay them out. 'He was doing it for thirty years. After his wife died, he said it kept him out of the pub.'

'So now, everyone just pitches in?' Nola changed the subject quickly.

'Something like that. A few of us came together, decided to take it on – everyone has their own day and we swap about if it doesn't suit.' He stood for a moment, counting up the stacks of chairs. 'What about you?'

'Me? Oh, I won't be here long enough to get my name on a rota.'

'Of course, but I just thought, when I saw you there, you seemed to be...' He stopped. He'd clearly learned the hard way what happened if he said the wrong thing around her. 'You were lost in... something?'

'Daydreaming?'

'Was it? It looked almost tragic.'

'Ophelia or Desdemona tragic?'

'I'm not sure.' He started to unstack chairs from the back and for a while they wordlessly went about the work of setting the place out, the clanking of metal on the maple wood boards filling up the echoing hall with crashing bellows. He worked fast, taking stacks of chairs and emptying them across each line as if they were little more than teacups being set out for a quick snack. Nola moved as quickly as she could but there was no making up ground once Aiden started.

'Is that it?' she asked when they finally met each other after she'd laid out less than a quarter of the hall.

'I don't know, is it?' he asked, a little too close to her for comfort. She stepped back deliberately. 'Even though you're only here for a short time, it's okay to make connections.'

'I'm going back to London soon, Aiden. I have a job at the school and commitments at home and I'm helping out with the Ballycove fete.' The fact was, she had more connections here than she'd left behind in London.

'You see, I think there's more to you being here today than just coincidence.'

'Well, it wasn't to see you, if that's what you're hinting at.' The very nerve of him.

'No, of course not.' He too took a step back and then walked away from her, towards the end of the hall. 'You miss this, don't you?' He nodded towards the stage behind him.

'I...' She sighed. There was no harm telling him what had been rattling about her brain for the last few days. 'Okay, so I had this crazy idea that maybe I could open my own drama club and...' She waved her hand to let him know that her thoughts had rambled off into something silly.

'So?'

'Well, of course I can't open a drama school.'

'Why not?'

'Because...' She stopped and took a long theatrical breath before exhaling softly, feeling that overwhelming sense of failure she had felt for the last few years – that everything she touched was bound to turn to failure. 'Because I don't know the first thing about running a drama school for one thing and…'

'What's that got to do with anything? I didn't know a thing about farming, other than the little day-to-day jobs I did to help out around the place when I was a kid at school, but I knew when I came back here that this was where I was meant to be. I made my own blueprint and it's worked out okay.' His gaze was unnerving, as if there would be no fudging or excuses that he would believe.

'It would probably be a complete flop,' she said, dropping down into the hard chair nearest to her.

'How do you know before you even try?'

'Because everything I do is a flop.'

'That's not what I hear from the school; they think you're the best thing that's arrived in Ballycove since yellow bananas.' He smiled at her and she couldn't help smiling back. 'Tell me a little about this drama school?' He walked over and sat in the row before her.

'There's nothing much to tell,' she said, but then she looked beyond him to the empty stage. 'I just came in here one afternoon, stood on the stage and, I don't know… I felt something.' Now she felt a bit silly, but at the same time, there was a knot in her stomach and she wasn't sure if it was induced by the idea of her own drama school or being sat here with Aiden.

'So far, that sounds a bit like my conversion on the road to Damascus.' His smile was bloody infectious and Nola had that sensation that she hadn't felt since she was a small child that she could soon be laughing and crying all at once.

'Yes, but you didn't have to return to London soon.'

'I had a job, a good job, a flat and a girlfriend in Dublin. None of which was going to wait for me indefinitely,' he said and his voice was hoarse.

'I'm sorry.'

'Oh, don't be sorry, I have no regrets. Moving back here was the best decision I've ever made. I mean, I'm probably not making as much money as I did before, but I have a quality of life that far outweighs the corporate ladder and there's no beating the feeling that my future is completely in my own hands.'

'Yes, I can imagine that's something all right.' For a moment, Nola remembered those long harrowing calls to her agent, knowing before she even rang to badger her that the answer was going to be the same again. There was no work; no-one was battering down her door to give her so much as a drop-by, never mind an audition and far less likely an actual role.

'Do you *have* to go back straight away?'

'My life is there. It's where I belong,' she said too quickly, so even she knew it sounded as if she'd just taken it for granted and not considered a possibility beyond what she'd believed to be the case since she was a youngster.

'Well, that's just a pity for Ballycove, I suppose,' he said, but he was still smiling. He studied the floor between them for a moment. 'Just so you know, I think it could be a great success. It's exactly what the mothers of Ballycove are crying out for, somewhere to send their kids that could build them up and let them have some fun learning how to perform on a stage. And you know, with the buzz you've created down at the school, I'd say word would travel so fast, you could open up a club in some of the other villages also. I suppose, all I'm saying is, you don't have to stick with what you've got, you can change your mind and choose a different life.' He smiled at her once more and got up from his seat. Only his footsteps echoed around the hall and then the door at the end closed with a whining creak behind him.

Nola sat there for ages thinking about what he said, but the fact was that he really didn't know what he was talking about. If Nola made up her mind to move back here, she wouldn't be walking out mid-career; the fact was her career had screeched to a halt. She had convinced herself that returning to London after this hiatus would be the start of her second career. She had gone to bed each night for her first couple of months here and nodded off to sleep with dreams of her reinvention. At this point, she'd practically brainwashed herself into the inevitability of her success. Yes, she was *almost* convinced of it.

But the reality was, without her share in the Delahaye legacy, she didn't have enough money to put a down payment on a parking space, never mind a flat. A drama summer club needn't be a long-term commitment. She could earn enough to get by until September. Hopefully, Georgie and Iris wouldn't object to her staying on in the house for a few more weeks and in the autumn, with a fat bank balance, she could go back to her real life in London.

That was it. She took a deep breath and looked up at the empty stage. The decision was made: she was going to set up the Delahaye Drama School. It was terrifying and exciting in equal measure, but her feet did a little happy dance, maybe because she loved the idea even more than she'd admitted to herself or Aiden.

13

Early June, One Month To Go...

The morning of the village fete dawned dark and thunderous. Iris lay in bed listening to the sound of a westerly wind blowing in off the Atlantic. An ominous weather forecast had woken her at seven o'clock. The Atlantic hurricane season was sending across an early summer gift; hopefully it wouldn't fully hit land until later this evening. She meant to spring out of bed and get organised for the day, but honestly, she'd turned over to the sound of the wind in the chimneys and drifted into a half-sleep, remembering that fete so long ago where Myles first noticed her. She could almost feel the sun on her skin, the taste of that first kiss on her lips. It filled her with a sort of yearning that she'd almost forgotten she'd ever experienced.

The unexpected sting of it made her groan. For a tantalising few seconds the memory of it all was so vivid, Myles looking at her with those deep blue eyes from under his floppy fair hair. It had caught her up, so it felt as if she was holding her breath for too long. He had done that to her, made her heart race, turned everything she thought she was and all she knew over in an instant. It had taken just one kiss. She had snuck an extra fairy cake on his plate and hadn't charged him. Their secret. God. It was a lifetime ago.

By the time she did tumble out of bed she was running late and her mood was as black as the sky hanging low over Ballycove in the distance. As she ate breakfast she tried to convince herself that the day would be fine enough for the fete to go ahead, now the winds had eased.

'Dry spells with the risk of thundery showers, moving in from the west and spreading across the entire country in late evening,' Nola repeated the weather forecast glumly. There was a pile of fliers before her for the summer drama club she was setting up.

'Oh, don't worry, they never get it right,' Georgie said with the determined forced smile of one who intends to stick it out to the bitter end.

Iris couldn't help feeling that they were in for a washout of a day, which was such a pity since the village fete was the event of the year in Ballycove. There was, to be fair, a limited calendar of events to choose from, but certainly, the fundraising fete was right up there with the vigil mass at Christmas and the spring concert in the little library, at which there were never quite enough seats or wine to go round.

In spite of the forecast, Iris enjoyed her walk to the village and soon she was happily arranging the assorted books and other donations on her stall. A small canopy covered over each table and when the rain came at least there would be room enough to stand beneath its shelter. She was intent on enjoying the day.

Her good humour plummeted further when she saw that her stall was full of what looked like the items they hadn't managed to sell last year or maybe for the last twenty years – you couldn't give this tat away, never mind sell it. Worse, the three sisters would be working on stalls right next to each other and she had a feeling that the whole village would flock for free samples of Georgie's gin and the chance to win a tonne of coal in the school raffle.

It was mid-afternoon before the crowds really began to arrive. Perhaps it was the long weekend or maybe the fact that between the villages that traced along the coast, there wouldn't be much more to do on a day like today, but Iris was surprised at the turnout for the fete, especially given the dark clouds overhead. She never remembered it being this busy before. The upside was bumping into a few girls she'd been in school with, which was lovely. Of course, everyone's life had moved on, but the thing that surprised her was, rather than being the only one who seemed to have lived a life only to return to the point where she'd started, the other women seemed to be in the very same boat. They'd either divorced or they'd reared a family and now, to all intents and purposes they were alone again – maybe even more so, because they were stuck in a house with a husband who they felt they hardly knew anymore.

They organised to meet up for coffee and Iris even agreed to join their badminton game, so they could make up a set of doubles. It was years since she'd played any sports, years since she'd had proper friends, but it was time to change that now.

Iris realised she must have nodded off in the afternoon sunshine because her phone woke her and when she looked about, she saw Georgie standing opposite chatting happily to some people Iris assumed worked in the distillery. She pressed 'accept' before registering the name on the screen.

'Iris?' She heard her name but was far too bleary-eyed to figure out who was speaking on the other end. 'Are you there? It's me – Myles...'

She groaned, suddenly wide awake. She hung up the phone before he said another word.

Half an hour later her solicitor rang. 'Hello!' Muriel was unfeasibly chipper.

'Hello, Muriel,' said Iris wearily.

'I'll get straight to the point: I'm afraid Myles is digging his heels in.'

'Can he do that?'

'He's asking for mediation, saying he wants you two to give things another go—'

'Seriously?' Iris felt her head spin and suddenly, rather than butterflies in her stomach, she felt hollow. 'His girlfriend is about to pop any day and he really thinks that I'm going to go for some sort of counselling with him?' The words as they flew from her mouth were a complete surprise to Iris. She looked around, suddenly conscious that she might be heard. Georgie and Nola were close enough to hear every word and she automatically lowered her voice. Although, even as she moved away towards the perimeter wall, she wasn't sure why she couldn't just tell them and get it over with.

'If we want to move things along…' Muriel cut through her thoughts. God, a month ago she'd have been jumping at the chance to get him back – on any terms.

'Will we be bringing Amanda and the baby along too?' Sarcasm wasn't something she did often, but this deserved it.

'It's a tactic, don't worry. Most likely he expected you to be a pushover and we've gone in with guns blazing. He's just trying to win some ground back.'

'Yes, well, I suppose I have been a sap for most of our married lives.' Iris sighed.

'And now, he can't understand what's changed. Actually, since I sent out those papers, he's done everything he can to track you down, even rang here pretending to be the new tenant in your house wanting to report a burst pipe directly to the owner.'

'He's just playing games.'

'Yes. But legally, we can't afford to hang about. After all, if your father's estate becomes part of this settlement, it could cost you dearly.'

'Of course.' Iris knew with certainty now, she couldn't bear the idea of the Delahaye fortune feathering Myles' new nest. Even hearing his voice on the phone earlier had made her stomach churn. Iris took a deep breath, watched as a narrow shaft of light tripped across the sea opposite her. Had she finally gotten over him? Yes. She absolutely wanted nothing more to do with Myles; she'd never been surer of anything in her life. 'The thought of even being in the same room as him just sends me into all sorts of panic.' Even now, she could feel her stomach erupt into disloyal somersaults at the idea of it.

'I do understand. Divorces are never easy. No matter how acrimoniously things have broken down, there's still a period of loss and in a way, mourning.'

'I thought I did my mourning during my marriage,' Iris said sadly; she'd certainly cried enough over the years.

'Sorry to disappoint you, but you have a few more tears left ahead of you, even after it's all over,' Muriel said wisely. Then she shuffled some papers around her desk. 'So that's settled. If you need to come across for one session with a mediator, it's possible for you to make it?'

'Only if I have to. I'll check out flight times and let you know what would suit.' God, even as she said it, the thought of sitting in the same room as Myles made Iris feel nauseous.

Georgie had spotted Iris snoozing in the afternoon sun. Of course, she was probably worn out. Being pregnant at any age was meant to absolutely floor you with tiredness, but at Iris's age – well, it was bound to be so much worse. That phone call had to be from Myles. Something in her bones told her that only Myles could evoke the sort of reaction on her sister's face that reminded her of the maelstrom of distress and, yes, utter anguish she would surely feel if Paul Mellon rang her up while she was snoozing contentedly. It struck her as odd how she could so easily equate the boss she disliked so intensely to the man her sister had adored for so long.

'You all right, sis?' she asked when Iris returned to her

stall. It was a pretty pathetic stall and a little part of Georgie felt sorry for Iris. Georgie had enjoyed manning the distillery stall, chatting to some of her colleagues who had turned up to volunteer alongside her. They were giving out free samples of gin and hoping for donations to the local tidy towns fund. The only downside was that her stall was directly under a loudspeaker system that blasted out occasionally, making her almost jump out of her skin when she least expected it. As the day wore on, she could feel the start of a raging headache and she wasn't sure whether to blame the thundery electricity on the air, the loudspeakers peeling off in her ears or just a general aggravation as she watched Nola convert every stranger who tripped past her stall into what looked like a long-lost friend.

She should be happy for her. It looked as if every child in the village was signing up for her drama summer school. It seemed no matter how she tried to move on from feeling jealous, sometimes it was hard not to remember how lonely London had been for her, while Nola swept up friends as if they were moths to her bright flame. By mid-afternoon, all Georgie wanted was to shake the day off with a long tramp across the fields and an even longer soak in the bath when she got home.

'Oh for goodness' sake, those bloody speakers,' Nola snapped across at her, as if Georgie was connected to the divine and there was a single thing she could do about them. 'You're next to them, can't you turn them off? Every time I'm in the middle of signing someone up to the drama school they get bloody louder.' Behind her Aiden Barry rolled his eyes and made a silly face, as if to make up for her.

'It's hardly my fault,' Georgie snarled back. 'They're driving me as mad as anyone. It's at full volume over *my* head after all.'

'Isn't there a plug there?' Iris had arrived back her table stacked high with unsold crocheted doilies. 'My nerves are rattled with it.' She looked completely shot, as if her patience was at empty and she was running on a reserve that could explode at any moment.

'Oh, yeah, because it's all about your *nerves*.' Nola rolled her eyes and Georgie tried to send her a warning glance. They had agreed they wouldn't mention the pregnancy until Iris did. In fairness, Iris hadn't uttered so much as a word, not a gripe about morning sickness and as to showing – well, she'd put on a bit of weight, certainly. But, apart from a little rounded paunch, she was hardly in danger of giving herself away at this stage and she must be at least six months gone. Sometimes, Georgie thought she'd burst if they couldn't talk about the baby soon – how on earth could Iris keep something so exciting to herself for so long? Suddenly, it seemed to Georgie that Nola was in danger of letting her temper spill it out in a way that would more likely end up in a fight rather than what should have been a celebration.

'What's that supposed to mean exactly?' Iris swung round, obviously just spoiling for an argument in which to vent her frustration at whatever Myles had said to her in that earlier call.

'It means' – Nola took a step out from behind her stall; her face was red now with pent-up rage – 'that your nerves have little or nothing to do with the speakers overhead and everything to do with—' Just in time, she caught the warning glance from Georgie and there was an awkward silence.

'Myles ringing you five minutes ago,' Georgie supplied quickly.

'How dare you say that?' No matter how worn out she looked, it seemed that she always had the energy to defend the man she'd sacrificed her family for.

'Why not? It's the truth, isn't it?' Georgie couldn't help it. 'All he's ever done is made you completely bloody miserable. He's spent your entire marriage treating you like a doormat and when you trot back to England again with the proceeds of our family's legacy, he'll only want to spend it on himself and you'll be a big enough fool to let him.' Georgie was shouting now, drawing a crowd, but it felt as if some reckless part of her had been let loose and she didn't care who heard her. Suddenly it didn't matter, because all she could think of was the work their father had done to build up the distillery, the farm and Soldier Hill House, and it was just wrong that it would all be sold off and the proceeds lavished on the likes of Myles bloody Cutler.

'And you're one to talk.' Nola was in like a flash. 'Dedicating your whole life to becoming a hotshot marketing executive. It was all you could see, even when some of us hardly had enough money to eat at the end of the week. You couldn't even throw a part-time job my way. What are you going to do with your share? Probably put it in the bank and never look back, because you're cold, Georgie, frozen to the bone. That's what you've let your ambition do to you. Iris might have been blind as a bat when it came to Myles, but you just put on tunnel vision goggles all those years ago and the only one you've thought about is yourself.'

It was like being doused with icy water and for a long moment Georgie was too stunned to do much more than stand there and take it. And now it seemed as if all of Ballycove had turned out to see them argue here in the middle of the village on the busiest day of the year.

'A doormat?' Iris's lips were trembling, her expression raging between anger and hurt. 'And I suppose I was blind as a bat, was I, when I saw you both together?'

'Oh, for goodness' sake, Iris, play another record.' Nola swung about at Iris. 'I told you at the time, that was all Myles' doing. I was just trying to get away from him when you walked in on us, but of course, you wouldn't listen then and you'll probably never see him for what he was...'

Georgie was seething, 'Can we not fight over Myles bloody Cutler again?'

'Yeah, well, he was the beginning of the end of us, wasn't he?' Nola screamed at Georgie. She was frantic with rage now. 'When she threw me out of the house, you were some great sister then, weren't you? Family indeed.' Nola shook her head, but there were tears in her eyes.

That's rich coming from the woman who walked out of Ballycove and never looked back. Once fame arrived, we were forgotten about faster than yesterday's breakfast, but you were back here fast enough when it came to the reading of Dad's will. Georgie was right up next to Nola now, the three of them standing in the middle of the green, squaring up to each other, like some crazy three-way sparring match.

'You forgot about everyone here because you were much too busy with your social life.'

'I had my career too and I...' Nola began, but there was something behind her eyes and Georgie should have seen it for what it was – not anger, but something far worse: complete and utter devastation and regret.

'Oh, yes, acting,' Iris shouted. She was ashen-faced and if Georgie hadn't been so caught up in this argument, she might have paused and thought about the baby for longer than a second. 'Acting with someone else's husband no doubt...' But even as Iris was spitting the words out, all Georgie could think of was all those times she'd been in London. Lonely. Bloody lonely, thinking that at least they both had relationships, friends, lives that had moved on from these petty jealousies. And now, worse than all that jealousy she realised that maybe none of them had moved on, not really, and that was just too sad to contemplate when she was this angry.

'For the last time, it wasn't my fault, Iris. I didn't lead him on; it was all him. Myles never let up from the moment I moved to London...' She sounded as if she might cry, but instead she tossed her hair back defiantly.

'I know what I saw.' Iris and Nola were at each other's throats, and Georgie knew they weren't here – instead, they were back there in that little terraced house in London all those years ago when Iris had come home early and caught her husband and her sister in a clinch that left her in no doubt as to where it might have led had she not arrived when she did.

'No, Iris. No, you don't know what it was like, what he

was like. I'd never betray you, never.' And then, as if fifteen years rolled by in an instant and all the buried feelings of that terrible time cloaked them from the rumbling clouds overhead, they both started to cry. Loud, gulping tears, the hurt of decades cascading down both of their faces. 'It was all him. He wouldn't leave me alone, even when I threatened to tell you, he still wouldn't give up...' Nola was hiccupping now, hardly able to get the words out. 'He made me feel...' She stopped, tried to catch her breath. 'As if it was my fault; but I never, Iris, I never would...' She was bawling now, like a child.

'I...' Iris began and perhaps she'd always known that Nola hadn't done anything wrong all those years ago, but it had taken until now for her to finally admit the villain here was Myles.

'Myles was always a scumbag. We tried to warn you before you married him. You never wanted to hear it, Iris. You believed him over your own sisters – how could you choose someone like Myles over your own flesh and blood?' Tears and snot were running down Nola's face. They combined to make her look like the little girl she'd been when their mother died and Georgie felt the guard around her heart crumble with a force of love she'd thought was long gone. It was only then she began to register some of the familiar faces in the large crowd gathered around them.

'Come on.' Georgie moved between them. She for one saw no need to air all their family secrets in public.

'And as for you, when I needed you the most, when I had nowhere to live, no-one to fall back on, where were you with your fancy career? You couldn't even make space for me in a lowly receptionist post,' Nola railed at Georgie. 'I was living in a squat and you were...'

'Come on, Nola, not here.' Georgie reached out to touch her sister's arm.

'Why not here, why not now?' Nola screamed. 'What is it? Can't you admit to everyone what a cold ambitious bitch you've been?' Nola pulled her arm away, was about to launch into another verbal attack when Georgie moved up close to her, kept her voice low.

'Excuse me, but if you'd bothered to return my call, if you hadn't been so busy partying with your mates every night of the week, I could have got you a really good job. I left a message with one of your mates and you...' Georgie could feel what little self-control she had left deserting her now and there wasn't a thing she could do about it. 'You never even bothered to turn up to the interview – it was in the bag, all you had to do was show up... And that was my reputation you were throwing away with your own chance, or did you even care about that?' Georgie remembered now, so clearly, she had begged for that interview for Nola. She'd talked her up so bloody much.

'What a load of total crock you talk, Georgie.' Nola stood for a moment, looking at Georgie, studying her in a way that maybe convinced her of the truth of all those years earlier. 'There was never any message from you.' Now it was Nola's turn to stand there like a fish taking in air while the world moved slowly past her. She opened and closed her mouth a few times, but there was no speech. There was nothing she could say, not really.

And then, instead of doing what their father would have

wanted, Georgie found herself doing the exact opposite, and the worst of it was that she was completely aware of herself as if looking on from outside and entirely mortified at what she was seeing.

'Admit it, you'd never wanted a real job, all you wanted was your glitzy career…' She stopped to catch her breath. '*Tea for me!*' Georgie mimicked cruelly in a sing-song voice. Georgie felt her head begin to swim, as if a tide of unspent resentment was carrying her far out into deep waters, unfathomable and defying any navigation back to land. 'Hah!' Her voice was so high-pitched, she startled herself. 'You can't even act like a grown-up and keep your cool for an afternoon on a stall at the village fete.'

And that was when the unthinkable happened; Georgie could see it coming but she was stuck to the spot, livid and maybe in shock that they could all let themselves down so badly. Nola reached down into some part of herself that maybe none of them ever thought she could reach and with every drop of disappointment and anger in her, she levelled a resounding slap across Georgie's face.

Iris was on them in a flash, trying to separate them, but she lost her balance and Georgie watched her career towards them, a slow-motion figure, her expression tied up in a mixture of alarm and embarrassment.

But everything had slowed down, so the noise of Nola's hand striking Georgie's cheek seemed to echo across not just the now-silent fete, but back over the village, out beyond the church spire and right into that tiny corner of the graveyard where their parents were meant to be resting in peace.

They landed in a sorry heap at an almost perfect midpoint between the three stalls they were meant to be working on, with Georgie at the very bottom. When she raised her head, her eyes were level with the assorted footwear and ankles of what felt like half the village. *Oh, my God – it was the centenary celebration all over again.*

Iris was the first to disentangle herself, with Robert English wading through the crowd to pull her to her feet. Next, Aiden Barry stepped in gallantly and yanked both Nola and Georgie off the ground with more thought for speed than decorum or their dignity.

'The storm is coming,' he stated gruffly as he shoved them both ahead of him between the open-mouthed villagers.

Georgie was dazed, as much by her own part in the argument as anyone else's, and Nola's shocked expression was enough to know that she too had taken herself by surprise. They stumbled back towards their stalls as a growl of thunder yawned out across the fete. Somewhere, Georgie was aware of people around her pulling the stall down, gathering up the samples, shoving everything into bags, pulling the cover from it, then two of the men dragging it to the perimeter of the green.

Suddenly, she was standing there, alone, with her bags at her feet as the heavens opened and rain came crashing down, spiky and unrelenting against her skin, so that before she could think, she was already soaked through. Someone pulled her up. When she looked up, she saw that it was Aiden. He was dragging her away from the centre of the green, towards his jeep and then bundling her into the back seat, next to Iris, who was weeping as if her life were over.

Nola was already sitting in the front seat, her neck rigid with tension.

The whole thing, this fight between them, this toxic connection felt as if it was falling away, disintegrating from within, robbed of the silence that had allowed it to ferment for far too long. It was melting like the witch in *The Wizard of Oz* with a glass of water, fizzing out of them. Georgie could feel it dissolving so it left her only with the gritty remains rather than the lifetime of simmering resentment that had marked out every moment since Myles Cutler had come between them all those years ago.

'Oh my God,' Iris murmured, because strangely, there was no need to shout, somehow the lashing rain on the windows was muffled so it was as if they were sitting in the deepest most drawn-out silence Georgie had ever experienced. 'What have we done to each other?'

Nola began to cry, a soft pathetic keening sound as if they'd lost their parents and each other all over again.

'It's all right, Nola,' Georgie said, reaching out to her, but Nola shook her hand away. And in that moment, Georgie wondered if anything would ever be all right again. They'd let themselves and their parents down. Among the faces of the crowd who had stood around them, Georgie remembered Stephen Leather. Oh, God, the look of disappointment in his eyes was enough to make her want to throw herself onto the ground and cry like a baby for all the damage they'd done to each other over the years. But it was too late now, wasn't it?

* * *

Nola pushed open the heavy door of the jeep. She couldn't get away from the fete or, more accurately, her sisters quickly enough. The truth was, she'd prefer to get double pneumonia than sit there for a moment longer with the pair of them.

Initially, all Nola could think was, *Thank God, it's the beginning of the summer holidays soon*. And then it struck her – the drama school. What parent would want to send their child for her to teach them now? The rain was driving down hard on her back, almost painful through her thin summer clothes, but it didn't matter. It felt to Nola as if nothing mattered anymore. By the time she'd reached the end of the green, she was soaked through to the skin, but she had no intention of turning back. It was horrendous. She'd actually hit her sister. She tried to make sense of what had just happened. They'd had a screaming match, at the top of their voices, like common alley cats and, worse, for the whole village to see. Nola was mortified. She'd never be able to show her face in Ballycove again.

She raced away from the fete, blinded by tears and shame, but it was no good. She became disorientated as a shriek of lightning struck the ground just beyond the village. She kept running, still racing towards it, knowing that it was the nearest route back to the house. In the middle of the village the streets were deserted. No-one but Nola would be stupid or desperate enough to be out in this storm.

'Nola,' a familiar voice cracked along the road behind her, making her heart sink even further, and she swivelled about to see the school principal open his car door to give her a lift and rescue her from the rain at least.

'Gary.' She wiped the tears from her face; she must look a complete mess now.

'Get in, I'll drop you home.'

'No, I need to walk…' She couldn't get into his car, not just because she felt so wet and weary she was little more than a standing puddle, but also, she wasn't entirely sure she could take even the tiniest amount of kindness at this moment.

'Are you all right? I saw what happened and I…' He moved the car forward, along the path beside her as another roar of thunder bellowed from the clouds, which seemed to hang so low now, she might touch them if she just reached up her hand.

'I'm fine. It was just… sisters, you know…' She tried to make light of it, but there was a growing emptiness inside her that she knew no acting could cover over.

'But you hit her.'

'Yes.' She stopped, examined the ground at her feet, biting her lip hard to stop herself from crying. 'It was nothing.' Then, from the bottom of her heart: 'It was terrible. It's been brewing up for years. We're as bad as each other really, but the air had to be cleared.' Her voice trailed off. It wasn't good enough. Not for a teacher who was meant to be an example to students. And today, this fete was filled with schoolkids and parents. Bloody hell. What on earth had she done?

'Well, if you're sure you're all right?' Gary said, but she felt him survey her in a whole new way. 'We need to talk about it when we get back to school. Will you pop into the office before taking your first class?'

'Of course,' she said, and then she knew her job at the

school, which she'd loved so much, was over. She'd messed everything up by being completely stupid. How on earth had she let Georgie and Iris bait her into letting herself down like that?

Her anger at her two sisters had dissipated by the time she reached the empty lane that was a shortcut to Soldier Hill House, and all she was left with was a deflated sense of failure. All was finally lost. She couldn't stay in Ballycove now – not that she had actually considered it beyond the summer, but maybe she'd been getting used to the idea that there was a choice. At least, for a short while, there seemed to be an alternative to the empty place London had become to her.

'Nola, Nola.' Another voice, not the principal this time, but instead, Aiden Barry running up the narrow road, as if he was out for a leisurely jog. 'Please, wait a minute – just let me check that you're all right.' He was beside her then, holding her away from him, the rain pelting down on both of them as if it might finally rub them out completely.

'I'm just…' She was too empty to cry, much less make any excuse for what she'd just done.

'I know, it was terrible,' he said and then he pulled her into him, his arms around her, holding her so tight that she imagined she could hear his heart hammering against his chest. He was warm, in spite of the freezing rain, and he smelled of soap and the merest hint of leather, as if he'd just taken off a jacket and the scent remained. It was calming, being encircled in his arms, in spite of the rain and the fact that they were meant to dislike each other and her ragged breath that made her whole body shake. 'But there's nothing you can do about it now, apart from maybe kiss and make up.' He was murmuring into her hair and, for a moment, it felt as if everything halted and Nola stood back, studying him as if he was some rare species. Their eyes locked; they were being slowly drawn together by some invisible magnet with a force she couldn't stop, even if she wanted to, just one more centimetre and their lips might touch. A crack of lightning, breaking against one of the tall trees in a nearby field, made her jump backwards, suddenly bringing her to her senses.

'I have to go,' she shouted and pulled away from him to race back to the house. She was running away, but there was nothing else she could do at this point, was there?

'Nola,' she heard him call after her, but she knew she had to keep running because staying near him could lead her into something she was certain that neither of them really wanted.

She leaned her whole body against the front door to push it open. She'd never felt so emptied out in her whole life, as if every last drop of her was spent physically, emotionally and spiritually. In her room, she peeled off her clothes, left them in a puddle on the floor. Even as she collapsed on the bed she felt her mind shutting down. She had ruined everything.

No matter how nice Gary was, he would have no other choice but to sack her. She had displayed a serious lack of judgement. It was unprofessional conduct and there was no getting around it; anyone who assaulted a family member in full view of the entire school was hardly a shining example to kids in their care.

Nola closed her eyes, sinking not into sleep, but rather

into a comatose state of unthinking. She just had to blot everything out; because she'd really hit rock bottom now and there was no hiding the mess she'd made of things from her sisters this time.

14

It was the strangest sensation, but the house had that same feeling that Iris remembered as a small child: safe and insulating, as if there was no danger that could penetrate its thick walls, no worry that couldn't be eased if she sat near the warm fire with her mother's arms about her. She moved automatically towards the kitchen. The ride home was little more than a blurry memory. Georgie had taken the wheel of Aiden's jeep and the storm was so incessant that they could see no further than a few feet beyond the end of the bonnet. And all the time, the devastating insults that they'd shouted at each other earlier played about her thoughts on a seemingly endless loop.

What if Georgie and Nola really did hate her as much as it seemed they did? Was there any way at all that she could make things right? The truth was, she was the architect of most of the destruction between them. It was her blind acceptance of every word – every lie – that Myles had told her over the years that had led them to this point. She shivered. What on earth had she done?

Looking back, of course Nola would never have gone after Myles. Nola was a young and beautiful woman and even then, Myles had been the sort of man who was a little too aware of the other women around them, a little too caught up with his own attractiveness to them. Wasn't that why she'd cut off every female friend who had ever come close to them – so they wouldn't be a threat?

Facing up to the reality of what she'd allowed her life to descend into over the years just so she could hang on to Myles, was not as devastating as she might have feared. In fact, it was even a little liberating. And for the first time in a very long time, Iris began to smile. Freedom from Myles's control over her was suddenly within her grasp; she knew exactly what she had to do if things were ever to be set right.

The rain outside still drove relentlessly against the thin window opposite and as Iris stood there, cold and shivering, with her clothes dripping into a small lake at her feet, in her mind she began to formulate the apology that was long overdue to her sisters.

First, though, she would change out of these soaking clothes. A long, hard shiver overtook her and she sneezed loudly. God, she'd never felt so cold too her bones. She raced upstairs, feeling lighter than she had in years.

It would mean eating a huge slice of humble pie. There was nothing else for it, if she wanted to rescue anything from this time and of course make sure that Myles couldn't touch Soldier Hill House or the Delahaye inheritance. She couldn't let that happen. Since she'd arrived back here, it had been like a balm, soothing as much as London had irritated the emptiness in her. She hadn't even known she needed healing. It was the village and the sea air. It was Soldier Hill House and the memories that wrapped around her and made her feel secure in a way she hadn't for years. She had to come clean with Georgie and Nola, even if it was the last thing she wanted to do. She had to face up to the resentment and jealousy she'd harboured all these years – against Georgie for her success and independence and Nola for the misconception that she wanted to steal Myles from her. And most of all, she had to tell them that her marriage was over.

Georgie knew it was D-Day when she saw Iris's expression as she stood in the doorway of the drawing room that evening. It was time to finally end this feuding that had festered between them for far too long.

Looking at Iris tipped something over in Georgie. It reminded her of when they'd lost their mother. They were young and they knew it was coming, but to this day, she could not dampen down the utter devastation she had felt when their father had sat them down to tell them their mother had died.

'I'm so sorry about earlier,' she said, dropping to the sofa and pulling Iris down next to her in an action of familiarity that took them both by surprise. 'I shouldn't have—'

'No, I'm sorry, really, about everything,' Iris said, and she was laughing and crying all at once, as much overwhelmed by emotion as Georgie felt. Georgie hiccupped and she too was crying, but it was with a remarkable sense of relief that she couldn't have imagined existed before, much less that she'd experience it. They sat there, on that sofa, surrounded by the trappings of their childhood with their arms wrapped around each other, just as they would have done so often as girls. When their tears subsided, only a sense of utter release remained and Georgie held her sister at arm's length for a moment. 'There's something you need to tell me, isn't there?' she said quietly. It was time to be open with each other and Georgie wanted to celebrate Iris's pregnancy news with her.

'It's Myles,' Iris said flatly.

'Oh? Is he all right?' Because Georgie's first thought was that there had been some terrible accident and she found herself thinking that no matter how much she disliked the man, she wouldn't wish anything bad had happened to him.

'No.' Iris laughed bitterly. 'No, Myles is more than all right. Actually, you might say he's never been better.' She looked Georgie in the eye, as if steeling herself for some big revelation. 'We're getting a divorce.'

'Oh, Iris. I'm…' She stopped, because she wasn't sure what she felt. 'I'm sorry to hear that. I mean, there's no point in pretending that I ever liked him, but I know you loved him and we both know what it's like to lose someone you love.' She glanced at the piano, thinking of their mother. Iseult Delahaye had been many good things, but at her centre was a simple kindness that drew people to her; it marked her out in a way that made people remember her, even now so many years after her death. And now, Georgie knew she had to draw on some measure of that kindness, which for so long had been beyond her grasp.

'It's funny. I thought I'd be devastated. I thought my whole world would fall in on top of me, but it hasn't. It turns out losing Myles is nothing like losing our mother or even our father. After the initial shock, which took a lot of getting over, well, who knows? Perhaps one day, I'll see it as a bit of a relief?'

'Still, though.' Georgie bit her lip for a moment, because there was something she knew she had to say. It was now or never, and she'd learned her lesson that night at the cottage. 'Iris, I'm sorry.'

'You're sorry? Myles is the one who should be apologising here.' Iris smiled.

'No, really. The way I've behaved over the years, it's been terrible, just because I didn't like him. I shouldn't have hurt you, just because... Well, the truth is, over the years, maybe in some ways I've grown to envy you and your marriage to Myles.'

'You envied me?' Iris's eyes had opened so wide it looked as if they might pop out of her head.

'Yes, of course. You seemed to have it all – or at least, everything you had set your heart on. Whereas I... well, all I had was a job where people hated me and an empty apartment that I dreaded going back to at the end of the day.'

'Yes, well, you know what they say, be careful what you wish for.' Iris looked towards the fireplace now, and as Georgie studied her side profile, she noticed the soft lines that had appeared about her sister's eyes. Suddenly, it was far more obvious that Iris's life had not been as easy as she'd always believed it was. 'Leopards and spots, eh?' Iris smiled sadly. 'Thanks, Georgie. The idea of telling you and Nola was actually the worst part of coming back here. I had hoped I wouldn't have to mention it at all, that we would all go our separate ways at the end of this and you'd be none the wiser.'

'When did it happen?'

'Oh, about five minutes before I got the news that Dad had passed away,' Iris said. 'He met someone else.'

'Of course he did. I told you, he was never good enough for you,' Georgie spat out and then she realised, the last thing Iris needed now was to hear *I told you so*. 'Sorry, sorry, you don't need to hear that, but you know what I mean. You deserved better than that.'

'I did. I do. Anyway, we both know that meeting someone else probably wasn't something new for Myles.' Iris looked down at her hands folded on her laps. She'd taken off her wedding ring this evening. 'The worst part is that he got her pregnant and...' A small tear ran down Iris's cheek. 'Oh, God. I knew this would be difficult.' She took a tissue from her sleeve and blew her nose loudly, mopping up the tears from her eyes at the same time. 'Anyway, Amanda – that's her name, by the way – is about to pop any day and Myles is demanding his share and most of mine, of all our assets.'

'Oh my God, and he's left you to be with her, when you're pregnant too...' The words had flown from her before she could stop them. Georgie could only see red now. 'That bastard.' She cursed. 'I'll go over there and wring his bloody neck myself, I swear.'

'Pregnant? Me?' Iris gasped.

Georgie winced. 'Sorry. We've known for a while. Nola spotted the app on your phone and...'

'You thought I was pregnant because of the app?' Iris

threw her head back and began to laugh. It was a strange sound and it alarmed Georgie. Had this finally pushed her poor sister over the edge? She waited a minute, wondered about getting Iris a drink, something to calm her perhaps? But the last thing she wanted was to push her sister into an early labour with gin on top of the stress of earlier. 'That's the funniest thing.' Iris wiped her eyes eventually.

'What is?'

'You thinking I'm pregnant.' She shook her head, but then she stopped laughing and a little sadness crept across her features. 'If only…'

'So, you're not pregnant?' Georgie felt a little tug. It was disappointment; she'd been looking forward to a niece or nephew.

'No. I'm afraid not. I sort of gave up on the idea years ago, but now I've had plenty of time to regret it and it's too late.' She shook her head sadly. 'It's stupid, I don't even know why I downloaded the app. It's only made me more bloody miserable knowing exactly what's going on with their baby and knowing I'm never going to have that.'

'It's never too late, Iris,' Georgie said softly, because it was the one thing she was absolutely sure of. 'Anyway, being free of Myles is probably the best thing if you wanted to have a baby, isn't it?'

'I…' Iris stopped for a moment and her features lifted into something closer to a smile. 'Oh God! I had that same weird notion only a few days ago,' she said softly. 'But the problem for now is that Myles is being a pig about the division of our assets and you can imagine what he'd be like if he realised that he might have a possible stake in this place.'

'Sweet divine and all that's holy, what a total mess. Talk about terrible timing.' Georgie sighed. 'Well, there's no way. There are things we can do to make sure he can't touch this place, I'm certain of that. We can talk to Stephen, we could make it so this place is tied up for as long as we need to or… I don't know, we'll think of something.'

'Myles doesn't know Dad has died.'

'Well, that's something, at least,' Georgie murmured.

'He hasn't a clue about anything to do with his will or he'd probably be over here demanding it be carved four ways if he thought he had a leg to stand on.'

'God, so he really is as horrible as we always thought,' Georgie murmured, although it wasn't really surprising. 'You need a good divorce solicitor.' She was thinking of Stephen Leather, but he would be hopeless up against some smart London lawyer who knew the divorce courts like the back of their hands.

'I have one. She's very good. She's very much out to make sure that Myles gets what he deserves, which is half the current value of the house and nothing more.'

'And what about this place?'

'Well, as long as Dad's will hasn't gone into probate by the time the divorce is finalised, there's nothing for him to claim against, is there?'

'And is it likely to be done and dusted by then?'

'It looked likely until today at the fete.' Iris sighed. 'The thing is, Georgie, I didn't tell him I was coming over here. I've rented out our house to keep the mortgage paid and I've thrown in my job, but he thinks I'm renting a grotty bedsit in London and nothing much else has changed.'

'Wow,' Georgie said. 'You've just gone up about a hundred times in my estimation. I can't believe you just walked away from everything like that.'

'It wasn't hard, believe me. I haven't been happy in London for years. When all this happened, I realised the only reason I was still there was because of Myles. Coming here was a great opportunity to clear my head, reset everything so I can start again.' Iris smiled and Georgie knew it was the first genuine smile she'd managed since they sat down.

'So when all of this is over' – Georgie looked around the drawing room – 'you might actually stay on here in Ballycove?'

'I just might,' Iris said, and Georgie thought, why wouldn't she? After all, when the bright lights of London began to fade, what was there to keep either of them there? Hadn't she seen it herself when she'd walked out of Sandstone and Mellon? What was there to do, but hang about her apartment? Step back onto the same treadmill again and keep on going until one day you prematurely dropped due to stress and feeling deeply unfulfilled? Georgie shivered involuntarily, and she pushed away the thoughts for another time – she needed to listen to Iris now.

'It would be the perfect place to bring up a baby...'

'It would, but *I'm* not bloody pregnant.' Iris started to laugh again.

'No, but it doesn't mean you couldn't adopt, though, does it?'

'Maybe...' The smallest smile twitched at the edge of Iris's mouth and she sat there, perfectly still for a moment until it grew into something more genuine than any spark of happiness Georgie remembered in her sister for years. 'In an ideal world, but I can't think about that at the moment.' Iris sighed. 'The thing is, Myles wants to go for mediation now.'

'Sorry?' Georgie was brought back to her words with a bang. 'He wants to go for mediation?'

'Yes.'

'But why? Hasn't he already done enough to you? Does this solicitor you have not realise what's at stake here?' Georgie thought she'd happily *mediate* him the right way and when she'd have finished with him, there wouldn't be a lot left for any more running about with other women.

'It's typical of Myles. He's playing games, but Muriel is not giving in on anything less than half of all our assets. He obviously thought he could wheedle a lot more out of me, that I'd just roll over and he'd take the house with a small payment in lieu of half the original purchase price. He wants the car – that I paid for. Let's face it, if he could organise it so I'd pop in a couple of times each week to make his dinner and do a spot of babysitting, he'd probably go after that too.'

'He probably would,' Georgie agreed ruefully.

'What's this about Myles? He rang here a few days ago and sounded a little strange.' Nola was standing at the door to the drawing room. She looked dreadful, pale and fragile; her eyes hollowed out as if she'd just escaped some sort of torture regime.

'He rang?' Iris echoed and she drained to the colour of death in an instant. 'What exactly did you say to him?'

***

Myles Cutler was at the very bottom of Nola's worries this evening, but of course, typically, when she walked into the sitting room, it was all about Myles and Iris.

Well, the truth was, after today, she couldn't give a flying monkey for any of them, least of all, Myles.

'Seriously, whatever he's told you, I was perfectly civil to him, which let me tell you is more than he bloody deserves...' she snapped, but she caught a warning flash from Georgie and stopped mid-sentence. 'Anyway, not that it probably matters to either of you, but it looks like I've lost my job at the school thanks to what happened today at the fete. I'll probably be suspended if not sacked.' Nola felt so disappointed she wanted to cry all over again.

'It can't be that bad,' Georgie soothed.

'Isn't it? I met Gary Cotter and he didn't need to say it exactly, but our behaviour – *my* behaviour – is hardly the example he wants his students following...' Her voice trembled with miserable humiliation. 'I basically assaulted my sister on the village green.' The job was coming to an end anyway, there were only a few weeks left in the term and the plan had always been to return to London. She wasn't sure what she was getting so upset about. 'I suppose, it's only meant to be a stopgap after all.' She was trying for bravado and failing badly. But maybe, it wasn't just the idea of losing the job she loved, maybe it was also the fact that she believed she'd scuppered her drama school plans for the summer also – and that was a very bitter pill to swallow.

'But you've really enjoyed working at the school and everyone says that you're brilliant,' Iris said in a surprising show of loyalty.

'What does it matter anyway?' Nola sighed.

'It matters a great bloody deal.' Georgie's head was high, as if she was ready for battle. 'Don't tell me that you're just going to roll over and let them sack you because of this.'

'She's right, Nola. I know our behaviour today was terrible and I probably feel worse than any of you for my part in it, but that doesn't mean that you can't go in there and explain the sort of pressure we've been under.'

'The way *we've* put *each other* under pressure,' Georgie murmured and this was met with silence, because of course it was completely true. 'I'd be happy to go in with you and take full responsibility for driving you to it,' she said and Nola hated to admit it, but she knew that with Georgie in her corner, she'd feel a lot stronger. 'The thing is, Nola, this was a blip. You're not the sort of person who goes about slapping people and it turns out you're a very good teacher, everyone says so. Those kids are getting so much out of the time you've put into them.'

'She's right: it would have been too bloody annoying to admit it before, but I can't go ten paces through the village but someone is singing your praises.' Iris managed a wobbly smile.

'Really?' Nola couldn't help but feel a glimmer of something hopeful in her. 'I suppose everyone was very nice at the fete. If all the families who signed up for the drama school showed up, I'd have to think about running several classes a week, and quite a few talked about how much they'd love something to run the whole year through as an after-school club.'

'Really.' Iris nodded. 'Gary Cotter would be a fool to lose you from his staff and I'm sure he knows it too. He might have to jump through hoops because of the school rules, but it doesn't mean you can't help him make sure that at the end of it all, there's a way of reinstating you.'

'I don't know, I mean, it's not as if I intend to stay on the staff team into next year.' Again the doubt was setting in. God, she'd love a big glass of gin now, but it wasn't fair having a drink when they were trying not to tempt Iris who seemed far too easily led astray considering she was pregnant.

'Well, I do.' Georgie said. 'You're not just giving up without a fight, even if we have to put your boxing gloves on and shove you into the ring ourselves.'

'Come on,' Iris said, as if reading her mind. She poured out three large glasses and handed one with far too much gin and not enough tonic to Nola, and then she smiled, taking a long lingering sip of her own.

'Are you sure you should be drinking when…' The words were out before Nola could help it. They weren't meant to know that Iris was pregnant after all and the last thing she wanted was all-out war tonight, it would be the final straw.

'Oh, dear Nola, we have so much to tell you…' Georgie and Iris both started to laugh like she hadn't seen them laugh in years.

'But first, I have to say sorry.' Iris cleared her throat. 'You were right – I should have believed you and not Myles all those years ago. Maybe, deep down in my heart, I even knew it then, but I didn't want to believe it.' She stopped for a moment, and Nola watched as a great shadow of remorse crossed her features, making her look older than her years for a flash. 'The truth is, even before I came in on him with you that day, I had my doubts that there hadn't been others, but he always managed to convince me. I suppose I was so blindly in love with him, I just wanted to believe him.'

'But not anymore?' Nola couldn't quite believe she was hearing this and yet, in some part of her brain, she knew that for Iris to have such a complete turnaround would have taken more than just a screaming match to make her see sense.

'No. My eyes have finally been opened. We've split up. He's been seeing someone. He's having a baby with her and—'

'I'm so sorry.' Nola dropped to the sofa next to Iris. She wanted to throw her arms around the sister that until this second she'd disliked so intensely for so long. 'That's...' Terrible, she wanted to say, but she'd seen first-hand exactly what Myles was like and the only surprise was that it had taken so long for Iris to see through him. 'At least you have the baby to look forward to...' The words slipped out before she had time to think of how many nets of irony might be caught up in Iris's own pregnancy now.

'Oh, Nola, Iris isn't pregnant,' Georgie said softly. 'We'll explain everything, but first, I owe you an apology too...'

'No, Georgie, if what you said was true at the fete – then it's me who should be saying sorry to you. I never got your message all those years ago and you were right, I was just floating along, surrounding myself with the wrong crowd. That squat... well, it was... not a good place for me. And

Benji…' Nola shook her head sadly, remembering a fleeting fling with a man who was probably still squatting and still forgetting to pass on messages. 'Let's just say, yours wasn't the only message he never passed along.'

'I should have called you back, checked why you didn't show up, but I just assumed you couldn't be bothered.'

'Let's face it, you were probably right to assume the worst. At that point, I was a total flake and even if you'd managed to get me the best job in London, I probably wouldn't have truly appreciated it anyway.' That was the truth. 'The thing is, even once my career *did* take off, I missed both of you so much. I wouldn't admit it at the time, but…' Nola stopped. It was too late to look back now. But she knew that later when she'd lost everything, there were years when she'd have given anything for an office job with regular hours and a decent wage.

'It wasn't even that you didn't turn up that bothered me the most,' Georgie said, staring at the faded rug on the floor at her feet. 'It was… well, the truth was, I was jealous of you too. I was jealous of both of you, because I was lonely, and you both seemed to have found people to share your lives with.'

'You were jealous of me?' Nola was stunned.

'Of course. Everywhere you go, you seem to gather up friends as easily as if you were collecting butterflies on a summer's day. I mean, even today, at the fete – people flock to you, whereas I've never had that.'

'Oh, Georgie…'

'It's true. At work, they hated the sight of me and I had no social life. There weren't any real connections with people.

It's one of the reasons I ended up coming over here so often. I'd have been completely alone, if it wasn't for Dad.'

'I never realised,' Nola said, but of course, how could she have, she had been so taken up with her own worries. 'It looks like we all made a bit of a mess of things...'

'But it worked out for the best in the end. I mean, you got that part in the soap and you were really famous...' Iris's words petered off.

'I suppose, it worked out exactly as it was supposed to,' Nola said. 'And now, tell me what's going on with your baby. I saw the app!'

'My baby app?' Iris spluttered and she began to laugh and then she pulled Nola onto the sofa next to them and began to explain exactly why they were laughing and crying all at the same time.

It felt like the reunion they should have had years earlier, but better late than never. It was only later that Nola remembered the call from Myles and she explained she'd only picked it up by chance. Who used landlines anymore? And of course, then, Nola had no idea that Iris's marriage had imploded. She'd just popped back to the house at lunchtime to pick up a book she'd borrowed from the library. The phone rang just as she was leaving. A London number, so of course, naïvely she hoped it was news on one of the many submissions she'd made to countless agents before she'd left the city. Myles Cutler was an obvious disappointment. Looking for Iris, of course, Nola had just told him he should try her mobile and then slammed down the phone.

The problem was of course, Myles could take her answer either way. He might just believe that Iris was wandering about London and Nola had absolutely no idea where she was, or he might twig to something in the impatience of her voice. And even Nola knew that no matter how things were between them, the last thing they needed was Myles here putting in his two cents' worth and cutting between them as he'd always done.

'I'll go with you,' Georgie said. 'To the mediation.'

'You can't come to mediation with me and Myles,' Iris spluttered, but Nola could see she was thankful of the support.

'Count me in too,' Nola said; she'd love to wipe the smug smile from his face and she might as well. It's not as if she'd have a job here after today's performance anyway.

'I can go along with you and sit outside in whatever reception area there is to wait. We can make a show of unity. If this solicitor isn't enough to intimidate him, it'd be no harm for him to know you have extra back-up that he isn't counting on,' Georgie said with determination.

'Really?' Iris said. 'You'd do that for me?'

'Absolutely, and I don't have to say one word. Just let him know that we're behind you.'

'She's right,' Nola said.

'Nola, pet.' Iris turned to her youngest sister. 'He knows you're here. It's probably better if we let him think you're back here for a while, not in London. You don't have to come, really.' She was probably right, even if she didn't have a job to turn up for, neither had she the money to fritter away on flights to London at the drop of a hat, especially if she wasn't teaching anymore.

Georgie nodded. 'There's no point in him twigging anything more than he might already suspect.'

It was only later, as she was turning in for the night, that Nola began to realise how hard it must have been for Iris to tell them about her impending divorce and finally admit to what a complete shit Myles had been all along. Nola had never liked him, even before he'd tried to seduce her. It had taken years to face up to the fact that she'd done nothing wrong, but now she could see that was a measure of the sort of manipulator Myles was. Somehow, she'd been left feeling as if she'd done something wrong, when all she'd done was push him away. Still, even she wouldn't have guessed he'd sink this low.

Georgie had really surprised her by being so nice about it all. Perhaps the old Georgie, the sister she'd loved so dearly, who had been her fearless champion when they were kids, the one she'd almost forgotten had ever existed, was still here. Deep beneath that hardened reserve, the sister she remembered looking out for her and holding her close when their mother died was almost covered over, but maybe she was there all along, only Nola had been too blind to see it.

Over the midterm break, calm descended over the house between the three sisters, as if they were each feeling their way along this fresh new start between them. For the first time in years, Nola felt at home, even if she had to face that meeting she'd been dreading since the fete. As usual, the timing was horrible – it was also the day that Iris was due to meet Myles in London.

'Don't worry,' Iris said. 'I'll drop you down to school in the car before we go to the airport.' Nola was grateful, especially since Iris was meant to be catching her flight in less than two hours. And she hadn't been relishing the idea of walking: the tail end of a storm from the previous evening was still battering away at the windows as they finished breakfast.

'I just wish we were at the other end of today…' Iris sighed before draining her cup of tea.

It was obvious Iris was dreading seeing Myles again, and Nola regretted she couldn't go with her and Georgie. 'It'll be fine. What chance has he got up against you two?'

'I'm only sorry we won't be here for you when you get home, Nola,' Georgie said, but then she smiled. 'Not that you'll need us, of course.'

'She's right. We'll be thinking of you, though,' Iris said, looking out the window. 'Oh look, Aiden is here.'

The most Nola could manage was an inelegant snort between mouthfuls of her cereal.

'Are you ready, Nola?' Aiden Barry was standing at the door, rain dripping from his nose, but probably otherwise dry, since he seemed to be wearing oilskins designed more for a salmon angler than a farmer.

'Excuse me?' Nola glanced from one expectant face to another. 'Are you here for me? Because I have to go to work, so whatever hare-brained plan you have, I can tell you right now…'

'And where else do you think I'd want to bring you at this hour of the day? Hollywood?'

'You've come to give me a lift?'

'I've come because you don't have a car and I'm giving a talk to the agricultural science class about the importance of organic farming to the environment. I thought you might prefer it to getting soaked to the skin.' Iris handed him a cup of tea from the pot on the table. 'Ta,' he said, smiling at her.

'Well, you needn't have bothered, because Iris is taking me.' Nola knew she sounded like a pampered brat, but after the fete she wasn't sure exactly where she stood with him and she wasn't keen to have any long and deep conversations this morning, when she had enough to worry about already.

'Not if I can help it,' Iris said disloyally, smiling at Aiden. 'You're welcome to her. I've a thousand things to do here and we both know that I'll only put them off if I have an excuse to get out the door.'

'So, it's like that, is it?' Nola smiled because she didn't want to stress Iris out any more than she already was. Honestly, she'd prefer to walk than sit in a car with Aiden, but then a huge crack of lightning lit up the room, dimming the lights for a long drawn-out moment.

'I'd say that wasn't more than a mile away.' Aiden looked out the window, but his voice was almost drowned by the roar of thunder that bellowed out long and threatening. And they all knew that regardless of what she said, there was no way Nola could walk to school in that.

It was a mercifully wordless drive to school. Conversation, if they'd been up for it, would have to be at full pitch anyway, since the roar of the summer storm was so loud that it would muffle out any sound.

Aiden pulled the jeep up in front of a side entrance that was little used, but was situated on a corridor near the headmaster's office. That was thoughtful, she admitted grudgingly to herself, rather than making her do a walk of shame all the way through the school to get to the principal's office.

'Listen,' he said as he switched off the engine.

'I haven't the time and if it's about the other day. Well, I'm not sure that there's anything more to say,' she snapped.

'No, well, yes maybe there are things we should say, but what I wanted to say to you was good luck, that's all.'

'Thank you,' Nola said softly.

'You won't need it, you know. You're the best drama teacher they've ever had here. Everyone says so and Gary Cotter knows it too. Go in there with your head up as if you have a thousand other offers waiting for you, and it'll be all right.'

Nola was temporarily stunned by his kind words.

'And as for the other day, I'm sorry, I didn't mean to... We're good? Yeah?' He leaned over and opened the door for her.

'Sure,' she said faintly, but when she heard the jeep door bang closed behind her as she ran up the steps in the pouring rain, she wasn't entirely sure that his words hadn't given her a feeling of disappointment, rather than relief. Had she actually wanted him to kiss her that day in the midst of all the other drama that her life had unfurled into? Had she really? Of course not. She shook herself off when she reached the safety of the corridor. That was madness. The last thing she needed now was to go falling for Aiden Barry. Soon she'd be heading back to London and a brand-new life a million miles away from the mortification of what happened in Ballycove a week earlier. That was what she had to think about now and forget about Aiden and any other nonsense like drama schools or staying in Ballycove when there was nothing here to stay for.

15

Iris wasn't sure how she could look and act normal for the mediation session with Myles. She'd been up since four-thirty in the morning and any notion of sleeping while they flew were dashed thanks to the worst turbulence she'd ever experienced on a flight. Even Georgie looked completely shattered after it.

Myles was already there when they arrived. It took her a second to place him, because he looked somehow strangely so much less of himself than she remembered. He was sitting in the corner, scrunched up defensively against the rest of the empty waiting room, reading a gardening magazine, when they both knew he had zero interest in any activity that meant getting his hands dirty. When she arrived, he looked slightly startled, obviously thrown by the presence of Georgie at her side. Iris didn't think she'd ever heard such grudging greetings between two people as she did between Georgie and Myles. How could she have chosen this pathetic excuse of a man over her sisters all those years ago?

'Right, let's get this over with,' Iris said, leading the way into the neutral greys of a room that was empty apart from three chairs and a pot plant. Catherine Dickson – the mediator – was a fragile-looking woman, with silver hair that marked her out as perhaps being in her seventies, but her eyes moved rapidly over them, as if assessing them and taking in all she needed to know with one quick glance. Catherine opened the meeting with a short time for reflection, an opportunity for everyone to catch their breath. Iris thought that she might faint; such was the pressure to relax. The silence of the room amplified each breath, making her feel claustrophobic.

'Now, so we're all clear. The intention of this session is not to patch up this marriage,' Catherine said in a way that brooked no discussion. 'The future of your marriage is of no concern in this space; what is of concern is that going forward you are able to communicate with each other in a more open and trustworthy manner.'

'That's right.' Myles smiled his smarmiest grin. Iris almost snorted.

'I'm given to understand that currently, there is some disagreement about the future distribution of your shared assets?' Catherine asked, looking at Iris as if she might have the definitive answer to her question.

'Yes. I thought that our assets at the end of our marriage would be divided equally. That seems fair to me, at least,' Iris said.

'And, Myles?' Catherine smiled at Myles and although

she looked like a harmless old pensioner, Iris could almost hear the soundtrack to *Jaws* gearing up from the far corner of the room.

'Well, yes, but here's the thing: I'm about to have a baby, and we're living in a tiny bedsit. It seems such a waste that we can't just move into my house and get on with things...'

'I'm sorry,' Iris interrupted and for a moment, she wondered if she shouldn't raise her hand like at school. 'But, it's not as if I'm living there myself and by renting it out, we're paying the mortgage.' She didn't add that she didn't think she could bear to stand in the place ever again. 'There's even a small surplus, which I've left there to make additional payments on the mortgage before it's sold or to split evenly between us, which I think is fair.' She almost sounded contrite.

'So, you're living elsewhere?'

'Yes, for now. With my sister,' Iris said evenly. It was not a lie, but it was hardly her fault if Myles construed that she was staying in some box room in Georgie's London apartment, rather than holed up with both her sisters in the west of Ireland.

'The lady who came along with you today?' Catherine asked.

'Yes. She's been a great support.' She enjoyed seeing Myles's face crumple into something that signalled the fact that he knew he was no match for Georgie Delahaye.

'So...' Catherine looked at her watch and Iris supposed you had to be a master at keeping things on time and on topic in this job. She had a similar agenda herself, if the truth were known. 'We were talking about your baby?' Catherine turned to Myles.

'Well, yes, you see, we have a baby due and there's no way I can afford to buy another house and now Iris is insisting that she wants to take the car off me and...'

'Can't you rent like the rest of London? Live within your means, or move a little further out? Have you thought about other ways to figure out your future living arrangements with your new partner that don't involve inconveniencing your soon to be ex-wife? And what's this about a car?' Catherine raised an eyebrow as she asked.

'Well, I need the car for work,' he said, jumping on the only part of that sentence that maybe didn't put so much pressure on him to take responsibility for himself and his future family. And in that moment, Iris looked at him and felt deeply sorry for Amanda Prescott and even more so for their as yet unborn child. Pity was the last thing she expected to feel for the woman who, until so recently, she blamed for causing her such pain. Of course, she'd been wrong; she could see that now. Amanda had done no more than become an exchange prisoner in the cell that Iris had for too long feared to leave. She took a deep breath, knew she had missed half of what he was saying.

'Are you okay? Would you like to take a break?' Catherine leaned forward and patted the armrest of the chair that Iris was sitting on.

'No. No need, I just... Sorry, can you say that again, Myles?' And he looked at her as if it was some sort of trick.

'I... well, I was just saying, that I need the car for work. I was explaining that I work mainly freelance these days for the news channel, and if I'm not there to cover the story first, they'll pick up the footage from whoever is.'

'Ah, yes, I see.' Catherine looked across at Iris.

'Yes. That's true, except I paid for the car. It took me three years to pay it off. I took out a loan in the credit union and paid for it each week from my wages, the same as I've done for every car since we got married.' She stopped for a moment, a flash of anger rising up in her. 'Actually, when I think about it, I basically paid for everything. I bought all the groceries, paid the electric, the gas and the insurance for both the house and the car.' How had she not added all that up before? When she was outlining her life with Myles, somehow the sundry details had become blurred or lost amid all the bigger-ticket items of their marriage, like fidelity, and honesty and, oh yes, love.

'Have you outlined all of this for your own solicitor?' Catherine asked softly.

'Actually, no.' Iris thought with the uncomfortable feeling that the woman was reading her mind.

'Don't worry. Mediation often brings up the most unlikely things. Lucky you came along, eh?' She smiled at Myles, who looked as if he was fit to burst with rage.

By the end of the meeting, Iris felt much better. She thanked Catherine sincerely while they stood at the doorway watching Myles stomp off, probably back to the car that he knew for almost certain now he was not entitled to keep without making some sort of contribution towards it.

'It's not about the money, you know,' Iris said to Georgie later.

'I know that,' Georgie said.

'It's more like, I feel he's already taken so much from me, I can't bear to walk away feeling as if he's just plundered and left me like some tragic victim,' she said, because she knew she'd been a fool for far too long as far as her marriage was concerned. If she was ever going to build up her own self-esteem, she had to see this through and feel she'd come out of it on her own terms. Then, Georgie laughed, the most irreverent sound, so people around them turned to see what it was all about.

'God, but hasn't he become very prune-faced?' Georgie said as they made their way out of the building, and it was as if they were young girls again, laughing at their own private joke and nothing else really mattered.

'Nola, take a seat for a minute.' Principal Cotter was sitting behind a pile of spreadsheets, looking as if he'd been buried beneath them for far too long. Nola settled herself in the chair opposite and looked around his office. It was probably typical of headmasters' offices all round the country, busy, but organised by a dedicated secretary who no doubt knew exactly where everything should be, if not where it was exactly. 'So...' He took off his glasses and pinched the bridge of his nose. 'The village fete...'

'Yes. The village fete.' Nola wanted to hang her head in shame, but she didn't dare with Georgie's voice ringing in her ears.

'We can't have our teachers making public displays of themselves, you know. The school rules are quite clear.'

'I understand.' Nola sighed.

'And there have been phone calls, from...' He stopped. Well, they both knew the holier-than-thou brigade – of which there were a few staunch members in the village – would have been out in force.

'I can imagine.' Nola wanted to curl up and die, but then, she remembered what Georgie and Aiden had said and she felt her spine galvanising. It was just enough to make her sit straighter and determined to keep her eyes off the floor and her head high. 'The thing is, there's no excuse for what happened, Gary, and I'm not going to try and make any. True, this last year has been extremely stressful.' Actually, if she was honest, the last couple of years were pretty crap; it was only since she came here that things began to improve. 'But my behaviour that day was completely out of the ordinary. It's never happened before and I can promise you it will never happen again...'

'The problem for me is that it has happened at all, in full view of the whole village, Nola, and I'm not sure that your promises are going to be enough to...'

'But what about my work here so far? Surely that counts for something? *Easter Parade* was the most successful play the school has ever produced and we managed it in little over one term.' By all accounts, her predecessor was a disaster and the last school musical had ended in little more than one act, three badly arranged songs, a broken collar bone and tears all round.

'Yes, I'll grant you, I've never had more calls from parents telling me how wonderful a teacher is...' He smiled at this. 'And even this morning, I've had two parents already call me to lobby in your favour.' There was a knock at the door. 'Not now,' he called.

'Sorry, excuse me.' The secretary poked her head into the

office. 'I really do hate to interrupt, but you need to know that the fifth-years are threatening to stage a sit-in protest unless their drama teacher arrives for class this morning.' A small twitch about her lips told Nola that the older woman was on her side too.

'This is most irregular.' Gary raised his eyes towards heaven and sighed.

'Look, Gary, I love this job, I mean, I'm not just saying I want to keep it, but I actually feel as if I've found my calling.' This was a revelation to Nola as much as it might be to anyone else, but as she was saying the words, she knew with all her heart they were true. 'I know it wasn't meant to be a permanent arrangement, but if you sack me like this, I'll never have the chance to start over somewhere else, don't you see? Even my summer drama school will be left hanging under a dark cloud.'

'It's not what I want either, but the school rules are very clear, Nola, I'm sorry. You've behaved in a way that I can't be seen to condone and by letting you back in to teach this morning, that's effectively what I'm doing.'

'I see,' Nola said, so that was that.

'Of course, you could resign your position...'

'And how exactly is that meant to make things any better?'

'There wouldn't be a disciplinary meeting. There would be no records of what happened outside the school on your employment file. It would be a simple case of filing parents' praise and a report from me about your positive impact on the school.' He smiled sadly.

'All right. Thank you very much. I suppose that's it, so...'

Nola sighed, she felt far more disappointed than she'd have ever expected to feel.

'Nola,' Gary said as she opened the office door to leave. 'I don't think this should affect your plans for a summer school; in fact, I'm so certain that I would like to enrol my two girls for the full summer term, if you have space.' He was smiling at her. It was a testimonial of sorts and Nola knew it was a huge vote of confidence against any naysayers in the village.

'Thank you, Gary,' she said, standing there for a moment. 'That's really sweet of you.' And it was with a very heavy heart, she had to face the fact that her career in Ballycove Secondary School was officially at an end.

By some minor miracle, when she walked out of Gary Cotter's office the first person she bumped into was Aiden Barry.

'Well, fancy meeting you here.' His voice was enough to send a rush of relief through her.

'Oh, Aiden, I've had to resign.'

'Come on, I'm bringing you home,' he said, moving her along the corridor before every student and teacher milled out to witness the state of her.

He had a strength about him that made her want to just be bundled up in his arms and be swept a million miles away from the stress of meeting with Gary Cotter or having to face the shame of forced resignation. Thankfully, she caught herself up before she joined one of his legions of fans. For now, all she had to do was pull herself together – not let herself down any more than she already had. They raced along the empty corridor, exiting through one of the side doors outside of which, Aiden had conveniently parked his jeep. Nola thought she'd never felt so relieved to sit into a vehicle, even if it did smell just a little of wet dog and diesel, in all her life.

As he turned over the engine, he said, 'I'm so sorry about what happened at the fete.'

'Oh God.' She felt that terrible rush of agony come over her again, as if the floodgates might open and she would never manage to lock them shut again. She took a deep breath. 'It wasn't your fault.'

'It feels as if every time I'm around you, I just get on your nerves...' He took a deep breath and when she looked at him, she could see he was embarrassed. 'And that day, I should have held you back, maybe said something, I don't know...'

'Yes, well I don't think St Patrick and all the saints of Ireland could have done much to stop me once it all got started, that's the ugly truth of it; the whole village has seen and heard it all.'

'Nola.' He said her name with a hoarseness that felt as if she'd never heard him say it before. 'There's nothing ugly about you and all of that' – he waved his hand as if he might brush the whole terrible episode aside – 'all of it, needed to be said. You can't move forward, not properly unless the air is cleared and there was a lot of air that needed clearing between you Delahaye sisters. A blind man could see that.'

'Well, it carried a heavy price. I'm finished ever having a chance to teach drama again.'

'What? Of course you're not finished teaching. Did Gary say that to you?'

'No, he was actually very sweet. I think he felt almost as badly as I did.' She smiled now, thinking of it. They were speeding through the empty streets of Ballycove; it was too wet today for even the most dedicated dog walkers. 'He said he'd enrol his own daughters in my drama school if I'd have them.'

'But that's brilliant, don't you see? You have to get that drama school up and running now. It's his way of supporting you. None of the naysayers can say a word against you. You've resigned with dignity in order to start your own business – there's no shame there.'

'It's hardly a business.' She shook her head; after all, she'd be returning to London hopefully at the end of summer.

'And what else would you call it? Look, when you go back to London, if you want to get a job teaching, Gary can give you a reference. He'll be signing it as a parent, but it won't hurt that he was also your previous employer.'

'I hadn't thought of that.' Nola felt a little lighter suddenly.

'And you know, I'm sure if you look all along the coast, it's not just this village that's crying out for something kids can get involved in. You and your drama school could be the best thing that happened to the place.' He smiled at her. 'Of course, you'll need to keep that temper of yours in check and use a little charm to get it off the ground.'

'I can be charming, when I want to be,' she said with a reluctant smile. 'Look, you and I, we just got off to a bad start.'

'Well, that might have been more my fault than yours;

after all, I did almost run over you, but…' His words petered off, they had pulled up at the back door of the house, but he turned off the engine, as if he was in no rush to leave just yet.

'Yes, well, it would have taken two of us to make an accident.'

'I tried to make amends by bringing you along to the pub that night.' He was laughing now and against all the odds of the morning she'd just had, she found herself laughing too.

'Yes, and then you left me sitting there while you went off to chat up the barmaid.'

'Whoa, I definitely wasn't chatting up the barmaid.' He held up his hand in defence and she half believed him; it didn't matter; it wasn't as if it was a date or anything.

'Water under the bridge.' She smiled.

'Hah. It looks like we're destined to always be at odds, I think, which is a pity.'

'It is?'

'Well, yes. I was very fond of your father, I get on well with most everyone in the village and I hoped we could be… *friends*, for as long as you're here.'

'Don't worry, I'm sure I'll grow on you too,' she said a little coyly.

'I think you already have.' His voice was coarse and when their eyes met, it felt as if time stopped and there wasn't so much as a sound to be heard between them except Nola could feel her heart hammering hard against her chest.

'Well, maybe you should do something about that,' she said breaking the spell before she hopped out of the jeep and ran into the house. Once inside she wasn't sure whether she felt excited or disappointed; after all, what good could become of falling for Aiden now, when before too long, she'd be packing her bags to go back to London?

'I would like to buy you both out of the distillery,' Georgie said to Iris as they made their way to a smart office, just about midway between her apartment and Sandstone and Mellon. 'I'm hoping to raise enough money, between my pay-off from Paul Mellon and selling my apartment, to take over both your shares.'

Iris turned to look at her sister. 'Wow. That's a great idea, Georgie. It's hardly going to cost that much, though, is it?' Iris knew too well the value of London property; even her own house in the suburbs would be worth a fortune.

'I intend to pay the market value.' They both knew Nola would need her full share. If she returned to London, every penny would count for her. 'So, I'll be taking over from where Dad left off.' Georgie beamed at the thought – it would be worth every penny. She'd never felt more fulfilled than she had these last few months working in the distillery. It wasn't just the work itself, but it was the people too – it was a new start, just what she needed, even if she hadn't realised it before she'd left London.

'But that's marvellous.' Iris hugged her. 'Dad would have been over the moon, wouldn't he?'

'I think he would, but I'm not just doing it out of sentimentality. It's a good business, with the potential to be a great business.'

'Well, I'm sure if anyone can make it into that, it's you.'

'Let's hope so…' Georgie said, because it was true, while she had no qualms about taking on the business, she had learned that it was the relationships around it that were most important. Without Iris, Nola and the people who had worked for Delahaye Distilleries for years, Georgie knew that any success would be as hollow an experience as her life in London had become.

'God, this place looks as if it cost an arm and a leg,' Iris whispered as Georgie pushed open the door to one of the swankiest estate agents in the city. It was a tasteful collage of modern art, deep pile mint rugs and walls that looked as if they'd been painted in ivory velvet.

'They'll get me the best price and they'll do it with minimum disruption,' Georgie said. It was funny, but being back here now confirmed one thing for her: she was finished with London.

The agent, Imogen, who hardly looked old enough to have finished school, took down all her details. Georgie called the management company who looked after her building to set things in motion. 'It won't take long. Properties like this are very much sought after,' Imogen soothed.

Out on the busy London street, Georgie and Iris stood for a moment and looked at each other. 'God, I can't believe I've just put my apartment on the market.' She felt a giddy combination of excitement and fear mixed through with a tremor of terror racing through her. But then, Iris reached out and took her hand and she looked into those lovely, kind eyes.

'It's going to be great,' Iris said with a rush of enthusiasm that was contagious.

'It *is* going to be great,' Georgie agreed, and she knew it in her bones. She was going home, for once and for all.

16

June, Two Weeks To Go...

It's never too late. It had become like a mantra between them at this stage. Iris was thinking about them one afternoon, as she tucked away the rocking horse in the little cottage after a family had booked out. The words rolled about in her mind and the horse slipped from her arms when she realised that the only thing stopping her was the notion that she was waiting for the time to be right. It seemed the whole world around her ground to a resounding halt. Wasn't that the excuse Myles had always thrown at her? The time never seemed to be right as far as having a baby was concerned.

Iris dropped into the narrow bedroom chair, feeling like she'd been struck by some profound understanding that had always been there, if only she'd taken the time to see it. Maybe there was no right or wrong time – maybe there was just time, and she was running out of it. She took a deep breath, threw her shoulders back and smiled. This was *her* time. And she was ready to have a family of her own.

A few days later, Iris was still mulling over the best way to go about things as she walked along the beach with Nola and Georgie. It felt like they were making up for lost time. They had decided, together, that there was no point regretting the years when they'd resented each other so much. All they had was the here and now, gifted to them by their wonderful father. They were making the most of it too, walking the beach together and staying up very late drinking too much and talking about all and nothing.

She'd told them everything. Far more than she would have if alcohol hadn't allowed her to lower her guard, and they had been just lovely. Nola had cried when Iris talked about how much she'd wanted children. It was still a physical pain, the fact that she had lost something that was meant to be a part of her life, resurrected to hurt her again now that Myles was throwing her sacrifice back in her face with Amanda.

It was time to think of making the most of her own life now and fashioning it into something she wanted, not just what Myles let her have. And so, with Georgie's help she began to look into what might just be possible. Night after night, it was Georgie who kept researching, emailing and filling in what soon seemed to Iris to be an endless number of forms. Within a week they had narrowed things down quite a bit.

It didn't matter how old the child was. At the end of the day, what mattered was that Iris could take care of someone, love them and feel what it was to be a mother. Age, or colour or sex was completely beside the point – Iris knew that whatever child came her way, she would love them with all her heart and she knew Georgie would also.

A week later, Iris's thoughts were racing about her mind because there had been an email from one of the agencies. It was tentative, maybe the first of many, which might lead to nothing more than a conversation, but she couldn't help but feel hopeful. She decided she would keep it to herself, at least until there was something more concrete to share – otherwise, Georgie could burst with expectation.

She had suggested a walk on the beach, as much to clear her own mind as to stop her rereading the email over and over again. Iris thought that walking along here was perfect. Summer had finally arrived in Ballycove. The waves had that salty smell of their childhood and even if they didn't have the beach to themselves, Iris loved the feel of the sand, soft and dry beneath her feet. They had walked for miles and were linking each other back up the steps to the main road when she spotted a familiar figure bent across the wall watching them. Iris blinked, not sure if it was a trick of the sunlight, but then her stomach turned over and that familiar feeling of dread rose up in her throat. 'Myles,' she said darkly, making her sisters look up, and it felt as if every bit of resolve and strength sapped from her in that moment.

'Where?' Georgie said, picking up pace and dragging Iris in her wake.

'I don't believe it. Surely he'd never have the nerve to turn up here,' Nola was saying, but she was almost out of breath, such was the steam with which Georgie was pulling them forward. If he was within a five-mile radius he'd be wise to turn and run quickly, before Georgie caught up to him.

'Sorry, it must be a trick of the light,' Iris said squinting towards the pier road. There was no-one there at all, or no-one that she could see at any rate. 'I need to get my eyes tested. I could have sworn I saw him standing against the wall watching us.' She shivered. The last thing they needed was him turning up here.

'Hopefully, you've seen the last of him now. From what you say, he won't want to dig up any more worms that might end up costing him more in the divorce,' Georgie said and somehow her composure was contagious and Iris laughed off the silly notion of him making his way to Ballycove of all places.

They walked on; up towards the huge boulders that formed a stout defence against the cliff face before the barrier wall had been erected. Iris loved it here, looking out across the vastness of the ocean. 'So, I've made up my mind too.' Iris said the words softly, but there was no breeze to carry them away today. 'I can't think of anywhere else I'd rather be.'

'You're going to stay in Ballycove? That's the best news ever!' Georgie's mouth drew up into a wide smile and they both looked at Nola then. 'So, it's up to you, little sister. What could we do to make you think about staying on in Ballycove?'

'Oh, I don't know if I'm quite ready to settle here yet,' Nola said, but Iris had a feeling Ballycove could be the best place for Nola too, if only she'd let herself see it. Still, if she'd learned anything over the last number of weeks it was when to say less and keep her opinions to herself. Even if Nola returned to London at the end of the summer there was nothing to stop her coming back here in a year or two, or ten if it came to it, so long as they never again lost sight of that promise they'd made years earlier and continued to remain close.

'What about you, Iris? Will you just run the gate lodge or have you plans to build a new Delahaye empire?' Georgie was joking, but Iris knew her sister was concerned for her.

'If all comes to all, I'll see if I can't get a job in the local distillery!' Iris joked. 'No. Seriously, I'll be all right. Whatever the future holds, I know I don't want to live in London anymore. I want to be here, with the Atlantic on my doorstep in a village where I know people and they know me.'

'Well, what with our inheritance as well, you certainly won't be on the breadline,' Nola said, then she bit her lip, because it was the one thing they'd skirted about – how they would divide the estate evenly between them.

'I won't be in any rush to get my hands on that,' Iris said softly. There would be enough to live on for some time yet with the proceeds from the divorce. 'I think we have a lot of talking to do before we decide how we're going to handle the Delahaye legacy.'

'So long as that soon-to-be ex-husband of yours doesn't get his hands on a penny of it, I think we'll all be quite pleased,' Georgie said, and then her eyes darted along the top of the wall behind them.

'Don't tell me, you're seeing things too?' Iris laughed.

'Old age, just like you. We probably both need to have

our eyes tested.' Georgie shook her head. 'It's a good thing we have Nola here or God knows where we'd end up.' They started to laugh at that.

'You'd better make the most of me while I'm here so,' Nola said, but it seemed to Iris as if her voice had broken off into that faraway sound, as if she was already drifting from them.

'You know, Nola…' Georgie pulled them all to a stop and stood for a moment looking out to sea as if she was gathering up the force of the Atlantic itself to say what was on her mind. 'You could always stay… if the numbers keep growing in the drama school, you could make a great success of it.' It was true, already having just opened for enrolments, it looked as if Nola would have to have three separate sessions and that was just in Ballycove. There was nothing to stop her opening up a class in any of the other nearby villages also.

'Oh, no.' Nola laughed. 'I couldn't possibly stay. I mean, I have to go back to London, and anyway…'

'Anyway?' Iris was pretty sure there was no other anyway, but she wouldn't say that for all the world.

'Well, what is there for me here? I mean, I can see why you two are choosing to stay what with between the distillery for Georgie and your plans for the cottage and a baby, but me? I'm just?' What? What was she? Drifting? Passing through?

'This is your home too,' Georgie said firmly. 'We don't have to sell up, you know; we could just keep on going like this.' She tore her gaze from the waves crashing far out in the sea.

'Don't be silly, of course we have to sell up,' Nola snapped. It seemed anything else was ridiculous.

'At least think about it,' Iris urged, linking her arm into Nola's. 'Just think about it.'

You could always stay. Those words hung about Nola like a melody she couldn't forget as she walked across the beach again. The fact was, she hadn't time to think about staying or doing much of anything else over the last couple of days. The Delahaye Drama School was much busier than she'd ever expected. Apart from enrolling what felt like half the kids from around the county, she also had lessons to plan. In a few short evenings, it had become clear to her that so many of the drama classes she'd paid a fortune for over the years, were little more than old rope.

The one thing she'd been clear about from the get-go of setting up her own school was that the students would get something out of it and the parents would see the value of it. That meant a lot of hard work and planning before she even held her first class. She would start with the basics, everyone would have a folder so there would be accountability and the term would end in a wonderful piece of theatre that the village would be talking about for years to come.

It was a strange thing. She felt so happy, almost complete, as if everything was just as it should be, but something still held her back from telling her sisters the whole truth of what her life had become in London. And maybe that was why she felt as if somehow the city was not yet finished with her. She couldn't think of going back without feeling a wave of loneliness for what she'd be leaving in Ballycove and it was funny, because after all those years, the only thing she truly missed was her friendship with Shalib. Dear, dear Shalib. But they talked regularly on the phone and she knew, he should be thinking of retiring one day soon anyway. There wouldn't be a job in the coffee shop forever for her.

Her sisters were right, even if they didn't say it exactly, but she had far more to stay for than she had to return to London for. Suddenly, it felt as if everything became much clearer to her. The difference between Nola and her sisters, now, as far as she saw it was that both Iris and Georgie had taken their lives into their own hands. They'd decided to steer a new course in a direction that until now hadn't even seemed possible. And yet, here they were, both ready to throw up everything to follow the simple dream of being content and happy. And maybe that was enough. After all, Nola herself, when she thought about being an actress, what was that all about, if not to be happy? Didn't she always believe that once she'd made a name for herself in the theatre or if she was lucky TV or film, then she'd think about settling down, doing the things most young girls expect to grow up and do one day.

That was when she knew what she had to do. If she was going to make a go of things here, there was one thing that would give her more security than she'd ever known in London.

The school had emptied out for the holidays, but she knew that the principal would be still here, trying to figure out timetables and teacher training for the following term. Gary Cotter was a teddy bear of a man, hardly suited to a life of laying down heavy discipline, but he managed to run a school based on values of nurture and excellence that had kindness at their core. Nola had experienced that herself and she knew that he'd only followed the rules when he'd forced her hand into resignation – he was giving her the easy way out and there were plenty who wouldn't have been so generous.

'Nola,' he said, looking up from his desk. 'What on earth are you doing here at this hour?'

'I had to talk to you,' she said, pushing through the door, suddenly aware of her windswept appearance. 'It's about...' What was it about? She wanted her job back, but there was no way that was going to happen. 'I've been thinking about next year.'

'Okay?'

'I hear you haven't been able to fill my post.' She plopped down into a chair opposite him.

'Well, I did tell the board you'd be irreplaceable.' He smiled at her now. 'If I can't get someone to fill it, it's going to be a nightmare to be honest. It'll mean no musical, it might even mean we have to cancel transition year and the parents will go mad over that.' He blew out a long, worried sigh.

'What if I was to propose taking on the musical as an outside contractor – a freelancer?'

'Oh, I don't know, Nola – it would be most unusual.'

'That doesn't mean it can't be done.' She sat forward in her chair, feeling as if she was somehow channelling Georgie's enthusiasm and driving force.

'Tell me what you have in mind.'

'My new theatre company,' she began. 'Right here in

Ballycove. You've probably heard it's already booked solid for the summer.' She smiled at him because she could see he needed her to pitch something he could take to the board. 'My suggestion is that you hire my drama company to complete production on the school musical. You can explain that it's just about getting you to the finish line in terms of keeping the timetable up and running. Then, you can take on a part-time teacher for the academic hours around that block on the timetable. It might get you out of a spot.'

'Bloody brilliant.' He clapped his hands together. 'I'll have to take it to the board mind, but when it's put in context of having to cancel classes, well…'

'Fantastic.' A frisson of excitement shot through Nola. She might actually be doing this and as she walked back home, filled with buzzy energy, she couldn't wait to tell Georgie and Iris. They'd be thrilled to hear she'd finally come to her senses and it looked like she was coming home at last.

It was early that evening when Iris heard the doorbell ring. Unusual in itself as no-one ever really used the front door anymore. She padded towards the hallway, half expecting it to be Nola having forgotten her key again. She pulled the door back to reveal the last person she expected to see standing there.

Myles was standing on the doorstep, suitcase in hand. For a moment, Iris stopped, dazzled, trying to figure out what he was doing – did he think he was coming on holiday? Iris looked at him, suddenly out of the familiar surroundings where for so long he'd held all the cards. Here, as night was drawing in, standing in the pool of yellow light that seeped out from the hall, he looked pathetic. And not even in a way that she could feel sorry for him either. No, the man she saw standing there trying desperately to make some sort of unspoken connection with her looked like a stranger to her.

'What the hell do you think you're doing here, Myles?' Georgie appearing at her side was like a lioness, cornered and protecting her cub. He took a step backwards.

'I... I... I...' he stuttered. 'I've come to see my wife.' Even his voice was smaller than Iris remembered.

'Well, now you've seen her, you might as well turn around and crawl back under whatever rock will have you,' Georgie said, moving forward, breaking away from inside the hall and standing, hands on hips between him and Iris. Honestly, Iris expected her to level a punch at him. Suddenly, she remembered them as kids. Georgie fought all their battles, happily taking on any kid who dared to mess with the Delahaye girls. She was fearless. Quite a few had been left with bloody noses thanks to her nifty left hook.

'Iris?' he wheedled, trying to peer around Georgie and make eye contact with her.

'I have nothing to say to you, Myles.' Iris stepped forward and she felt an unexpected surge of confidence.

'Yes, why don't you toddle on back to your *pregnant* girlfriend, Myles?' Nola said now from behind him. She and Aiden Barry had just pulled up in that huge jeep on the drive outside. Iris knew that the way she leaned on the word meant Nola would never forgive him for doing her out of a brood of nieces and nephews.

'Oh, we're all so very smart now.' Myles's voice dipped in a menacing tone that resurrected memories in Iris that until now she'd managed to bury so well she'd forgotten that side of him. 'Well, what if I was to say I'm going to talk to my solicitor and make sure that I take half of *everything* that my not so saintly wife has been hiding from me?'

'I don't know what you mean.' Iris managed to keep her voice even.

'Oh, don't you? You see, Iris, I'm not as stupid as you might think. I saw your plane ticket at the top of your bag at that dippy mediation session. It didn't take a lot to figure out where you were planning on running to and when I arrived here, the first person to greet me couldn't wait to pass on his condolence at the loss of my father-in-law.' He shook his head as if he'd just figured out the mystery of the Bermuda triangle.

'You think for one moment you're going to get a look-in to our family's life's work?' Georgie moved towards him again and this time there was no sidestepping her. 'Listen to me, Myles Cutler. You've done enough damage to last us a lifetime, and it's like this. First off, there is no inheritance. Our father has tied up the lot in so many conditions it's going to take forever to sort it all out and even if he hadn't, we'd throw every last stick of it into the ocean before any of us would see you get your hands on one penny.' She was almost spitting the words into his face. 'So, I'm telling you one last time, either you get out of Ballycove this minute and we don't hear one more word from you, or it won't be Iris and her solicitor you'll be dealing with. It'll be me and I'll be going after you with the intention of leaving you with less than nothing, and mark my words, you'll be begging me to take your last penny from you by the time I'm finished.'

'You can't—'

'Oh, can't I?' She laughed; a strange scary sound that Iris figured came from a place within her sister that was almost spent, although Myles Cutler didn't know that. 'I'll contact every news station executive in London for a start. Do you know how much money my firm spends on advertising every year, Myles? That's effectively your wages I'm talking about. I'll make sure you never work again.'

'I never planned on things turning out this way.' But he wasn't talking to Iris now; he was sobbing the words at Georgie. 'It wasn't like that. Tell her, Iris.' He couldn't make eye contact with Iris, as Georgie and now Nola were standing between them. He didn't realise it, but Aiden Barry stood square behind him as well. Aiden was a tree of a man compared to Myles, who looked like little more than a lonesome weed in the wind before him.

'You never planned it?' Iris moved forward. Suddenly she felt as if the years of sadness and emptiness and uncertainty propelled her along the hallway, so she was standing facing Myles not as they would have been six months earlier, but rather with a new perspective she'd never had before. They stood for a long moment, inches away from each other, but it seemed suddenly as if they'd travelled many thousands of miles apart. And in that instant of looking into his face, Iris recognised the distance for what it was. She had become a different person, a stronger person, a woman who was no longer dependant on a man for her happiness, but was ready to make something of her life on her own terms.

She felt a surge of anger rise up in her for the years she'd wasted on this pathetic scrap of a man. 'You never planned to take the best years of my life from me and then throw them back in my face – is that what you're telling me?' She took a deep breath, because there were things she should have said before and she'd never had the courage. 'You never planned to do me out of having a family of my own? And worse, put such a wedge between me and my sisters that I've missed out on them too? You've spent our entire marriage lying to me. You lied to me about Nola, poisonous lies when that evening was all down to you. I see now that Nola would never have betrayed me like that, but you? And even Georgie, you spent years criticising her for the success you couldn't even begin to hold a candle to and instead, you lived off my earnings and squandered your own.'

'Oh, so they're perfect now, I suppose? Well, you were the one who turned your back on them, I never made you…' But he trailed off, his voice shaking with temper but mostly with defeat. 'I always said we needed to keep our feet in the door of this place…' He looked up now at Soldier Hill House. For a moment, it seemed to Iris as if he was seeing it for the first time, or maybe he realised he was looking at it for the last time.

'None of that matters now.' Georgie stepped forward again. 'The fact is, she's finally seen through you.'

'I'll never forgive you, Myles.' But even as she said the words, Iris knew she was already beginning to heal. Being here, with her sisters, with so much to look forward to, a child of her own, a good life – she knew, carrying bitterness in her heart would only keep repaying a debt to Myles that she'd never really owed him to begin with.

'And you think I'm going to lose sleep over that?' He sneered at her. 'It'll be a lot easier to sleep when I have my head on a pillow feathered by the sale of this place, that's for sure.'

'I don't bloody think so.' Iris stepped forward, right into his face. 'This place has never been on the table for you, Myles. Our father saw to that.'

'Oh?'

'Yes. And even if he didn't...' Iris stopped for a moment '...I'd throw away my share to make sure you don't get a penny.'

'You wouldn't—'

'Now, if you want to get what is rightfully yours, you need to agree to half of everything we accumulated during our marriage. I'm not going to go after you for any more, even though we both know I could.'

'How do you mean?' He took a step backwards, stumbling on the step and landing on the next one down with a wobble.

'Seriously? Do I need to remind you who paid every bill that came through the door? Who bought the car and paid the insurance? Who cooked and cleaned and generally held things together – while you flitted about London from one woman to the next probably, when you were supposed to be earning a decent wage.' She was standing over him now, looking down on him, something that had never happened in their marriage.

'I...' He cleared his throat. 'I just want out of it. That's all,' he stammered; his bluster was evaporating and Iris had a feeling that whatever he'd come here for, whatever he thought he'd get out of her, he knew now that with her sisters united behind her, he had no choice but to take what she was willing to give.

'You run along now,' Nola said. 'Before Iris changes her mind and decides to make things really awkward for you – or worse, you get on Georgie's nerves too much.'

'You're nothing but a shower of sour old crones, the lot of you,' Myles shouted as he made his way to turn around, but he walked straight into Aiden, causing him to shriek before sidestepping him and picking his way as quickly and carefully as he could back down the avenue, cursing and stumbling.

'I'm not sure,' Georgie said, 'but I think that's the last we'll be seeing of Myles Cutler.'

'Well, thank goodness for that,' Iris said, and they watched as he disappeared into the darkening night.

17

Time's Up...

It was late evening when Muriel rang Iris. Outside, a light shower of rain was just moving off out across the Atlantic. The evening orange sun kicked glints from rain-covered leaves, but there was a feeling of cleanliness to everything that Iris felt put the world at rights.

'I really can't understand it,' Muriel said. 'I mean, I know Catherine is good, but I've never seen such a sudden and complete turnaround.'

'Oh?' Iris asked. Muriel was on speakerphone to let Georgie and Nola hear everything. She had no secrets from her sisters now and she had them to thank more than anyone else for Myles's unexpected moment of enlightenment on his road to Damascus.

'Yes. His solicitor contacted me earlier. They're happy to settle. They'll agree to every condition we've put in place, just so long as it's all done and dusted as quickly as possible.'

'So?'

'So, you're going to be free much more quickly than we could have hoped for,' Muriel said, and then she laughed as she heard the sound of whooping excitement on the other end of the phone. Iris knew the tears she was shedding as her sisters embraced her were sheer joy – this really felt like a whole new beginning.

Georgie wasn't sure if it was just her, but it felt as if a sort of calm had descended on Soldier Hill House once Myles Cutler had been washed from their lives. Iris's solicitor had moved things along with admirable speed. Stephen Leather had been happy to put off finalising their father's will until whenever the divorce was through. Now it seemed that all they had to do was help Iris celebrate her freedom.

Georgie went to bed that night feeling very satisfied with life. It looked as if the last few weeks had not only washed Myles from their family, but Iris had taken her destiny in her own hands. Regardless of what happened with Soldier Hill House, she had the cottage and she'd have enough money from her divorce settlement and her share of the distillery to give her little family a good start in Ballycove.

It took no time at all to sell her own apartment in London. That hadn't surprised Georgie in the least, but for the quick sale, she'd expected no more than the market value. The phone call from the estate agency had been a doubly pleasant surprise then to let her know that it had gone well above the asking price with a provision that the sale be closed immediately and so all she had to do was empty out her remaining belongings. She was ready to say goodbye to

London. Two days to pack a lorry full of boxes was as much time as she wanted to spend there now.

When Georgie arrived back she decided it was time to make her announcement formally at the distillery. She gathered all the employees and she and her sisters passed around glasses of champagne before raising a toast.

'To the future,' she announced. 'But to the past also.'

'And the present,' Iris cut in.

'Yes, very much to the present.' Nola raised her glass.

'So, there's something we're celebrating?' Robert asked and she noticed how lovely his eyes were, kind and sensuous when they creased up in a smile – how had she not noticed that before?

'Yes.' Georgie looked around at the familiar faces gathered about her. All colleagues, friends, family. These people did not feel as if they were employees; rather they were all on the same side. They were all pulling together and Georgie knew they liked her, maybe they even loved her. And she felt the same about them. 'I wanted you all to hear it from me first – I've spoken to my sisters and I'm so pleased to tell you all that they've agreed to sell me their shares in the distillery…'

'And we're delighted you agreed to take it on.' Nola put her arm around Georgie's shoulder and it felt good, warm and loving. 'You're going to make it even more successful than ever.'

Robert threw back his head and laughed because maybe he'd known all along it would come to this.

'So we have a new boss?' one of the wags shouted, holding up his glass. His eyes were twinkling.

'Well, I hope we can carry on just as we have been for the last few months…' Georgie said, and she meant it. She'd learned a great lesson since she'd come to the distillery. Good business was done on good relationships and being happy meant getting along with the people in your workplace. And maybe too, working *with* people was much more fun than having people work for you. It certainly meant that Georgie was having the time of her life and it was something she'd never forget again. 'As a team.'

'To the future of the Delahaye Distillery.' Robert held up his glass again. The cheers and laughter that rang out around the stills were like opening music to a whole new chapter.

A week later, Georgie was chatting to Robert over a cup of coffee in their shared office.

'I'm divorced,' he'd told her when she enquired if there would be anyone waiting up for him at home on those nights when it seemed that there was no rush to finish up. 'One of those things,' he said a little sadly, 'but it was a long time ago and perhaps there is only so much time anyone needs to mourn the end of a relationship. And you? Ever tempted to tie the knot yourself?'

'There never seemed to be the time or the right one to get tied up to!' she said, and she realised that maybe that had been her loss.

'Well, maybe you should make the time now, you know – there are some good men in Ballycove…' He smiled at her and held her gaze just a little longer than perhaps he should, but it made her stomach turn over in a way it hadn't for years.

'Are you trying to fix me up or flirt with me?' She

laughed now, because really, wasn't it too late for her to be entertaining thoughts of romance?

'Would it be so terrible if I was?' His voice lowered so she had to bend closer to listen. She squinted slightly, for once really looking at Robert. He truly was a lovely man, maybe not movie star good-looking, but he was certainly attractive in a way that resonated with her. Perhaps he would like to meet someone too? He was too old-fashioned for Tinder, too proud to go to a matchmaking festival. He wasn't even a man to spend his evenings in the pub and how on earth did he expect to meet a nice woman if all he did was walk his dog along the beach or across the bogs?

'No, it wouldn't be terrible at all,' she said, and then she leaned just a little closer and met his lips before either of them had a chance to say another word.

Afterwards, he smiled at her shyly. 'I should ask you on a proper date before you get snapped up on me!' He leaned in and when he kissed her it felt as if some deep part of her was being loosened. His kiss was long and lingering, opening her up so she wanted so much more. Butterflies in her stomach – *God, it was forever since she'd felt anything like this.*

'I think you should.' She didn't want him to stop kissing her, but it was late. Iris would be putting dinner on the table. Iris! Wait until she told Iris and Nola that she'd kissed Robert!

It was time for them all to move on. For the first time in years, Georgie felt as if she deserved her shot at happiness as much as any of them and, maybe now, that happiness might mean more than just owning the distillery; maybe it could mean so much more than she'd bargained for when she came back to Ballycove.

As far as Nola could tell, the following days and weeks just sort of rolled into each other. It was probably contentment, although she'd never have had the confidence to call it that before. Life was good, she had work she enjoyed, she had a home that felt like home. She had friends, real friends, in the village and time to meet them unlike when she'd lived in London. And she had her sisters – a family – something she was valuing more with every passing day.

'Can you believe that we've spent over six months here?' she said to her sisters as they sat down for dinner after meeting Stephen Leather in the drawing room that afternoon. Having officially made it to six months meant that he could now execute the next stage of their father's will as soon as Iris's divorce was through.

'It's flown and yet, sometimes it feels like we've been here forever,' Georgie said, topping up their wine glasses while Iris ladled out the casserole.

'God, this smells so good,' Iris said, tucking in once everyone was ready.

'Have either of you thought about what happens next?' Georgie asked, taking a sip of her wine and watching her sisters. 'I mean, once the dust settles and the sale of your shares in the distillery have gone through…'

'I don't know,' Nola said. 'To be honest, I haven't had time to think much further than the opening night of the summer play.' She laughed at this, but it was the truth. She was investing her heart and soul in the production because apart from the fact that Georgie called it her shop window for parents enrolling their kids in her drama school for the rest of the year, she absolutely loved every minute of it. 'I suppose I'll just carry on…' And she caught herself up and smiled at Georgie, who would no more allow her to drift aimlessly as she once had than she would herself.

'We'll see,' Georgie said. Earlier in the week, Nola had spotted her working on a website design for the drama school – honestly, she was so lucky to have such a clever sister.

'I suppose you could always pop back and see your friends in London and act during midterms…' Iris said softly.

'Hah!' Nola heard the sound just after she made it. She took a deep breath. It was time to be honest with her sisters, finally. 'The truth is, Iris, I haven't worked properly since that awful tea advert. Once all the commotion kicked off around that and the court case, the call-backs stopped coming, hell, even the auditions dried up. Just before I came over here, my agent closed up shop and my flat is probably little more than a heap of rubble now.' She began to laugh at it all, because, absurdly, from where she was currently sitting it all sounded so tragic that, with the way things had worked out, it was rather funny.

'I don't understand.' Georgie leaned forward and reached for her sister's hand.

'The best way I can describe it to you both is that over the last few years, my life had just started to slide off the side of a cliff.' That was pretty much it. 'After they killed off my character in the soap, my so-called friends disappeared, my boyfriend dumped me and it didn't take very long until I couldn't make the payments on my nice flat and I had to move into a bedsit. I was lucky to get the job with Shalib, but that was all I had in London. Just before I left, my landlord handed me an eviction order; they were tearing down my building for high-end apartments and then, to cap it all off, my agent announced she was running off to Spain.'

Iris looked as if she might cry. 'I'm so sorry, I thought—'

'It doesn't matter. When I actually hear myself describing it all, it's almost the stuff of a bad movie. I can't really believe that I even wanted to go back there now, I mean, seriously, I am so happy here, I love my job and having you two back – no soap opera could compare to living with you pair.' She started to laugh when Georgie elbowed her affectionately.

'Well, I'm glad you're here too and this chapter of your life is shaping up to be a lot more successful and happy so far.' Georgie raised her glass.

'What about you, Iris?' Nola asked, happy to step out of the spotlight for a moment.

'Me?' Iris squeaked, and they both looked at her, because it was obvious that she had something to tell them, even if she hadn't been planning to share it just yet. She cleared her throat and sipped her water before placing it down on the table carefully. 'I'd like this house,' Iris said softly. 'I don't know if I can afford to buy it, unless of course Georgie is planning on paying us an awful lot of money for our shares in the distillery, but I'd like to run it as a top-class guest house. Maybe in summertime hold small, intimate wedding parties in a marquee on the lawn?' She studied her fingernails, hardly able to make eye contact in case they'd laugh at her. 'Madness, right?'

'Not at all.' Georgie said exactly what Nola was thinking. 'I think it's a great idea and you'd hold onto the gate lodge as well?'

'Oh, no, that would be too much,' Iris said. 'I'd be happy to let that go to either of you and of course, there'll always be space here if you want to stay. This will always be home.'

'You'll definitely have enough to get the work started on this place, if that's the dream,' Georgie said, reaching for her phone and flicking through her emails. 'I've had the distillery valued, properly, at the sort of prices that it would make if it was bought up by one of the big distilleries.'

'Oh, I didn't realise.' Iris looked at Georgie now, too. 'Well, go on, don't keep us in suspense.'

'Fine, but it's not good news for me I'm afraid.' She smiled before throwing her head back to laugh. Georgie had learned the cost of being miserable, and no amount of money could refund her on lost happiness. 'If I am to buy you both out, it's equal to the apartment in London and all my savings.' She smiled ruefully now.

'Ooh, so that's…' Iris exhaled slowly.

'It's a lot of money, that's what it is.'

'It's a million each,' Georgie said coolly. 'I just need to get my finances organised.

'God, and there she is wading about the place in a forty-year-old jacket belonging to Dad.' Iris was making gentle fun of Georgie now.

'Yes, and even if I end up with too many millions in the

bank to count, I don't think I could be any happier than traipsing across those fields to work every morning.'

'I can understand that,' Nola said and then she looked across at Iris. 'There's definitely something you're not telling us.' She topped up her sister's glass of wine.

'About that...' A small smile crept across Iris's lips. 'I wasn't going to say anything just yet, but one of the agencies has been in contact.'

Georgie screamed excitedly. 'Why didn't you tell us immediately? Go on...'

'Well, it's early days and nothing is guaranteed but they've found a child who seems to be just perfect...'

Epilogue

One Year Later…

They had been walking along the seafront when Nola heard the call above their heads. Wild geese returning home for winter, late this year, but welcome all the same. They were walking more slowly now, three sisters – friends, arm in arm.

'We really should be getting back.' Georgie looked at her watch. She was nervous, trying to keep her excitement and apprehension buttoned down, so it didn't overflow into this precious quiet time before they went back to get ready for the launch of Iseult Gin. It was hard to believe that finally, after their father's years of dedication to getting it just right, it was about to go out into the world.

It was strangely moving, even seeing the final packaging. Georgie had used a photograph of her mother, faded into the deep velvety blue packaging. It seemed to be so luxurious, but Georgie had made sure it all came in well under budget. The whole thing had brought tears to Iris's eyes.

'I can't believe we're finally doing this,' Nola said softly.

'Yes, it feels as if we've come full circle.' Iris looked down at the little girl holding her hand. Isolde had arrived six weeks earlier. She was already one of them; perhaps she had been long before she arrived. Her hair was a tangled mess of red curls; in fact, Iris thought, if Georgie had a daughter, she couldn't be any more like her. But she was a lot quieter and more reserved than Georgie. Already, Nola was trying to convince Iris to let her join the Delahaye Theatre Company, but there was lots of time for that.

It was hard to believe that they'd been back over a year. So much had happened since their reluctant and grudging agreement to fulfil their father's final wishes. Iris had dived in with her usual energy and enthusiasm to create the guest house that she wanted. She planned it with precision; it would come to life, room by room. As each room was completed, she opened it up to guests. The summer months had far exceeded her expectations and there had been one or two nights when she'd been in the happy position of being able to send her overflow to the local hotel, much to her own and their amusement. The main part of the house remained very much as it had always been. It was scrubbed and cleaned, but retained the sense of old-world cosiness that appealed to nostalgia lovers who just wanted to escape the similitude of everyday life. 'It's a work in progress,' she would tell anyone who asked, and it would be, for a very long time, and she was happy with that. She had lived long enough, or maybe deeply enough to know that happiness was about the journey, far more than the destination. For a short while, when it became apparent that the kitchen would not pass muster, she'd moved in with Georgie to the gate lodge.

It turned out that once Georgie unpacked her things, she knew that she had finally arrived home. The little cottage was everything Georgie could want even if she'd never realised it before. She was looking forward to the dark evenings drawing in, so she could light a roaring fire and enjoy the rain beating against her windows. It was all so different to London. Here, when her work was done, she was not alone. Robert was such a regular guest, he'd almost moved in permanently and every other day someone dropped by to say hello or to ask for her help. She had become involved in the local tourism committee, who were thrilled to have her marketing skills, and she in turn was learning how to make friends, some of whom she had a feeling might last a lifetime. Georgie still occasionally pinched herself to make sure she wasn't dreaming that this wonderful life was unfolding so easily before her.

'You're miles away,' Nola said, bringing Georgie back to what she was saying.

'I'm thinking of what Father used to say, you remember, that quote, *There is another world, but it is in this one.*'

'He said that to me before I left Ballycove all those years ago.' A shadow of sad recollection passed across Iris's features. 'It's taken a long time for it to make sense.'

'It's not about how long it takes though, is it?' Nola said. 'It's about remembering and what we learn along the way.' She reached down and stroked Isolde's beautiful hair.

'You are getting far too wise, little sister,' Iris said. 'Are you all right, Georgie?'

'I'm just going over everything for tonight.' She smiled.

'Everything is sorted, you've checked your to-do list a hundred times over, and we'll all be there, supporting you.'

'You're both only coming for the gin,' Georgie joked.

'True, but it's very good gin.' Nola smiled. She was a little nervous too, but it was a pleasant feeling, butterflies before a performance, only better. A few of her students had agreed to put on a short excerpt from the play they were due to stage in a few weeks' time.

'Do you think they'd be proud of us now?' Iris's voice sounded as if it was very far away.

'I think they'd be very proud,' Georgie said easily, because she knew it as truly as she knew the tide would turn each day and the sun would set. By being here, by mending the bridges that had almost been washed away, they'd fulfilled the terms of their father's will. But more than that, they'd come together in a way that meant the Gin Sisters' Promise would be something that would sustain them for the rest of their lives, and maybe that was more than any of them could have ever wished for.

Acknowledgements

My thanks to the following people who have helped to shape this book into what you hold in your hands today.

The Aria/Head of Zeus Team editing wonder women beginning with Thorne Ryan, Laura McCallen, Helena Newton, Bianca Gillam, Laura Palmer and ending with Rachel Faulker-Willcocks – thank you for sound advice, fresh eyes and brilliant suggestions. The HoZ sales and marketing wizards Nikky Ward, Jessie Sullivan, Jade Gwilliam, Victoria Eddison and Amy Watson – all of your help and hard work is very much appreciated. In Ireland – thanks to Simon & Declan and all at Gill Hess for all the work you put in getting the books on shelves.

To my wise and brilliant agent, Judith Murdoch – what fun we've had this year, in spite of not being able to travel very far.

On the home front, thanks to my family – Seán, Roisín,

Tomás and Cristín. I know, it's not cool, but you gang are the icing on my cake! To Bernadine, David and Stephen for stepping in when I sometimes couldn't, and to Christine Cafferkey for keeping us all in line. Thanks as always to James for far more than I can list out here.

Thank you to you, my reader – I hope you enjoyed this book and I look forward to hearing how you got on with it, whether that's on Twitter, Facebook, Instagram or maybe, with a little luck when we meet one day to chat about books and stories. Now the world feels as if it's returning to where that's a thing again!

Finally, I've dedicated this book to the Scannan-Beehive gang – it's a big list so, one deep breath and here we go... Denise B, Michelle L, Mary G, Louise M, Louise (LouLou), Niamh G, Kevin M, Kevin R, Martin B, Martin and Jack D – the loveliest people to work with. And to the following, who over the years have made it seem as if it's really not work at all... Silke, Olivia, Michelle, Mairead, Pamela, Pauline, Karen, Sharon and Gerard.

Author's Note

There are two things I would like to mention as I let this book slip from my hands into yours...

The first is that, yes, Iris has managed to get the quickest, quickiest divorce ever! But hey – this is fiction and after you've read the book, you really wouldn't wish another minute of marriage on poor Iris to her pathetic weed of a husband, would you?

The second is that I know, we're all thoroughly fed up of that little C word that has disrupted just about everything and caused such pain and heartbreak to so many. I wrote this book in 2021, when we were weary of lockdowns and nightly case numbers and so many other atrocities going on in the world. Each time I opened the manuscript, Georgie, Iris and Nola took me to a place where there were no masks, no social distancing and no terrible tragic stories that defy making any sense of.

It's for this reason that I've left out any mention of the

dreaded pandemic, as it was categorized at the time of writing.

I hope that you the reader will enjoy escaping to Ballycove and being uplifted too. If I've managed to give you a little break from whatever worries you're currently carrying, that will make me very happy indeed.

Love,

Faith xx